the *white*
body of evening

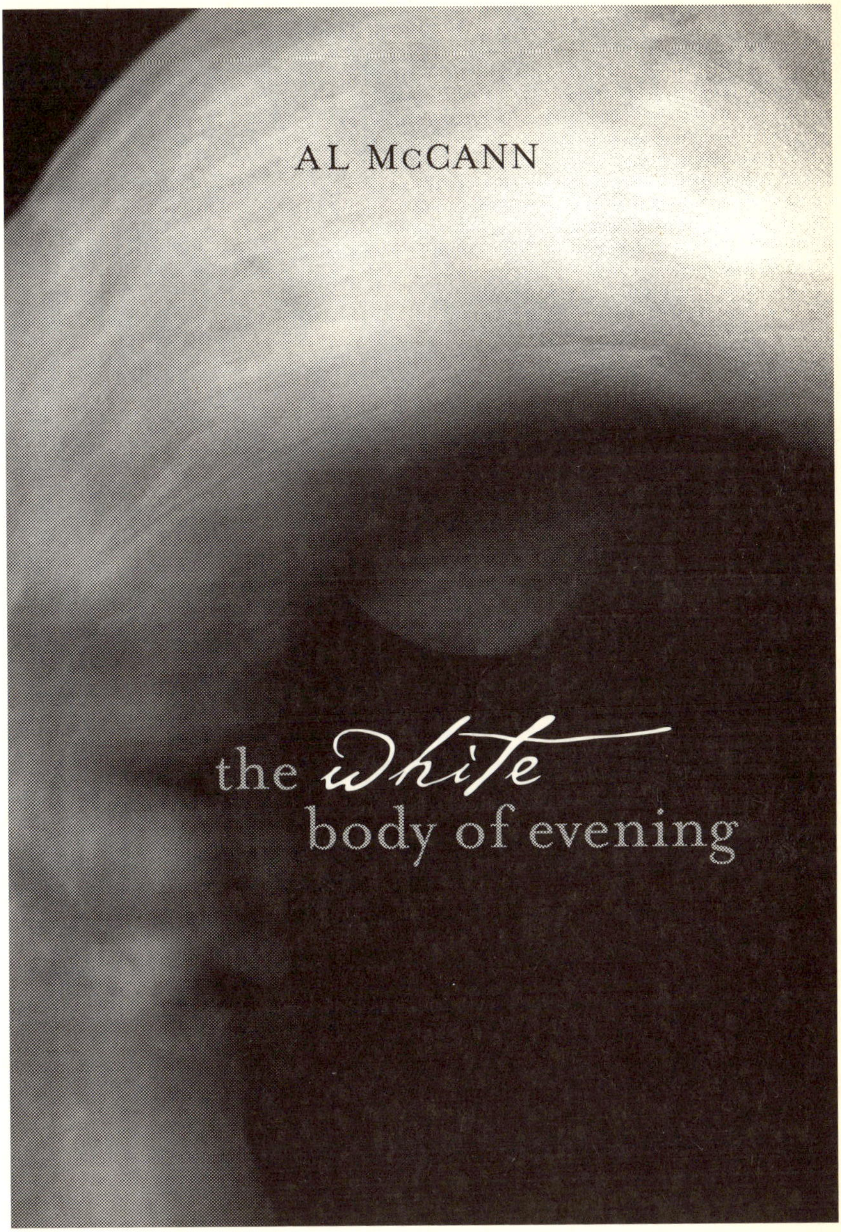

AL McCANN

the *white*
body of evening

An imprint of HarperCollins*Publishers*

Excerpt from "Sunsets" © The Estate of Richard Aldington.
Reproduced with kind permission.


**Flamingo**
An imprint of HarperCollins*Publishers*, Australia

First published in Australia in 2002
by HarperCollins*Publishers* Pty Limited
ABN 36 009 913 517
A member of the HarperCollins*Publishers* (Australia) Pty Limited Group
www.harpercollins.com.au

Copyright © A L McCann 2002

The right of A L McCann to be identified as the moral rights
author of this work has been asserted by him in accordance with
the *Copyright Amendment (Moral Rights) Act 2000* (Cth).

This book is copyright.
Apart from any fair dealing for the purposes of private study, research,
criticism or review, as permitted under the Copyright Act, no part may
be reproduced by any process without written permission.
Inquiries should be addressed to the publishers.

**HarperCollins***Publishers*
25 Ryde Road, Pymble, Sydney NSW 2073, Australia
31 View Road, Glenfield, Auckland 10, New Zealand
77–85 Fulham Palace Road, London W6 8JB, United Kingdom
Hazelton Lanes, 55 Avenue Road, Suite 2900, Toronto, Ontario, M5R 3L2
*and* 1995 Markham Road, Scarborough, Ontario, M1B 5M8, Canada
10 East 53rd Street, New York NY 10022, USA

National Library of Australia Cataloguing-in-Publication data:

McCann, Andrew Lachlan, 1966– .
 The white body of evening: a novel.
 ISBN 0 7322 7467 2.
A823.4

Cover and internal design by Katie Mitchell, HarperCollins Design Studio
Cover photograph: Getty Images
Typeset in 11.5/17 Bembo by HarperCollins Design Studio
Printed and bound in Australia by Griffin Press on 80gsm Bulky Book Ivory

5 4 3 2 1    02 03 04 05

*for Rosa*

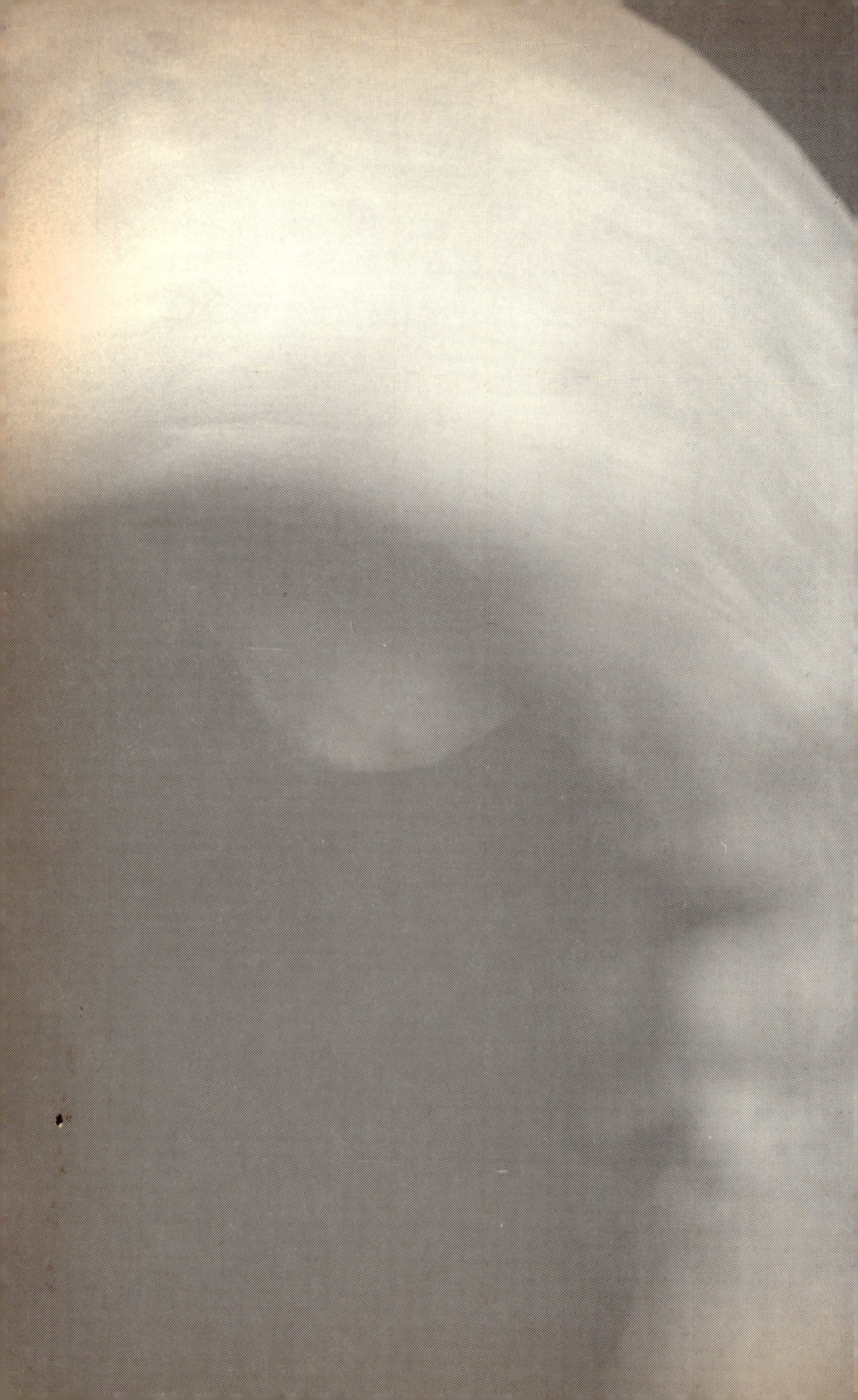

*The white body of the evening*
*Is torn into scarlet,*
*Slashed and gouged and seared*
*Into crimson,*
*And hung ironically*
*With garlands of mist.*

FROM "SUNSETS" BY
RICHARD ALDINGTON (1892–1962)

the *white* body of evening

part ONE

## chapter one

On the day of his wedding, Albert Walters conquered his fear of strong spirits and drank everything that came his way. What, after all, was the point of restraint? Every step he'd taken towards the altar had been reckless and now, after an engagement of barely a fortnight, the thought of decorum just for the sake of good form seemed absurd. Anna, sure enough, had reverted to a demure Lutheranism, despite being two months pregnant, and the small bluestone chapel in East Melbourne had lent itself to the illusion of considered matrimony. But by late afternoon, as the party left the tranquillity of the ceremony behind it and headed to a wine saloon in the Eastern Arcade, Albert was ready to cast off the pretence and, with embittered enthusiasm, embrace the comedy of his fall into rectitude.

The wedding party's short journey to the Australian Wine Shop could not have involved a sharper contrast. In the spring of 1891

East Melbourne was a calming place, protected from the city by the Fitzroy Gardens and at a safe enough distance from Richmond and Collingwood not to be disturbed by the larrikin element. It was an appropriate place for an afternoon marriage. A dignified Lutheran chapel in a quiet street, followed by a pleasant stroll through the neatly laid out gardens should have supplied a leisurely sense of ceremony in keeping with the demands of middle-class propriety.

The Eastern Arcade, in the city proper, belonged to a different world. Connecting Bourke and Little Collins Streets, a narrow passage of shops and saloons formed an enclosed court covered by a domed glass roof. Rickety wooden stairs at either end sagged and warped underfoot as they led to a second storey, where another lot of shadowy businesses framed a balcony overlooking a flagstone pavement turned black with filth. The shops on both levels were of a dubious character. Spiritualists and phrenologists with exotic names, nondescript booksellers and stationers, a billiard parlour and a few unmarked windows draped mysteriously with crimson velvet, vied for the attention of the loiterers who, initiated into the dreamlike caverns of the city, were disinclined to hurry through to the more populated streets.

The Australian Wine Shop was a double-fronted saloon divided into a bar and a parlour by a makeshift curtain. In these shabby surroundings the wedding celebration was attended by no more than a dozen people selected without much conviction from Albert's meagre circle of acquaintances. Most of them were clerks and salesmen from Citizen's Insurance. Sid Packard, Albert's immediate superior in the accounts department, had brought his wife Sadie, and a couple of other blokes were accompanied by sullen-looking young women too lazy to conceal the occasional yawn.

Both of Albert's parents were dead, and apart from his older brother, Robert, there was no one present who could be considered family. Anna found this disheartening. Her parents were still in South Australia and could not afford to come all the way to Melbourne for a wedding they thought hasty and ill-considered to begin with. She hadn't expected a conventional wedding, but nor had she expected the whole thing to be as perfunctory and disenchanting as it was. By the time the party had walked through the gardens to the edge of the city, the hot sun, the utter lack of civility, the lukewarm congratulations from people she hardly knew and the weary sense that the day had turned out to be just as tiresome as every other, left her on the verge of tears. But walking into the half-light of the arcade was like entering the crystal world of a fairytale, and for a moment she was overcome with its fantastic squalor. Murkily refracted rays of sunlight dripped down from the ceiling and slid off the plate-glass shopfronts and she imagined she was in a subaquatic city. But a moment later, led into the wine saloon by her new husband, her heart sank again.

The men gathered around the cramped, horseshoe-shaped bar drinking Albert's health, a few women congregated by the window and Anna was left alone, between the two, desperately wanting to be part of something on her own wedding day.

"Are you all right there, love?" Albert shouted.

Anna smiled limply and tried to work her way closer to her husband, to take his hand in a gesture of warmth.

"What have you got planned then, Bert?" a pimply young man asked with a suggestive smirk.

"Booked over the way, haven't we, Anna?"

"That ought to be a bit of luxury," someone added.

"Not that residential job on Bourke Street?" someone else said with a laugh.

"Don't be crass," Albert said.

Anna slunk back towards the women. Her mother had warned her about the boorishness of Australian men. According to a kind of mental reflex, she always spoke about this in conjunction with her first image of South Australia as a place of hard, dry ground, denuded eucalypts and miserable slab huts that made the simple peasant cottages of the German countryside look like palaces.

"What would you like to drink then, love?" asked Sadie Packard as she gently led Anna into the parlour. The two other young women, Mavis Day and Sophie Adams, had already cautiously retreated, suggesting that an arcade wine saloon was uncharted territory for them as well.

At the sight of the nervous, unfamiliar faces welcoming her, Anna began to sob.

"They don't do it like this in Germany then, love?" asked Sadie, trying her best to console her.

"No, not really."

"Never mind then. They don't do it like this here either."

For a moment the sound of festive male voices from behind the curtain overwhelmed the four women, and an awkward silence ensued.

"What part of Germany are you from, Anna?" asked Mavis, finally.

Anna wiped her nose on a handkerchief. "I'm not really from Germany. My parents are. But I was born in Hahndorf, near Adelaide."

She spoke crisp, accent-free English. Yet the absence of local idiom and inflection still suggested a vague kind of foreignness that, to the uninitiated, would have been impossible to trace.

"So you're a native of the place, well and truly."

"Yes, I suppose so."

She wondered what it would mean to be a native of a country like Australia. The thought had never occurred to her before, but it met her now with an unnerving clarity.

"I've never thought of myself as Australian," she said. "I suppose I always thought we'd one day go back to Europe. My mother always talked about it, though she's lived here now for more than twenty years."

Now that she was married and, more to the point, expecting a child by the winter, Anna wondered if she'd ever see the German countryside for which her mother pined.

"Well, it's a mighty good time to be an Australian anyway, ain't it?" Mavis said.

"Yes, I suppose," Anna said, not quite following her drift.

"How'd you end up over here?" Sadie asked. "Coming from so far away, I mean."

"My aunt moved here with her husband years ago. They went to Ballarat first, but soon gave up prospecting and settled in Melbourne. After her husband died, she fell ill. She was too sick to travel, so I came down here and looked after her."

"That was good of you," Mavis said.

"She didn't really have anyone," Anna went on. "No children, I mean."

"Is your aunt well enough now?"

"She died during the winter." Anna hadn't wanted to say this. She knew it would cast a further pall over the proceedings and again the women fell silent.

A few moments later, Robert Walters, her new husband's brother, appeared at the table, lightly touching Anna on the shoulder.

7

"I've got to get going," he said. "Have to be at the paper by four. Albert won't be much longer, I made him promise. I hope it works out well for you both."

"Thank you, Robert," she said.

"Look, Anna, I'm sorry about all this. I should have had more of a hand in the whole thing."

"Don't be, Robert."

With a hunched posture he walked back through the curtain and out into the arcade. He touched his hat at her through the window and slowly moved off towards the street.

"I think he might be carrying a flame for you, Anna," Sadie chirped.

"Might have fancied it himself, you reckon?" said Sophie, following Sadie's lead.

Anna tried not to take much notice, but was grateful for the attention of the three women who now seemed determined to make the best of a bad situation. Sadie went into the bar and a moment later reappeared with a bottle of champagne and four glasses, fending off the vulgar attentions of her husband, who lingered for a moment at the parlour entrance.

"Get back in there, you lout," she said, pushing him away with her foot.

It might have been the effects of the sun on her pale skin earlier in the afternoon, but after her first glass of champagne Anna felt giddy and hot. As the mood became more relaxed she knew she was still delicately poised on the edge of some melancholic slough, and strove to hold herself clear of it. She could have hugged Sadie, who guzzled down glass after glass of champagne with a stoical commitment to the spirit of debauchery coming from the bar.

It was twilight by the time the toasts were made and Albert, red with whisky and reeking of cigars, was ready to leave.

"C'mon love," he said, holding his arms out to Anna as they stumbled from the saloon into the musty gloom of the arcade.

Leaving the others assembled at the entrance, the newlyweds walked back towards Bourke Street to the cheers of the little crowd gathered behind them. Out on the road Albert hailed a hansom and ushered Anna onto the worn leather. As they started moving, he worked his lumpish hands into the folds of her dress and over her thighs. She kissed him. She felt it was the right thing to do, though her heart wasn't in it, not right now. She was tipsy, and could sense the tiredness that comes from disappointment welling up in her again.

"Do you really love me, Albert?" she asked, pushing him away from her.

She knew the question was both contrived and conventional, but still it seemed important to try to summon forth the ideal conception of love and marriage, if only to reconcile herself more quickly to the fallen reality.

"What kind of question is that? Of course I do."

"It's not just the baby?"

"Of course not," he answered, though he too knew that his words were part of a thin surface barely concealing his doubt.

He proceeded with his clumsy groping, to which she submitted in a passive, distracted manner, glancing out the window at the crowds moving along Bourke Street. He could see she had lost interest and followed her eyes out onto the passing verandahs, noticing the building that used to house the waxworks he'd go to as a boy. Sohier's it was called.

Albert sank back into the leather, lazily swaying with the movement of the carriage, thinking about the displays that used to fascinate him all those years ago. He remembered a smooth, bald head split open by an axe still embedded in the skull, and a beautiful young woman lying on a bed in a state of partial undress with her throat hacked through to the spine, and two knife-wielding Chinamen lingering like vultures over the bloody corpse. The image still unnerved him. He couldn't get the frozen stare of the murdered woman out of his mind, the dead eyes fixed obsessively on his.

He looked back at Anna, who was still gazing out the window, and was impressed by her gentle pallor, coloured by the sun and the glow of pregnancy. He couldn't help but compare it with the hard, jaundiced skin of the two wax murderers. Anna's flawless, white complexion and her occasional wandering look of indifference fascinated him. It was what had attracted him to her in the first place. Someone had said that she looked pagan, and though he didn't really know what that was supposed to mean, the word had a mysterious implication which drew him to the pale German. Initially he dreamt of her giving in to a sterile, depraved kind of lust. But when she finally did surrender, in a moment of weakness or perhaps apathy, it was with a prudish frigidity that he hadn't counted on. Later, when she told him that she was pregnant, he was moved by her nervousness and replied, with barely a moment's hesitation, that he was in love with her. At the back of it all, through their brief engagement and now the day of their marriage, was the dull regret, a longing for the brutal act of conquest that she had never quite allowed him.

As they made their way into a drab hotel foyer on Elizabeth Street, and then into the beige wedding suite, it was this regret that ate into him. He looked at her long, lithe body in the darkened room and firmly caught hold of her wrist, drawing her towards him.

"Albert," she said, surprised at this fervour. "Albert, are you very drunk?"

He didn't say anything, but yanked her down onto the bed where he rapidly began to undress her. She lay back, unintentionally hindering his progress, unsure of herself. He was mauling her. Touched by the awkwardness of his desire, she giggled to herself. The laughter, so slight, so unobtrusive, washed over him like a drug. He lay back on the bed and she fell beside him, nestling into his arm, feeling more affectionate than she had the entire day. At that moment he thought again about the waxwork corpse, the white skin, the slit throat and the leering Chinamen. It was as vivid in his memory as it had been when he was twelve or thirteen years of age. Something in him ached. He was drunk enough for the room to spin as soon as he was still.

"Anna, love," he said, "I think I need a bit of air."

"I'll be waiting for you," she said with a hint of regret as he stood up and moved towards the door.

For a moment she felt foolish, having to negotiate his drunkenness with this trite token of affection. But as the door closed she was relieved and grateful to be alone. She quickly drifted to the edge of sleep, overwhelmed by the exhausting jumble of emotions and sensations that had assailed her during the day and that now danced before her in a confused montage. For a moment she was stunned at how thoroughly she had lost control of her life. How had it happened? Albert hadn't forced her to have sex, but she hadn't exactly sought it out either. Afterwards he had kissed her tenderly and treated her well, and so it seemed all right. But now that they were married all she wanted was the obliviousness of sleep.

Albert walked back down Bourke Street into the heart of the city, which was alive with activity as young men and women began to assemble at street corners, at coffee stalls on the pavement and around the entrances to the theatres and the dance halls. It was a warm night, almost the beginning of summer, and there was a carnality about the unfolding evening that overwhelmed him. He meandered through the crowds and in a few minutes was walking down Little Bourke Street, where he imagined wretched opium dens hidden away in back rooms and wasted addicts lost in frightful dreams of ancient cruelty played out amidst pagodas and burning paper lanterns. At Russell Street he turned north and shortly after was on Little Lonsdale Street, watching an itinerant patterer trying to sell chapbooks to uninterested passers-by. He walked aimlessly for a block or so until he came to a row of decrepit cottages fronted by a pair of ragged young women. In his impaired state they looked to him like visions dragged up from the depths of a troubled dream.

"Why don't you come inside, Sir?" said the bolder of the two, stroking the cuff of his jacket and gesturing towards a dirty brown building with sagging gutters and boarded-up windows.

The girl was standing directly in front of him, looking unflinchingly into his eyes with a subtle hint of malevolence.

"What's your name?" he asked, laughing. But he knew already that he wanted to touch her, to grip her arms in his hands, to draw her to him. His heart was beating furiously as he struggled to remain aloof.

"Angelique," the girl said.

The name had a delirious quality that swirled like an elaborate arabesque. Hadn't he married Anna for the sake of appearances? Surely she didn't expect him to sacrifice all of himself to that lie?

Angelique's eyes were murky green, the colour of the ocean, and shaped like two perfectly symmetrical almonds. Her gaze paralysed him with indecision. Again he thought of the two wax Chinamen and the bleeding body.

"Anything you want, Sir," she said, taking his hand. "Suck and swallow, anal buggery. Anything you want."

Stunned by this frankness, he was on the verge of following her into the hovel when, quite unconsciously, he shook himself free and turned back towards the hotel.

He stumbled along the crowded streets with only the barest recollection of what had just happened. The noise of the city, the din of the trams, the frenetic movement of rushing bodies swept him up. It was only a matter of moments before he was outside the hotel on Elizabeth Street, mounting the stairs and opening the door to the room. Anna was in bed, stirring drowsily as he walked past her into the bathroom. He looked at his haggard face in the mirror, quickly turned on the tap, thinking that he'd wash away the smell of the streets, and proceeded to vomit into the sink.

"Are you all right?" Anna asked, half asleep.

"Yes. A bit seedy. Tired."

"Come to sleep then."

She was so trusting, so unsuspecting. How was it possible? He felt sick at the thought of his own potential for depravity. But as he lay down beside his wife and closed his eyes, the thought of the girl – malevolent and vulgar – smouldered away within him until the embers caught again and the darkness of sleep was consumed with flames.

## chapter Two

Anna tried to look at ease as she sat on the couch and read a novel about the perils of love. She could hear Albert stomping impatiently around the bedroom. He's too big for the house, she thought. When he appeared at the threshold of the cramped living room, her eyes wandered away from the page in search of his, but he walked past her as if she were not there. She returned to the novel, so anxious she couldn't concentrate on the words. They skipped and blurred in front of her as she listened to her husband groaning into the kitchen.

"Are you all right, Albert?" she asked, dropping the book on her lap.

"Hmm, hmm," he said groggily, as if he'd just woken up. "Headache. Just a headache."

She closed her eyes, resting her hand on her stomach, pressing it for signs of life. Only the thought of the child let her pull herself above the loneliness of her marriage, the fear lurking at the bottom of her.

At times she suspected he felt trapped, as if he had been tricked into marrying her, or that living in her house offended his pride. When her aunt died Anna inherited her small cottage in South Melbourne, and Albert had moved in shortly after the marriage. It was a dank little place in Brooke Street, a narrow, curving lane crowded to the point of congestion with similar single-storey cottages. There was no sewerage in the area and the yard at the back of the house was often plagued by puddles rising up from the swamp beneath it. Compared with the larger brick and stone houses with nice wide verandahs only blocks away from them, it felt dilapidated.

Albert muttered something to himself. When she stood up and went to check on him, he was sitting opposite the sink. She put her hand on his shoulder.

"What's the matter?" she said gently. She knew it was futile asking.

He shook his head and shrugged off the question. "Nothing, love," he said. "Just work. I'm feeling worn out." He couldn't look her in the eye as he said it.

She thought it prudent not to push him, sat back down on the couch, and gave in to the atmosphere of unease he generated, deciding to make the best of it, for the sake of the child.

Sometimes, when a mood of tenderness overcame him, her gratitude seemed to embarrass him back into his usual remoteness. Only when they had company did his spirits seem to lighten. When Sid and Sadie Packard came over, or his brother Robert, he was comfortably distracted and regained some of the simple amicability he'd had when they'd first met.

Usually Sid and Albert discussed politics, but in a language that was alienating to Anna. Early in the new year Sid had started talking about joining an anti-Chinese league. Cheap Chinese and Kanaka labour was putting real Australians out of work, he said. Anna thought that Albert merely kept up the tone of these conversations to save face, and in fact she pitied him when she suspected that he was being pulled along by Sid's sense of urgency.

She thought it was strange that people could talk about real Australians in a country that was so young, in a country that, in fact, was not even a country at all, at least not in the old European sense of a *Volk* with a shared history etched so indelibly into the landscape. It seemed so wishful to her, innocent even. At the same time she was bewildered by her own lack of connectedness to the place. Sometimes she felt that she was floating just above the ground, light enough to be blown away altogether, while others around her were walking with their feet firmly planted on the solid terrain.

"Don't you think it's a little odd to talk about an Australian people," she ventured timidly, "at least if you mean a people other than the original blacks?"

Albert poured another beer, deferring to Sid.

"That might have been true once upon a time," Sid explained patiently, "but nowadays a real change is occurring. White Australians are standing up for their rights more than ever. For the first time we're coming together as a people."

"It's different, of course, for you Barossa Germans," Albert added. "I mean not really speaking English and all."

"I suppose," said Anna.

"But on the other hand," Sid went on, "the English and the German races are really the same. And here we have a chance to protect ourselves from the low influences of Latin and Slavic peoples that have mixed everything up in Europe."

Unconvinced, Anna decided then and there that she'd have to teach her child to speak her parents' language, as a bulwark against people like Sid. She had noticed him glancing quizzically at the tattered volumes of Goethe and Heine on the shelves and the wistful Rhineland vistas on the wall. The banality of the coming Australian nation, concentrated in his suspicious eyes, filled her with dread.

"How's the tummy coming along?" Sadie asked, patting Anna's knee.

"You can't really see much," said Anna.

"Well, they say the muscles are firmer the first time."

As Sadie examined Anna's unobtrusive belly, there was a knock at the door. Jack McDermott, a next-door neighbour who worked on the wharves, peered in through the open front window.

"I say, Albert, you wouldn't have a bottle of disinfectant, would you? Hamish has damn near cut his bloody hand off."

"Oh, poor kid," sighed Anna, moving into the bathroom while Albert let Jack inside.

"What did the young fella do?" he asked, welcoming the new visitor with a friendly pat on the shoulder.

"I don't know. Bloody idiot was mucking around with a penknife and sliced his finger."

Anna and Sadie accompanied Jack next door, determined to be of assistance. In the kitchen of the neighbouring cottage Sarah McDermott was clutching the bleeding hand of her three-year-old son, who whined with a look of petrified shock on his pale face.

"We've got some alcohol and a bandage, Sarah," Anna said. As she spoke the child stopped crying and looked at her blankly,

17

apparently distracted by a new face in the house, though he had seen his neighbours several times before.

"*Ach, Liebchen*," said Anna under her breath as she doused the boy's hand in spirits. Hamish winced, but didn't cry as she wrapped the bandage tightly around his hand.

"Probably needs a stitch or two," Sadie said.

Jack had already vanished in search of a doctor a few blocks away in St Vincent Place. Hamish clutched at Anna, who tried in vain to pass him back to his mother once the bandage was secure.

"Little bugger won't let go," Sarah said nervously. "Thanks Anna."

"*Lieb*," the child lisped as Anna finally managed to unload him.

When Dr Winton arrived he lifted Hamish onto his knee and slowly undid the bandage that Anna had worked so hard to put on. The cut on the child's hand opened again and in a second or two filled with blood, which the doctor tried to conceal with the bandage.

"This is going to need a few stitches," he said calmly, rummaging about in his leather bag. "Mustn't let the little man here get his hand infected, must we?"

Jack held Hamish on the kitchen table while the doctor swabbed the wound and then, with no more finesse than a short-sighted seamstress, proceeded to sew the folds of skin together.

When the operation was complete, and mother and child had both been lulled into a tentative calm, the doctor strolled out onto the pavement in front of the McDermotts's house. Albert and Sid were leaning on the fence, smoking cigarettes.

"Hello there, Albert," Dr Winton said in a subdued, but good-natured tone of voice.

"Hello there yourself, Doc."

Anna and Sadie had walked out onto the pavement behind him.

"Feeling all right then are we, Albert?"

"Fine, thanks."

"I'm glad to hear it."

He bowed respectfully at Anna and then walked off down the street with a curious, self-satisfied swagger that put one in mind of an old-style dandy or flâneur of the sort that might have flourished when Melbourne was still a gold rush city able to afford such social extravagances.

"What an odd bloke," said Sid.

Anna had noticed it too. The doctor seemed to be amused at Albert's expense, as if there were a secret understanding between the two that played to his advantage. She wondered if Albert had been ill recently. Anyway, it was inconsiderate of Dr Winton to insinuate like that, and she resented him for it.

"You know," said Sid after a minute, "that doctor bloke reminds me of someone, but I don't know who."

"Let's go in," said Albert, rubbing out the butt of his cigarette with his shoe.

It was twilight and the hot afternoon had faded into a warm, but dull grey. The street was silent and motionless. It put Albert on edge and he felt a tension arise in him that, he knew, was related to this strange sense of inertia as evening approached. He would have liked to have gone out somewhere, the Limerick Arms for a drink or a stroll along the bay, but knew he'd feel the inertia of nightfall all the more intensely as he tried to wrestle free of its clutches. The world took on a flatness that offered nothing but the same old amusements, frayed and threadbare, over and over again. It left him feeling empty and finally a bit hateful.

"We got to get going, Bert," Sid said. "Going to walk back through the gardens. Look after yourself, Anna."

Sadie and Anna hugged, then Sid took his wife's hand. Anna and Albert stood on the street watching them walk away.

"They seem very happy," said Albert listlessly.

"Yes they do," said Anna.

Albert felt bored and tired. It wasn't anything to do with Anna specifically. Not really. But she was there, in the midst of the drabness, and that made him indignant.

"Are you all right, Albert?" she asked, noticing his remoteness.

"Yes, I'm fine." He took her hand and they went inside.

Something in him throbbed. He thought about the prostitute. Was he in love with her? The wretched, cobbled alleys snaking off Little Lonsdale Street had the sickening smell of brimstone seeping up through the pores of the city. The stench was palpable. Only in those filthy, labyrinthine streets, he imagined, would he find love. He would have given anything to possess that girl, anything to know her shameless, impersonal surrender, the dreamlike compulsion of commerce and carnality, the pleasure of places so remote they will never see the light of day.

He watched Anna move about in the kitchen, putting on the kettle, washing up a few dirty dishes. The sounds of such ordinariness grated on him. Weary, he threw himself down onto the couch and closed his eyes. He admired the beauty of his wife as one would admire a handsomely painted portrait. But on the other side, in the dark, frantic city of his dreams, he'd forget all about her. Maybe this is the beginning of madness, he thought. He imagined himself as a raving idiot at Yarra Bend.

Anna had moved to the edge of the living room, and watched as his mouth curled into a smile.

"What are you so amused at?" she asked, smiling herself.

"Nothing, darling," he answered calmly.

"Would you like a cuppa before dinner?"

"Nup, but I'll help myself to another beer."

He sat up on the couch, opened his eyes and looked at her, feeling momentarily refreshed. Yes, she was beautiful. His German wife was a domestic angel of the sort that was celebrated to the point of ridicule in the papers and popular journals. A slight neurotic tremor rippled out along his arms all the way to his fingertips.

"Isn't that Dr Winton a strange man?" Anna said as Albert stood up and walked into the kitchen.

"Haven't thought that much about him, to tell you the truth."

"But the way he talked to you just now was so mysterious."

"That's just his manner I suppose. You know he's a literary type as well. Writes little pamphlets about social issues. I reckon he likes making a bit of a show of himself."

"Have you read anything he's written?"

"Wouldn't waste my time."

Albert poured himself a beer and took the *Herald* off the sideboard, returning to the couch.

"This Crimea Street business is a nasty piece of work," he said, scanning the paper. "They say the woman was probably locked in the wine cellar for days before the bloke strangled her and, well, it says here he must have 'tampered' with the body. It's like something from a horror story."

Anna looked at him as he read the paper. How do they know all that, she wondered. A terrifying image of bleeding, white hands clawing at the earth and stone of the cellar wall sent a chill through her. She closed her eyes. The thought of the violated corpse, still dirty with clay soil, hovered at the limits of her imagination.

"I hope you don't do anything like that to me," she said after a moment's silence.

"Don't be absurd," he said. He knew she was being deliberately perverse, that it was her uneasy way of expressing affection.

As she sat down beside him he didn't notice her anxiousness. Without moving his eyes from the paper he took her hand and kissed it.

A few weeks later on a warm March day, Anna was walking through Emerald Hill past the South Melbourne Town Hall, on her shopping rounds, when she bumped into Dr Winton on the corner of Bank and Clarendon Streets. He had appeared out of nowhere, almost as if he had been waiting for her, his auburn moustache neatly trimmed, his hazelnut eyes sparkling with a mischievous delight. He was, she guessed, in his forties and handsome, in a way. She acknowledged it despite herself. Behind him a cable tram rattled towards the river, disturbing the eerie silence of the afternoon, while an old beggar woman with a wicker basket shuffled across the road in its wake.

"Hello Anna," said the doctor, lifting himself out of his repose and, with a twirl of a gold-handled cane, positioning himself at her side.

It struck her as forward of him to use her first name like that.

"Hello Doctor," she said, repressing the faint unease she felt at his open, unflinching, but still very gentlemanly manner. She noticed a large ring on his hand, a golden claw clutching a round, turquoise stone.

"My husband tells me that you're a writer," she said, afraid of the silence that might engulf them if she let the conversation flag, for Dr Winton was now walking beside her with a confidence that suggested a more familiar acquaintance.

"Well, yes. I do write a little. I translate short pieces as well, from the French and the German."

"You speak German?" she asked, barely able to conceal her interest in the idea of a fellow speaker.

"Read it would be more accurate."

"I'd like to see something you have written."

"I'm not so sure you would. I don't mean to be condescending."

"You don't believe me?" she said with a laugh.

"I think beautiful young women like you, Anna, would have better things to do."

"You're mad," she said, blushing.

"And your husband is doing well?" he asked.

"Quite well."

"That's very good."

"But I wasn't aware he had been ill."

"No?" the doctor asked. "Well, who's to say that he has?"

"You. You said as much just then."

"I'll tell you what, Anna. If you would really like to read something I've written, there's a bookshop in Flinders Lane, quite close to the station. You can normally find the odd book and a pamphlet or two there. In fact, I'd be flattered to think that you'd seek me out like that." He stopped himself. For a moment he seemed ill at ease. "But they're dry works," he said with a dismissive wave of his hand. "Written for medical men. Dull stuff for a lay reader."

"I'm stopping here," she said, pausing in front of a haberdashery. She was embarrassed at the suggestion of the illicit in the idea of seeking him out, but her curiosity was also aroused by his sudden reserve.

"Well, good day then," he said, tilting his hat politely and resuming his course with a strut and a twirl of his cane.

What an unusual man, Anna thought to herself. All intrigue and innuendo. He certainly does fancy himself. She watched him move away from her down Clarendon Street until he vanished into the sparsely populated shade of the wide verandahs covering the pavement.

But when she was alone again she suddenly felt aroused. He had called her beautiful, and his completely unabashed manner left her with a sense of well-being. She lingered in front of the haberdashery for another minute or so, looked up ahead to make sure the doctor was not coming back, and then with a truant's guilt stepped towards the side of the road to hail the next tram into the city.

Half an hour later she alighted at the corner of Queen and Collins Streets and, with a sense of excitement at being driven by a secret purpose, made her way towards Flinders Lane and the bookshop the doctor had mentioned.

She hadn't expected to find such an odd collection of industries thriving in the narrow alleys of the city. Amongst the warehouses and businesses dedicated to the city's rag trade, a shop selling glassware cradled undulating pools of multi-coloured light in its dark interior. An optician's store was marked by two enormous, sombre eyes looking down at her. There was a place selling casting irons and another selling fishing tackle. There was a fancy dress shop with a grotesque collection of masks leering through the glass and a bric-a-brac merchant whose window was crammed with obscure, dust-covered artefacts. As she strolled down the lane she dwelt upon the magical possibilities of what seemed to her a forgotten part of the city into which the bustle of the larger streets had not yet reached.

By the time she found the stationer's store, which she presumed to be the bookshop the doctor had mentioned, she was feeling a bit light-headed. She looked around the collection of writing materials, stamps and magazines that cluttered the shelves of the dingy shop.

A thin, middle-aged woman with yellowish skin appeared at the counter from behind a black curtain, looking as if she'd rather not be disturbed by customers.

"Can I help you, dear?"

"I'm after something by Dr Charles Winton," Anna said.

"Winton?" the woman said, turning the name over in her memory. "You probably mean Dr W. In that case you'd better follow me."

She led Anna back through the curtain into a small parlour area lined with bookshelves. A short, pudgy man sat in a corner smoking a cigar, reading Zola's *Thérèse Raquin*. He nodded indifferently at Anna as the woman gestured towards a shelf of thin volumes.

"Here are our syphilographers," she said without the faintest trace of irony in her voice.

Anna read the titles: *Morbid Anatomy and the Generative System, Syphilis and its Diffusion Popularly Considered, Satyriasis: Causes and Cures, Syphilitic Madness and the Modern City*. She opened one of the books and studied the sketches of diseased genitalia blossoming with bright red pustules. She put the book back and took another: *Sexual Pathology* by Dr W. Upon opening it she tried not to dwell on the sketches and photographs that shimmered before her. Her hand trembled as she put it back on the shelf, and walked out into the front of the shop. As she left she thought she could hear laughter coming from behind the black curtain. "Not for you then, love?" the woman said. In a moment she was out on the street again, her heart racing and her head reeling. She felt a hand catch her by the arm.

"Anna," a man's voice said solicitously. It was Dr Winton. She didn't look at him but saw him standing beside her, reflected in the window of the stationer's shop. He gently led her back inside and sat her down in a chair by the counter.

"You look flustered," he said. "Quite normal for expecting mothers."

"You followed me," she replied coldly.

"I'm sorry, Anna. It was not my intention to offend."

He seemed at a loss, grasping for an explanation that eluded him. The woman appeared again from behind the curtain, took a look at the doctor and quickly withdrew.

"Why don't I call you a cab?" Dr Winton said.

"No, thank you." She regained her composure and stood up, leaving the shop for the second time.

She walked swiftly back onto Collins Street and then, not wanting to wait for the doctor to reappear, continued towards Spencer Street Station, looking over her shoulder every few paces until she was sure that he wasn't following her.

What was she afraid of? She hurried her step, as if in doing so she could avoid the question. She understood just how effortlessly he had compromised her and shuddered at how easily she'd been drawn in. She could never tell Albert. How could she without implicating herself? It was the kind of thing that would simply widen the gap between them. She started sobbing, wiping her eyes with the cuff of her blouse, and kept moving through the din of the afternoon.

Nearing Spencer Street, she thought she'd take a ferry back over the river to South Melbourne, but as she approached the Collins Street Police Station she could see a crowd gathering outside and noticed that the haphazard movement of people along the pavement beside her had become a steady flow moving towards the same point.

"What's going on?" she asked the woman marching along purposefully next to her.

"Ain't you heard, then?" the woman replied. "They've just got that Howard fellow, what strangled that poor girl in his cellar."

"And what do all these people want with him?" she asked.

"I reckon they're going to give him what for."

A little way ahead people were spilling onto the road. Quite mindlessly, she let herself drift along with the throng. Someone near the door to the building yelled something inaudible that kindled the fury of the mob. As the hint of violence rippled out through the crowd, people pressed harder against the narrow bluestone entrance. There were shouts of rage and the muffled sounds of breaking glass as the police attempted to hold the angry mob at bay. Anna moved to the opposite side of the street, looking on with both wonder and horror. Next to her, two elderly women were holding banners that read "An Eye for an Eye" and "A Tooth for a Tooth".

"I hope he gets what's coming to him," one of them said, leaning close to Anna.

The two old women had leathery, weatherworn skin. Anna imagined a pair of ancient vultures lingering over the scene of some public catastrophe, croaking the verdict of a terrible, unforgiving law. For a moment the image in her mind obscured the horror of the murder itself.

"I only hope the man will have a fair trial," Anna said.

"What's got into you? Don't pity the bugger. Makes me sick the thought of it, what he done with the body."

"Molested the corpse," the other woman said vindictively, as if she would have liked to see the same thing happen to Anna. "The horrid little pervert!"

The word "pervert" made Anna think of the doctor's book. She saw the golden claw wrapped around its turquoise orb. An instant later she pictured Albert reading about the murder the evening after the doctor had put stitches in Hamish's hand. This confluence haunted her, but its logic, so strongly intuited, also eluded her grasp. She felt as if she were trying to pursue the pattern of a dream that had once seemed perfectly plausible, but that upon waking had unravelled itself into a confused and scattered array of fragments, impressions and insinuations that appeared like blurs of light or shapes obscured in the shadows.

She continued to Spencer Street, pushing against the bodies rushing past her in the direction of the police station, and then turned towards the river. A fishmonger had littered the pavement and gutter with tiny pieces of offal and bone that stank in the hot sun. Before her, the river trembled yellow and brown, and as the ferry groaned across it she thought she could hear the cries of a delirious mob venting its rage in an atrocious act of collective retribution, hacking away at the body of the prisoner until it was an unrecognisable mass of bleeding limbs and the street a sickening shambles.

## chapter three

As Anna grew larger in the final months of her pregnancy, Albert began to hope that the birth of the child would help him effect a positive change of outlook. Anna held his hand on her belly as the child kicked and turned inside her, but he felt the little rumblings with a sense of confusion that fell well short of her own enthusiasm.

He sat silently next to her, watching her smile as she rested her hand on her stomach.

"It's wonderful," she said to herself.

Something in the ease of her manner grated on him. She seemed oblivious to him, unaware of just how much he struggled to keep himself together for the sake of the child.

He stood up and straightened his jacket. "I'm going to be late," he said.

She didn't say anything. She just smiled, or tried to, as he hurried away from her.

It was a relief to leave the house in the morning. Albert couldn't wait to exchange the stench of damp for the fresh air of the bay. But as he got closer to work, bumping along through the city with other clerks and shop assistants, all worn out even before the day had really begun, he felt himself tensing up again.

He hated Citizen's Insurance. The tedium of it had eaten into him, leaving him bitter and anxious. He had even begun to fall out with Sid Packard as he showed his increasing impatience. The daily routine of checking accounts, balancing books, calculating bills and issuing letters of payment made him ill with its banality. He couldn't conceal his temper. Sid tried to tolerate this as much as possible, sensing that Albert was not himself, but when he muttered something insulting to Rodney O'Dell, the young nephew of a co-owner, Sid upbraided him and told him to display a healthier attitude. Albert turned the word "healthier" over in his mind for the rest of the day, wondering exactly what it might mean to display a healthy attitude to work so utterly meaningless.

His hands trembled as he typed up another letter of request. His fingers hit the keys with unusual force. Finally, at the end of his tether, he bashed the machine with his fists until the letterhead was an incomprehensible mass of inkblots and lacerations. In a blind rage he took a pencil off the desk and slammed it down into the open palm of his hand. The shock of it, and the stinging pain, returned him to his senses. He gazed numbly at the small, graphite-tinged puncture mark in the skin, clenched his hand around a crumpled piece of newspaper and walked into the bathroom to wash the wound.

After that Albert forced himself to think about the child more insistently. It was an exercise in self-discipline. He'd have to keep his head down, for a while at least. He knew how difficult things could get if he lost his job. All year the streets of South Melbourne had seen groups of unemployed men loitering around the factories and workshops, or making their way to the Sandridge wharves, on the off-chance of finding work. He read newspaper articles daily about the destitute of the city, and the Benevolent Ladies Society talked up a city-wide suicide mania, after an insolvent had secreted himself away in a Fitzroy boarding house to blow a hole through his brain in peace. At the back of Albert's mind were desperate schemes, like joining Lane's New Australia expedition and shipping off to Paraguay, or moving up north where they still had gold.

Of course Anna would never be in it, and with the house and all they wouldn't be badly off as long as he could stay in work. He told himself this constantly, rehearsing the conditions of the minimal form of sanity that would let him shuffle along the surfaces of life without stumbling too heavily. He swallowed his pride and apologised to Sid who, harbouring a natural affection for Albert, patted him on the back and suggested that they have a drink after work.

Albert also apologised to the co-owner's nephew, claiming that he was having some trouble at home. He said this so genuinely that it surprised him. But wasn't that the truth? While he could tell himself that he loved Anna, after a manner, he was also remote from her, unable to satisfy himself with her, unable to bend her in the way that he secretly craved. Something lurked within him. A clammy, shapeless thing that shifted suddenly out of its repulsive slouch according to its own primitive needs. When Albert felt it move he cowered from himself. It was always there, at the bottom of him, waiting to stir, waiting to grip him.

"You are suffering from an instinctual deviation," Dr Winton had told him. It was shortly after the debacle of the wedding night.

He had visited the doctor at his rooms in St Vincent Place, complaining of lethargy and weariness. All he was looking for was a tonic or some pills, something to pick him up a bit.

Winton looked at him, folding his hands over his knee. "Tell me what's wrong, Albert," he said. "I can call you Albert, can't I?"

Albert fumbled for an answer. He said he had trouble concentrating, tired easily and felt frustrated. Sometimes he felt himself trembling.

Winton exhaled through his nose and nodded. "What about your private life?" he asked. "Recently married, I understand."

"Yes," Albert said.

"Tell me what it's like for you, and your wife. Anna, isn't it? I knew her aunt."

Albert pushed out his lower lip, then quickly sucked it in. The questions kept coming. They were intrusive and humiliating, but the doctor's authority held him there and impelled him to answer. Albert suddenly felt as if he'd had the wind knocked out of him.

"Have you ever desired a man?" the doctor asked.

"No," Albert replied.

"Do you associate sexual pleasure with violence?"

"No," he replied again.

"But you have visited prostitutes?"

He didn't answer, feeling as if he had been backed into a corner. He tried to explain to himself what exactly had happened on the night of his wedding. They had only talked, but Angelique's voice lingered with him more powerfully than any physical sensation he'd known.

"You are aware that syphilis is a disease that can be brought back and spread through the home?" Winton looked into his eyes accusingly.

Albert sat silently, trying to avoid the doctor's stare as if he were a criminal awaiting judgement.

"Your wife is a beautiful woman, Albert," Winton said. "Any man would desire her."

Albert already hated him. Winton seemed to take a sadistic pleasure in articulating his diagnosis and explaining the necessity of self-restraint. "Instinctual deviation." The phrase filled Albert with guilt.

And then there was that incident in the street, when Winton had almost let things slip in front of Anna. He might have to kill the doctor, Albert thought. He could wring his neck or crush his forehead, or beat him to a pulp with his own gold-handled walking cane.

In such thoughts he found a perpetual nightmare weaving through the monotony of his daily life. Lying in bed, thinking about what Winton had said to him, Albert was afraid of his own rage, his own propensity for violence, the secret life seething within him. For a long time he couldn't close his eyes. He felt sullied by the doctor's verdict, accused by the strangeness he felt beside his pregnant wife. He listened to the rhythm of her breathing, sensed the darkness and the creaking of the house descend upon him. For hours they pressed closer and closer and he retreated further and further into himself until, finally, he slipped away into an abyss where the burdens of consciousness and guilt faded, and the darkness came alive with the wanton voices of the fallen and the lost. Every night he returned to this prehistoric dung-pit, a wilderness of bones and seashells and gaunt skeletal bodies languishing outside the city walls. This was his home, his resting place. He was an outcast, a stranger, a shadow.

~

In May 1892, Anna gave birth to a son. To see such raw, helpless life convinced Albert that his place was out in the world fulfilling his function as a breadwinner, and for a moment it seemed as if the mantle of responsibility had fallen so squarely on his shoulders that there was no time for anything else. For the first few weeks after the birth he doggedly went off to the city offices of Citizen's Insurance in the morning and returned promptly at 5.30 p.m. to take care of the household chores. The simple realities of the situation had a gravity about them that he found comforting and distracting.

Slowly Anna's body resumed its usual litheness and her breasts became softer. But by then there was Paul to compete for her attention as well. In the evening Albert sat on the couch and read the *Bulletin* or the *Boomerang*, trying to distract himself, while Anna nursed the baby and chanted endearments in childish German. The sound of the language rankled.

He noticed that Anna was speaking more German than English, and began to feel marginalised by the bond, codified in another tongue, between the mother and the baby. He wondered what she was saying about him, wondered whether he was being betrayed by the words he couldn't understand. Exacerbating this was the constant presence in the house of Hamish McDermott, the child from next door. Since the day Anna had bandaged his hand and called him *Liebchen*, the child had developed a fascination with her that now, as he was old enough to walk about himself, had him constantly appearing at the front door or sitting attentively on the living room floor while Anna breastfed Paul. With both his parents often working, Anna had agreed to mind the child during the day and in the process had started teaching him her parents' tongue, which he took up with all the alacrity that children have for new languages. Hamish had acquired a smattering of German from Anna and was now trying to communicate with the baby using a rudimentary German vocabulary. Albert soon felt more alone than ever, and imagined that he'd have to tear this remote language out of his wife's mouth before she could truly be his.

One evening he met his brother Robert at the Limerick Arms and brought him home to see his new nephew. When they arrived, Anna was in the living room with Paul and Hamish rehearsing vowel sounds as if she were conducting an actual classroom, gradually shaping her lips and tongue into words which Hamish repeated to her obediently.

"*Bald ein Blümchen, bald ein Stein, bald erfüllt ein Vögelein dich mit innigem Entzücken.*"

The child mimicked this almost perfectly. Albert stood at the door, dumbfounded.

"Shouldn't Hamish be getting home?" he said.

"Sarah said she'd come by when she gets home from work," Anna replied.

"But she's already home. The light is on. Hamish, why don't you run and see if Mummy is home already?"

The child scooted out into the street as Albert assumed command of his living room, leading Robert, who looked a bit sheepish, inside.

"We hear nothing but German these days," Albert said by way of apology to his brother.

"Well, there's no harm in that," Robert said.

"Of course not," said Albert soberly.

Robert stayed for dinner and after Paul had fallen asleep the three adults had a supper of corned beef and potato salad which Anna had prepared that afternoon. Robert was a writer at the *Melburnian*, a weekly publication that blended factual reportage, trivia and society gossip, so their discussion meandered around the news of the day. But Robert was anxious not to let his younger brother feel overshadowed, and constantly returned the conversation to the insurance firm, the baby or something calculated to draw Albert out a bit. Anna was relieved that Robert had come. She knew that Albert was more likely to be amicable in company. As if the presence of a third person formed a liberating breach in the usual routine of the evening, Albert spoke easily and with a degree of good humour. For a moment she felt as if things were quite normal.

"Rob, tell Anna about that forgery," he said to his brother as he poured three glasses of warm beer.

"You mean the Howard thing?"

"Of course."

Anna remembered the awful day she'd been followed by the doctor and ended up watching the crowd prepare to rip the murderer apart. Throughout the week of Edmund Howard's trial it was impossible not to feel the horror of the crime, as one tumid euphemism after another cloaked the image of the violated corpse. Because the man had once performed a hypnotist's act at the Polytechnic, people said he must have mesmerised the girl – Edith Joyce was her name – and then killed her when the trance was broken. Stories about the "Jew's eye" did the rounds (so much so that the *Australian Israelite* published an angry rebuttal) and books on mesmerism were briefly in demand at the Coles Book Arcade. But the interest died out as quickly as it had started. By the time Howard was executed, fact and fiction were so thoroughly confused that one wondered whether the whole thing had been some fleeting, common hallucination, as ephemeral as a daydream. The execution had a profoundly purgative effect on the press and the public alike.

The murder was soon a sombre memory and the city quickly found other atrocities and scandals on which to sate its hunger for sensation.

"I don't like hearing about that man," Anna said calmly. "I was glad when the whole thing died down."

"Why is that? Do you find it frightening?" asked Albert.

Anna looked at him, as if the question were obtuse.

"Who wouldn't be frightened?" said Robert.

Anna recalled the impression she'd had on the ferry, when she'd felt as if the waking world were animated by a sinister logic that was only truly accessible in dreams.

"It's not simply the facts of the case that are frightening," she said. "It's the sense that something dreadful, just out of sight, is living side by side with commonplace things. I read in the paper that the girl was due to meet her sister and her brother-in-law at the Follies the day she went missing. In ordinary details like that there is something unspeakable that terrifies me more than the thought of the murder itself."

What she said touched Albert directly, yet in a way that she could not have anticipated. He was keenly aware of his own ordinariness, the banal fact of his body, perched on a chair in the kitchen of a cheap worker's cottage. His stomach had begun to sag a bit. He had become sedentary. At night he stretched out on the couch and read the paper or a journal and drank a glass of beer before dozing off. On the surface he was a fairly typical bloke. It was somewhere else, in nightmares and in waking dreams, that he met his double, the dim presentiment of all his possible crimes.

"Tell her about the forgery," Albert urged, eager to keep the conversation moving.

"Well, it's not much of a story. But I suppose it is indicative. A few weeks after the execution, a man turned up at the office with a manuscript. It was a collection of poems, about twenty in all, made out to look as if they'd been written by Howard. Awful stuff. Smatterings of Poe, dank, subterranean prisons, lascivious sexual details, necrophilia, the voices of the dying ringing out like suffocating muses from beneath the ground. Awful, obscene stuff."

"But you don't think they're authentic?" Anna asked, concealing a shudder of revulsion.

"Well, we've tracked down Howard's sister, who's adamant that her brother could barely even pen a letter."

"Are you going to publish them?" asked Albert.

"God no," said Robert. "Completely unsuited for public consumption. Even as oddities. With writers like Maupassant, Daudet and Zola banned by the *Customs Act*, we'd be certain to end up in court."

"The whole thing is so mysterious," Albert said. "Where did the poems come from in the first place? I mean, who is the bloke who brought them in? Did he write them himself?"

"He's a man called Dacre, a crooked little fellow with a broken accent. He claims to have known Howard. Some murky connection. Something to do with spiritualists in Bendigo. Sounds like nonsense to me. He keeps possession of the poems, of course, and is evidently thinking of publication for profit. When he brought them into the office he wouldn't let them out of his sight. Hovered around like an old fart and made sure that we only got a look at the first few. You'd think he had the deed to the Midas mine itself."

"But surely whoever publishes these is going to make a mint," Albert said, his eyes lighting up at the thought of such a lucrative little sham.

"I dare say these poems will find their way to the public, but it will have to be through some disreputable, back-room publisher or one of those nasty little dives, hidden away in your arcades, that sell those French novels."

Anna blushed. She remembered the pudgy man sitting like a bloated toad in the corner of the parlour reading Zola and the withered, jaundiced face of the woman highlighted against the black curtain.

"I'd like to read those poems," said Albert absentmindedly, in between mouthfuls of potato salad.

"I think they'd be quite out of place here, Bert," Robert said, smiling. "Howard was sick and so was the mania around him. The sooner we get him out of our systems the better, lest the infection spread into decent homes and families."

Albert listened calmly, impressed at how well his brother spoke and in a way loving him for the rectitude and certainty of what he said. Anna also found a certain comfort in his words. They would both have liked to believe in this vision of the home he conjured, but they knew, in their own very private ways, that it was a lie. They had both fallen away from this myth of righteousness, and if they could have spoken about this directly, they might have been able to fall away together. As it was each had stumbled off alone and the further they went along their own dark paths, the less, it seemed, they knew about themselves or each other.

A few nights later, after Robert's calming influence had subsided, Albert propped himself up on a pillow watching his wife prepare to turn in. Anna tried not to look at him and hurried under the counterpane, as if to avoid his gaze. Albert resented the thought of her untouchability. Decent homes and families, he thought sardonically. When he put out the lamp next to him, he leant into her and kissed her on the neck. Anna started, almost as if he'd bitten her. The baby was already screaming in the next room. She wriggled away from Albert and got out of bed.

"I'm sorry," she said impatiently, hugging a shawl around herself and hurrying out of the room.

He folded his hands on his stomach and lay as still as a corpse. She didn't seem to care about him, didn't see how his life was ebbing away, he thought. It surprised him to think that he was even really married to her. He listened to the creaking floorboards. He could hear her through the darkness, whispering to the baby.

When she came back half an hour later, he touched her nervously, moved his hand over her thigh and rested it on her hip, waiting for her to respond. But she lay still and he began to imagine the puritanical deadness of her acquiescence, her passive obedience to a sense of marital duty, the hollowness of her physical pleasure. Like Winton's diagnosis, the thought of it filled him with guilt. His penis went flaccid and the anxiety gathered in the pit of his stomach, twisting through him as he dropped away from her. He felt as if he'd swallowed a bag of nails.

"Albert," she said, sleepily. She sounded relieved to be left alone.

As he lay there his eyes began to ache. He wondered if he were slowly going blind or developing a tumour behind his sockets.

He suddenly wanted to sob. The urge came from nowhere. He felt the cruel distance opening up between himself and the body that he dragged through this impersonal domestic routine. It seized him and wouldn't let go. He yearned for his own resurrection while he imagined the sound of dirt falling on the lid of his coffin. He longed to feel his body come alive again, but knew the magic charm that animated the flesh had been snatched from his mouth. He trembled as he looked back at himself, heavy and stolid, barely alive.

How much longer could he bear it? In the kitchen, clutching the knife in his hand, he seemed to see everything clearly again. It was a sluggish afternoon. The light coming in through the back was sepia-tinged, like an old photograph, and he was hypnotised by the crisscross patterns on the dirty linoleum. He closed his hand around the handle, and touched the sharp blade with his thumb. He saw the way forward, and the certainty of a victory over his misery was so complete that no trace of doubt clouded his resolve. He shuddered with the conviction of his vision. She would scream, "What have you done?" and he'd reply, like the voice of judgement, "What have *you*?"

For a while he watched Anna cooing in German to their son. The child's eyes sparkled with delight. "*Holdes Kind*," he heard her say with love in her voice. Albert's loneliness stabbed at him. His hand hesitated for only a moment. He willed the rage into his heart until he thought it would burst. Fist white around the handle, he dug the knife into his skin, just above the hip, and felt himself flooding back into his body through the dull pain of the wound.

"*Sieh doch selbst!*" Anna said to Paul, pointing to a picture book on her lap.

Albert stumbled towards her, clutching his side. She heard the knife fall to the ground as she looked up at his white face and at his shirt wet with blood. For a moment she saw nothing and then, almost choking on her own breath, caught him as he fell into her.

"*Was hast du gemacht? Was hast du gemacht?*" she screamed, looking at his blood on her bare arms, as he sunk onto the floor beside the child.

A moment later she pulled herself together and ran next door, telling herself to say it calmly in English so that they'd understand that her husband had tried to kill himself. For the second time in his life Jack McDermott ran the two blocks to Dr Winton's, returning in a hansom, while a distraught Anna knelt over her husband and Sarah hurried Paul into his bedroom.

When Albert saw Dr Winton appear above him he almost laughed out loud. He was bleeding steadily, but of course he'd never meant to kill himself. He still saw everything as lucidly as he had at the moment of his decision, but now feared that somehow the sinister presence of the doctor would bring him undone. He began to weaken and feared that he really might bleed to death. The doctor was ready to usher him away. His teeth glistened like fangs under his fine, auburn moustache, reminding Albert of a cat or a rodent or some dreadful hybrid of the two – a hairy, carnivorous scavenger. Finally he shut his eyes.

Anna's fears, for a moment, reflected those of her husband. As Jack and the doctor carried Albert into the carriage, Anna watched Dr Winton uneasily. If Albert should die, she thought, that man will come for me. She dared herself to think it, only to smother the thought the instant it had formed. She left Sarah looking after the baby and got into the cab.

"I don't think you need fear, Anna," the doctor said as the carriage jolted into motion. "Your husband is bleeding very slowly and the wound is not a deep one. When he gets to the hospital he'll be fine."

He patted her arm. She was too exhausted to refuse his sympathy, concentrating her attention on her husband, feeling herself go blank with the shock of his pale face, the blood, the horrible implications of his act.

She held Albert's hand as she watched the houses flash by. The carriage was moving rapidly. Its chaotic motion made her feel ill. If he dies, she thought, she'd be to blame. She had forced him to marry her, she told herself. Her distance, the unconscious wish to be free — but she stopped herself. It was too horrible. She wanted to love him. She knew that she wanted to love him.

Albert was convalescing on the couch within a few days. The wound, as Dr Winton had said, was not a serious one. Albert's mental fragility, however, was another matter. A doctor at the Homoeopathic Hospital recommended that he see someone at Yarra Bend, someone with experience in the treatment of hysterics and neurasthenics. Anna and Robert, both harbouring an instinctive fear of mental illness, insisted that he'd be all right at home for the time being, but nevertheless agreed they should consult an expert.

Anna, deep down, doubted Robert's private insistence that he'd be fine under their supervision, but she was also sufficiently convinced that, because she was partly to blame for what had happened, she could also restore her husband to health simply by being more willing to meet the demands of their marriage. She knew now that she had entertained a kind of distance from the whole thing. She was barely aware of it until the sight of her husband bleeding on the floor tore the scales from her eyes and she stared into the giddy emptiness of their relationship.

"What have I done, Albert?" she asked him as they sat on the couch together.

"Nothing, Anna," he said in an apathetic manner that, far from consoling her, suggested that he didn't have the energy to implicate her in his breakdown.

She clutched his hand as tears ran down her cheeks. "I'll be better, Albert," she said. "I'll be a better wife, a better lover. I promise."

"It's not your fault. Don't blame yourself." He stood up and walked gingerly into the kitchen, careful not to disturb the stitches. A moment later he came back with a recent issue of the *Bulletin*, which he began reading while Anna dried her eyes with a handkerchief. His easy assurances merely reinforced her sense of guilt and she felt heavy with remorse. He could see her unease and knew that she was becoming the penitent he had intended her to be.

But she was also getting paler and thinner. She was no longer so peacefully and blithely absorbed in the welfare of her child. Her hands shook as she washed dishes, dusted the sideboard or cut up vegetables. She needed Albert to accept her, either to punish her or finally to convince her that she had nothing for which to atone. Her guilt consumed her, as if it were a poison that she carried in her veins and couldn't purge. She was wasting away under its steadily corrosive influence. Her breast milk dried up, her ribs began to press through her chest and her cheekbones slowly became more prominent.

"You're not really eating much these days," Albert said to her coldly. It was twilight, about a month after his stitches had been removed.

She looked at him, almost at her wit's end. "I'm too bloody nervous to eat."

She was standing in the fading light of the front bedroom window, her silhouette hanging in front of him. He walked up to her and held her thin hands. She turned to him, her eyes red but expressionless, and kissed him on the lips, tasting faint traces of beer and tobacco as she pushed her mouth into his. He could feel her shivering as he took her arms.

"I'm sorry, Albert," she said to him.

He kissed her harder. He could still sense her subtle resistance to him, the distance opening up between them as he drew her closer. He looked at her in the half-light of the approaching evening, noticing how tired she looked and how worn.

"I love you," she said, and began to unbutton her blouse, looking at him steadily.

But something in him didn't trust her. He took a small step away.

She stood in front of him, and now the indifference in her vanished. Her eyes were almost pleading and he felt himself change too, as if something horrible in him were making its way to the surface. He knew she had given in to him. For a second he imagined that he had put her into a trance.

"Do . . ." she said, and swallowed, ". . . do what you want to me."

She looked away from him as he stepped towards her, tore off her blouse and pushed her onto the unmade bed. He furiously pulled her skirt down over her thighs and then, when she was naked, held her beneath him, looking into her frightened eyes.

Neither of them heard the baby crying, or the front door creak open. As Hamish McDermott wandered into the narrow hallway he heard strange rutting noises that seemed oblivious to the distressed sobbing of the child in the next room. He followed the noises into the front bedroom. The door was open and he could see Albert's white backside jerking itself into a chaotically splayed mass of limbs that looked to the child like pieces of a disassembled shop mannequin. The place stank. Like a toilet, he thought. Soiled pieces of clothing littered the floor. Then he saw Anna's face, turned to one side. Her eyes were closed and she was panting with exhaustion. The smoothness of her skin, the high cheekbones and the blankness of her expression, all made him think that she was wearing a mask, and that underneath it wasn't really her, but a stranger. And when the eyes of the stranger opened and looked at him, he knew that they were not her eyes. They were dead, like hollow, burnt-out sockets.

Frightened, Hamish ran out into the street. It was grey outside, the very edge of nightfall. He could still hear Albert's animal groans, the shrill squeaking of the mattress and the cries of the baby filling the stifling atmosphere of the bedroom with a desperate breathlessness. But when he stopped, everything was calm. He breathed deeply, measuring the silence around him until he regained his composure.

"If little boys don't go to bed on time, they have their eyes plucked out," he remembered his mother saying to him.

He went back to his own house, with the vague fear of punishment for having looked in the dead eyes of the stranger. Later, in his bedroom, with all the lights out, it was as if a queer absence lay in wait for him. The darkness trembled and he longed for the fresh, clear light of morning.

part TWO

## chapter *four*

On the last night of the nineteenth century crowds gathered around the clock towers of the Melbourne Town Hall and the central post office. Flags had been stretched across the main streets. Banners attached to the light posts bore the names of the federated Australian states, and handmade posters, draped from upper-storey windows, prophesised the moment of national becoming that was just hours away: "One Flag, One Hope, One Destiny".

As night settled, the city was aglow. Caverns of white light shone from shopfronts through the densely packed footpaths, illuminating a tangled mass of black silhouettes. Some of the revellers blew toy trumpets and banged drums, such that when people forgot themselves or drifted absentmindedly in the throng, the sounds of these rude instruments returned them to their sense of a shared purpose. As midnight approached a calm descended on the streets.

Gradually eyes everywhere turned to one of the two clock towers as the minute hands slowly approached their zeniths.

"It's nearly time, Paul," Robert Walters said to his nephew. "Can you see the clock?"

The child, eight years old, was too engrossed to answer. Exhaustion and the constant shock of so much noise and movement about him had produced an abstracted state of mind that bordered on the ecstatic. Next to Paul was Hamish McDermott, who had grown into a stout, freckled child of twelve. The three of them stood on the corner of Bourke and Elizabeth Streets, opposite the post office. From their vantage point it looked like a crowded amphitheatre about to witness a gladiatorial combat or a triumphal procession. The arc light at the top of the post office flagpole cast a crimson glow over the celebrations.

A moment before midnight the first of twelve chimes rang out. Before the second had sounded the crowd let out a deafening cheer. A small cannon atop a roof on the other side of Bourke Street let off a round that was swallowed up by the noise.

"This is the first day of the Australian nation, boys," Robert said, eager that they understand the gravity of the moment. "After this, everything will be different."

As he spoke, Roman candles were ignited on both sides of Bourke Street and a mass of glittering golden sparks cascaded above the crowd.

Hamish wished Ondine, Paul's younger sister, were with them to witness this. He was besotted with her, and had been put out when Anna hadn't allowed her to accompany them. He would write something capturing the occasion, he told himself, and give it to her. How would he describe it? There were people, and moments of weird, clanging noise, and trumpets, as if they were at a strange circus. Then there was light, red light, and the street exploded into a shower of sparks that looked as if it were burning the people of the new nation. But whether it burnt or not, it was beautiful.

"It's ridiculous to be in love when you are twelve," his mother had told him. "You won't need a girl for another ten years." But Hamish still wished that Ondine had been allowed to come too. He wished she could have seen it all. He would have held her hand, and maybe told her that he loved her. What did it matter to them, all this talk of Federation? They weren't real Australians anyway and the three of them – Paul, Ondine and he – were going to Germany, to live in the forest, just as soon as they were old enough. It was their pact.

To Paul, the arc light made the whole scene look as if it had suddenly been bathed in blood. In a miraculous transformation the celebrating crowd had become something frightening and hateful, yet the boy was mesmerised. The play of darkness and light and the postures of jubilation and drunkenness before him invited his imagination to run wild as he saw things that he had never dreamt of before. Men dressed like clowns capered along the street and beggars stumbled in and out of gutters; some of the faces looked like skulls, others like dogs' heads, or masks, or people he thought he knew but couldn't place. People drank, vomited, kissed, jostled or just moved through the crowd like lunatics or oblivious sleepwalkers. They were all jammed together, moving as one, yet still so alone, and the whole seething mass was soaked in the ghastly red light of its own blood.

But then, as some time passed, the crowd thinned and another transformation occurred. At first it had been a violent sea of bodies, but now it was a series of gentle flows and eddies. Slowly the flood dissipated and, as Robert took Paul's hand and made to leave, the boy was engrossed by the sight of a sparse assortment of stragglers inhabiting a deserted, rubbish-strewn street. There was something eerie about it. It made him think of a painting he'd once seen depicting the aftermath of a great battle in which the field was strewn with bodies and debris. He wanted to stay and keep looking at the carnage and the forlorn sight of lost souls, but his uncle was now anxious to go and gently pulled him away from the street.

"We have a bit of a journey back home, Paul," Robert said.

"Will Ondine still be awake?" Hamish asked.

"I doubt it, young fella," he replied, smiling to himself.

In the distance, somewhere near the river, a cracked voice was singing, hopelessly out of tune.

*With no thoughts of 'er yesterday,*
*But dreams of a mighty state,*
*Great 'mid the old grave nations,*
*Divine in 'er aspirations,*
*Blessed be the men who brought 'er,*
*Freedom's starriest daughter,*
*Outa the night, inta the light.*
*The power and the glory,*
*For evermore.*

"Amen," another voice yelled out at the conclusion of the song, prompting a burst of boisterous laughter that rippled along the banks of the river.

As the century ended, as the clock struck twelve and other people cheered and hugged, Anna held her daughter on her shoulder.

Ondine had wanted to go into the city as well, but her mother, not feeling hardy enough to tackle the tumult, decided that Robert would have his hands full with the two boys. Albert was scheduled to work the Melbourne–Geelong line and wouldn't be home until late, so rather than spending such a significant night alone, Anna went next door to the McDermotts', where a group of men from the wharves and their families had gathered to celebrate the arrival of Federation.

For a while Ondine played with the other children, leaving Anna to chat and have a glass of cider. She was taken by the easy sociability of these working men and their open, if slightly uncouth manners. Since Albert's troubles, Jack and Sarah had been warm and supportive neighbours. When Albert lost his job at the insurance company they continued to interact with unembarrassed candour, and when he found work again as a train conductor, Jack slapped him on the shoulder and congratulated him on his return to the "ranks of the Southern Cross".

The fading hours of the nineteenth century had gripped Anna with nostalgia, homesickness and regret. She thought about her father, who had died two years earlier, and her mother who, at the age of sixty-three, had refused to move to Melbourne and instead raised herself in revolt against a country she hated and planned her return to Germany to pass away in peace. She died of pneumonia in Port Adelaide, waiting for the *Gothland* to sail to Bremen.

As twilight fell Anna knew she couldn't bear to be alone with these thoughts and gratefully accepted Sarah's invitation as they watched Robert escort their sons towards their encounter with history. But now it was as if the passing of midnight had broken the spell. The century had turned and she finally felt able to leave the party and go home.

When she tucked Ondine into bed she knew she wasn't looking forward to Robert's return. Since Albert's suicide attempt – she still called it that – and his subsequent breakdown, which saw him convalescing and then unemployed for almost three years after the birth of Ondine, Robert had helped her no end. He was always there to take a hand in the raising of the children and the running of the household affairs. He did this with such chivalry and commitment to his brother's family that soon his mere presence, as surely as anything, reminded Anna of the desperate nature of her situation. She would almost have preferred to have been left alone with her enfeebled husband and their two small children, rather than encounter Robert's good intentions at every turn. He made her feel as if she were living in some protracted state of hopeless dependence. He tried to sympathise with her and to help Albert along, but he had no idea what it was really like. Her husband had worn her out, living off her like a parasitic strangler vine, turning her into a shell of herself. She knew that, in a way, she had given up.

While Albert was unemployed he occupied himself with incessant writing. At first he wrote letters to newspapers complaining about larrikins on Clarendon Street, prostitutes around Albert Park, and the sorry state of the Hanna Street drain, "the river of the dead", which had become a dumping ground for animal carcasses. Not one of these diatribes was ever published, but the act of writing seemed to mollify his anxiety and distract him from what the doctors had described as "nervous exhaustion and enervation". Then he started going to the library in pursuit of other projects about which he remained secretive. She almost never saw him during the day. In the grip of his graphomania, Albert was more complex than she had first thought, and it was this complexity on which she focused when she sacrificed herself in the hope of appeasing his obscure and sometimes violent inclinations. She was almost used to it. She'd learnt how to tame her fear and forget her shame, how to numb herself and act out her part.

And then, one day, there he was, standing in the living room wearing a train conductor's uniform.

Anna felt her chest tighten. The children's wooden train set was spread out at his feet. Paul pushed the red and blue carriages along the tracks, choo-chooing as they went.

"I got a job," Albert said, morosely. But then a grin crept over his face. He grabbed her as if she should have been happy, mocking her with the irony of his celebration.

Something in her gave out, and though she was aware that she didn't betray herself, she felt as if she were about to dissolve in the acid of her anguish.

"Dad's a conductor," he puffed out to the children.

Anna looked at the train set, the children and then at her husband's uniform. She put her hand to her mouth, stifling a shudder as Albert's hands ran down her spine. The man who hid himself away in the library all day and virtually raped her at night now revealed himself as a grotesque and regressing man-child. She was living in a nightmare.

That night, when he hauled her carelessly towards him, it was all she could think about. She forced herself to quieten her revulsion, becoming a pliant, but dead thing as he crushed her into the sagging mattress.

Why on earth should she feel guilty at having run to Winton? As her husband tore away at her like an animal, she knew there was nothing left to accuse her.

Paul was only three and Ondine was about to turn two when it first happened. With no money coming in but for the little Robert could afford to lend Albert, they were getting by on parcels of food relief from the Benevolent Ladies Society. One morning there was a knock at the front door. A messenger had an envelope for Anna. She opened it in front of him and found a ten-pound banknote.

"What's this?" she asked.

She turned the envelope over. It had a St Vincent Place address. She knew straightaway it was from Dr Winton and the blood rushed to her face.

"Please take this back," she said.

"Can't do that, ma'am," the boy said. "The doctor said that you could return it in person, or not at all."

She left the children with Sarah McDermott and, flustered, hurried over to the doctor's house, determined to return the money and let him know that his assistance was not required. He opened the door as if he had been expecting her.

"Hello Anna," he said shamelessly. Not wanting to make a scene on his verandah in full view of the picnickers sunning themselves in the gardens opposite, she let herself be drawn into the darkness of his hallway. "I'm glad you came, but I'd implore you to keep the money."

She looked at him, speechless. Her resolve failed her and, suddenly, she didn't know what she was doing in this strange man's house. He led her into a sitting room and positioned her in front of him on a leather couch, still standing while he spoke to her.

"I would like to help you, Anna. You and the children. And Albert, of course."

She looked at him with suspicion and said nothing. She remembered the book by Dr W, the confronting illustrations, the sense of the illicit that had led her on as she walked through the city in search of some obscure thing that she could not possibly have put a name to.

"Will you allow me that?"

She tried to remain calm. She knew she was vulnerable, and as she admitted this to herself she scrutinised the doctor's cultured, gentlemanly demeanour, searching for a hint of something more sinister, a propensity to exploit perhaps, a clue that would give him away and release her. Could it be his intention to humiliate her? He continued to speak and she endeavoured to listen, but the words rushed past her despite her efforts. Money, the children, his sincere desire to share his good fortune. Her heart was pounding so frantically it was all she could hear. She couldn't bear it. The cool of the room caressed her and her skin prickled. She stood up. She had to get out, but his eyes seized her as she moved and held her just long enough for him to make his play.

"Any man could fall in love with you, Anna," he said in an abrupt and impassioned turn. "But the thought of you loving *any* man is a travesty, an utter travesty."

This sudden change startled her. Finally, the secret implication of Winton's meandering, the secret she'd known all along, had worked its way to the surface.

"What are you talking about?"

The doctor paused, collecting himself. He breathed deeply for a moment, drawing in the air through tightly clenched teeth before regaining his composure.

"You wander from place to place," he said. "One day you meet a man and stumble into a certain intimacy. How does it happen? What distinguishes him? Before you know it you're doing the block with 'your boy', your heart's idol, the romance of it all is overwhelming and in this realm of shadows you fancy that you are happy, contented, fulfilled. Good Lord! Only an idiot could put up with it, Anna."

"It wasn't like that," she said, unable to disguise her annoyance.

"Of course it wasn't. So why go on pretending? For the sake of respectability? A respectability that no one but yourself believes in?"

She met his stare and then quickly lowered her eyes again.

"I have no wish to, to . . ." But he couldn't finish the sentence.

She wasn't sure whether he was acting a part or not, but she didn't let herself linger over the question of his sincerity. She thought about Albert, about how powerless she was in his hands, how vile and humiliated she felt. How dead, dead to her own pleasure. She was about to leave, but compelled by a sense of abandon welling within herself she remained in front of him, waiting for the certainty of her own desire to seize her. Winton appeared so vulnerable, as if his mask had fallen and she had seen something else underneath it. She had never seen this, this other thing, existing in a man, save for the moment at which Albert had stabbed himself.

"To live with our eyes open," he mumbled. "That's all."

She touched his hand. She didn't know what she was doing. But at that moment it didn't matter. She had glimpsed something. It might have been freedom. It might simply have been the space to breathe. Whatever it was, she embraced it.

She touched his mouth. Her lips parted slightly as she held herself for him, his hand on the back of her neck, running up through her hair.

The next day, when Robert offered her money for groceries, she said casually that she still had some of the inheritance her aunt had left her, and that, for the moment, they could manage well enough.

"Very well then," he said, relieved for her sake, and for his.

She turned away from him, unable to conceal her lack of composure as she thought about the doctor. Wasn't she already prostituting herself? Albert had saved her from the disgrace of being a single mother left to raise a bastard son. He had also saved her from the shame of having to confront her parents with this guilt. And in return she repaid him with constant, abject submission. The shadow world of love had dissipated. She could clearly see what she had become, and it had happened well before Winton had sent her his ten-pound banknote.

In the early hours of 1901 the calm of the house gave Anna the pause in which to trace out the tangled threads of this existence. As she waited for her brother-in-law and her husband to return home, she watched Ondine sleeping, praying that her daughter might see with her eyes open right from the outset.

When Albert first began working out of Spencer Street Station he took umbrage at not being able to spend such long hours in the public library where he'd grown fond of the dim, yellowish glow of the old gas-jet lamps, the polished wood, and the musty smell of accumulated dust. As he slowly recovered his strength he had traded the banality of the accounts department, where books and figures had a deadening sameness, for the seductiveness of novels, poetry, essays and more obscure treasures fished out of the deep recesses of history. The secret knowledge of the library, which he imagined forming some vast, intricate system linking all the disparate faculties and inclinations of man, held him entranced as each of his obsessions ran its course, only to see another emerge in its place. The library, he came to believe, was the place in which the authentic being of man was possible, because in it all the tendrils of human possibility coiled around the essential but impossible core of authentic understanding, absolute knowledge and truth. These were, of course, literally out of man's reach, but were nonetheless perceptible in the idea of the library – a vast, material metaphor for truth as resonant with meaning as any cathedral in the city. Behind the hundreds of thousands of words was a beginning, a world of soot and steam and shadow that stirred convulsively through the earthly endeavours of man. The word obscured this pure, sensual, brutal world, but it was also the key to it. With the faith of a religious maniac seeking insight, Albert buried himself in the library, reading books about the fall of ancient civilisations, the cults of tribal societies, the building of great cities, the secrets of nature, the powers of magic, the miracles of technology, the death of God, the birth of man and the perverse depths of the human mind.

At first the trains had been a poor substitute for this devotion to the absolute. Robert had urged him to apply for the job when it was advertised and Sid Packard, against his better judgement, had warmly recommended him to the Rail Board. Albert loathed the thought of working again. He saw work, in fact all forms of merely utilitarian endeavour, as ultimately futile and worthless.

"You have a family, Albert," Robert urged him one evening in the Limerick Arms. "You have to take responsibility for them."

Albert, who was always at his calmest and most reasonable in the presence of his brother, didn't disagree, but merely avoided direct eye contact, sulking in a way that acknowledged his high aspirations would have to be put aside for the time being.

"I should have lived in another century, Robert," he said.

His brother looked at him, but Albert sensed that Robert, a mere journalist after all, a scribe more than a writer, a simple recorder of the everyday rather than a quester for the truth behind it, would never understand him.

"What century would that have been?"

"Never mind. It's curious to think that we are so worn out. The place is barely a hundred years old and the country seems completely exhausted. All that settling, felling and digging has taken an awful toll."

"You used to sing a different tune. You and your mate Sid."

"Did I?" Albert asked, looking at his brother with an expression of mild surprise. "I can barely remember."

"Albert, you need to take that job. You can't expect Anna to keep spending the little bit of money she has supporting the children while you fritter away your time in the library. If you wrote articles I could maybe organise some sort of freelance work for you, but ... "

Robert knew he couldn't finish the sentence without insulting his brother. With the thought still hanging he signalled to the bartender and ordered another round.

But working as a conductor was not like working in an accounts department. At the insurance company there had been a constant stream of bureaucratic detail to attend to. There was no relief from it, no time to think, no time to be oneself. As the trains swayed and bumped between Melbourne and their various provincial destinations, however, Albert found that he had time to spare. In the contraction of space between two points, as the locomotive sped between cities, a contemplative expanse opened up in which he could meander from one abstraction to another. The regimentation of the railway, the constant adherence to schedules and timetables, was also a relief. The administrative erasure of free will in the measurement of miles, hours and minutes, meant that he was spared the burden of having to concentrate too hard on the job at hand. It was simply a matter of turning up on time and then letting the mechanised ensemble of man and machine run itself. Whereas the work of a clerk involved the constant exercise of will, until there came a point at which will gave out altogether, the life of a train conductor was an automatic one. As the machine moved through space, the conductor moved anonymously through the train's compartments and carriages without the burden of identity or responsibility.

Later, after his shift had finished, Albert struggled to remember what he had done. He was usually physically exhausted by the time he got home and could recall only strange, disjointed impressions of landscape, darkness and rushing light, of sleeping passengers, the sound of his own footfalls, the vision of a beautiful woman alone in a compartment gripped by the motion of the machine, the light caught in her hair like a nimbus.

# chapter five

Towards the end of summer Albert took Paul with him on a trip to Ballarat, thinking that the novelty of train travel would interest his son. It was a quiet weekday and the train was almost empty, enabling him to spend a good few hours sitting with his son instead of patrolling the carriages. Paul was a taciturn and self-absorbed child and had brought a pad and a handful of coloured pencils with him. Even before the train started moving he was drawing what he could see through the window.

"What are you sketching, Paul?" Albert asked.

"Just tracks and stuff. And people."

As the train gathered speed the child's hand became less steady. At first Paul gripped his pencil and concentrated more earnestly on the integrity of line and form. But the jolting motion of the locomotive became more intense and the scenes passing outside the window more rapid, until finally the cityscape rushed by in a blur. His hand gave in to the movement of the carriage, producing a chaotic series of jagged, plunging lines. Having finished with something that looked like a record of seismographic activity, he gave up, letting his eyes settle on the stream of images outside the window.

"How *do* people draw on trains?" he asked his father.

"Usually they don't."

"That's because everything moves so fast and the train is always bumping you," he said sagely.

Albert looked at his son, wondering what the boy knew. He could divine little from the child's features, which as yet were too unformed to reveal much of his character. Ondine was, if anything, more opaque to him, but the fact that she looked so much like her mother suggested that the girl would grow up to have the same remote demeanour, the same passivity, the same dread-inspiring aura of Lutheran purity. That Albert barely knew his wife didn't occur to him. He was confident that he understood her thoroughly, despite the obvious distance that separated them. Empathy wasn't necessary for him to grasp the deadening, Nordic chill of such women.

When Paul got used to the movement of the train he tried drawing again. This time he didn't bother looking out the window, but drew from his imagination. He didn't try to exert a strict control over the movement of the pencil either, but let the train exert a degree of influence on the shapes and forms he drew.

"What's that, Paul?" Albert asked, looking at the crude farrago of faces and bodies that his son was producing unselfconsciously before him.

"It's the arrival of midnight in the city of Melbourne," the boy said.

Albert could make out the post office clock tower, the streamers and banners, and the rudiments of a crowd. The whole thing had a grotesque, comic energy that could have been the result of the boy's lack of skill, or of the train's chaotic effect on the steadiness of his hand. The faces in the crowd were outlandish, warped little blobs stuck on bloated bodies. Some had animal fangs, chattering skeleton teeth, hollow eyes, or sharp, vulture-like beaks. Some looked like bears, wolves or dingos. Some wore top hats, carried swords, waved flags or were busy vomiting a nasty melange of liquid and assorted garbage into the street. The sky was dark and in the distance the child had drawn flames dancing around the revellers, and a scarlet moon. Paul's hand jerked with the jolts of the train, adding further distortion to the brutality of the scene, as forms closed in on each other creating a menacing jumble of activity. As Albert watched his son's seemingly random pencil strokes he saw the relentless chaos of plummeting movement. Coherence gave way to disintegration, ordered form to compulsive distortion, yet the drawing had more life in it than anything he could imagine producing himself.

When Paul and Albert arrived home in the evening, Hamish was in the living room playing dominoes on the floor with Ondine, while Anna and Sarah drank tea in the kitchen.

"That's an eight," Hamish said gently.

"Oh," the girl said, snatching the tile back and replacing it with a matching nine.

Paul sat down beside them. "You wanna see what I drew on the train?" he asked.

Ondine put her arms around him and diverted herself away from Hamish, who was clearly peeved at his demotion in her attentions. Paul showed them the picture, which now had the title written in crude letters underneath it.

"That's awful," said Hamish.

"I think it's beautiful," said Ondine.

"No it's not, it's ugly." He might have added that Ondine herself was beautiful, that her mother was beautiful, that each of them was the embodiment of a beauty more radiant than any of the princesses or sprites in the stories that Anna had read to them.

Albert watched the children debate the merits of the picture and then strolled into the kitchen where his wife stood up, kissed him on the cheek and poured him a cup of tea.

"Did Paul behave himself?" Anna asked.

"He worked most of the day and sat quietly in the depot office in Ballarat. Good as gold, so to speak."

The ease with which they both slipped into the rhythm of the evening sometimes astounded Anna. She would have preferred it if Albert had looked at her like a quivering madman, but he didn't. His usual manner had nothing really exceptional about it, the demeaning uniform aside, and the casual observer would not have sensed that there was all that much out of the ordinary.

"Hungry?" Anna asked as Sarah finished her tea and made to leave.

"Yes," Albert said.

"I've got some chops, fresh."

"That sounds good."

The surface of things had its own comforts, and sometimes they could both feel at ease in it, as long as neither of them dwelt too long on the deception.

"Can Hamish stay for tea too?" Paul asked from the living room, catching the mention of food.

"He's got to come home to his own dinner," Sarah said before Anna could consent, as she inevitably did in these situations.

"These children are really inseparable," Sarah said under her breath.

"You can say that again," said Albert.

Anna liked Hamish and the way in which he interacted with her own children. The boy had taken to German and once, when she read them a Heine poem about the Lorelei, he asked her whether Australia had a Lorelei of its own, which she took to be a revealing question, indicating the boy's intelligence. While other children played cricket in Draper Street, Hamish was content to read or be read to, and his presence turned what might have been the loneliness of a mother and her children into something like the feeling of company. That, years ago now, he had looked into her eyes, seen her so cruelly exposed and then concealed the fact of such intimacy within him, never mentioning or even hinting at what he had witnessed, also filled her with warmth at the thought of his loyalty. Paul, Ondine and Hamish had grown up together, and though Hamish was older, the bonds between them seemed quite unbreakable.

Albert, on the other hand, was not so trusting. He thought a boy of twelve, nearly thirteen, was too old to be playing dominoes with a girl of seven. He could see that Hamish was infatuated with Ondine and it troubled him.

One evening Albert had come home to find Hamish nervously looking at an old issue of the *Bulletin*, fixing upon a provocative illustration by Norman Lindsay depicting "The Poet and the Muse". The former was a forlorn, world-weary man, leaning bent and broken over a writing desk. The latter was a winged maiden, her rounded breasts drawn with precise detail, leaning over the poet sympathetically, as if to guide him. Hamish quickly closed the magazine when Albert appeared at the door, but not before he could guess what the boy had found so engrossing.

Later, according to Sarah, the boy had asked his parents what a muse was.

"What did you say?" Anna asked.

"Well, I don't really know. Like an inspiration, wouldn't you say? That's what Jack said to him anyway."

Albert promptly produced the very issue of the *Bulletin* that contained the sketch, which he showed the women, and read the accompanying poem about the sacred secret of infinity burning in the beauty of the rose, and the soul of the radiant maiden who breathes light and meaning into the visible world.

"Overblown rubbish," he concluded.

"But better than the usual woman-hating stuff they come up with," Anna rejoined, snatching the magazine out of his hands. "Listen. This from the wisdom of Nietzsche on the Red Page: 'Is it not better to fall into the hands of a murderer than into the dreams of a lustful woman? Mud is at the bottom of her soul.'"

She blushed as she read it, wondering why it seemed so repulsively resonant to her.

"He was a lunatic," Albert muttered.

Anna dropped the magazine on the table sensing that Albert felt exposed.

"Anyway, it's nice to have a muse," she said finally. "Hamish has a romantic temperament, which in this day and age is a good thing."

Albert slouched into a chair, resenting Hamish all the more. Anna treated him as one of her own children, not perceiving the stranger so close to their daughter. At the back of his mind Albert harboured the tremulous thought, which he knew he dare not explore, of the boy, chubby, freckled and with lumpish white hands, and Ondine, only seven, yet still on the verge of the cold sensuality that he imagined in his wife.

Years later, when Hamish McDermott dwelt upon his childhood, he'd recall parts of the city as if they were enchanted. He couldn't be sure of the extent to which his imagination had invented the phantasmagoric city of his youth. Sometimes, when he had time, he'd go for walks through the streets and lanes looking for places that he had known as a child – a cyclorama, a dilapidated arcade, or a used-book stall selling banned literature – and not find the place, which made him suspect that it had never been there at all. Even so he never tired of the streets, which would wink at him with the promise of his childhood and draw him out into forgetfulness. To the casual passer-by it must have looked as if he walked in a completely aimless manner, with no apparent destination. And in a way the aimlessness of these walks was their pleasure. With no ostensible goal or object in mind, he'd meander off the main thoroughfares and find himself confronting some unfrequented lane or dusty window where time seemed to have stood still and an eerie calm prevailed.

"*Ich weiß nicht, was soll es bedeuten, daß ich so traurig bin.*" He recalled the poem about the Lorelei that Anna had read to the three of them, Paul, Ondine and him, when they were children. In the poem a beautiful maiden with glittering jewels in her hair sits on a cliff overlooking the Rhine and sings a song of such intoxicating power that a sailor is lured off his course onto the rocks and drowns. The poet who tells this story describes it as a tale from olden times. In the gloomy absence of the Lorelei's song, the song of death, he is inexplicably sad, and this sadness is the mystery explained by the description of the song's violent power.

When he was thirteen Hamish and Paul had run off into the city to look at near naked mannequins in the window of a ladieswear store in the Royal Arcade. The plaster figures stretched their smooth, white limbs into various postures of arousal. Behind the glass window, which caught reflected light from the other shops and the glowing white orbs suspended from the ceiling, they seemed to be swimming in a sea of stars.

"That must be what the Lorelei looks like," Hamish said to Paul. He paused. He was on the verge of adding that he loved Ondine. He wanted to tell someone. He was bursting with the secret of his innocent desire, but put off by the closeness of the brother and sister, and the awkwardness he felt being excluded from their blood bond, he caught himself.

Instead he put the question to Paul: "Do *you* love Ondine?"

The younger boy smirked at him, shrugged and said nothing.

When a passer-by disturbed the moment of reverie the boys withdrew from the window and headed back towards Bourke Street. Hamish couldn't remember what happened next, but the image of the mannequins and the tension he felt would often resurface, luminous with its promise and possibility, through all the dark times that subsequently crowded around it. It was a moment that never left him, even though he knew, in the years that followed, how delusional it had been. The celestial shopfront of naked female forms, the glassy mystery of the arcade, flooded with light, yet still harbouring a darkness that had been gathering for decades, might have been what he was searching out on his many walks through the city. Whenever he returned to the arcade it was heavy with the memory of those mannequins. Even though the place had fallen into disrepair, he still imagined that, amidst the flaking paint, the cracked walls and the broken windows, he could hear the song – pure, primal sound, calling him away from the profane shimmer of electric lights and the din of motor car traffic into some watery Rhineland dream.

After this visit to the arcade Paul returned to his pencils with a head brimful of imagery. He was almost frantic as he sat down, dangling over the clean, white page before him, anxious about the appearance of the first line. Ondine sat opposite him on the floor, moving a toy spindle around her hand, occasionally glancing up at her brother. The two children looked alike at a fundamental level. Both were pale and slender, both had delicate hands and faintly freckled skin, but Ondine's flaxen hair was a stark contrast to Paul's jet black. Nevertheless they barely noticed this difference, instinctively dwelling on the sameness between them as a source of enormous comfort and security.

Paul looked at his sister, who was careless of his attention, and then looked down at the paper again. The arcade, he thought, was like a cathedral, or a cavern, or a vast grave site, a catacomb full of aloof figures ghosting up and down its length. He imagined crosses and candles. If he drew the arcade it would be a place that had a large crucifix at one end, that was lined with candles and bathed in a weird, orange light. He drew the smooth, hairless pudendum of the mannequin in the shop window with long lines curving around the pristine whiteness of the page. Then, on another sheet, he tried to draw the arcade itself, using straighter lines and angles. But he found the control and the economy of these drawings tiresome and soon his hand began to move faster and more erratically as he jerked the pencil in short, sharp movements across the page, drawing the shopfront as a chaotic ensemble of lines and limbs and hastily composed objects. He tried to capture the effects of the light, starting with simply drawn rays emanating from a lamp and then, unsatisfied, tried to shade in parts of the window with heavier, more densely concentrated pencil lines until the whole composition seemed far darker and more crowded than he had wanted it to be.

The drawing turned out much like his picture of midnight in the city of Melbourne, entirely destroying the sense of light and glass he had wanted to capture, turning the mannequins into fearful things of terror, leering out of the thickly drawn darkness like ghouls. Realising his error he decided to finish the picture by adding more extreme and grotesque features to the figures, giving them bulbous red eyes and exaggerated, gaping mouths. In the space around the window he drew a mass of tiny objects hovering in the air like a cloud of insects. Diamonds, coins, combs, scissors, a dagger dripping with blood, a crucifix on a chain, a gun, a glove, a little doll with its hair sticking up erect, a spider, a snake, a pair of bloodshot eyes, a coffin, a skull, a saucer and cup, could all be made out of the frantically drawn minutiae encircling the harpies in the shop window like a halo of detritus. The picture finally nauseated him. It was as if something had gripped him and his hand, quite mechanically, had run out of his control. He had wanted calm, and instead he'd drawn a kind of sick, sensual anarchy.

Ondine put down the spindle and moved over to Paul looking at the picture as she took up a piece of paper and started on her own. She drew his face, concentrating on the pale freckles standing out against his white skin, giving the cheeks a greenish glow as she shaded them, and the eyes a deep blue, with a faint, yellowish outline. She drew calmly, changing colour quickly and pedantically, as if just the right amount of each were the essential secret of her portrait. Paul watched her, noticing that the skin tones looked better when they were tinted with blue or green, rather than red or brown, which was his instinct. He returned to his first picture, which he began to amend following his sister's use of these colours, smudging them with his thumb into a mysterious, fleshy form, the promise of a garish vitality that, for a moment, pulsed with life on the page before him.

~

Later, when the children were asleep, Albert paced the house scrutinising the drawings his children had left lying about on the floor. Anna sat on the couch reading Ada Cambridge by the light of an old oil lamp, trying to ignore Albert's agitation, which was grating on her nerves. He was on the verge of saying something to her, but caught himself, realising that he didn't have the words to express succinctly the sense of anxiety that mounted in him as he looked at the sketches. He had detected certain tendencies in himself, but detection and a degree of understanding did not render him capable of self-mastery. Accepting his own failure in a resigned and apathetic manner he was still, nevertheless, hopeful that Paul might be able to summon the powers of concentration and self-control, the absence of which had unhinged him. My son should be able to keep his head down, he thought to himself, and at that moment Albert glimpsed the vortex to which he had slowly sacrificed all the sounder principles of life and wondered at the folly of his own delusion.

He wanted to say something about this to his wife, but the formulaic rhythms of their life together precluded confession as surely as it did intimacy. The sense of their partnership fulfilling itself according to the remote and automatic logic of hollow contractual agreement, in which man and wife were simply the masks they adopted for the sake of convenience, was now so apparent to him that he would have felt foolish and even a little bit insensitive reintroducing something of himself into their intercourse. There was no telling what it might have sparked in her. She seemed to sit there on the edge of hysterical self-revelation. Albert had no idea about Dr Winton, but in moments of clarity he hoped that Anna had been able to find something more than what the four walls of their cottage offered her, that she had been able to stumble after and perhaps lay hands on her own chimeras and draw life out of some secret source untouched by the poison that slowly seeped through the crevices of their marriage.

So Albert said nothing much about the drawings. He just placed them gently on Anna's lap, not wanting to disturb her reading. "Take a look at these," he said.

She looked them over, one after the other, until she came to the smooth, formless genitalia Paul had drawn. The drawing put her in mind of the afternoon she had gone to the stationer's store in Flinders Lane. That afternoon she had resented Winton, more out of a thoughtless deference to convention than to anything she sincerely believed or felt. She imagined that his hands would be sweaty and that his gold-handled cane would be a tool for the exercise of cruelty. Why had she thought this, solely on the basis of the books assembled in the stationer's shop? Because the body was such a filthy and compromising object? Because one couldn't dare probe its workings in a disinterested manner? What a stupid prude she had been. She smiled inwardly at her former self, picturing a child with an utterly fantastic set of fears and hopes about the workings of the natural world.

"He is certainly ahead of his age," she said calmly.

"You don't think it's inappropriate?"

"Oh, perhaps," she said, waving off his concern. "It's probably quite normal."

Albert looked at the picture again. It troubled him that Anna was so blasé about it. For a moment he felt emasculated, thinking that he would take the situation in hand but realising, as Anna spoke, that his assumption of paternal authority was something in which she was not prepared to collaborate. What was the point of him getting all anxious about it and trying to talk some sense into the boy if his wife were not remotely interested in the moral danger so emphatically embodied in the chaotic little sketch? He resented her anew, but said nothing.

She went on reading for a moment or two and then began to hum a song to herself as her eyes wandered away from the page. "*Wie soll ich fliehen? Wälderwärts ziehen?*"

He turned to her again. He hated the sound of her speaking German, the awful sense of words existing under other words, the beautiful mocking melody of her voice.

"Anna, did you ever think . . . ?"

She looked up at him blankly.

"Did you ever . . . with German . . . I . . . I mean the children . . ." The words failed him.

She still looked at him and he looked back thinking, for a second, that her eyes were not her own and that this woman, sitting in front of him, was someone he had never even seen before.

## chapter six

Without another word about it to his wife, Albert decided to take things into his own hands. The next Saturday, wearing his conductor's uniform, though he wasn't scheduled to work a shift that day, he led Paul through the city towards the Eastern Arcade, not bothering to explain to his son the purpose of their odyssey into the queer end of Bourke Street. It was a long time since Albert had set foot in the arcade, and even he was a little surprised at the extent of its decrepitude.

Outside it was a humid day with grey clouds hanging over the city. As a result there was almost no natural light in the passageway, giving it the appearance of a cavern or a tomb illuminated only by the occasional light visible behind a plate-glass window. In the gloom strange figures sauntered and loitered about, gazing lazily at their own reflections in the windows, vanishing into or emerging out of the mysteriously cloaked depths of the arcade as if the whole place were an elaborately staged magic show, a hall of mirrors, of false surfaces and hidden trapdoors.

Albert led Paul into a small shop, down a short hallway and then into a maze of rooms lit up by bright electric lights. At the entrance of the hallway was a booth attended by a young bloke selling admittance tickets at a shilling apiece. As Albert paid the youth, Paul could see one or two men ahead of them shuffling along the hallway, casually crossing from room to room.

The place had been called an anthropological institute for a brief period in the previous century. In those days showmen boasted of the medical benefits in acquainting the masses with the formation of their own bodies, inviting the public to explore the maladies it needed to guard against. They vehemently opposed the sentimentality that objected to their efforts on the grounds of taste and propriety, insisting that the admirers of the works of God would find no immorality in an open display of His divine craftsmanship. In this school of moral instruction, they claimed, parents might teach their children the very principles of health and purity that would shield them from temptation. But public outrage soon reached a sufficient pitch to force such displays off the main thoroughfares and into the moist, fungal depths of the city. There they could regenerate, cross-fertilised with numerous other gametes of bourgeois deformity, spawning outgrowths that would never share the sunlight with respectable citizens strolling down the posh end of Collins Street.

In the Eastern Arcade what had once been known as Melbourne's Grand Anthropological Institute had reappeared as the Cabinet of Anatomical Curiosities, a warren of oddities with a brothel on one side and a photographic studio on the other. Despite its changed appearance and status Albert Walters still recalled the horror he had experienced as a boy when his father had led him through its previous incarnation, explaining the models with reference to the criminal deformity of the onanist and the "sisterhood of shame" in Little Bourke and Little Lonsdale Streets. Albert didn't have the energy or the inclination to repeat this sermon to Paul as the boy gazed at the models. He didn't know what he would say. His own moment of failure, when he had fallen in love with a whore on his wedding night, still gripped him, and a vision of his own monstrous lust rose up before him as if to mock his good intentions. He hoped that the horrible sight of syphilitic ulcerations, blisters, pustules and cancers would speak for itself, filling the boy with dread at the thought of the dangers lying in wait for him.

Paul lingered in front of a model simply described in the catalogue as "A Monstrosity". It was an old woman with a sharp horn growing out of her forehead. Next to her were the "Malformation Termed 'Hermaphrodite'" and the natural apron of the Hottentot. He lingered over the anatomical Venus, diseased vaginas, virgin breasts, and a jar full of glass eyes until the obscene paraphernalia of the place had overwhelmed his senses and he felt in desperate need of his pencil set to record the vivid colours and luxuriating flowerage not of the models, but of his own desire.

Across the way, a pale man with a neatly waxed moustache and tight black gloves nodded at him. His glistening, bloodshot eyes, which seemed so moist that they might overflow with tears at any moment, held Paul fixed on the spot in front of the open lips of a swollen, syphilitic mouth gaping up at him from the display case. The man approached a little closer, moving gently with barely audible footfalls.

"Young man, the train conductor is calling you."

Paul turned around to see his father looking bewildered at the edge of the room.

"Of course," the man continued, "you are under no compulsion to oblige him."

Albert could plainly see that the display had stimulated rather than discouraged his son. As he guided Paul back out into the arcade, the boy was mesmerised.

"Paul, those diseases are caused by our sins," he said earnestly, putting his hands on his son's shoulders, shaking the boy as he spoke. "The drawings you did are sinful as well. I can't make you stamp out impure thoughts. But I hope you have the good sense to … to …"

Albert faltered, not really knowing how he had intended to finish his speech. The boy looked at him blankly, just as Anna had done when she sang to herself in German. Was Paul secretly laughing at him? The boy sucked in his cheeks. For a moment Albert felt like slapping him.

"Purity and health, Paul," he said finally, in a more resigned tone of voice. "Why don't you try to draw purity and health?"

"What does purity look like?" Paul asked.

Albert pondered. His eyes were suddenly aching again. "It could be a pretty picture. Like a mountain and a fresh stream."

"Like Mum's picture of the Rhine?" Paul asked, thinking of the painting that had been on their living room wall his entire life.

"Yes," said Albert. "Or something else good and innocent." As he spoke he glimpsed the rot within him. How much longer could he keep up the façade? He grimaced, rubbing the palms of his hands against his temples.

At that moment, the door of the Cabinet of Anatomical Curiosities opened and the man who had spoken to Paul emerged, giving them both a meaningful glance, before ambling off towards Little Collins

Street. A few doors along he stopped to greet a young woman wearing a tattered purple dress and black stockings, who had propped herself up next to the window of a fancy dress shop and now swayed precariously at the man's side, leading him back down towards Paul and Albert. The woman had lush red lips and a powdered face. As Paul watched her approach he felt a weird thrill course through his veins. The woman looked at him shiftily as she opened a door and led the pale man into a dimly lit foyer. Paul caught a glimpse of crimson and mauve and imagined that he had seen something glitter like crystal. Albert took his son by the hand and hurried him out onto the street.

That night, under his father's curious but averted gaze, Paul sat on the living room floor and began to invent a landscape after the image of the Rhine on the wall. He drew mountains and a valley with a blue stream running through it and a bright sun overhead. Ondine, as always, sat opposite him, flicking through a picture book of *Hansel and Gretel*. What if she and Paul were thrown out into the woods and into the evil clutches of some old witch, she wondered. How would they make do then? Next to her was a crude doll's house made out of cardboard and plywood. The structure was so flimsy and the materials so inferior that its roof had begun to sag and its walls warp, giving it a distorted appearance like a reflection in a trick mirror at a fairground.

"Albert," Anna said from the kitchen door, "why don't you get out of that uniform? It's not as if you don't have regular clothes."

"I know, I know," Albert replied.

Anna withdrew again and didn't say another word about it. While Albert and Paul were at the Cabinet of Anatomical Curiosities, she had left Ondine with Sarah and Hamish, much to the latter's delight, and hurried off to meet Winton in St Vincent

Place. Inside his large, stone terrace house they barely spoke. She glued her lips to the older man's and felt her body come alive under his subtle caresses. Sometimes he only had to begin touching her and she'd feel compulsive spasms slowly rippling through her. She felt no shame now, only happiness and relief. In the aftermath of these surreptitious encounters she experienced a calm that fortified her for her return to this slow travesty of a marriage.

Under the spell of this calm she was able, at first, to forget the fact that Albert had worn his uniform all day, though in the back of her mind she knew that it portended another stage in his gradual disintegration. She wondered where it would all end, the utter tedium of this breakdown by degrees, and then, thinking about her children, began to fret. She sat down in the kitchen and burst into silent tears, which she quickly stifled. A moment later, with an appearance of practised tranquillity that would have done credit to the most accomplished of actresses, she stood up and joined her family in the living room.

Aware of his father's interest, Paul tried his best to focus his attention on the completion of the landscape, but the large expanses of white, the sense of the land as untouched, was too much for him. He looked at his sister, who was holding a tiny wooden doll in her hand, toying with it, twisting its arms and legs into irregular postures. Paul bided his time and added minute touches to the drawing, until he noticed his father dozing off. Then he attacked it. A fever of red pustules blossomed out of the pristine snow, transforming the smooth white surface into a pockmarked wilderness of ulcerating sores and lacerations. Paul felt the tension that had been mounting in him dissipate as he disfigured the drawing. When he finally put it down he was careful to conceal it at the back of his sketchpad.

Albert's jaw had sagged slightly as he dozed, giving the two children a glimpse of the roof of his mouth and his yellowing teeth. Ondine giggled, concealing the sound of her laughter with her hand. She sat with her legs carelessly stretched out almost at right angles. Her blond hair fell into her eyes and over her face. Paul remembered what Hamish had asked him about his sister, and surmised then that he might secretly want to marry Ondine. Of course the thought of it was silly, but just to test this out Paul said, "Ond, you know Hamish wants to marry you, don't you?"

Anna looked up from her book, Albert stirred but didn't wake, and Ondine reeled with laughter.

"He's a fool then," she said, red with mirth.

"Hamish is a very nice young man," Anna said.

"But he's still an idiot," Ondine insisted.

Albert opened an eye, winking at the word idiot. He had caught it right on the edge of sleep and it stuck in him like a hook. He squinted at Ondine and noted again the uncanny resemblance between daughter and mother. So she thinks I'm an idiot, he thought, the cruel little bitch.

He shut his eyes again. The house was driving him mad. It was a closed-up den that smelt of damp and mould, that creaked all night, that groaned as if it were alive, as if the miserable little façade had eyes and a mouth that was constantly chewing away at him. He imagined Ondine's cold eyes as she cut his skin, her hand over his mouth as she stabbed into his heart. For a second he lost his breath. He shut the image away where it couldn't touch him, buried it under the calm exterior he showed them when he roused himself to find them all sitting there, closed in their silence.

Most nights he would sit up after the others had gone to bed, writing down his thoughts until the exertion of it tired him out.

Every now and again he'd get up, go to the door of his children's room and check that they were asleep. Paul and Ondine shared a room at the back of the house. Their two small beds were pushed into opposite corners and separated by a large chest of drawers. Albert would crouch at the keyhole or even walk outside into the yard and gaze in through the window if the curtains were not pulled tightly closed, until he was confident they were slumbering. Sometimes he did this two or three times in a night. After viewing Paul's sketches of genitalia he secretly altered the curtains so that they couldn't be closed completely, giving him a peephole from the yard. It excited him to spy on his children, though he was afraid of what he might find.

That night, after Paul and Ondine had gone to bed and Anna had fallen asleep on the couch, Albert crept off to the keyhole at regular intervals, peering hopelessly in at the darkness. By the time he was ready for bed he'd been writing in his notebook for another few hours. Anna had already retired and he stood up from the kitchen table ready to unbutton his shirt, feeling exhausted and barely able to keep his eyes open. The house was dark but for the oil lamp he'd been using in the kitchen. He smarted again at the thought that his own daughter would call him an idiot. The image of her dead stare as her hand smothered his cries slipped back into his mind. Again his chest tightened.

Somewhere in the darkness of the still house he heard a giggle. It was Ondine, he was sure. He put the oil lamp down on the kitchen table, took off his shoes, and walked quietly across the kitchen to the back door and out into the yard. There was a light on in the children's room. Through the crack in the curtains he could see an oil lamp burning on the top of the chest of drawers, casting a pale, yellow glow over Ondine's naked body. The girl was staring at the ceiling trying not to laugh, holding her hand in her mouth while Paul crouched over her, examining her genitals with a magnifying glass, pushing gently at the fatty skin with the rounded end of a lead pencil. Albert drew back a little, careful to conceal himself at the edge of the frame, his blood coursing through his veins, his breath shortening as it did every time the whore on Little Lonsdale Street stepped towards him out of the squalor of his imagination. He watched Ondine writhe under her brother's careful examination. The whole scene was bathed in the eeriness of hallucination: deep shadows and slithers of light filled the room like entwining serpents that might have been thrown up by a swirling magic lantern. For a moment the girl seemed to be looking right at him, her eyes twinkling with shamelessness.

At least that was what Albert remembered as he put on his boots and walked out into the street, his body shaking. A moment later the whole thing seemed like an intoxicating dream. The night filled him with its poisonous possibilities and he walked towards the river, thinking that he'd find his prostitute again. But when he imagined what she would look like all he saw was Ondine laughing at him, calling him an idiot, confident that he wouldn't plumb the depths of her secret life. What was he, after all? A nothing, a mere cipher, a bit of clay barely conscious of itself.

As he walked, he knew with increasing certainty that he would never return to that warped house with its crooked floorboards and its sinking foundations. And he knew that his wife would be indifferent, perhaps even relieved. She had never really loved him. It was comical even to contemplate. He thought about the day he stabbed himself, in a moment of perfect sanity and clarity, because he desired to the point of madness. Now his wife and children were strangers and he was going to find his Angelique again and follow her to the end of him. Only she could bring him back to life.

It was an unseasonably warm night, and as Albert walked he became hotter, until the sight of the river was a balm and he watched a single light on the opposite bank winking at him in its inky surface. On Princess Bridge he paused and gazed down into the water.

A soldier staggered past him, drunk.

"Been to fight the Boers?" Albert said, in a voice that he didn't recognise as his own.

"Been – to – fight – the – Boers," the soldier repeated, not even bothering to raise his eyes from the pavement.

The city in front of him was dead. Nothing moved. The entire place was completely still, like a vast graveyard. He couldn't bring himself to disturb its solemnity, and realised how thoroughly inconsequential he was to the sleeping mass of brick and stone and mortar.

Barely conscious of what he was doing, he climbed up onto the bridge's railing. Only thirty-five, he told himself, and this filthy river will be here forever. As the town hall clock chimed some ungodly hour, he let himself drop into the darkness below.

# part THREE

# chapter seven

Three years after her husband's death, Anna Walters dashed her brother-in-law Robert's earnest hopes when she turned her back on months of gentle courting, married Charles Winton and moved into his opulent residence on St Vincent Place South. There was only a civil ceremony, which took place in a registration office in William Street, with Winton's housekeeper, Mrs Norris, and a quiet but chagrined Robert, as witnesses.

Winton made it clear that Paul and Ondine would be comfortably accommodated. He promised Anna that he would treat them as his own, and had legal adoption papers in place almost before the marriage certificate was signed. To make the transition easier for them all he had arranged that Anna and the children would move into the house while he was on a lecture tour of country Victoria, where he was scheduled to speak about various aspects of social hygiene in the gold towns of Ballarat, Bendigo and

Castlemaine. It was a tiresome trip for Winton, who as a city-dweller showed no affection for what he liked to think of as the provinces, and who looked forward to the arrival of his wife with the excitability of a much younger lover. Since he had made his fortune out of prudent investments in the area twenty years earlier he felt he owed the goldfields some sort of debt. But with his one-time hope that success as a popular medical authority might pave the way for lecture tours to Europe and America long since abandoned, the opportunity to let Anna and the children relocate unfettered and at their leisure was the only thing that justified his absence. He was gone for eight days, and when he returned Anna had tentatively assumed control of the house. A picture of the Rhine hung unobtrusively in the sitting room that she had appropriated as her private retreat.

For Paul and Ondine, then thirteen and twelve respectively, the affluence of their new home far outweighed the inconvenience of having to move. For the first time they each had their own bedroom, side by side along a wide hallway on the second floor. Winton had made sure that both rooms were lavishly furnished so that the two children fancied themselves royalty as they leapt onto each other's deep, soft beds and unpacked their meagre belongings.

When Winton arrived home he appeared happy to see them both. They feared he would be an old-style tyrant, the sort of demented aristocrat they had encountered in the fairytales and Gothic romances which their mother had read to them when they were younger and which they both still avidly consumed, frequently reading out loud to each other at night before they fell asleep. When Anna first mentioned moving to St Vincent Place, Ondine wondered about tombs and crypts where she might be locked up as punishment and imagined that Winton, a doctor after all, might try to hack out their eyes like Coppelius in "The Sandman".

Her fears, which she had deliberately nurtured as a way of giving rein to her melodramatic temperament, were almost immediately allayed. They met the doctor in his new capacity as stepfather at dinner the evening after his return, and though he was evidently tired, he was in such good spirits that his warmth succeeded in melting the children's reserve. They ate a meal of roast lamb and vegetables, which Mrs Norris had prepared, had a glass of wine from fine cut-crystal, which made both children a bit tipsy, and finished with spotted dick. The doctor politely inquired as to the children's interests, talked about painting with Paul and the possibility of him studying it in a few years' time, and chatted about novels with Ondine, who was delighted to find that he had read the writers she adored — the Brothers Grimm, Tieck and Hoffmann. She suddenly felt very grown-up.

Anna was quiet, but glowed with secret satisfaction, confident that they would all be secure here and that her children would benefit from the advantages of wealth and education. She and Winton were careful to avoid explicit displays of their amorousness, and this cult of secrecy lent their interactions a coyness that charmed them both when they were in public and heightened their passion when they were finally alone together.

After dinner, as the four of them retreated to a sitting room of leather-upholstered couches arranged in a semicircle around a fireplace, Winton presented each of them with a gift. He had bought Ondine a gold necklace and Paul a new set of paintbrushes and oils. Both were thrilled. Ondine put on her necklace immediately, shivering at the touch of the cold metal on her skin.

"She is quite a princess," the doctor said softly to Anna as they watched the girl sit very upright and throw her blond locks over her back so that she could more easily link the chain.

"Haven't you anything for Mum?" she asked.

"Ondine!" Anna said.

"Why of course," the doctor said. "But she'll have to wait a little while to receive it." Anna looked at him. She was self-conscious about the prospect of her children confronting the fact that a new husband was also a new lover.

But before Paul and Ondine had time to ponder the implications of this mysterious deferral, Mrs Norris brought in a tray of coffee, tea and chocolates, which they lingered over with feigned reserve until Winton urged them to help themselves, waving them on towards the sweets with his ringed hand which, Anna remembered, had once seemed so menacing.

In the week or so before the doctor's return the children had made a habit of creeping into each other's rooms after they were supposed to have gone to bed. The size of the house and the rugs running along the hallways made it easy to walk around at night without the slightest fear of detection. They sat up together and read stories or ate the sweet food they had hoarded during the day. It was a marked contrast to their old house, especially when their father was alive. In Brooke Street rickety floorboards shifted with every footfall, and the thin wooden walls carried a ghastly range of effects. Mattresses would squeak, doors slam and muted groans of pain or deep, troubled breathing would sometimes reach the children in the dead of night, putting them in fear of an intruder stalking around the yard. Their old house was a claustrophobic shanty of trapdoors, secret panels and peepholes, presided over by a clownish father in a conductor's uniform. It was a place to be ashamed of and neither of the children looked back on Brooke Street with any nostalgia whatsoever.

Nevertheless, they had both cried when their father died. Two policemen had knocked on their door around midday. Paul heard them tell Anna that Albert's body had been fished out of the river near Yarraville. The children were shaken, but their tears were as much a response to the grotesqueness of the situation as an act of genuine grief. The whole thing seemed so strange, ugly and, in an intangible way, demeaning. Afterwards the shame of their father's death hung around the Brooke Street house like the unwholesome odour of rising damp. Ondine dreamt repeatedly of the bloated, blue body floating under the water's glassy surface and both children imagined they could still hear their father's footsteps outside their door. The house would creak in the night and they'd both start, almost simultaneously, and listen to the troubled silence around them. It was only now, in the comfort of this new home, that they were completely free of this haunting. The sense of relief they both felt as they stretched out together on Paul's bed the night of their arrival was enough to obviate the unease of living in a stranger's house. A week later, when the doctor turned out to be so genial and solicitous, their apprehensions were banished altogether.

Neither of them suspected that their mother would have been capable of betraying their dead father, though this faith was born of idealism and a sense of convention, rather than an understanding of the distance and sometimes the hatred that had existed between their parents. They were both young when Albert had died, and the enchantment of childhood had been strong enough to protect them from the thorns that entangled them. What they remembered as unpleasantness they now attributed to the weird powers of night, the melancholy of childhood, the spectres of the imagination. They could dismiss these easily enough as they grew older, whereas the starker realities of disintegration, breakdown and adultery would have been so much more intractable had they ever managed to displace this half-remembered realm of shadow and light.

Anna seldom retired before her children. On the rare occasion she did, she retreated to the room that preserved the half-fiction of her celibacy, which she carried on with an almost superstitious insistence, though she knew she was being old-fashioned. It was an austere but comfortable chamber that she in fact only ever used as a place to dress. It opened into a bathroom, which in turn opened into Winton's own room. The second floor of the house was laid out so that the hallway connecting the children's rooms was entirely sequestered from the other rooms on the floor, which were accessible along another hallway running off at a right angle, and usually closed off by a locked door. The house had two staircases. One was attached to each hallway so that the top floor was in effect divided into two discrete sets of sleeping quarters. This suited everyone. Paul and Ondine, as soon as they became familiar with the layout, moved about their own part of the house with an increasingly careless freedom, while Anna and Winton could carry on with no fear of being intruded upon.

When the doctor turned sixty, a few years after his wife and the children had moved in, Anna arranged a lavish birthday dinner. She wanted to preside over a bigger, more public function, but the unusual circumstances of her relationship with the doctor made this awkward in a society still labouring under a morality that had survived the previous century and that, despite its moribund character, seemed destined to survive her as well. Winton didn't care in the least. As he concentrated his attention on his wife, he'd also shed many of his old acquaintances. A private celebration was entirely in keeping with his own inclinations.

When the four of them sat down at the table, Ondine couldn't help but notice her mother's devotion to the doctor. She had never seen her so radiant in his presence. Anna glowed with satisfaction and Ondine felt uneasy in their midst.

At twelve, when they'd first moved to St Vincent Place, she had an inkling of what it meant to live as man and wife. But back then her sense of this was abstract, innocently astray. She still looked up to adults as if they were faultless, semi-divine creatures unsullied by the elements. Her own father, of course, was an exception, but even there the mystery of a grown-up's motivations, unfathomable to a child, preserved her idea of adulthood as an unassailable state. Now, at fifteen, she had begun to see her mother and Winton quite differently. There was nothing in particular that she could put her finger on, no one thing that could account for it. Rather it was the slow accumulation of detail that revealed to her intimations of their sexuality – intimations that were increasingly graphic and estranged.

It was not merely the thought of Winton being so much older. It was her awareness of his calm, confident possession of her mother, his easy command of the dinner table, and the rich, overpowering smell of his cologne. She imagined that such a pungent, artificial scent could only be used to mask the hot, musky odour of bodies frantically groping and pawing like animals. She imagined them languishing, swooning in each other's arms, or rutting away at each other like the dogs she'd seen behind the Punch and Judy show on St Kilda beach. Her vision of their enjoyment might well have cast the familiar dinner gathering in a changed and disturbed light, but it couldn't explain her sense that she was being pushed away from herself. It was a surreal feeling, as if the self she were used to was falling away, leaving her exposed, vulnerable.

For a moment there was an awkward silence. Anna smiled sweetly at Winton. The flickering candles cast a warm reddish glow over the room. The polished oak table, the chairs upholstered in Utrecht velvet, the gleaming silverware, the crystal glasses and the decanter imparted a heaviness to the proceedings which pulled against her mother's incongruous lightness of manner. Ondine was startled by this contrast. It was as if the room, which had become so comfortable and familiar, were suddenly foreign, hostile even, as if it were questioning her presence in it. Her mother's attention concentrated around the doctor, who seemed intoxicated by it and proud of the little gathering. For a second, an expression, partly of anxiety, partly of loathing, disturbed Ondine's serene demeanour. Paul noticed the change and when she saw him staring at her she immediately resumed her customary prettiness, sipping the half-glass of claret she was permitted in the interests of cultivation and breeding.

After they'd finished the first course of watercress soup, Mrs Norris served a dish of glazed duck, the preparation of which Anna had supervised that afternoon.

"May I have some more wine, Mother?" Ondine asked after she had finished her ration. It was the first time she had referred to Anna as "Mother" instead of "Mum".

"As it is Dr Winton's birthday, you may," she said, determined not to be put off by the hint of disdain in her daughter's voice.

"Might one inquire as to the doctor's age?" Ondine returned.

"The doctor's age is an open secret, my dear," Winton replied, smiling in a way that revealed his sharp, white teeth under his auburn beard.

Ondine, of course, knew very well how old he was, but thought she could embarrass him by drawing attention to the twenty-two-year gulf separating him from her mother. Her attempts, for now, came to naught. Anna and Winton carried on the atmosphere of geniality, and Winton again broached the topic of Paul attending classes at the Gallery School, which was now only a year away.

They've bribed him with all that art school nonsense, Ondine thought to herself, as the doctor talked enthusiastically about his connections at the academy and his acquaintance with many of the city's leading art critics and reviewers, some of whom divided their time between medicine and the press.

"James Smith, in fact, was a close friend before he went off the boil and became religious," the doctor said with a smile.

Ondine looked at Paul, who was evidently going to pretend that he knew who James Smith was. Thinking that she could deflate the doctor a bit she said, with an air of affected nonchalance that sounded childish, "And who exactly is James Smith, Doctor?"

Winton answered her in his stride. A girl of fifteen, he told himself, was not about to ruffle the feathers of a man who had been reinventing himself, across virtually the entire social spectrum, for the last forty years.

"Smith was the critic who tried to sink the impressionists. Streeton, Roberts, Conder and the like. A conservative really, but very influential for a time. I suppose history has run on ahead of him, poor chap."

"So what use would a poor chap like that be to my brother?" Ondine said.

"Use?" rejoined the doctor, still smiling. "Ondine, we all have our uses." He might have added that he was sure he could find a particular use for her, but held his tongue, not wanting to disappoint Anna and undermine her touching attempt to create a real family atmosphere.

Ondine drank her wine, aware of her mother's disapproval.

"I think you've had enough for one night, dear," she said.

"Oh, let the girl celebrate with the rest of us," Winton said jovially.

Ondine again fixed upon his quietly assured control of the table, his effortless authority, his neatly trimmed beard, his studs and that ring, a tiny golden claw clutching at a ball of turquoise, he'd been wearing for years. Her sense of something repulsive in Winton, the outline of something ugly and even bestial concealed in his accomplished manner and impeccable grooming, became more emphatic, until she imagined she could see a primitive wolfishness glaring back at her from across the table. The man is old, she thought to herself, yet he fancies himself young. He behaves as if he were a man half his age. How is it that my mother could love him? Was she fooled by all this finery and talk of literature and art?

It only took her a second to piece this puzzle together, and the ensuing explanation cut right through her. That man has bought us all, she said to herself. A nice little family to put on display. All paid for in full, like figures in a doll's house or parrots in a gilt cage. The house, the money, the polish, it all represented a right of dominion over them. It was as clear to her as the threat of overt violence.

She regained her composure instantly. It was as if she had lived through a revolution. She knew that the world she was inhabiting had not changed. She was simply looking at things with her eyes open, and had found the clarity of her vision startling. She regretted that it had affected her and now hoped that her rudeness had not undermined their position in the doctor's scheme, had not offended his assumption of sovereignty. Like a creature capable of magically changing its form, Ondine cast off her look of distracted contemplation as if it were a piece of old clothing, and assumed an expression of gentle bonhomie as the doctor spoke about a performance of *Hamlet* to which he wished to take them the following week.

"Doctor," Ondine said with deliberate melodiousness, "could we play Schubert Lieder on the graphophone?"

"By all means," he replied.

"Thank you."

The girl got up and walked to the corner of the dining room, where there was a new disk graphophone positioned in an oak cabinet designed specially for it. Ondine wound the machine and the record crackled into life, filling the room with the mechanically tortured strains of "The Wanderer's Nachtlied".

As she returned to the table she passed by the doctor and kissed him on the cheek, aware of his heavy scent.

"Happy birthday," she said.

Anna blushed on her daughter's behalf.

"Thank you dear," he said.

After the usual round of coffee and chocolate, during which Anna presented Winton with a leather-bound edition of Dante's *Inferno* illustrated by Gustave Doré, the children retired to their rooms.

Paul kissed his sister goodnight in the hallway, realising that she was drunk from the wine. He sat on his own bed, fully expecting her to appear as soon as the light in the hallway was put out by Mrs Norris. On cue Ondine opened the door, wearing a full-length nightgown, and immediately flung herself onto the bed in a fit of consternation.

"You know what's happening," she exclaimed, leaning on her brother's shoulder.

"What's wrong, Ond?"

"I hate them both."

"Mum and Dr Winton?"

"Who else? The mere thought of it makes me sick."

"Ond, they're married. What do you think married people do?"

Paul thought he had already intuited what she was upset about, thought he'd seen her curious naïvety clearly written in her countenance at the table.

"Oh, don't be stupid. I don't mean that. Not just that. I'm not a child."

She was on the verge of explaining herself to Paul as she glimpsed the difficulty of revealing exactly what she had seen. For a second she lingered over the word "prostitute". She didn't want to say it, didn't want to sully them all with the thought of it.

"We could creep in and catch them at it," she said, diverting herself. "Only it would disgust me too much."

"Winton is not a bad man," Paul said. "And he has made Mum very happy."

"And of course *you're* happy, going off to the Gallery School," she said. "Oh, I don't care a damn about him anyway. Not really. It'll have to be us against them. A secret alliance."

Ondine turned to face him, leaning back on her elbows and pulling her legs up around her brother's waist.

For a moment he was surprised by the frankness of her body and he blushed. Her thighs tightened around him. He slid his hands over her shoulders, resting his palms on her ribs, just touching her breasts with the tips of his thumbs. Years of longing welled up in him. All the lascivious detail he had accumulated in his mind, the seething carnal mass that spilled over onto his sketchpad, now blinded him in a moment of dazzling possibility. He put his arms around his sister and kissed her playfully. Ondine seemed to melt into him as she kissed him back, gently biting his lower lip.

"Do you love me, Paul?" she asked with a contrived coquettishness.

"Who else would I bother loving?"

At that very moment, in another part of the house, Anna looked at herself in the mirror. She was thirty-eight years old, still pretty, but the weight of years had begun to etch itself around her eyes. Her face, she fancied, had a hardness that reminded her of worn stone. She turned over in her mind the image of her daughter kissing Winton. She was ashamed to admit that it made her jealous. Ondine was beautiful, more beautiful than she had ever been. What's more, she was going to have all the advantages of Winton's money. The doctor had already willed the house and nearly two-thirds of his portable capital to Anna, who would see that her children lacked nothing. It was a vague and petty anxiety, she knew, but she imagined she'd be happier when her daughter was married and securely settled.

A part of her knew that she was being trite clinging to this fiction of domestic tranquillity. When Albert was alive she read novels about marriage, domestic romances and the like, partly as a way of seeking refuge from her own situation. She was never really taken in by them. She always saw through the optimism of the fairytale. And she wasn't foolish enough to take her own good fortune with Winton as proof of anything more universal either. Still, the thought of Ondine happily married was one she harboured for all their sakes. Though Anna didn't credit theories of hereditary madness, the fact that her daughter shared her father's blood still made her anxious. Ondine's stateliness and her occasionally condescending air put Anna on edge. There was the hint of excess lingering in her capacity to parody the conventions of family life, and Anna was convinced she'd sooner see Ondine happily reconciled to these than up in arms against them. She hoped that her daughter would not need reining in.

## chapter eight

St Vincent Place was a wide crescent bordering pleasantly sculpted gardens of winding paths, flower beds, Algerian oak trees, palms, lilly-pillies, and, in season, apple and cherry blossoms. Before Federation the outer rim of the street, divided into St Vincent Place North and South by the gardens, housed some of the most prominent and well-to-do families in the colony. This was not Toorak wealth mind you, not a matter of stately mansions or of antipodean aristocracy built on vast pastoral leases, rather it was what Australians respect far more – the modest opulence of professional classes and shrewd investors. But just as the new rich of the colonies were never far away from reminders of their humbler origins as opportunistic settlers, St Vincent Place was only a matter of blocks from places like Brooke Street. It was a vagary of South Melbourne's early design that a street of such solid middle-class prosperity could coexist side by side with a tangled nest of lanes and alleys that might, without much chance of melodramatic exaggeration, be described as squalid.

Hamish McDermott was increasingly aware of these differences. The miraculous social elevation of his childhood playmates had been a bitter lesson in the awkwardness of class distinction, one that he bore with moroseness and resentment. Some afternoons, if he had an early shift at the Homoeopathic Hospital where he worked now as an orderly, he concealed himself in the gardens opposite Dr Winton's house and watched as Ondine arrived home from Albert Park Ladies' College, wondering at her lithe, graceful beauty and the way in which she had assumed the mantle of her new position with such theatrical imperiousness. She learnt the piano and was taught French and German by expert tutors. Sometimes Hamish would stay out in the gardens until well after dark, gazing at the faint orange glow emanating from within the house. On rainy days he wore his thick, black overcoat and imagined, without a trace of humour, that he had become a sad, Quasimodo-like figure, a lumpish young man with thick worker's hands, unkempt red hair, freckles and an awkward gait, waiting forlornly to dash his hopes at the feet of an Esmeralda corrupted and made cruel by money.

Despite the amount of time he spent furtively lurking outside it, Hamish was in fact no stranger to the interior of the house. Paul frequently invited him to peruse Winton's library and study, which had a marvellous collection of the Romantic poets and some fine pieces of early colonial art. The two of them still kept up a healthy friendship. Paul craved Hamish's company after putting up all week with the sons of financiers, bankers and, worse, the squattocracy, at Wesley College. Anna too was happy to accommodate Hamish, treating him almost as one of the family.

Still, the finery of the place put him on edge and he never felt able to relax in the way that he had in the old Brooke Street cottage. Winton's library seemed an uninviting place to him. There were volumes of Wordsworth, Keats, Shelley, Carlyle, Browning, Tennyson and a complete set of Sir Walter Scott, as well as Australian authors like Harpur, Kendall, Gordon and Clarke. There were, of course, other obscure tracts on medicine, social hygiene, sexual pathology and tribal customs, but none of these books, not even the most familiar of them, seemed to Hamish as if they were meant to be read. He was afraid to take the books off the shelves and didn't want to borrow any of them for fear of damaging or losing them.

The sight of these books, so elaborately bound and preserved, with their gilded spines, reminded him just how much he actually disliked reading. The thought of sitting down in a comfortable study to read one of these volumes was deadly. When he first began reading in earnest he hated the way the sentences, paragraphs and pages strung out meaning interminably. He was too impatient and wanted a book to reveal itself straightaway. He imagined himself cutting up the lines until he was left with a mass of words that he could consume in one intoxicating act of understanding. He had turned to poetry for that reason. The dreamlike brevity, the condensation of meaning, the concentration of multiplicity in a single, primal word, were correctives to the lethargy he felt when reading larger works. The order and authority of Winton's library seemed to mock this need for spontaneous revelation. It was like a tomb built out of books by comparison.

When he was asked to stay for dinner he often felt pushed to the margins of the conversation despite the doctor's attempts to draw him out. He hadn't seen any operas and his family didn't own a graphophone, so he was unable to comment intelligently on the quality of this or that performance, or debate the relative merits of German and Italian music. He imagined that Ondine must be sneering at his vulgarity and lack of refinement. Like an expert mimic she had learnt the rules of taste and conduct that distinguish the upper classes from their inferiors. She sipped wine like a lady, held herself perfectly erect and touched her brother's hand affectionately every so often as if, in proper aristocratic fashion, she had assumed the gestures of a subtle decadence. In public she and Paul had even begun to speak to each other like two characters in a contrived comedy of manners. When they carried on with this kind of talk, so artificial and pretentious, Hamish felt excluded and cut off, lacking the intangible quality they so greedily hoarded between them. If Ondine still spoke to him in her old familiar way, everything else about her had changed so visibly that he knew he couldn't place any stock in this intimacy, which he was sure she would soon forget as she distanced herself even further from her past.

After these evenings Hamish threw himself into what he now saw, mockingly, as his own milieu. Instead of the opera, he watched vaudeville and fairground entertainments at the Mechanics' Institute with workers from the wharves who knew his father, or other orderlies and cleaners from the hospital. Hamish hadn't been an outstanding student at the state high school, but he had only narrowly missed out on a scholarship to university just the same. He hadn't given up the idea of attending university, but knew that he would first need to save some money and so he hastily took a job at the Homoeopathic while he waited for a public service position to open up. He bridled at the way in which wealth seemed to translate into cultural attainment and didn't doubt that Paul would eventually become the famous artist he had always dreamt of being, while he'd be stuck as a drudge in an office or a factory.

Galled at the thought of his own mediocrity, Hamish would drag himself along to the popular theatre at the Mechanics' Institute and howl disingenuously at the juggling clowns, applaud the man doing bird whistles and feign wonder when a ventriloquist made a dog read Shakespeare. Once he saw a professor, claiming descent from the great ghost-seers of Europe, project a lightshow of spectral polyps around the walls of the hall. It pleased him to think that he was doing something that would so thoroughly debase him in Ondine's eyes, and he imagined that the next time he dined at St Vincent Place he'd shock them all by describing these wonders.

After one such evening in the Mechanics' Institute, where he'd witnessed an unconvincing display of telepathic communication conducted by an enthused and excitable spiritualist who claimed to have lived as a Roman slave in the days of Nero, Hamish walked over to St Vincent Place, where he intended to wallow self-indulgently in the frustration of his unrequited devotion to Ondine. In good romantic fashion he hoped that this might galvanise him in one direction or another, jolt him towards some sense of resolve or purpose. He sat down on a park bench in the middle of the garden. It was a cold, cloudless night, and he could see the steam of his breath in the moonlight. He fell into a trancelike state in which, but for an awareness of his own misery, his mind was empty. In this stupor the garden came alive with the mystery of its stillness. He felt that he was being watched, that other forms moved in the night, that the garden was peopled with shadows come to lose themselves in darkness. Then a figure glided past him, oblivious to his presence. It paused, almost in front of him, gazing at Dr Winton's house. At first Hamish doubted his own eyes, then wondered just how many other suitors were troubled and pursued by the thought of Ondine.

He didn't have to wait long for the mystery to be resolved. As the figure turned despondently away from the house, the moonlight betrayed Robert Walters, Albert's brother. Hamish remained motionless, hoping against hope that Robert hadn't noticed him. He seemed to be looking straight into his eyes, but registered nothing, slowly dragging himself off in the direction of Clarendon Street. It was a moment of awful self-recognition. Robert looked pathetic, as if he'd been sapped of life and left to wander as a kind of human shell, a hollow vessel. Was the man pining after Anna? Hamish got up and walked swiftly in the opposite direction, confident that his lonely vigils in the name of thwarted love were over.

He was, however, to allow himself one final act of remembrance. The house the Walters family had lived in on Brooke Street had been rented for a few years after their departure, but for the last two had been vacant, a home only to the occasional drunk or vagabond. Anna eventually sold it and the place was about to be demolished by its new owners, before it collapsed of its own accord. At the hospital the next day Hamish decided that he would walk through the place one last time, drawn by the mystery of his childhood and the hope of rekindling some of its enchantment.

He thought about the house the whole day, the better to forget the corpse he had wheeled towards the undertaker's van almost first thing that morning. An old bloke he had pushed around in a wheelchair from time to time had died of a cancer that had eaten its way into his lung and finally through an artery wall. He drowned in his own blood during the night, coughing up a horrible clotted mess. By the time Hamish arrived in Brooke Street he had spent almost eight hours wrestling with the image of the dead man, the bloody evidence of his dreadful death rattle, and the memory of the cold, cancerous coughs he had heard as he pushed the breathless patient around the wards.

The Brooke Street cottage had fallen into such a state of disrepair that Hamish feared he might fall through the rotted floorboards. The place smelt like urine and was littered with old newspapers, rags and odd pieces of clothing – a single worker's boot, a pair of football shorts, some soiled underwear. In the living room there was straw scattered about and the blackened remains of a makeshift fire. A few empty bottles had been tossed into one corner. In the kitchen the linoleum had been torn up and many of the floorboards had decayed, leaving a view of the dark underside of the house, the moist, swampy soil of the bay that looked as if it had been coated in treacle. In the front bedroom there was only a mattress with the stuffing leaking out of its side. Hamish recalled the sight of Anna's naked body that afternoon and how it had been twisted out of shape beneath Albert's. But it was not Anna that he saw in his mind's eye, it was Ondine. And in the scenario he now pictured to himself it was he and not Albert humiliating the girl on the piss-stained mattress before him. He felt himself go hard and wondered if he had it in him to masturbate over the mingling of fantasy and memory that now overwhelmed him. He foresaw himself spraying like a tomcat into the mattress and then anticipated the shame he'd feel walking back out into the light of the street, wet with his own semen.

As he withdrew from the room he noticed a curious thing. A floorboard buckled under his weight and flipped out of place, suggesting it had been deliberately loosened. There was something underneath it, wedged into the shallow space between the sagging floor and the ground. He pulled out the adjacent floorboard and then, kneeling over the hole, lifted up a brown leather satchel from the house's foundations. It was damp and mouldy, and so stretched at the seams with papers and books that when Hamish dropped it on the floor it literally burst open, vomiting forth its contents with a host of spiders, beetles, and other crawling insects which raced at various speeds towards the extremities of the room.

Hamish brushed away the last of these creatures and examined the satchel's contents. There were obscene photographs, erotic drawings and lithographs that depicted women copulating with the devil, with monkeys, with writhing, tendrilled sea monsters, whores peeking out from behind dominoes, black masses and Oriental harems, all drawn with lascivious detail and exactness. Some of these pictures had then been copied, crudely, without the tawdry economy of the expert pornographer, on loose-leaf sheets of paper. There were also several notebooks containing writing in a small, steady hand that must have taken concentration to maintain. There were poems, fragments, diatribes, ruminations, lists of words and phrases. Skimming through these Hamish found fragments of written pornography, the violence and perversity of which made him colour. He found poems written to the powers of night, accounts of mythical cities, fantastic dream-states, and descriptions of familiar parts of Melbourne that were shrouded with an uncanny sense of menace.

When he came across some old copies of the *Bulletin* folded into a collection of newspaper cuttings describing the trial of Edmund Howard, Hamish had no doubt in his mind. The satchel had belonged to Albert Walters.

## chapter nine

Winton realised that the children had been slow to catch on, and had given him and Anna a merciful few years in which their relationship could be pursued without the worry of their disapproval. While Paul and Ondine acquired all the trappings his wealth provided they were content, and it almost seemed that the four of them together had succeeded in forming quite a conventional family. Winton, with a stepfather's instinctive animosity towards the natural son, had always feared Paul, believing that a rebellious adolescent eager to redeem his father's name might begin to see ghosts commanding him to vengeance. For this reason he had been especially solicitous of the boy's confidences. He'd promised that he'd send Paul to the Gallery School when he left Wesley, and made every effort in the meantime to construct a genial, cultured ambience that would triumph over whatever Oedipal animosities might be festering within his stepson.

On the night of his sixtieth birthday dinner, however, he saw that he had miscalculated. It was Ondine who had been the first to look at him accusingly, and the girl had not been sophisticated enough to conceal her disgust. Late that night Winton sat in his study and closed his eyes, trying to quieten the spectres that now rose up around him. The girl's revulsion accused him not simply of sleeping with her mother, but of all his past indiscretions as well. His days as a man about town were well and truly over. Falling in love with Anna had seen to that. But in his past lay incarnations that might be dredged up at his dinner table by the girl eager to humiliate him in front of the woman who, alone, sustained the thought of life unsullied by the fear of aging and ultimately of death.

As an author and an occasional lecturer Winton was always confident that his proclivities were justified in the interests of science, health and hygiene. Anna already knew about his public face, the progressive man of science. It was the thought of what lay beyond the public mask that now had him writhing away from his own guilty conscience. He dropped his head into his hands and tried to shake the memories loose. How many times had he done it? A dozen? He didn't remember. An accommodating consultant, that's what they called him. Aborted pregnancies, foetuses wrapped in bloodied sheets, the backblock stench of those brothels. He was another person then, before the Midas mine had made him rich and let him wash his hands of the whole business. Had Ondine somehow found him out? He knew he was being childish but her disgust, glimpsed out of the corner of his eye earlier in the evening, now gripped his innards like a talon. In a moment of acute anxiety he imagined her preternatural knowledge and the danger it put him in.

Later, when Anna casually suggested that her daughter might be married and taken off their hands, the doctor was immediately gratified at his wife's unconscious sympathy with him and promised to set about finding a suitable young man. After a long discussion they decided that he should settle money on the girl, ensuring that she might marry into a secure family with decent prospects.

"This is not the old world," Winton assured Anna. "There are no end of simple, adventurous settler families who have made themselves rich in this country, not through inheritance or the privileges of the blood, but through honest hard work and a bit of luck. Any one of them would be happy to have a beautiful, cultured creature like Ondine gracing the drawing room." The girl will make a fine ornament, he thought.

"Charles, you have been so good to us," she said, holding his hand, her voice faltering.

"You have done more for me than I could possibly repay, Anna."

She kissed him and he wrapped his arms around her, still confident that he could do so with the zeal of one much younger.

By the time Paul was lodged at the Gallery School, Winton had found a potential match for Ondine. It was the edge of winter, 1910. Ondine had another six months of school and was about to turn seventeen. Winton foresaw a lengthy and gradual courtship in keeping with the legacy he'd given the girl, and hoped to see her engaged by her eighteenth birthday.

The young man in question was Ralph Matthews, the son of a retired grazier who still held a property in New South Wales, but who now lived comfortably with his wife and son in Toorak. Winton had met Bruce Matthews and his son Ralph at a private club in the city and decided, with a mixture of benevolence and malice, that the lad was handsome and wealthy enough to be acceptable to Ondine, but that he also had an edge to him, a touch of brusqueness that might finally unnerve the girl. Deep down Winton wanted to punish her, ever so slightly, for her rejection of his friendship and generosity. Perhaps this urge was unconscious. He certainly didn't confess it openly to himself. But when he thought about Ralph his approval was inevitably tainted by this impulse. In this young man's money, his unpretentious patriotism and in his love of the land, Winton saw Ondine's future and imagined that it might not be completely forgiving of the delicacy and cultured sensibility she'd developed since moving away from Brooke Street.

The news that Winton had invited Ralph Matthews to St Vincent Place for lunch the last Sunday in May put Paul on edge. He knew that Ralph had not been asked for his benefit. What interest could he possibly have in a grazier's son? The information had been directed at Ondine, who barely seemed to register it as she sipped her tea.

This ominous intrusion, combined with his first few months at the Gallery School, succeeded in making him despondent. The School of Painting was tiresome and conservative, full of diligent but weak-minded students who had effortlessly assimilated the director's distrust of the imagination. At his insistence, the tenor of the school was oriented almost exclusively to portraiture. Paul felt the point of the school was to bore students senseless with months of rigid discipline and then, when their spirits were broken, turn them into professional lackeys, trained like dogs to flatter society matrons and politicians.

The path from charcoal to monochrome sepia had been painstaking. And then, if one's creative instinct were not already defeated, there were weeks of still life to be endured. It was only near the end of a full term that the students were allowed a brief flirtation with a full set of oils, as long as they understood that this was a luxury not to be taken for granted. How could Paul's frustrated ambition not get the better of him?

Lindsay Bannister, the director, looked at his first canvas disapprovingly. While the other students with any ability used unobtrusive brushstrokes, drab colours and subtle variation to represent the model in the centre of the room, Paul's painting had sacrificed precision and control for wilder brushstrokes and a garish use of blues, green and reds knitted into the flesh to give the body a morbid, diseased appearance.

"It's not really working, is it?" the director said, as if he could gently warn Paul away from what he evidently regarded as a dangerous tendency.

"I don't follow you, Sir," Paul replied.

"We encourage a certain discipline here, Mr Walters," Bannister said. "Look at Priestley's canvas, for comparison."

The other first-year students tried to conceal their interest in this ritual of humiliation as Bannister directed Paul's attention towards the second-year student's easel on the opposite side of the studio. It held a beige portrait of a middle-aged woman sitting rigidly on a chair, hands folded on her lap, set against a window out of which one could see a nondescript landscape of brown and faded green. The woman was expressionless, her dress was a chocolate colour, to match her hair, and her face was the colour of oatmeal.

"There is a certain level of control, which I find admirable. An orderliness, I suppose."

"But it might as well be a photograph, only a photograph would look sharper, and be more exact," Paul said, feeling his blood boil at the injunction to take seriously such a mediocre painting.

"Oh, I disagree. Photography has no room for the artist's hand and eye, for elegance and form. It is merely art for the masses, with no regard for the genius, the unique vision of the painter. The camera is purely mechanical, the photograph a function of the machine. That's one of the things we must guard against, Mr Walters. This painting, by contrast, is controlled and tonally realistic, but also distinguishes itself from a mere copy in the complexity of its workmanship."

Paul bit his lip. He could sense the others secretly laughing at him. But what rubbish, he thought. Priestley's painting was barely art at all. It was a bad copy of a banal moment that had no business being recorded in the first place. He'd rather work on the photographer's book of beauty, with the fake backdrops of the ocean or the Alps, than participate in the sycophancy of portraiture and the farce of good taste.

"Beauty is what we strive for, but beauty is also a matter of restraint and precision," Bannister said, leading Paul back to his own painting. "Art is, after all, a discipline."

Paul was ready to explode, outraged at the presumptive ignorance and gross insensitivity of the man. He began to imagine some of the ways in which he could use photographs in his paintings in order to travesty the dogma of the studio. He wanted to deface Priestley's horrible, dead picture, slashing at the canvas with streaks of red so that it bled through its lacerations.

"Bad luck there," the student at his side whispered. "Bloody awful of the old bloke if you ask me."

Paul looked at his neighbour's painting. It was a badly proportioned botch-up. The upper part of the body was so large that the legs and arms had to be shrunken in order to fit on the canvas. There was no anatomical logic to it and the features of the face, painted in a series of monochrome blocks, were merely gestures towards the generic forms recognisable as eyes, a nose and a mouth.

Paul couldn't wait to get out of the place. He'd arranged to meet Hamish at Fasoli's later that afternoon, and by the time he got there he was wet with rain, exhausted with the frustration of it all and light-headed from hunger.

Fasoli's was their established meeting place, even though it would have been far more convenient to meet at the Limerick Arms or the Railway Hotel. It was a little restaurant on Lonsdale Street where, so it was said, one might be able to imagine oneself in Soho or Montmartre. A narrow hallway led off the street into a cramped, dilapidated room and, out the back, an asphalt courtyard surrounded by ferns. As night fell the place filled with a motley collection of characters. Students, artists, journalists and assorted bohemian night-birds drifted in to eat richly sauced pasta dishes served on cracked plates and to drink red wine from glass tumblers. In one corner a couple of Italian girls lounged about inscrutably, blowing smoke rings into the air as they pursed their coral-red lips, occasionally rousing themselves to deliver some food or to wipe down an empty table.

Hamish was already seated, his wet hair plastered against his oversized head. Paul sat down, eager to unburden himself.

"Bannister will be the fucking death of me," he blurted out. "The man is a bloody philistine who imagines us feeding off Toorak mansions, painting portraits of old crones. And the students there! My God, you couldn't imagine the utter lack of talent."

"Actually I could," said Hamish. "I'm surrounded by a lack of talent most of the time."

They ordered a bottle of wine, which restored Paul's energy. Hamish was on the verge of mentioning the satchel he'd found. When they'd arranged to meet that was what he had on his mind. He couldn't think of a better place to broach the subject than Fasoli's. But as Paul launched into a tirade about the Gallery School, something held him back and he realised that, for a while at least, it would be prudent to keep its contents to himself.

"I don't know if I can stick it out for three years," Paul said.

"How onerous could it be?" Hamish said. "You could be pushing corpses about the Homoeopathic."

"Did you send the poems off?" Paul asked, realising he was getting painfully self-absorbed.

"Yes. I expect I'll hear within a few weeks, though I really don't know if they're the sort of thing the *Bulletin* is looking for."

"Why not? I thought they were fine."

"I don't know," Hamish said despondently. "Besides the Red Page all they publish these days are eulogies to the nation, satires or bush vignettes."

"I suppose. Perhaps that's why artists are fleeing Australia like rats from a sinking ship. It's hard to feel grounded here. Nobody really feels like they belong, not in that Henry Lawson sense, anyway. 'Natives of the land' and all that."

"Lawson's 'natives of the land' are a lot of rot. But we are grounded in a different way," Hamish said, gulping his wine in a manner that suggested his interest had been piqued. "Right here. In the city where we've grown up. It's just that there's not much room for heroism and romance in the city. What people will find here is likely to offend them."

He was thinking about Albert's poems as he said this and wondered whether Paul had any inkling.

"Maybe. You're forgetting that Ondine and I, well, I'm not sure what we are. Not Australians, not Germans either. We're caught in the middle, which is nowhere."

As he said this he realised he'd touched upon the basis of their bond. In his sister he recognised a creature of his own blood who, like him, was rootless, trapped between two worlds, suspicious of the ease with which Australians so loudly proclaimed their kinship.

As they spoke, an older man called out across the room, his mouth sucking in a loose strand of spaghetti.

"'Scuse me. 'Scuse me," he said. "Either of you blokes know about the Kulin?"

"Afraid not," Paul replied.

"Thought as much," the old bloke said. "Heard you talking about being grounded. Well it's pretty bloody hard to be grounded if ya don't know nothing about a place's history, ain't it?"

"What's he on about?" Paul said, looking at Hamish.

"Haven't the foggiest."

"I'm talking about being grounded, ain't I?" the old man said. "Ah, never mind."

Concentrating on his meal the man lost interest in them and resumed eating.

"Well, tell us about the Kulin, then," Hamish said.

"Nah, never mind about it."

"He's talking about the Abos," a man sipping coffee in the corner said, putting down his newspaper. "Ain't ya, Les?"

"Never mind. Never mind. I ain't a bloody history book, am I?" Les said, shaking his head.

"The five tribes of Port Phillip were the Kulin nation before Melbourne was settled. The Bunurong and what not. That's before you blokes were even born." The man in the corner smiled at them.

"Too right, Peter. Before youse was even born. That bloody long ago," Les croaked through his laughter.

The man in the corner returned to his paper, Les returned to his food and a waitress with piercing black eyes and a Mona Lisa smile stood over Paul and Hamish ready to take their orders. They both sat in silence, puzzling over the thought of Melbourne before there was a Melbourne, when the city was the violence of its own becoming, building itself out of blood and bone.

They didn't order any food, but got another bottle of wine. In the meantime the man in the corner settled his bill and gave Les a friendly tap on the shoulder as he left.

"You know, I meant to ask you over to lunch Sunday week," Paul said, rousing himself. "Winton has some screwed idea that he's going to start introducing suitors to Ondine. He's lined up some bloke from the bush."

Hamish felt himself colouring and hoped that Paul hadn't noticed. Of course Paul's invitation was a calculated one. He hoped that Hamish would come to nullify the presence of Ralph Matthews and maybe even fight him off altogether. He didn't dwell on it though, affecting an air of casualness that aroused Hamish's curiosity and left it so unsatisfied that he couldn't help but accept the invitation.

By the time they were getting up to leave, the old man, Les, was quite drunk and making a bit of a goat of himself with the waitress, who sat him down again in his chair and offered to bring him a cup of coffee.

"Kulin nation, young fellas!" he shouted out after them as they stumbled out onto Lonsdale Street.

"What about that old bloke, eh?" Paul said.

"Suppose he has a point," Hamish said. "A hundred years ago there was none of this. No city I mean. It's like the whole place has been dreamt up almost overnight. It might vanish just as quickly."

They walked through a decrepit arcade, a dark, deserted cavern that sold a bit of old furniture and bric-a-brac, and then made their way through Little Bourke Street and the Eastern Market, which but for a few peepshows and a tattoo parlour was closed up for the day. The occasional forlorn figure skulked about in the drizzle or vanished through a door. Stray cats prowled about the rubbish and fought over the odd morsel of offal, disturbing the gloom with their hissing. Hamish thought about Albert's poems, which had conjured the city as a place of cruel dreams and obscene fantasies written, he imagined, in blood and semen and shit. At the same time Paul remembered the day Albert had taken him to the Cabinet of Anatomical Curiosities and the whore who'd stumbled down the Eastern Arcade.

"So you'll come Sunday week?" Paul asked again, wanting to be sure.

"Yes, I'll come."

At Swanston Street they climbed onto a tram and headed back to South Melbourne. It was already dark and as the tram rattled over Princess Bridge they both imagined, as they often did, a body in a train conductor's uniform fading through the water.

## chapter Ten

The family was already seated for lunch, and Mrs Norris was on the point of serving, when the doorbell rang again. Ralph Matthews looked so sheepish sitting opposite her that Ondine nearly laughed into her serviette.

"I forgot to mention," Paul said apologetically, "that I asked Hamish along as well."

Winton twisted uncomfortably in his seat at the head of the table and frowned. He knew Anna still thought of Hamish fondly and so said nothing that might upset her. But Anna herself was annoyed at Paul for inviting him, and glanced searchingly at Winton. Hadn't he understood that Ralph Matthews was a guest on whom they'd wanted to make a good impression? She looked at Paul as if he were conspiring to undo the plan she and Winton had stitched together.

Winton had Mrs Norris hastily set another place as Hamish

stood at the threshold of the dining room, looking a bit buffoonish in his crumpled checked jacket and mismatched beige trousers, and with his usually dishevelled red hair plastered down onto his skull with brilliantine. Anna was taken aback to see the boy she always remembered transformed into the heavy young man of twenty-two standing before her. He walked strangely, as if his feet were flat or his ankles inflexible. She noticed it as he approached the table. She felt sorry for the fact that he had made himself so ridiculous as a homage to the gulf that now existed between him and her own children. She tried to make him feel at home as he sat down, but the unusual sense of ceremony around the table, which focused itself on the stranger now sitting next to Hamish, clearly conveyed to him that his presence was inappropriate and, at least unofficially, unwanted.

"Ralph, this is Hamish McDermott, an old friend of the family's," Anna said politely. "Ralph is . . ." she continued, turning to Hamish, fumbling after a way to finish the sentence. "Ralph is tossing up between the country and the city."

Ralph had barely looked at Hamish during this introduction. He was engrossed with Ondine, awed by her languid beauty and cultured distance. She had immediately put him on edge as he sensed that even the fortune he was set to inherit would be a meaningless bait to this girl who seemed animated by her own inexplicable, utterly alien needs. In the past, his good looks and the promise of his father's wealth had made Ralph a favourite at the South Yarra Tennis Club, at the races or at city balls, where he never had any trouble attracting the attention of society matrons anxious to secure a connection for their daughters.

Compared to Ondine, whose obscurity now revealed the obviousness of their designs, these women seemed vulgar. He fidgeted as he wondered how to begin a conversation that might redound to his credit, but before the calm, almost haughty silence of the girl he was at a loss for words.

"How is your father, Ralph?" asked Winton, noticing the lad's reluctance to venture forth.

All eyes turned to poor Ralph, who knew how thoroughly he was being scrutinised.

"He's fine thank you, Doctor. Bored in the city, but fine nevertheless."

"Bored in the city?" echoed Paul. "It might not be Paris or London, but I'd imagine Melbourne must make country New South Wales look pretty grim."

"Not if you've grown up in one and not the other," Ralph answered.

"What on earth is there to do out there?" Paul continued, a slight jeer in his voice.

"Well, one works, principally. And then at night one sits by a fire or looks at the stars from the verandah."

Paul glanced at Ondine, as if to pass a preliminary judgement on the suitor in conjunction with his sister, who simply looked back blankly, giving little away.

Mrs Norris placed a tureen of pumpkin soup on the table and poured out a bottle of claret, which Hamish immediately took to, thinking that he'd have to bolster himself if he were ever to insert himself into this awkward drama and make an impression on Ondine.

"Doctor, may we put on the graphophone?" asked Ondine.

"Certainly, dear."

Paul leapt out of his chair and moved to the oak cabinet in the corner of the room.

"What would you like to hear, Ralph?" he asked. "Dr Winton has an up-to-date collection." He passed a pile of disks back to Ralph who, much to Paul's delight and Ondine's more muted amusement, looked befuddled as he read the labels.

The doctor glanced again at Anna, thinking that this trial would not end well for Ralph. Before he could intervene with an appropriate suggestion of his own, the guest, as if driven by nervous unease, began reading the labels under his breath.

"Schubert, Verdi, Dv-or-ak."

Paul and Ondine giggled at Ralph's ignorance. The young man flushed indignantly and handed the records back to Paul.

"Why don't we listen to Caruso?" the doctor said, unable to conceal his annoyance. "This machine is more trouble than it's worth."

It occurred to Hamish for the first time, though he was amazed that he hadn't thought of it earlier, that Paul himself loved Ondine, not simply as a brother loves a sister, but in a way that was profoundly threatened by Ralph's presence. Paul's carry-on around his sister was not mere affectation. It pointed to feelings too dangerous to own except in the disguise of the play-acting that had begun to sicken him. Hamish realised just how marginal he was to this battle for the girl's attention and resigned himself to a gloomy afternoon in which the best he could do would be to get thoroughly inebriated at the expense of the doctor and his well-stocked cellar.

Ralph was stung by his inability to pronounce Dvořák, and a moment later, realising his error, tried to compensate with a clumsy declaration of his preference for the Czech composer which also had Paul glancing slyly at his sister.

Abruptly, Ralph changed the subject, resolving not to take this little humiliation lightly.

"The doctor tells me that you are at the Gallery School studying painting," he said to Paul.

"Yes, the doctor tells you correctly."

"Personally, I'm not one to waste my time with art," he said, "but I'm sure, if you cut the mustard, Mother would love to have you paint her portrait. She has a weak spot for that kind of flattery."

"There's more to the art of painting than portraiture," Hamish volunteered, thinking that he'd have to deflect attention from his friend, who looked as if he were on the verge of tossing his claret into Ralph's face.

"I'm sure there is," Ralph continued, "but there's not much of a living to be made from art unless one is prepared to flatter well-intentioned patrons into buying the odd picture, is there?"

Paul gulped his wine sullenly, refilling his glass and topping up Hamish's.

"You have a point there, Ralph," said Winton, who was relieved to see him holding his own. "The question is how art can exist outside of these forms of patronage."

"In a benighted country like Australia, full of beer-guzzling cattle barons and bush nationalists, art is probably going to wither away altogether," Paul said. "As soon as the memory of Europe fades there'll be nothing except the dead images your mother sticks up on the walls to distract herself from the ugliness around her."

Again Ralph prickled and flushed at the arrogance of the little upstart beside him. I could wring your bloody neck, he thought to himself. Ondine looked at him, sensing the violence surging within. She was amused by the tussle unfolding in front of her, flattered that her brother and her potential suitor would be so willing to fight over her.

Anna was surprised at how closely Paul's rancour echoed that of her own mother, who always insisted that Australia was an ugly, barren country. Her constant complaining had dragged her father down. He, at least, was determined to scratch out a living for them. For a long time Anna also had felt as if she didn't belong and imagined that she too saw the ugliness from which her mother shrank. But now, as she listened to her son launch into a diatribe that seemed to speak the legacy of some inherited animosity to the new world, she realised just how out of place it all was. Times had moved on and she pitied her son, with his mannered speech and pretensions to a Europe he had never seen. By contrast, she admired Ralph's bluntness, but looking at her daughter she feared that Ondine was too much like her brother to see the virtue in this.

"To tell you the truth, I've never felt less like a European and more like an Australian than I do now listening to you say that, Paul," Anna said.

Paul looked flabbergasted. For a moment he was speechless.

"Still," he insisted, "it's hard to say that we, whatever we are, belong here in the way that the Kulin tribes do. Australia is all an illusion. A trick with smoke and mirrors, performed by demagogues and balladeers."

Winton looked at him uneasily.

"What are you talking about?" Anna said.

"The Kulin peoples were the original inhabitants of the bay area. If there's an Australian *Volk* around here, they're it, only they've been decimated. Killed off by disease, dispersed or murdered. The rest of us are interlopers."

Mrs Norris's reappearance gave them all an excuse to fall silent. She cleared the first course, replacing it with a rack of roast lamb and a plate of vegetables, then refilled the empty wine decanter with another bottle of claret that had been breathing on the counter.

Ondine, who up until this point hadn't said much, decided that she'd better, at least for the sake of appearances, show some sort of engagement with Ralph.

"Ralph, the doctor tells me you're quite a horseman," she said. "I've never been horse riding. We are such city-dwellers."

"Well there's no shortage of horse riding to be done on a farm," he said, still flustered by Paul's animosity and his own belligerence.

"Do you whip them?" she asked.

"No," he said with a laugh, "spurs will do the trick, but mostly they know we're there to ride them. Horses are intelligent animals and don't take much prompting."

"I'm glad to hear that. I've always thought whipping horses cruel. When I was a girl it used to scare me, looking at the cab drivers in the city, listening to them abuse those poor animals."

Ondine noticed Winton again glancing at her mother. For the duration of the luncheon they communicated like two mutes with a secret language of eye movements. Ondine was careful not to betray her animosity. A few weeks earlier Winton had called her into his study to discuss the question of her inheritance and his wish that she should "marry well". She imagined that he was a procurer preparing to sell her off to the highest bidder. After that discussion, she and Paul took to referring to him as "Monsieur Souteneur", the implication of which, they both knew, did not spare their mother any less than it spared him.

Hamish listened to Ondine talking to Ralph with a mounting ire. He felt ostracised by good breeding. Again he wondered how he could insert himself into a conversation that meandered from horses to cattle runs, from country balls to a country boy's first glimpse of the city. He listened for an opening, but none seemed to come and the whole thing was, after all, so interminably boring that he wondered how Ondine could have the patience for it. Finally his own patience gave way.

"You know, I've had a poem accepted by the *Bulletin*," he blurted out. It was a blatant lie.

They all turned to him. At the centre of their attention, he felt foolish.

"That's wonderful, Hamish," Anna said brightly. "I knew you were a poet when you asked me those tricky questions about the Lorelei. I even said so to your mother."

He sank away under the heavy shadow of his deceit, still hoping desperately for a word of praise or even acknowledgment from Ondine. But before she could say anything Paul, by this time quite drunk, remarked that Australians don't care a fig for poetry.

"I don't think that's quite true," Ralph said.

"Poets make a worse living than painters, don't they?" Paul said. "And that must make them pretty damn pitiful."

"Not if they capture the mood of the land, like Lawson or Paterson."

"My God," said Paul. "What on earth is the *mood of the land*? Since when has the *Zeitgeist* made it this far south?"

Again Anna felt pity for Paul. Winton was now amused rather than annoyed, but didn't seem to have the energy to take a side.

Hamish, feeling ignored, thought about the satchel he'd found under the derelict Brooke Street house and wondered if he should say something.

"Where is the *Zeitgeist* if not in the new world?" he said finally. "Doesn't history move west?"

"Sure," Paul waved off the question dismissively, "but that's not what Ralph here means by mood, is it? Does he even know what the word *Zeitgeist* means? He's thinking about the spirit of the land, isn't he? And what the hell is that anyway? A drab wilderness drenched in Aboriginal blood. Is that the mood that hacks like Paterson are after?"

"What are you on about, mate?" Ralph said.

At this point, Winton calmly accepted that the afternoon could officially be described as a disaster. He felt suddenly tired and was content to watch the two young men tear each other apart out in the street if that was what it came to. Instead of worrying about it he simply took his wife's hand, and kissed it.

Anna, however, was eager to defuse the situation, if only for the sake of her daughter's prospects.

"I am from the Barossa, you know, Ralph, of German descent. Paul and Ondine have always seen themselves as not quite belonging here. It takes time to find one's feet in a new country."

"My God!" said Paul again, outraged. "Who insisted that we speak German until it drove my father mad? Who taught us to read Goethe and Schiller, hoping that we'd be saved from the barbarity of Australia?"

The outburst shook Anna to the core and for a second she was shocked that her son would accuse her in this way. Paul saw immediately that he had overstepped the boundary of propriety, and rather than continue at the table with the shame of having humiliated his mother, stood up manfully, apologised, and left the room.

There was a moment of strained silence in which Winton and Anna both wondered if Paul were beginning to display the patterns of behaviour that undid Albert. Winton held Anna's hand again.

"Ralph, I'm sorry about all of this. We've behaved rather badly for you. You must think you've come to lunch at Yarra Bend."

Ondine, aware that this new sense of awkwardness accused her brother, directed her attention, finally, towards Hamish.

"Could you recite your poem for us, Hamish?" she asked, her limpid blue eyes fixed on him.

At that particular moment there was nothing he wanted to do less than recite a poem that imagined his final, impossible union with Ondine in some remote, hyperborean landscape of childish magic, secret signs and aberrant choral chanting.

"I really don't want to. It's embarrassing."

"But we'll read it anyway when it's published. Or will you try to hide that from us as well?"

"By then it will have the impersonality of print."

"Oh, all right. How are you going to be a poet if you never share your writing with your friends? We are practically family, aren't we?"

The candour of this convinced him that he truly loved her, but no sooner had she said it than she was again focusing on Ralph.

"Maybe after lunch we could all go for a stroll through the gardens? It looks like quite a nice day."

"You could try to coax your brother into a better mood," Winton said.

"Yes," she said. "I think I know just how to do that. He's not always so horrible."

After lunch, with the party waiting for her on the verandah, Ondine rushed upstairs to talk to Paul. She opened his bedroom door to find him sitting on the edge of his bed, his head in his hands.

"Hello there," she said, red with the exertion of the staircase.

"Has he gone?" Paul asked.

Ondine went to him, took his hands and looked into his eyes.

"Do you have any idea what it does to me to see you so hatefully jealous?" She had a girlish grin on her face. Before he could say anything she kissed him on the lips. "Now come down, walk with your mother, and be civil."

He did as his sister commanded.

Later on Paul apologised to Hamish, whom he felt he had wronged more intensely than either Ralph Matthews or his mother. Paul knew that Hamish was insightful enough to realise that he had invited him as a way of conveying his disregard for Ralph's presence, which Winton had clearly arranged with some sense of ceremony. He felt sorry for his friend who had come in good faith, only to be buffeted into the margins of the conversation, and systematically ignored by all of them. After Ralph left and the others had returned to the house, they walked together to the Montague, where they each had a beer and a cigarette.

"My behaviour was pretty dreadful, wasn't it?" Paul said sheepishly.

"Nothing that won't blow over."

"It was pretty dreadful where you were concerned as well."

"I can handle myself, Paul."

They were silent for a moment, both watching the pretty Irish barmaid serving a bloke at the other end of the bar.

"Are you still carrying a flame for Ondine?" Paul asked.

"Of course not," said Hamish as nonchalantly as he could. "But I didn't know that you were."

"Steady there, old man. That would be *Blutschande*, as they say in the old country."

Paul and Ondine had once looked up the word, as if they were looking for a code that would contain the excitement of their clandestine affections.

"Paul, she's going to have to get married sooner or later. If not to Ralph Matthews, then to someone else."

Paul wondered how much Hamish really knew. He looked at him pensively, blowing a swirl of cigarette smoke out over the bar, turning over in his mind the fact that they had known each other virtually their whole lives, shared the same fairytales and probably dreamt the same dreams.

"You've always loved Ondine, Hamish," Paul said. "I'll bet, ten to one, that your poem has some sort of murky connection to her, even if it might be invisible to everyone else."

"Perhaps you're hoping that I'll challenge Ralph Matthews to a duel or something. Is that it?"

"He'd probably do us both without thinking twice. No. I wouldn't be worried about him. Ondine won't look twice at such a philistine."

"But she will marry eventually."

"Bullshit. Marriage is a plot designed by the weak to enslave the strong. If you're awake to it you can stand well away. Ondine sees things too clearly to fall into the clutches of some nobody pleading that he loves her, that he'll cherish her until death do them part. You know my sister, Hamish. She's highly developed. None of that nonsense about child rearing and self-sacrifice for the good of the nation. None of that rot about the 'mood of the land'. She can see the end, the world in flames, and looks on without flinching."

Paul had worked himself up and drew heavily on the cigarette to calm himself.

Hamish, as if in obedience to a childish reflex, was on the verge of saying something glib at Paul's extravagant image of his sister, but the truth of it was that it engrossed him. He knew he couldn't be derisive about it without being false to himself. He loved Ondine, he realised, exactly for the quality that Paul had summed up as only one caught in the grips of obsession could. The thought of the fire in her dreams, the world reduced to burning rubble, left him almost breathless. Isn't that what Albert had tried to write about as well? The forsaken creatures of his fevered imagination, the filthy streets of the city, the labyrinth of death and desire. Hamish knew it all by heart. They were all fellow travellers in some futile quest for an intensity that defied mere being. It wasn't love, it was fire. Maybe that's why Albert killed himself, he thought. For the second time, Hamish was on the verge of saying something about the notebooks.

"But what about your poem? The bushman's bible, eh?" said Paul, trying to resume some semblance of normality.

"I sent them five poems, but they didn't accept any of them," Hamish said, relieved to be coming clean. "Too self-consciously romantic. Who the hell would have thought it from a bloke who works in a hospital cleaning up shit and disposing of corpses? They also said something about my 'Grecian' posing, and advised me not to become a master of the second-hand. On the whole, you could safely say I was torn to shreds."

Paul breathed deeply. He didn't need to ask Hamish why he lied about the poem. The two of them drank and smoked until closing time, content in the silences of each other's company, each unwilling to disturb the promise of empathy and understanding they contained. They had, after all, known each other since they were children and for the moment each knew about the other all he needed to know.

## chapter *eleven*

*A* few weeks after the catastrophe with Ralph Matthews, something took place in the Gallery School that was unprecedented. A man in his fifties appeared in the painting studio and proceeded to inspect the canvases. He cut a curious figure, with his smooth, bald head and blubbery features. He wore a monocle, which magnified his eye, and a cloak, which he swirled around with dramatic effect as he sailed through the room scrutinising one inept painting after another. Lindsay Bannister greeted him by asking, suspiciously, whether he could be of any help.

"My name is Reuben Gines," the man said in a slight European accent, shaking Bannister's hand. "I believe we met in Antwerp."

"Quite possibly," Bannister replied, dazzled by the oddity of the fellow before him. "I've certainly been there."

"I won't waste your time," the man said. "I've come to talk to one of your protégés."

"One of *mine*?" Bannister asked. The students in the studio were by this time all ears, wondering what surprise the cloaked man was about to spring.

"I'm representing a private collector, Sir, who has instructed me to offer twenty pounds to Mr Walters in exchange for..." The man paused, looking around him, searching out the exact piece of work.

"Mr Walters is this way," Bannister said in disbelief.

Paul shook the man's hand, and no sooner had he done so than Gines seized upon the garishly-coloured figure that Bannister himself had criticised so publicly.

"For this you'll pay twenty pounds?" Bannister asked.

"Not me, Sir. I'm acting only as a proxy. Paul, do you have any objections?"

Paul was stunned. He accepted the money gratefully and Gines said that he would have the painting picked up by the end of the day.

"Paul," Gines said as he handed over the bank draft, "I'm told that were you to offer a series of paintings along the same lines, you might be reasonably confident of a significant return. My employer is a gambler. Likes long odds, and isn't afraid of the future."

After Gines left, the class burst into applause. Bannister shook his head and asked to speak to Paul in private. As Paul followed his teacher into his office, the one could hide his annoyance as little as the other could his elation.

"You've had quite a windfall," Bannister said. "Evidently there is someone out there who's willing to take a gamble on something that, were you to ask me, is radically out of step with every canon of taste we currently hold dear."

Paul sat there silently, chuffed to have the money in his pocket. He looked at the tattered, dog-eared books on the shelf behind Bannister, waiting for him to warn him away from the prospect of a public exhibition, and steeling himself to resist the advice of his teacher.

"It is highly unusual for a student at your level to be selling paintings, Paul, and I'd warn you not to get carried away, especially given the, well, the unorthodox nature of the work. If this fellow, Gines — quite frankly I have no recollection of him from Antwerp or anywhere else — is going to bribe you into stylistic excess, well, I'd be thinking very carefully if I were you."

"I will think carefully, Sir," Paul said. He'd already made up his mind to sell what he could and send Bannister's monotonous tonal realism the way of the dinosaurs.

That evening Paul began sketching nudes in his pad, refining and expanding upon the style of the painting Gines had bought. The pictures were crude, contorted, needlessly abstract, but their mockery of discipline, control and the sterile cult of formal accomplishment excited him. He imagined that he had been put in touch with the elemental forces pulsing through the history of art. They gripped him, rendered his hand unsteady, and ruptured all harmony with their violent convulsions. The coherence of the image was ripped open. It was always an act of sacrifice in which an ideal conception of the body — pristine, celestial, transcendent — was conquered by the power of the artist. The images were torn, bleeding, unclean things and in them Paul possessed his sister more completely and more brutally than he ever would when she held him in the thrall of their all too chaste intimacy. He thought about the stillness of her room, the light in her blond hair, the sharp crystalline casing that closed around his pulsing heart as he touched her. What powers did he serve as he imagined the violation he could inflict with paint? His lust poured onto the page exalting all impure, adulterate things. His obsession plunged him into the formlessness of his own violent urges.

In the weeks that followed, Paul struggled to maintain his composure in class. Aware of the director's disapproval, he still had trouble keeping his impulses in check. Since the appearance of Gines he had become the one the other students looked up to. Even the older students welcomed him to their table at Fasoli's where he'd smoke and talk confidently about art and the elemental as if he were a fêted café philosopher. In the studio some of the students had begun to imitate him. Bannister looked on impotently as tonal realism degenerated into rhapsodies of abstract colour and anamorphic form. In art history classes Paul began to explore the precedents for anarchy prevailing over order, the Dionysian impulse over the Apollonian. He was mesmerised by Bosch and Breughel. In "The Triumph of Death" he saw the apocalyptic engine driving the creative spirit and his heart beat uncontrollably at the revelation.

All the time he was waiting for Gines to reappear. He even tried to will his presence. How else were his plans to come to fruition? Weeks and weeks passed, leaving him in a state of heated expectation. And just as Paul felt his energy ebbing away, as if his enthusiasm had run its course, there he was outside the studio, waiting as if not a day had passed since their first meeting.

Gines hugged himself inside his cloak like a vampire.

"Paul," he gestured with a nod of his head and an impish grin, "a word if I may."

"I should thank you," Paul said. "I don't think I managed it properly the other day."

"Not at all. Not at all."

"You said —"

But Gines cut him off. "I said, if you were to come up with another half-dozen canvases my employer would consider purchasing them. Without much effort you should clear at least a hundred pounds. There are some rooms at the top end of Little Collins Street under the Mercantile offices. You can hire them, I'm told, at a very reasonable rate for such a flash location, on the promise of a future return."

"Your employer," Paul asked, "won't buy privately?"

"Dear, dear, where's the fun in that? Why hide your light under a bushel? I think we're after a bit of notoriety, don't you? The art of the future must strike out like lightning — burning the timid like tinder."

The man spoke with fervour. His eyes lit up with a demonic sparkle and it was all Paul could do to subdue the flames they lit in his own heart.

"Can I ask the name of the buyer?"

He didn't expect an answer, and in any event the absence of one was not about to blanket his resolve.

"You can, but for the moment it will get you nowhere. Imagine a wealthy, middle-aged woman, beautiful in her own way, who has noticed what a promising chap you are, Paul. Or, if you like, an old rake collecting curiosities for his candle-lit den. Now I'm not giving anything away, but we should probably take our patrons where we can find them."

Gines wrote down a Little Collins Street address on the back of a calling card, and shook Paul's hand. "Congratulations, young man. You have been chosen." And with that he turned towards the river, his cloak billowing out behind him.

A moment of doubt crossed Paul's mind. Gines's personal oddity made him wary. In his fustian cloak and monocle he could have wandered out of the pages of some Satanic fable in which the tempter preys upon the flaws of gullible youth with promises of adulation and erotic fulfilment. If Paul had harboured a superstitious presentiment of the magical powers of allegory, he might have turned his back on Gines. But such things were unthinkable in the twentieth century. Satan was merely a figure of speech. Paul told himself to seize the moment chance had given him, for chance alone was at stake.

Before his doubts could resurface, he promptly marched over to Little Collins Street in search of the address Gines had jotted down. The shopfront under the Mercantile offices consisted of a large, open room connected to another behind it by a narrow hallway. A round man in a black suit busied himself sweeping dust onto the street.

"Can I help you?" he said without raising his eyes from the steady motion of the broom.

"Thought I might be interested in taking these rooms," Paul said boldly, determined not to take a backward step.

"Too right?" said the man. "Young fella like you."

"Yes. Young fella like me. Thought I'd use them as a studio."

"That right? You're not the young fella I was told about, are you?"

"Depends."

"Mr Gines's young friend?"

"I suppose I am," Paul said, wondering at the extent of Gines's influence.

"Yes, I suppose you are. Come in then. John Perryman, pleased to meet you." The man thrust out a sweaty hand and gave Paul's a vigorous shake. He led Paul through to the second room, concealed from the street. It contained an old, threadbare couch, pushed into a corner, a few chairs and a small writing desk.

Perryman opened a back door which led onto a filthy alley running onto a slightly wider lane that linked Little Collins with Collins Street proper.

"Private access, of course. The soul of discretion. This would do nicely as an atelier," he added with a pretentious flourish of French vowels. "And the main room, fronting the street and exposed through a large plate-glass window, would make a very decent exhibiting space. I'm told that you will want to show some of your work there."

Paul was overwhelmed by the possibilities. By the end of the week he had arranged to rent the two rooms, paying Perryman up-front for the first two months. As soon as he could he showed Ondine his new retreat and the two of them, like overexcited children, converted the back room into a lavish fantasy of bohemian living. They bought an Oriental carpet, a large cut of velvet to throw over the old couch, an antique Venetian lamp with a deep red shade, a second-hand graphophone, some cheap lithographs depicting scenes from classical mythology and a host of other useless miscellanea all of which conspired to turn the studio into a rather tawdry expression of the artist's rich inner life.

Ondine threw herself onto the couch, naïvely charmed by the transformation. "So, you are going to be a famous painter, after all," she said. "Of course, I never doubted you. But I may end up being envious. What am I going to do when you've outgrown me?"

The sight of his sister's long, elongated form reclining on the velvet excited him. He sat beside her and held her hand.

"We are like two children in a fairytale, Paul," she said. "Like Hansel and Gretel. You, because you are a man, will be able to remain a child as long as you wish. In a way this is the privilege of art. But I, because I am a woman, will have to stop this sooner or later."

He looked at her, barely comprehending. He kissed her gently on the lips. She returned the kiss, but then smiled weakly at him instead of pursuing his ardour. There was no envy in her expression. Without being able to explain why, she felt pity for her brother, and feared for his happiness, wondering why he would stake so much of himself on such a grand, but transparent illusion.

The next morning, Paul arrived at his studio and found a haggard young woman ensconced on the couch, admiring the crimson velvet and the accompanying effects.

"Hello," she said brazenly. "I hope you don't mind. Mr Gines asked Mr Perryman to let me in. He said you'd be needing a model and that I shouldn't have to wait on the street. Might embarrass you."

Paul was startled and took a step back. The young woman's appearance had something both miraculous and comical about it, as if she'd been conjured out of thin air. The room he'd decorated only the previous day reeled in front of him as the young woman stood up. She was bedraggled but becoming, with a vampish appeal that he attributed to her pointed, triangular face.

"Bit of a chill in here. Mind if we light up a fire?" she asked, suppressing a shiver.

The earthiness of her voice convinced him that she was real. It was the voice of the street, not of some enchanted forest.

"Not at all. There's a gas heater."

Paul crouched down at the small space heater built into the wall and momentarily filled the room with the deathly smell of methane, before managing to summon the flicker of gentle blue flames inside the ceramic frame.

"What's your name?" he asked.

"Roxanne," she replied. "Mr Gines said that you might make me famous, or my body at least." She giggled. "I said I'd not come, but he promised me your intentions are respectable."

"Respectable. Yes, of course," Paul said distractedly. He still hadn't quite recovered from the shock of finding a stranger waiting for him in his own studio.

"What other surprises does Mr Gines have in store?"

"Oh, he's full of surprises, that one."

"Tell me what you know about him," he asked, sitting down and lighting a cigarette.

"Mind if I smoke?" she asked.

He offered her his case and a silver lighter he'd bought the day before along with his other purchases.

"What would you be wanting to know?"

"How, for instance, he found you."

"Well, if you must know, Mr Nosey, he found me at the Arcadia, where he's been coming by from time to time."

"What's the Arcadia?" Paul asked.

"Well, it's a place, ain't it. A place where men come to make themselves at home."

"I see."

A brothel, Paul thought to himself. For a moment he couldn't take his eyes off Roxanne, and was fixated on the idea that this woman in front of him, close enough for him to touch, would exchange herself for money.

"What else do you know?" he asked, still lingering over the shape of her legs, the way she held a cigarette, the hint of a dimple, the purse of her lips.

"Not much. I know he's in the theatre. I think he manages something. Not sure what."

"Nothing else?" Paul asked sceptically.

"I ain't going about biting the hand that feeds me, am I?" she said.

"He's paid you?"

"'Course he has. He said I'm to serve in the name of the art of the future."

Paul tried to take this declaration in his stride, concealing his discomposure at the thought of her capacity to serve, and of Gines's hand in the orchestration of their meeting. He was conscious of maintaining at least the fiction of the artist's aloofness.

"All right then," said Paul. "Have you modelled before?"

"I'd say we're both new at this, wouldn't you?" Roxanne said with a smirk. "Where do you want me?"

The varying hues of the woman's skin worked their way into Paul's vision as she undressed before him and, still shivering, sat back down on the couch, affecting an air of casualness as she lifted one stockinged leg towards her chest and stretched the other out across the Persian rug.

Paul felt the blood rushing into his penis as he fidgeted indecisively at the easel. He tried not to stare, acting as if he knew what he was doing, and endeavoured to push the fact of her nakedness from his mind. Finally he squirted some paint onto a palette and started dabbing at the blank canvas. He worked quickly, eager to be done with it. The play of shadow looked more like a series of greenish bruises on her mottled skin. His abrasive, reddish brushstrokes might have been scratch marks weaving through sallow flesh, circling around the tonal intensity of black vulva and florid purple lips dominating the centre of the image. Her limbs were like extended, sinewy knots or the gnarled branches of a dead tree twisting around her torso. He made her neck disproportionately long, extending it forward into an erect posture that highlighted her sharp chin and the unnerving symmetry of her clear, green eyes. Paul smoked as he painted, mixing greens and blues and reds into the flesh tones, barely paying attention to the background at all, which was little more than a mess of errant brushstrokes.

When he paused and Roxanne stood up to look at herself she was appalled. "My God, I don't look nothing like that. You've turned me into a hag."

"Don't be stupid. I've turned you into the thing of flesh and bone that you are, not tried to hide you under a contrived, artificial surface."

She looked again. "I'm hideous."

"Call it what you want," he said, enthused. "I could have painted you like a corpse. A smooth white surface with still, lifeless limbs. Would that have flattered you more?"

"I'm not sure about you," she said, sitting down again. "You're weird." She smiled at the thought of it. "Do I really seem hideous to you?"

Paul's head was buzzing. The heater had taken the chill from the room and Roxanne's body gradually lost its reserve as she held herself in front of him, dissected by his maddened, increasingly frantic stare. He could channel his lust for her into the paint for only so long. Finally he put down his brushes. Roxanne rolled over onto her stomach and rested her head on her arms. He sat down beside her and stroked her back.

"Do you want it, then?" she asked.

He didn't answer.

She sat up and fondled his collar, running her forefinger along his jaw. On cue she leaned into him, sighing theatrically as he groped her buttocks, sliding her hands up inside his shirt, tossing her head back, losing herself in the performance. The urgency in her movements made Ondine seem so hesitant by comparison. Paul pushed his sister from his mind and threw himself at Roxanne. She stifled a laugh at his ineptitude and kept her mind firmly fixed on the quiver in her breathless gasping.

For the next month Paul worked feverishly, neglecting the Gallery School and avoiding Bannister, who sensed that the boy had ignored his advice and recklessly struck off on his own path. Paul kept Ondine away from the studio on the days when he'd arranged to see Roxanne, and treated his model with the freedom that came from the low esteem in which he held her. In four weeks he finished six canvases, each a full-body portrait in the same expressionist style, each with a crudely patched-up background of soft yellow or pearl white that was inconsequential to the violently arranged bodies in the foreground. Roxanne figured in three of these paintings. Other women from the Arcadia Club had posed for the remaining three. In consort with Gines he arranged an evening for a public showing in the Little Collins Street shopfront and placed advertisements in the *Argus* and the *Age*.

A few days before the appointed night, Bannister appeared blocking the narrow footpath as he knocked on the glass door and peered into the dark hallway that led to the studio. Paul was surprised, but let him in and nervously showed him through to the paintings, fully expecting the teacher's disapproval.

Bannister paused and surveyed the room with its exotic, somewhat exhausted sense of opulence. The six canvases were pushed up against the wall. He glanced at them and shook his head.

"Paul, I've come to try to stop you."

"What do you mean?" Paul pretended to be puzzled.

"If you make an exhibit of these, these *works*, you'll be a laughing-stock."

"A laughing-stock?" he replied with a callow puffing of the chest. "If I sell them for over a hundred pounds I promise you that no one will laugh."

"And who's going to pay that sort of money?" Bannister asked, shaking his head in disbelief. "Money like that just doesn't materialise out of thin air."

"Gines has assured me they'll all sell."

"And who in billy-o's name is this Gines?"

"Clearly someone with a keen eye for the contemporary."

"Please Paul. This is Melbourne, not a Henri Murger novel. The dreams of the artist have to be tempered by some harsh realities. What's more, the public taste hasn't even learnt to accommodate a Norman Lindsay. You'll be lucky not to be charged with obscenity and dragged before the magistrate's court."

Bannister glanced around again at the naked limbs, the crimson pudenda visible underneath raised skirts, the abrasive, flushed features that reminded him of consumptives, and the sinister, serpent eyes of a wild, reptilian sensuality. For a moment he saw something he couldn't quite describe. He couldn't tell himself that these were accomplished paintings. On the contrary, he thought them vile and impure. But at the back of his mind was some half-formed sense of paint and flesh, a vision of intensity just beyond his reach.

"Paul, these barely get beyond the visual gimmicks of pornographic illustration, though with none of the poise and control. As for Gines, I've never seen the man before in my life, though he claims to know me from somewhere or other. I'd say the man is a charlatan, though God only knows what he's playing at."

The two men were quiet and Bannister knew his efforts were defeated.

The day before the exhibition opening Paul was so anxious that he didn't sleep for a whole twenty-four hours. As his moment arrived he was both frantic and fatigued. Anna and Winton appeared early with Ondine, but almost immediately decided that they couldn't be seen anywhere near such compromising images. They awkwardly withdrew, insisting that Ondine, who was also embarrassed for her brother, leave with them.

"I would like to stay. It's so important to him," she remonstrated, secretly confident that her mother and her stepfather wouldn't be persuaded. She couldn't quite admit it, but the canvases were insulting. She wondered whether her brother hated the women he had painted and wondered whether that was how he saw her as well.

"Come along, Ondine," Winton said. "I'd drag Paul out as well if he weren't the one responsible for these abominations. What on earth was the young man thinking?"

Anna was already on the street, careful not to look back through the plate-glass for fear of catching her son's disappointment. A tremor of disgust ran through her. Once she had looked at Paul's drawings and dismissed them as the innocent works of a child. Now his paintings made her think of Albert pushing her down and raking her body like a wild beast. Is that what men see? She caught her breath and stood there in the twilight, frozen in horror at the thought of the correspondence between the father and son. It was not mere nakedness that shocked her, it was the violence intimated by the brushstrokes. It was too awful to think about. They would have to get help for him. Charles would know of someone good.

A doctor or an alienist who could talk Paul through his ghastly visions towards a healthier state of mind. She regained her composure as Winton led Ondine towards her. He took Anna's hand, but ashamed of her son she couldn't look into his eyes.

Paul was in such a stupor that he barely noticed them leaving or, at least, pretended that their presence was a matter of little consequence to him. Other people glided in, students from the Gallery School, faces that he recognised from Fasoli's, and nightbirds from the queer end of Bourke Street or the peepshows at the Eastern Market, all helping themselves to wine and champagne. Hamish was loyally slouched in a corner, happy that his lowly occupation at the hospital rendered him anonymous to the passers-by who gazed through the window or took a timid step or two into the exhibition only to withdraw in disgust. He'd watched Anna leave and realised that the whole exhibition was in such bad taste that it would be difficult for Paul to regain his family's confidence.

The evening took on a delirious, dreamlike atmosphere. Paul felt unsure on his feet and as the tobacco smoke got the better of him he became faint. When Roxanne appeared, draped in a fur and made-up with a thick layer of rice powder, carmine cheeks and glistening red lips, he thanked his lucky stars that Ondine and his mother had left, and glimpsed for the first time, with a sense of shock that would grow more pronounced as the night wore on, what dissipated company he was keeping. Roxanne looked like a garish china doll.

"Hello there, handsome," she said, embracing him. "Is my cunt famous yet?" She'd brought the three other models from the Arcadia Club with her. Maggie, Violet and Minuette, faded flowers miraculously resuscitated by the powers of night, mingled through the crowd, effortlessly holding its attention as they posed theatrically before their portraits.

"Not famous just yet," said Paul gloomily.

Where the hell was Gines, he wondered. He'd expected him to magically appear, rescuing him from the ignominy into which he was fast sinking with the promise of a three-figure banknote for his trouble. The crowd seemed to swell around him. Young men, larrikins most probably, were now jostling past to admire the paintings. One almost stumbled right over him. Roxanne clung to the lapel of his jacket, pushing her breasts into him, while Paul almost had to prop himself up against her. Her skin gave off a poisonous, artificial scent that overwhelmed the room's rank, asphyxiating mixture of sweat and smoke.

The gathering was getting rowdier and Paul cursed the second-rate throng of the colonies. He was staggered at the uncouth individuals, some no better dressed than swaggies or street urchins. The night dragged on and still there was no sign of Gines. In the studio Roxanne entertained her friends on the velvet-covered couch, holding court in front of a host of leering young men. Who are these people, Paul thought.

He was on the verge of throwing everyone out, which would probably have been impossible, when in through the front door walked Ralph Matthews. Paul shrank in front of the confident, unabashed step of his sister's suitor. He wished he could say Ralph was a fool, but the casual detachment with which he made his way through the mêlée towards Paul, who knew he was looking haggard and tired in the glass by comparison, made a mockery of these wishes.

"Hello, Paul," said Ralph, offering his hand.

"Come to find the *Zeitgeist*, have we?" said Paul, trying his best not to slur his words.

"I'd hoped to find your sister here, but on reflection," he said looking around him with subdued amusement, "it's not really a place for a decent young woman, is it?"

Paul was enraged. The room was spinning around him as if the alcohol he'd been steadily consuming had suddenly rushed from his stomach to his head, demolishing his sense of balance and proportion. He fell against Ralph, who picked him up and, with the help of Hamish who had just appeared from his corner, led him into the studio.

"Jesus," Paul heard Ralph say on beholding Roxanne and her ilk sprawled about the room, half-hidden in the deep crimson shadows thrown off by the Venetian lamp. The scene before them – the dim lighting, the bloodstained darkness and the ghostly white of the women's make-up – had the aura of a monstrous pantomime. Paul lifted himself up to attention and shook his head in his hands, hoping to regain his focus.

"What d'ya say?" Paul mumbled aggressively.

"Can you take care of him?" Ralph asked Hamish. "I guess I'm not wanted here."

Before Hamish could answer he noticed Paul dribbling a viscous yellow liquid from his mouth and hurried him to the back door, where he vomited into the darkness of the alley. Hamish, hand under his stomach, eased him onto the cobblestones.

"Just leave me for a bit," Paul said, on his knees. The cool night air had already revived him and he felt his stomach purge again, contracting into a short, violent spasm of anger that yielded nothing but a string of saliva tainted with bile.

"Doing some painting out there, are ya?" he heard a voice roar above the general din behind him. There was the sound of glass smashing and another roar of laughter mingling with the shriller giggling of a woman, maybe Roxanne, he couldn't tell. In a moment of resolve Paul picked himself up and went back inside, determined to throw this horde of freeloaders onto the street.

"I've ruined my fucking life," he said to Hamish, who was standing just inside the door.

"Don't be absurd," his friend said. "You want me to kick this lot out?"

But the crowd was already thinning of its own accord, as if the blister had burst and its poison were dissipating. The alcohol had run dry and the night-birds of the city had begun to move off in search of other pleasures. Ralph approached Paul again.

"Why don't we just close up the front, eh?" he said calmly.

Paul couldn't look into his eyes, but nodded despondently. He sat down beside Roxanne, who wrapped a leg around him and kissed him on the mouth, herself too drunk to taste the vomit on his breath. Paul hoped that Ralph wouldn't reappear to accuse him with his good-natured, even-headed attitude. By the time Hamish returned to the studio, without Ralph, an exhausted silence had descended on the room. Besides Roxanne and Maggie, only Hamish and, of all people, old Les from Fasoli's remained.

Paul was surprised that he hadn't noticed him before. Les was sitting on the floor with his back to the wall, lazily sucking on a bottle hidden in a brown paper bag. Maggie had taken to him and was stroking his rough, unshaven chin with a drowsy affection, both treacherous and condescending. The place looked as if it had just hosted a riot.

Paul dragged himself up and went to the basin, splashing some water on his pale face.

"Like a swig?" Les held the bottle towards him.

Paul took it without a word and choked back a mouthful of whisky, spluttering like a consumptive.

"That's bloody good Scotch whisky, young fella," Les said.

Paul fell back down next to Roxanne.

"I take it you ain't sold a cracker, eh?" Les croaked from the floor.

"Leave off, Les," said Roxanne, "we can't all be fucking big-wigs."

She'd noticed Paul's depressed state and, with a degree of sympathy that surprised him, modulated her own mood accordingly.

"You know him?" Paul asked.

"'Course. Don't you know who that is? His eminence? How's that, Les? One person in the city that don't know ya."

"Leave it off, ya cruel bitch," Les said.

"That's Christopher Leslie Collins," Roxanne went on with pomp in her voice. "A genius forgotten by the twentieth century. Can't afford to buy his own books back from the second-hand stalls. Lives on the charity of whores."

"Leave off, ya cruel bitch," he said again, this time in a cracked, lifeless monotone.

"*The Life of Charles Whitehead*," said Hamish.

"Hurray. You read it, then?" Les said ironically.

"Heard of it," Hamish corrected, feeling awkward and out of place.

"Well good for you, young man. Good for you." Les's voice tapered off into resignation.

"You're a writer?" asked Paul.

"Was, mate. Now I'm a drunk." He said this with a finality that suggested it would be futile to try to talk to him about his work.

Paul shuddered. The skeleton of a man in front of him, the wasted cheeks, and the sad eyes reddened with alcohol and the life of the streets, offered him a vision of the misery that now clawed at him out of the crimson half-light of the surrounding shambles.

"You feel like coming back to the Arcadia?" Roxanne said. "At least we'll find something to drink there."

"What else does the place have to recommend it?" Paul asked.

"Ya never been there?" Les said, perking up.

"No."

"Never?" Les addressed Roxanne.

"I didn't think he'd be the type, did I?" she protested.

"By God girl, take a look at his paintings."

Paul's interest was piqued. He was already feeling wretched and almost fancied a good dose of self-mortification as a way of completing his fall.

"All right then, let's go," Roxanne said.

"Where is this place?" Paul asked.

"Not far, just off Little Lon."

The group roused itself. Les walked arm in arm with Maggie, who had almost fallen asleep on his shoulder. Roxanne draped herself around Paul and seemed to be both dragging him down and holding him up. Hamish reluctantly tagged along in the wake of this odd collection, determined that he'd keep watch over Paul until he was safely away from the underworld and back at St Vincent Place, which now seemed as remote as the surface of the earth to someone trapped at its sulphurous centre.

"I can't face Winton or Mother again," Paul moaned to Hamish.

"Winton?" Les repeated.

"My stepfather."

"D'ya hear that?" Les tossed the question back to Roxanne.

"What of it?"

"Charles Winton, eh?" Les asked.

"That's right."

The streets had a moist, greasy sheen under the dim illumination that leaked out of the occasional window or dripped down from an overhead lamp. On Little Lonsdale Street a pair of turbaned Indians hauled crates of fruit down from a creaky wooden cart, unbothered by the solicitous murmurs of a woman slouched languidly on the corner of a nearby alleyway, flicking the ash of her cigarette into the gutter.

As they turned past her into the lane and entered the Arcadia Club, Les sidled up to Paul, as if he had something to confide. "And how d'ya get along with your old stepdad?" he asked.

"Right now I'd imagine I'm just about cut off."

"Well," Les said, "I'd be happy to be of some use to you, after all. I ain't much of a writer these days, but I can still tell you a bloody good tale or two."

## chapter *twelve*

The next morning the *Argus* ran a mercifully unobtrusive column under the headline "Bohemia at the Paris End":

Our laws against the dissemination of indecent and obscene materials are not wanting in their severity. Vigilant policing along the main thoroughfares of the city has forced the sale and exhibition of pornographic material into crevices, where it is at least kept away from the unsuspecting and the gullible. Yet the dealers in this illicit trade don't lack in ingenuity when it comes to finding new ways of presenting obscenity in the guise of art, education or science. We have long been aware of a certain museum flourishing in an obscure arcade of ill-repute under the banner of medical science, and a collection of wax models, thought to have been outlawed, which occasionally reappears in slightly altered costumes for a week or so at a time, before our law-makers can catch up. Last night obscenity again reared its ugly head, in the most respectable part of town. To call it the Paris end of Collins Street is all very well, but we don't welcome the riot of the left bank as a result. The occasion was a so-called art show of paintings by Paul Walters, under the Mercantile offices in Little Collins Street. These crude, almost childishly constructed canvases represented women of the filthiest kind in various postures of lewdness. There was no artistic merit here of any kind, save the art of attracting the prurient interest of passing larrikins, and before long the exhibition itself had degenerated into a disgusting debauch that had passers-by eager to cross to the other side of the street. Mr Walters is, we are told, currently studying painting at the Gallery School, where we hope his work and his crude showmanship are the exception, not the rule.

Anna and Winton both had the displeasure of reading the article. They sat silently in the sitting room like a couple in grief as Ondine went up to look in on her disgraced brother. When she came back down she was visibly disturbed.

"Doctor, I think you'd better look at him," she said, and took Winton's hand, the quicker to get him upstairs. "He seems to be raving."

Paul's room smelt of alcohol and cigar smoke. He was sleeping uneasily, muttering weird, incoherent imprecations, his face was pale, almost bloodless, and his lips were cracked and showing the first signs of ulceration. The doctor looked worried. When Anna appeared at the door she flew to his side.

"He has a fever," said Winton, feeling the heat on his forehead. "He's also probably still drunk and I'd say his body is quite run-down."

"What's he saying?" asked Ondine, trying to make some sense of her brother's mumblings. But nothing made sense, save the words "Mr Pussycat", which he said distinctly a number of times.

"What on earth does that mean?" Ondine asked, pondering the possible corruption of some childhood story they'd been told, like "Puss in Boots" or "Tomcat Murr". The words sounded dirty. They sullied the thought of the serene nights she had shared with her brother for so long. The sores appearing at the corners of Paul's mouth also repulsed her and she shuddered at the thought of her own snow-white complexion being disfigured by those weeping, red scabs.

"He's going to need rest," said Winton.

"Mr Pussycat's coming," Paul muttered.

"Did you hear that?" said Ondine.

Neither Anna nor Ondine noticed that Winton had gone suddenly pale.

"He's in no danger," the doctor said again. "We should leave him for a few hours and see how he recovers when he wakes up. I'll check on him every hour."

"Poor boy," said Ondine.

In the hallway, out of Ondine's earshot, Anna clutched at Winton's sleeve.

"Charles, those sores on his mouth. You don't think . . .?"

"No I don't, fortunately, though it's too early to tell. He doesn't have any other symptoms just yet, and I'll bet they are merely the result of a fever and exhaustion. Nevertheless, I don't think Ondine should be spending too much time in there."

Later, as Paul's sleep became lighter, he found himself lying in a dank, dark room with walls made of clay. Outside he could hear voices arguing and the sound of ceramic pots being smashed against the ground, one after the other. He thought he was in an eastern city

– in India or Egypt – but he couldn't be sure. He'd just come from the Arcadia Club and his sleep was full of the ghoulish theatre he'd seen enacted in that brothel, where whores performed scenes from the madhouse or the torture garden, inviting customers to act out their morbid fantasies in inspired flights of horror. When he heard a voice somewhere in the distance, soft at first, moving towards him through the streets, he knew he was asleep and that the voice was merely the sound of his own dreams. "Mr Pussycat's coming," the voice whispered, but it wasn't one voice, it was many, a chorus of whispers in the darkness around him getting gradually louder until he could hear footsteps mounting the stairs and edging towards the door. His blood turned to ice. He was paralysed with terror and struggled to wake himself up as the steps got closer. The door moved ever so slightly. His body tensed at the certainty of an evil presence waiting behind it. With one last terrified effort he roused himself out of the nightmare, clawing desperately at the liminal state between sleep and wakefulness until he could feel himself slipping clear of its grip, falling back into himself, his heart still braced for the horror of the thing left brooding at the threshold of consciousness.

When he opened his eyes the room was quiet. The voices had stopped but the door to the clay cell was ajar. He could see the subtle shift in the density of the darkness, the trace of a light crawling up the stairwell from the street. Then something stirred in the room beside him. He tried to raise himself but couldn't move. Little animal paws scampered across the floor. He tried to scream out but his mouth was shut tight. He tried to wriggle like a worm but it was as if his limbs were numb and he were strapped down to the mattress. The thing leapt onto the bed near his feet and its red eyes glistened at him. When the terror finally tore itself free of his body, he screamed and woke up in his own room in St Vincent

Place. It was dark and outside, in the street, he could hear the hateful sound of cats hissing at each other, and imagined their tiny fang marks festering with infection in the matted fur.

Paul spent a week recovering his strength and his will to face the world following his humiliation. While he convalesced, a letter arrived from the Gallery School informing him of his expulsion on the grounds that he had undermined the standing of the institution.

Ondine was frequently at his side, but his sister's pity convinced him that something between them had changed irrevocably. She hadn't assumed a position of superiority, but it was clear to both of them he had humiliated himself by giving in to a vulgar sensuality that had no place in their clandestine encounters. He felt dirty in front of her, as if he still carried upon him the traces of Roxanne's lip paint, or the stench of her body.

Ondine, infallible, unassailable, assumed the aura of the sacred in his eyes, while he, a pitiful, fallen creature, had given into the lure of the street, the obscene riot of the city, the sickening dance of pleasure and boredom in which drunks and whores courted each other in a nauseating parody of human intimacy.

When he had regained his energy he sold the furnishings he and Ondine had bought for the studio back to a bric-a-brac man in Flinders Lane. As he was clearing out, Perryman showed up with a note from Gines.

> Dear Paul,
>
> Sorry to inform that my employer has had a change of heart. I can't think why. I've been called away on urgent business to Adelaide, where I've read the Melbourne papers and learnt of your great success. Reuben Gines

With Hamish's help, Paul took his paintings, all six of them, to Spielvogel's pawnshop on City Road, where he received a pound for the lot. It was like waking from a dream. The phantom of inspiration had fled and he found that the clarity with which he'd glimpsed the secret of the elemental in art was utterly delusional.

No one had told Paul that in the week or so of his convalescence, during which he was seldom out of his room, Ralph Matthews had become a regular visitor at St Vincent Place. He had been to lunch, taken Ondine on a stroll through the Botanical Gardens and had driven her to the Exhibition Building where, on a whim, they had seen the much-talked-about "Maori Village", in which a group of dancers in straw skirts stamped out their rhythms to the polite amusement and disdain of the crowd.

The circumstances around Ralph's reappearance at St Vincent Place, after such an unfortunate introduction, cast the young man in a very positive light. To begin with, Anna and Winton were both relieved that Paul's public disgrace had not diminished his readiness to court Ondine. Neither of them suspected that Ralph was in fact present at the fiasco, and he, of course, was not about to mention it. The article printed in the *Argus* continued to trouble them all, and as there could be little doubt that Ralph and his father had read it, Anna and Winton believed his considerate avoidance of the subject to be very much to his credit.

As for Ondine, Ralph's brazen reappearance both flattered her and impressed her as an act of courage. He confronted her with a subtle disregard that showed no trace of the nervous, sheepish demeanour that had made her laugh on the occasion of his first visit. In fact he was very direct, and though clearly solicitous, also curiously uninterested. He made out as if her beauty were a matter of little consequence, insinuated that he had better things to do than join her in the sitting room, and that he could do no more than tolerate a walk through the gardens at her side. Anna and Winton saw none of this. It was only visible to the mind's eye of a young woman who was used to adoration and whose interest was aroused by one who treated her not as a goddess, but as an equal. A week of this careful neglect had her studying herself in the mirror, arranging her hair and carefully selecting the right dress in anticipation of his arrival. Then she'd sit downstairs and try not to notice the doorbell ringing, looking bored at the prospect of his appearance when Mrs Norris introduced him.

"Oh, it's you," she said, feigning surprise.

"Yes, don't look shocked. Who else were you expecting?"

She shrugged, as if the question were not worth answering.

"Are you ready to go? If you don't mind I'd like to pay my respects to your parents."

"Be my guest." She twirled the end of a long blond lock nervously about her finger as she stood up to led him into the yard at the back where Anna and Winton had taken to the cultivation of a rose garden.

Later, as they walked down Victoria Avenue towards the beach, she said, "You don't much care for walking, do you?"

"Not much," he said. "I find it boring."

"Boring? How can trees and birds and people and the sky stretching over the water be boring?"

"It seems so petty to me," he said with the hint of a smile. "Compared to the landscapes I've seen, it's petty and small."

"Am I boring to you as well?" she demanded.

"Of course not."

"Then why do you keep coming to see me only to carry on as if you couldn't care less?"

He laughed out loud.

"Why?" she demanded. "It's true."

"You simply aren't used to being treated as an adult."

"An adult?"

"The others worship you as if you were the totem of some primitive cult. Your brother and that Hamish, nice fellow that he is, have an idolatrous devotion. You're an article of faith to them. Even Dr Winton is scared of you. Now you're offended because I treat you with a dignity to which you're not accustomed."

"What a ridiculous thing to say."

He said nothing.

"Absurd, and arrogant," she insisted. "Do you think you are that much smarter than everyone else? Take me home now."

"You're capable of getting home by yourself, if that's what you want."

He kept walking towards the water. She followed sullenly.

They arrived at the beach in silence. Ralph looked out over the bay while Ondine fumed.

"You're hardly the chivalrous type, are you?" she said dryly.

"We're living in the twentieth century. Do you really expect a man to fall down on his knees in front of you, or write sickly, devotional sonnets?"

"Of course not," she said, blushing under her wide-brimmed hat, which now threatened to fly off in the breeze.

"Good, because I'm not about to."

"If you did I'd have you whipped with your own riding crop," she said impetuously.

"And I'd do the same to any woman capable of tolerating such nonsense."

"Well I'm glad we agree on that."

Her heart was pounding as they walked awkwardly over the sand to the pier, where men threw their fishing lines into the water and lazily smoked while they waited for the tackle to start showing signs of life wriggling at the other end. An old man yanked a flathead out of the water, threw it down onto the wood and pushed his penknife through its head. The creature struggled as dark, oily blood leaked out over its wet, green scales. Ondine watched as he tugged the hook out of its mouth and dumped it into a bucket of suffocating fish.

"It seems so cruel."

"I hate to think what you'd make of life on a farm," Ralph said.

"I should hope I'll never know. You're not planning on marrying me and turning me into a squatter's wife, are you?"

"The first time I saw my father slaughter a lamb it seemed so ordinary. He pulled it up and cut its throat and then let it simply bleed to death. To tell you the truth I didn't think much of it. It was only after, when I went to look at the entrails and the head, that I felt sick."

"Why are you telling me this?" she asked, squinting at him.

"Because if you're to see the property you'll need to know what to expect."

She looked at him, bewildered. "I'm a city girl, Ralph."

"You call this a city?"

They walked back towards the sand, each retreating into their own thoughts, yet each still reluctant to leave the other behind.

"Why don't you come to the opera next Friday?" Ondine said.

"I don't much care for it."

"Oh, why not bend a little? You're becoming a caricature. Besides, you'll have the pleasure of ignoring me in front of a great crowd. Won't that satisfy you?"

He laughed out loud.

"Why?" she demanded. "It's true."

"You simply aren't used to being treated as an adult."

"An adult?"

"The others worship you as if you were the totem of some primitive cult. Your brother and that Hamish, nice fellow that he is, have an idolatrous devotion. You're an article of faith to them. Even Dr Winton is scared of you. Now you're offended because I treat you with a dignity to which you're not accustomed."

"What a ridiculous thing to say."

He said nothing.

"Absurd, and arrogant," she insisted. "Do you think you are that much smarter than everyone else? Take me home now."

"You're capable of getting home by yourself, if that's what you want."

He kept walking towards the water. She followed sullenly.

They arrived at the beach in silence. Ralph looked out over the bay while Ondine fumed.

"You're hardly the chivalrous type, are you?" she said dryly.

"We're living in the twentieth century. Do you really expect a man to fall down on his knees in front of you, or write sickly, devotional sonnets?"

"Of course not," she said, blushing under her wide-brimmed hat, which now threatened to fly off in the breeze.

"Good, because I'm not about to."

"If you did I'd have you whipped with your own riding crop," she said impetuously.

"And I'd do the same to any woman capable of tolerating such nonsense."

"Well I'm glad we agree on that."

Her heart was pounding as they walked awkwardly over the sand to the pier, where men threw their fishing lines into the water and lazily smoked while they waited for the tackle to start showing signs of life wriggling at the other end. An old man yanked a flathead out of the water, threw it down onto the wood and pushed his penknife through its head. The creature struggled as dark, oily blood leaked out over its wet, green scales. Ondine watched as he tugged the hook out of its mouth and dumped it into a bucket of suffocating fish.

"It seems so cruel."

"I hate to think what you'd make of life on a farm," Ralph said.

"I should hope I'll never know. You're not planning on marrying me and turning me into a squatter's wife, are you?"

"The first time I saw my father slaughter a lamb it seemed so ordinary. He pulled it up and cut its throat and then let it simply bleed to death. To tell you the truth I didn't think much of it. It was only after, when I went to look at the entrails and the head, that I felt sick."

"Why are you telling me this?" she asked, squinting at him.

"Because if you're to see the property you'll need to know what to expect."

She looked at him, bewildered. "I'm a city girl, Ralph."

"You call this a city?"

They walked back towards the sand, each retreating into their own thoughts, yet each still reluctant to leave the other behind.

"Why don't you come to the opera next Friday?" Ondine said.

"I don't much care for it."

"Oh, why not bend a little? You're becoming a caricature. Besides, you'll have the pleasure of ignoring me in front of a great crowd. Won't that satisfy you?"

"I don't think I've been ignoring you."

"Well, you can treat me with your much vaunted dignity then, while others belittle me with their adulation."

"I'm just not much cut out for high society." He said this without a hint of self-deprecation, as if it were a point of honour.

High society, she thought to herself, picturing the house she'd grown up in. Brooke Street was only a few blocks from where they were standing. She could easily lead him there and show him that she was, if not exactly a child of the slums, then at least from a less exalted background than he imagined. Would that impress him? Or would something in him rebel against the thought of those ramshackle cottages and the mad father who threw himself into the river?

She wondered what she was going to do with Paul. Before she could marry Ralph Matthews, as she was now almost sure she would, she'd have to drag herself clear of her brother. For the first time, she was conscious of just how much she had been longing to be free of Paul, just as she had longed to be free of the house on Brooke Street and the shadow of their father.

A matter of a few weeks had worked a dramatic change in her. Watching her brother stew in the mire of his creativity had convinced her just how necessary it was to wrench herself clear of him and embrace the world as it was, not as it was dreamt. Ralph Matthews looked at things with none of Paul's idealism, and none of his childish illusions. What did Paul think he would get from her? At any rate, he had betrayed her to the lurid enthusiasms embodied in his paintings. She was not going to demean herself in the company of the whores who flaunted themselves in her brother's imagination. She was not one of them, was not about to be reduced to the simple, throbbing thing – the crime, the breaking of a taboo, the ritual of transgression – she imagined Paul wanting from her.

*Blutschande*. The word had begun to weigh on her. It was heavy and crude in its directness. She wanted to forget it, to erase it from her mind for fear that it might leak some unctuous liquid that would stain her or drown her in her own shame.

If she were to see Ralph at the opera the following Friday evening she'd know that his presence was a concession to her. But when the night arrived she had to sit through the last act of *Madama Butterfly*, disappointed that she'd not seen him at the interval, during which she'd felt too trapped by Paul's presence to go off searching for him directly. Her brother had regained his strength, but still looked haggard. He clung to her side, watching the crowd move around them, at once disdainful and paranoid. Ondine wanted to push him away. How she longed to be free of him, free of the contrived, demeaning role that now seemed to have been forced upon her. The way her brother simpered in his crude performance of old world manners and tastes was pathetic. Suddenly the uncomplicated directness of Australia seemed like a positive relief.

"Well, here's trouble," Paul sneered as they left the auditorium and found Ralph dawdling towards them across the vestibule. "Let's shaft the cad."

"Don't be stupid."

"I suppose I'm not a man of my convictions," Ralph said as he took Ondine's hand.

"That depends, doesn't it?" she said.

"Hello Paul."

"Ralph."

They reluctantly shook hands.

"Did you enjoy it after all?" Ondine asked.

Paul became instantly irritable as he beheld their familiarity.

"Not much," Ralph said.

"Not even Sorel singing '*Un bel dì vedremo*'? Don't tell me you're that heartless. I'll have to start calling you Pinkerton."

"Perhaps you'd be preferring the Kremo family acrobats at the Gaiety?" Paul said.

"Well, to tell you the truth I don't see a great deal of difference between the melodrama of an Italian opera and that sort of thing. There's a certain childishness in both, isn't there?"

"Oh, now you're being perverse," Ondine said.

"Don't suppose they have much of anything in the bush," said Paul, bored with the conversation.

"They don't have much of anything here either," Ralph said. "It all seems rather thin on the ground to me, and getting thinner. Melbourne's fortune was made out of gold, and now that there's not much of that left you can see the place grinding to a halt."

Ondine looked into his eyes and smiled to herself. Paul seemed ready to argue, but Ralph, thankfully, was quite uninterested.

"I didn't realise you had a basis for comparison," Paul said defensively.

"Well, I think I'd like to get out of here for a bit."

"Back to the farm, eh?"

"No. Thought I might take off for the Continent. If your sister marries me, then I'll take her with me."

Ondine turned crimson and her eyes flashed at him. "Don't be silly, Ralph," she said.

"That's a damned insult!" Paul swelled with anger. "Are you trying to make us look ridiculous?"

A few heads turned at the sound of Paul's raised voice.

"Not at all."

"You'd expect my sister to marry you?"

"If she wants to."

"You'd have to ask me," Ondine said vaguely. She was too nervous to look directly at him. Her eyes wandered about the vestibule and finally fixed on a point suspended safely behind his shoulder.

Paul took his sister's hand and led her firmly towards the door. As they stepped out onto the pavement, still thronging with people leaving the opera, Ondine shook him off and rushed back inside. Ralph was rooted to the floor where she had left him.

"To tell the truth, I feel quite sorry for your brother," he said.

"Ask me then, you stubborn idiot," she said, ignoring this evasive comment.

"All right then, I'm asking."

"Are you? Don't make a fool of me."

"Marry me then," he said with a smile.

"All right then, I will."

She squeezed his hand, and then walked back onto the street, where Paul had turned pale with rage. He caught her arm and led her to a cab.

"You can't be serious, Ondine," he said. "The man is a philistine."

For the moment, anxiety about how Paul might react was swept away by her happiness. They rode silently back to South Melbourne, each careful not to look at the other.

"I'm going to have to marry one day," Ondine said as she climbed out of the cab. "And after all he is rich."

"I hate him. And if you're serious, I'll hate you as well."

"You're behaving like a child," she said as she mounted the steps, leaving him on the street.

She went straight up to her room and flung herself on her bed, confused and excited. The tranquillity of the bedroom brought with it memories of her brother's warmth and despite her resolve she felt uneasy at the prospect of turning her back on him. She'd only been there for a moment when he materialised at the door. He looked weak as tears welled up in his eyes. At the sight of him she burst into tears as well, her body convulsing uncontrollably. But the fit passed in a second. Before he'd walked the width of the room to comfort her, she had regained her composure. Paul stood in front of her with eyes that pleaded for sympathy. As if animated by a force beyond her control she pushed him against the wall and held him there, her hand firm under his jaw. She stared at him, feeling the blood course through his neck, amazed at his fragility. She could crush his windpipe with one hand, and not think anything of it. She slapped him, laughing, then kissed him on the lips and threw him away from her in disgust. Then she burst into tears again, sitting on the bed, cradling her face in her hands.

Paul went to her and tried to hold her hands.

"Please leave me alone," she said, pushing him away.

"I love you," he murmured.

"If you ever say that again to me, in that way, I'll hate you forever. It makes me sick."

He drew back from her. "So you are going to marry him, then?" he said.

"Yes."

Paul turned his back on her and left the room without another word.

## chapter Thirteen

The next day Ralph was speaking to Winton and Anna confidentially in the study. A day later the entire family was invited to the Matthews's Toorak mansion, where the engagement was formally announced. Bruce Matthews, though now amongst the city's wealthiest inhabitants, was not the sort of man to entertain notions of his own importance or to imagine himself belonging to an antipodean version of the British aristocracy. On the contrary, he was happy to snub the Anglophile anachronisms of Toorak and South Yarra by marrying his son into such a bohemian family. He knew, of course, that Ondine stood to inherit a great deal of Winton's capital, but wealth alone couldn't attenuate the sense that she entered Melbourne society as an exotic, and this pleased the old man no end. He toasted the engagement with liberal sentiment and good humour, and welcomed the union of the two families.

The wedding was planned for spring the following year, after Ondine's eighteenth birthday, and with the odious transaction all but signed and sealed, Paul decided to talk to Winton about his own future. Since the night of the exhibition, they hadn't spoken much. In fact they had done their best to avoid each other. Paul was embarrassed and felt the sting of his disgrace acutely. No amount of bravado could mitigate the shame he experienced in the presence of his stepfather and mother. Winton, for his part, already knew just how thoroughly he had fallen under his stepson's power. As Paul muttered incoherently the day after his exhibition, there was no doubt in his mind.

The evening after the engagement was announced Paul sat in front of Winton in the study, flicking through a volume of Keats's poetry.

"He had syphilis, you know," Winton said, sitting down. "At least those are the rumours."

Paul closed the book and replaced it on the shelf. "I've never heard that," he said.

"Of course, there was nothing very chaste about his writing."

Paul noticed how nervous Winton seemed, how he fumbled with the little bust of Shakespeare on his desk and refused to make direct eye contact with him.

"You know we've invested a great deal of energy in your educations, Paul, yours and Ondine's," Winton said. "I've always believed that education is the way forward, that it civilises and satisfies, equipping us for a peaceful and fulfilled life, enabling us to integrate the disparate aspects of our personalities into an harmonious whole. That's the ideal, at least, and it seems to me like a good one."

"I agree with you there, Doctor."

"Of course, most of us are in reality more complicated than the simple psychology of this allows. And society itself, moreover, develops very unevenly. What might look like progress and civility from one angle, could appear as barbarity from another. Progress in medical science or social hygiene, for instance, might be well in advance of progress in morality or jurisprudence. Or certain tenets in philosophy might be well in advance of the prevailing artistic sensibility of an age, creating dissonance and confusion. Some of us are living not for our own time, Paul, but for the future."

"Yes, I follow you," said Paul.

The doctor fell silent, waiting anxiously for his stepson to say something decisive and reveal his hand. When it was clear that Paul was not about to volunteer his secret, Winton suspected him of unnecessary cruelty and he resumed with a note of desperation in his voice.

"Paul, I'm getting old. I'll live a little longer, but soon enough your mother will inherit a fortune which will eventually devolve to you and your sister. I've adopted you as my own. You can bear my name if you wish to. I've provided for you all, and I love your mother to distraction. As far as it is in the power of a mortal to do so, she has made me young again."

"I'm grateful, Doctor," Paul said. "We all are."

It struck him as odd that he still called Winton "Doctor" after all these years, as if paternal authority had vanished with the death of his actual father, and then reappeared as a colder, institutional knowledge that kept vigilant watch over them.

"You could show me that gratitude by promising that —" But Winton broke off, not knowing quite how to broach the subject. "Paul, when you were delirious, you said something, a name, a nonsensical name."

"I don't remember."

"But you do know what I'm talking about?"

"Yes I do. In fact I came in here thinking that I might try my hand at a bit of blackmail." Paul's voice assumed an unusual calm as Winton fidgeted again with the bust, not quite knowing whether this was an attempt at levity or not.

"Really?"

"Well, in a manner of speaking."

"What is it you want? Money?" A shudder ran through Winton as he realised that the young man sitting opposite him, whom he'd tried to look upon as his own son, looked back at him not as a father, but as a resource, a means to an end that could be ruthlessly exploited. "Do you have such little regard for me, Paul, to come here wanting to extort what you could freely ask for as my son?"

"I think you're taking it all a bit to heart, aren't you?" Paul said. "I understand that you're anxious to keep aspects of your past hidden, but I'm not in the business of extortion either."

"What do you want to talk about, then?" Winton asked coldly.

"Well, I think that things have pretty much run their course for me here," Paul said. "I've had it, to be frank, and imagine that it might be better for all of us if I were to leave for a bit. I thought I'd try to study painting in Europe somewhere – Munich or Vienna. I'm a disgrace to the family, after all, and could easily end up being a rather unpleasant skeleton hidden away in a closet."

Winton folded his hands, collecting himself. "I need your word, Paul, that the things you've heard about me will be forgotten. I'll arrange an allowance, to be paid twice yearly. You can spend it as you wish, whoring in Melbourne or in Vienna. I don't give a damn. If our agreement is broken, the allowance will be cut off and you'll not be getting another penny out of me. Tell me one thing, and I'll go to the bank tomorrow. Who mentioned that name?" Winton couldn't bring himself to utter it.

"The thing about the cat?" Paul asked.

Winton closed his eyes and nodded.

Now Paul felt a pang of remorse. The doctor's bluntness presented him with an unflattering image of what he had fallen to, and he shrank away from himself in disgust.

"Doctor, I just want to leave here. I don't care a whit about your past and I'd never disturb my mother's peace or yours by telling her about it."

He spoke as if he'd been sapped of his strength and now stood in front of an accusing judge nervously awaiting sentencing.

"Who told you, Paul?"

"Les Collins. Christopher Leslie Collins." Paul spoke the name as if it were a curse. "Do you know who he is?"

"Yes I do," the doctor said.

"Have you seen him recently?"

Winton shook his head.

"The man is a corpse. A sack of bones. A gutter-crawler. That's what will happen to me if I stay here. This country will crush me. It will turn me into dust."

His voice shook with conviction, and Winton saw the father in the son, the same failure to accommodate, the same propensity for regression. Instinctual deviation.

"If you think like that you'll always be a child, Paul. A country can't decide your fate for you, unless you join with it wholeheartedly."

"I'd like to leave early in the new year."

"Before your sister's wedding?"

"As soon as possible."

~

When Paul went back to his room Ondine was sitting on his bed, waiting for him.

"What do you want?" he said sullenly.

Since the night of the opera their exchanges had dwindled to embarrassed formalities.

"I wanted to apologise," she said.

"There's no need."

"I'll never hate you, Paul. I'll never not love you. As a brother, I mean."

He sat down, not beside her on the bed, but in the reading chair on the opposite side of the room.

"I'd sooner see you marry someone like Hamish," Paul said wearily.

"Hamish is a fool. His romantic temper is sickly."

"You've suddenly become very respectable, haven't you? You'll be a pillar of the establishment soon."

"Oh, I don't care about that," she said.

"So you really love him?"

"Yes I do. Won't you accept that?"

"I don't know."

"I hope you will."

Paul rubbed his eyes, which had begun to ache. He squinted at her, trying to screen out the glare of the ceiling light. He was on the verge of saying that he couldn't look upon her simply as a sister, but the mere possibility of articulating that had vanished. She was about to take the name of another man, to be branded with his mark, to embrace the law they had together denied. Or had they? For the first time, the remoteness of his sister struck him as undeniable. It was he who had longed for her, he who had dreamt of possessing her, his hands that had timidly roved over her body, while all along she'd remained at a distance, granting him nothing more than the occasional performative flourish, just enough to keep him hanging on, enthralled.

"Ondine, I'm tired. Please leave me."

She stood up silently, stretching her long body in what seemed to him a gesture of mockery.

"Goodnight then." She walked across the room and, with ceremonial candour, kissed him on the cheek.

When she left, Paul hurled himself onto his bed and smelt the subtle odour of her body still lingering on the counterpane. Why hadn't he told her about his plans to leave Melbourne? She'd be as pleased to get rid of him as he would be to go. He could only embarrass her with an image of the thing – the perversity – she'd have to forget in order to marry and live out the mundanity of a respectable bourgeois existence. The thought of it made him sick. He would always gravitate to the covert, and imagined concealing himself in obscure nooks and alleys, away from public view, away from a life of unending tedium. The horror of the everyday gripped him and he saw himself fleeing its perpetual, accusing gaze – a gaze as insistent and as tireless as the sun itself. If it were the one thing he'd do in his life, he vowed, he'd drag himself clear of the monotony, the utter, soul-destroying monotony of the everyday.

When he closed his eyes he saw the events of the last month flowing before him in a confused torrent of possibilities. Faces leered at him, twisted into various expressions of lust and drunkenness. He imagined Les Collins rubbing mercury into his diseased body until his teeth fell out. He saw the tawdry theatrics of the Arcadia Club and the bland, mocking smile of Reuben Gines, whose false promises had crushed him. And he saw his stepfather cowering from his past.

The story Les Collins told him had the aura of a nightmare, precisely because it had to coexist with the knowledge of Winton's humdrum domesticity. Paul pictured the old man pruning his roses, and then saw the same man, thirty years earlier, hacking out unwanted foetuses in the brothels of Little Lonsdale Street. Les Collins had described Winton's array of hooks, pumps and rubber tubes, the callous disposal of babies that were still living when they were pulled out of the womb, and the botch-up that killed a girl, barely fifteen. Collins didn't spare him the details of her death. In those days, Winton's smooth features, his auburn, whiskery moustache, his sharp little teeth, and his pleasant, old world manners combined with his grisly calling to earn him the nickname "Mr Pussycat". The very mention of him inspired terror, the equal of that felt by small children at the thought of the bogeyman. Thirty years later, Paul discovered, his stepfather was the basis of an ongoing urban legend — an image that the prostitutes at the Arcadia Club still summoned to caution each other about carelessness or just deserts.

When he dwelt on the hypocrisy of it he was appalled. His stepfather, when it came down to it, was little better than a murderer. Regardless of how he justified his actions, he must live in constant fear of himself, of his own past rising to meet him, walking towards him on a busy city street, ready to demolish the illusion of safety his wealth had created. It was no wonder Winton was ready to grant him an allowance. Like his sister, the doctor would be happy to see the back of him.

Gradually these thoughts lost their clarity and tapered off into a playful but treacherous forgetfulness on the edge of sleep. Paul saw his sister taking her marriage vows and the branding iron, bearing the name of the husband, glowing with the heat of the fire. There were hints of gold in the air as if they were all standing in a great cathedral of glittering light. He felt his penis growing into an erection as the branding ceremony neared. In the distance, the powers of the law, Truth and Justice, looked on benevolently, with pity for the sinner led into the clammy arms of Judgement. The tentacles of the monster wrapped themselves around Paul's naked torso and drew him to its cold, slimy surface, where one inky eye looked blankly into his. "Thus you are judged," said a voice and Paul, desperately struggling against the huge octopus, twisted himself out of sleep to find the bedroom light still waiting to blind him.

Meanwhile, Winton had retired to his bedroom where he watched his wife sleeping. His eyes were fixed on Anna, but all he could see was the girl – Maisie was her name – who'd bled to death in a filthy sty off Little Lonsdale Street. The colour ran out of her cheeks and she turned cold while the soiled bedsheets soaked up her life. Later, after Winton had left, Madame Bruges ordered some lackeys to disfigure her body and dump it in the Yarra. When the corpse snagged under a landing and a couple of rowers almost tripped over it climbing out of their scull, the case became the focus of public outrage and horror. Barely a week later, the police uncovered a suitcase with a dismembered body stored inside it and, soon after, a decapitated cadaver in Brunswick. The whole city seemed full of bodies. People soon forgot about the girl in the river.

Winton told himself that one day society would realise the social benefits of abortion and would reform its archaic laws. With a cultivated objectivity he recounted the chain of events that had led not just to the girl's death, but to the discovery of her mutilated body, convincing himself that his part in the tragedy had been that of a man of medicine, trying to act in accordance with the demands of science and social hygiene. It was only after the scandal had dropped well away from the public consciousness, and he realised that he'd be safe from prosecution, that he relaxed his efforts at self-justification and found that his role in the girl's death was even harder to specify than he remembered. But now the memory of the incident had been rudely disinterred. Les Collins was perhaps the one person left in Melbourne who still had an inkling of his role in the death. He began to fear its implications with renewed intensity, amplified by the sight of his sleeping wife, who was completely ignorant of his misdeeds.

In the early 1880s, Christopher Leslie Collins was still somebody in the city of Melbourne. His *Life of Charles Whitehead* was a moderate success, admired by influential critics in Melbourne and Sydney, and he had begun work on an epic recounting the destruction of the Kulin nation by white settlement. Winton had met him in the Yorick Club, where writers, lawyers and doctors frequently assembled to fortify themselves against the boredom of colonial life. Collins already had a problem with drink and was struggling to meet deadlines. When his wife died of consumption and publishers baulked at the bleak, caustic tone of his book on the Kulin, he let himself drop more directly into the mud of the city and sought forgetfulness in the back streets off Little Lon. Until Paul had mentioned him, Winton was not even sure that the man was still alive. In the 1890s one still heard rumours about Collins sleeping around the Eastern Market, under Princess Bridge, or in a drain near Spencer Street Station. By the turn of the century the man was already a ghost, an obscure memory of old Melbourne to be dug out of the archives a hundred years hence.

Now the thought of this ghost walking the streets filled Winton with horror. He looked at his wife, oblivious to the dark possibilities perhaps already closing in on them. He didn't care how he'd be judged by posterity or in the hereafter, but he couldn't live with the shame of thinking himself a criminal in his wife's eyes.

As if troubled by her husband's anxiety, Anna stirred and opened her eyes. "What did Paul want?" she asked sleepily. It was a question that seemed to spring directly from the depths of sleep, as if she had been dreaming her son's future and her husband's past and sensed the atmosphere of unease that now hung over both. For a moment Winton felt accused by her question.

"Your son sees himself in Vienna," Winton said. "The Academy of Visual Arts."

"Vienna," she murmured. "I'd like to go to Vienna." She propped herself up on her elbow and thought about this. "My poor boy," she said. "Paul will be a wanderer, like the Flying Dutchman."

"He is determined to succeed, despite his setback."

"That determination is also a curse," Anna said ruefully. "It'll keep him sailing forever."

As she reached out and took her husband's hand, seeking reassurance, he was mortified to imagine the loathsome tendrils of his past now reaching up through the ground, searching him out, embracing him and pulling him back into their murky depths. He would make sure that Paul left them. He could buy his silence. But for Collins himself, there was no accounting.

## chapter fourteen

The weeks preceding Paul's departure slowly turned into months. At first the time ran away in single grains of sand, each needing to fall before the next seemed ready to move. But by the spring of 1911, time had spilt out around him with such a wasteful extravagance that he felt his future being sucked away and wondered if he would ever leave at all. With the news of his imminent departure, Ondine's resistance to him had softened. She humoured him with her caresses, kissed him with her old affection, and coddled him like a child, anticipating that his leaving would bring a decisive close to their troubled relationship. At his mother's insistence, he agreed to stay for the wedding and see his sister married to Ralph Matthews. He toasted the couple with the knowledge that he'd soon be spared the indignity of their happiness.

On a cold day in early October, Paul finally took possession of a cabin on board the *Abendstern*. His mother and sister surveyed it warily, but nevertheless were impressed at its size and took this as a sign of the ship's seaworthiness. The next morning, as sheets of rain battered the bay and wind rattled the corrugated iron roofs of the houses along the shore, the ship pulled out of Port Melbourne. Paul stood on the deck. He had already lost his mother and sister in the sparse crowd along the pier and wondered if they could still see him. He hung over the railing and waved on the off-chance that they could. It was the last courtesy of a son not to turn his back on his mother until the ship was out of her sight. But it was only obligation that held him there. He had no desire to watch the shoreline of his birth and upbringing fade behind him nor to reminisce as his past slipped away. On the contrary, he was already thinking of the future with an excitement that completely obliterated his feeling for the city he was leaving.

As the pier receded behind a mist of drizzle, Melbourne had already become unreal. It was like a vision of Edwardian torpor from which he had just awoken. What he carried with him as its most palpable moments were the ones that had seemed most ethereal. It was only where the imagination had struggled to overcome the monotony of the city that Melbourne left him something tangible to hold onto. In the arcades he had walked through since he was a child, in gruesome wax images and the desperate yearnings of fetid alleys and lanes, he found a passage back to himself. But in the grid-like uniformity of the city, in the emptiness of its streets and the crushing conservatism of its terracotta-tiled villas spreading out into a vast suburban wilderness, the imagination, if it wasn't beaten flat with national sentiment and the spirit of the land, could only turn in on itself and devour its host like a parasite. The future of Australia lay in either individual sickness or collective subservience to the blandest and most brutal invention of modern times: the nation.

Paul had already glanced at the notebooks containing his father's writings. Hamish had given them to him at the Montague the night before, along with a battered, second-hand copy of *The Life of Charles Whitehead*. His skin prickled and his heart thudded as he looked into his father's inspired madness and pictured his mind ruptured by sphinxes, apparitions and dancing shadows. Looking over his father's writing was like gazing into a mass of particles slowly forming a shape that he could see clearly only by squinting or averting his eyes. It was there, and yet it wasn't — a huge, dark form on the periphery of perception. His father had stumbled over the drunken song of midnight, where the poet, the lunatic and the criminal are one, and had rewritten it in a hundred variations, each a futile quest for finality, an end to desire itself.

Paul wondered what his mother had really known about his father and what she really knew about Winton. Both men moved through the netherworld of the city, following a map sketched out by their imaginations until they found themselves confronting their own shadows. As he scanned the grey coastline that now stretched itself around the bay, these shadows were the substance of the place he was leaving. He could make out nothing except the varying shades of grey that distinguished the water from the sand, the sand from the buildings along the foreshore, and the buildings from the sky overhead.

Anna took Ondine's arm and allowed her daughter to lead her reluctantly away from the sombre vision of the *Abendstern* shrinking into a turbulent horizon. She didn't feel that she had the resolve simply to walk away from her son on her own, even though the two women were getting wet, and the rain seemed a suitable pretext for their departure.

"I envy him," Ondine said, thinking that she'd like to forestall her mother's sadness. They took shelter in a rotunda overlooking the beach and waited for the rain to pass.

"Do you really?" Anna asked.

"Of course. Haven't we always wanted to travel?"

"But he's not travelling, at least not in the usual sense."

Ondine didn't need this explained to her. She pictured her brother on a vain quest that would see him lost in a distant land, never to return to them. Her esteem for him grew with the thought of his misguided grandeur.

"We may have to go and find him," she said absently. "When Ralph and I travel to the Continent we will check on him."

But she knew that she and Ralph were not about to sail for Europe, that all that senseless motion was in fact futile and unproductive. They'd honeymooned in Queenscliff and moved into a house the size of Winton's in South Yarra, next to the Domain, but Ralph was already making noises about returning to New South Wales. His instinct was not to flee the familiar, but to gravitate towards it. The thought of travelling to Europe was merely a distraction for him. He wasn't one of those Australians who refer to England as "home". On the contrary, he saw himself as a native of the land, an inhabitant of the Monaro existing in a state of exile. He knew that if Ondine saw his home, then she too would be overwhelmed by the ambition that had created it. When he told her this she feared that she might not care for the ambition of his forefathers.

"What did you dream of doing when you were a girl?" she asked her mother as they walked along the beachfront after the rain had stopped.

Anna's eyes were searching for the ship, fading away from them in the distance.

"I don't know," she answered. "I think I've only ever wanted to have time, time simply to be."

"To be?"

"Yes, to be."

"Have you found it?"

"Yes, I have."

"So you have been happy?" Ondine knitted her eyebrows as she asked this, trying to round out her mother's uninspired responses.

"Yes." Anna took her daughter's hand. "Yes, I've been happy, as you will be with Ralph."

Anna could honestly say that she had been content with Winton, but she also knew that she was being disingenuous with her daughter, discounting so much that Ondine must be aware of, even though they had never explicitly talked about Albert or discussed his drowning. As the grey sky cleared and a few jaundiced rays of sunlight caught the edge of a dark rain cloud drifting out over the heads, both women overlooked the emptiness of Anna's assertion, and found momentary comfort in its naïvety.

# part FOUR

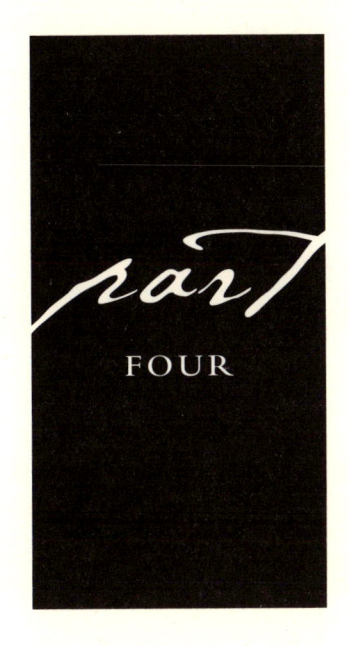

# chapter fifteen

October 9, 1911

Dear Hamish,

I have read the family archive from start to finish. I don't know how you managed to part with it, but I must thank you again for doing so. There is much to be frightened of here, though of course it is difficult to know where to draw the line between fact and fiction. I doubt that my father was a pervert, at least not a real one, though the manner of his death might tell us something on that account. Anyway, I'm not about to indict someone for his fantasies. We all live in various degrees of evasion, desperately (or maybe just lazily) clutching at the surface of things, which stops us from going to "the other side". I suppose spewing it all out like that is one way of being with oneself. I mean living with oneself, of getting beyond the illusion. Maybe there are people who already embrace their own horror as a matter of course, like criminals or the insane. Short of that, art is the language in which the self unfolds and I suppose it's the best we can do to have some inkling of ourselves.

Being at sea leads one to think in this vein. There's nothing else to do. Travel is a kind of blankness, between the place one is escaping from and the place one is fleeing to. Put like that it seems a waste of time really, and bound to end in disappointment. I don't know what it would have taken for me to stay in Melbourne. A good old-fashioned plague perhaps. I often think that I'd be happy in a plague town (perhaps that's what I think I'm going to find over there). It's the kind of thing that occurs to me late at night, when I'm having trouble sleeping. Wet cobblestones, dead rats underfoot, the stench of something rank, bodies torn open by pustules and thrown into the street. There wouldn't be much point in going through with the formalities then, would there? It would be "come as you are". But then I suppose the disappointment would be that nothing much would change, that people have been coming as they are all along, and there's simply not much there.

Paul broke off from his letter, thinking of something he had read in his father's writing. Is the child on the beach — the child and the "filthy streets of her sex" — Ondine? He remembered a day when they were all on the sand and his father was looking around, distracted. Ondine was mucking about in the seaweed and then he was staring at her, talking about how he could smell sewage leaking somewhere. Paul recognised the smell. It was the smell of the bay: seaweed and shellfish, the ocean mingling with the corruption of a port town. He saw his father look at his sister as if he were smelling her. Perhaps he'd write that poem out and send it to her, Paul thought. God knows what she'd make of it now. He imagined his sister had changed, but maybe it was simply that he never knew her.

At the pier as they had said their farewells, all he could see when he looked at Ondine were the traces of his incursions – Matthews's – imprinted on her body. Afterwards, when the port had receded from view, he lay awake listening to the waves, imagining her in her husband's arms, wondering whether she still looked chaste.

He dismissed the thought and returned to the letter.

The Whitehead book has also been a revelation to me. The whole thing is thick with the atmosphere of hallucination. The streets, the ghost of the wife, the nightmare of alcohol, poverty and failure. Of course Whitehead, though I suppose he really lived like that, is Collins himself. The two are doubles of each other. Perhaps you could write *The Tragedy of Christopher Leslie Collins* and make it an epic of modern Melbourne. God knows, that is what the city is short on – its own myth-makers.

But what can you expect from a place that seems to be ending before it has even really begun? That's the true tragedy of Australia – a country arrives at the moment in world history when the very concept of the nation has almost run out of steam. What is left to it but clichés and jingoism? Perhaps the odd blood sacrifice. National identity in Australia is already a layer of dead tissue. You probably don't quite agree and I may be exaggerating. If I ever come back I suppose I'll have to swallow my words. Will post from Fremantle.

Yours, Paul

October 20, 1911

Dear Hamish,

If you get a chance, look in on my sister and tell me what you find. I'm curious. I suppose I would like to know whether she is in good hands or about to let her rootlessness get the better of her and jump on a ship as well. I have visions of Matthews abusing her, taking his coveted riding whip to her and breaking her indomitable spirit as if she were one of his colts. He seems the type to me – an old-style sadist or a military man in uniform strolling brashly through a public garden with the smooth, clean look of a wife-beater. But I'm probably underestimating my sister. She is no doubt his equal in pride, strength and imperiousness. Perhaps it is she who has taken the riding whip to him.

My father seems to have had a fanciful sense of geography. He writes about South Melbourne Beach and St Kilda as if they were in North Africa, the Yarra River as if it were a Venetian canal, and the Block Arcade as if it were St Germain. He reconstructed virtually the entire city as a phantasmagoria of exotic possibilities, as if he were constantly in flight from it and living in his imagination.

Melbourne is a place given over to fantasy anyway. The streets are lined with oaks, elms and plane trees, and native plants have been carefully removed, creating the atmosphere of a northern city, or at least one that is not specifically Australian. Of course, when the last shadows of winter dry up and the place is drenched in sunlight, choking on dust and infested with blowflies, where else could it be but the south (and not the south that Keats imagined)? Even the most intense fantasies wither in such heat. The place is unwilling to confront its natural habitat, its antipodean reality, and would go to any lengths not to have to look inland at the grey, hacked-up earth. It seems futile really, and a bit infantile.

But then all those stolid realists who want to embrace the harsh spirit of the land are living in a dream as well, imagining that a few generations of bloodshed and genocide could be the basis of a robust national identity. They can't smell the blood on their own hands. Better to throw the whole thing in, if you ask me, and start again with the freedom of not having to be bound to a place at all.

But I suppose the sea is the epitome of this freedom, and it is monotony itself. On calm days one can look out on one side of the ship and see an eternity of still, flat water, and think that here is an image of one's own exile and homelessness. It makes me feel slightly nauseous, the light and the gentle, persistent swaying of that great, empty expanse. You long for a good bit of earth to pound your feet upon, something with a stable point of gravity, a city of brick and stone. In Fremantle I went ashore for a day and spent most of it in a drab Italian café, trying to avoid the sun. I must have smoked a packet of cigarettes, and watched the smoke of each of them drift on the blades of sunlight that pierced the tattered curtains. It was a relief to be still for a while, but by the evening I was anxious to be back on board the *Abendstern* and moving again, feeling as if the dry heat and the still streets were working their way into me and hollowing me out as surely as the ocean had.

My fellow passengers all seem to be suffering from this malaise. Perhaps this accounts for their dullness. There are some members of a scientific party from Freiburg who have been in Queensland studying the Lamington Plateau. The poor fellows are red as beetroots and about as interesting. There are some vaudeville performers heading for Cape Town, a couple of newlyweds who keep to themselves as if they were fugitives fleeing a scandalous past, and a woman from somewhere near Colac taking her gawky daughter on a grand tour to see the great galleries of Europe. There is also a funny little man from Adelaide, Arthur Hume, who claims to be an antiquarian book collector. He had me in his cabin the other night drinking sherry and talking about Byron's love of young Greek boys. The whole thing was a bit distasteful, but a distraction from the usual round of dinner, drinks and cards, or worse, an evening in the ship's casino wondering when the shoddily made wheel of fortune will come spinning off its bearings.

I have no love for travel. In fact I detest the farcical conversations one becomes inured to, the triviality of non-space, where the best one can hope for is to be mildly amused and forgetful of the tedium. What else can one do? Of course there is a limit to the amount one can read. Since Fremantle I've read Hoffmann's *Die Elixiere des Teufels*, hoping to revive my German, as well as Poe, Melville and Clarke – but I won't bore you with a reading list. We will be docking in Cape Town in about a week or so.

Yours, Paul

On a warm morning in early November, Paul sat on the deck of the *Abendstern* resting an unfinished letter in his lap, watching the coast of Africa glide by. Opposite him sat Laura Thomas, the girl from Colac way, and her mother, Eleanor. His eyes wandered back to them every so often as he puzzled over how he might describe the pair to his friend in Melbourne. He tapped his pen lightly on his knee and re-read his last few sentences: "The daughter's name is Laura. She's seventeen and is shaped like a gazelle. Or do I mean a giraffe? I don't know. Awkward but not unsightly. She's taken by the fact that I'm off to study art, and thinks it the height of romance."

In the company of this pair, Paul had found himself drawn out into endless discussions about European splendour based on the prosaic guidebook the two of them had memorised. Because he was going to study art they wanted to defer to him on every conceivable matter of taste that might confront the eager tourist. Did he have a preference for the Impressionists? Would he bother with the provinces? How long in Paris? Where in Italy? The questions were never-ending.

He couldn't make up his mind about Laura. He quizzed her about her family's farm. Her father was dead and her two older brothers were running the big property. Her mother, never entirely content with the country, had implanted in her daughter a gentle disdain for virtually everything about rural life and a longing for whatever lay beyond it. They were travelling to Europe, like so many Australians, to find culture. Her mother considered it an essential part of Laura's upbringing.

As the ship laboured along the vast, seemingly endless coast of Africa, Paul listened to her chatter on about spiritual quests and aesthetic education. He bristled at the thought of such a wholly unrealistic attitude to things, until he found his own reflection right there in front of him. Then he cringed. How many times had he complained to Hamish about cultural wastelands? He couldn't condemn Laura without also condemning himself. Unwilling to shatter her illusions, he played along with her romantic notions of European travel.

"Well, you must visit me in Wien," he said, conscious of the pretentiousness of using the German name.

"Oh, I will. We are certainly going there. Certainly. It's all arranged. It will be so nice to be shown around by a real artist."

And on it went. Paul soon felt sorry for her, and a bit sorry for himself too. When she referred to him as "a real artist" the pathos of both their lots was overwhelming. "The whole thing is really a bit of a farce, isn't it?" he wrote to Hamish later on. "I mean the fantasy of escape – to be an artist. It's as transparent in its own way as the Thomas family odyssey to discover the treasures of European culture so that the daughter will be better equipped to live out her days in some rural penitentiary. I felt like a mountebank flaunting the magic of these fantasies as if it were snake oil. If I've learnt to loathe Australia, I may end up loathing myself more for the self-deception involved in fleeing it."

He made up his mind to avoid Laura. Lord knows there were enough people on the *Abendstern* to hide behind. He imagined the ship must have packed on the passengers like cattle through a turnstile. But despite his resolution, made over and over again, he invariably found himself sitting beside her on the deck, running up against the same impasse. At times it made him sick and he was gripped by a kind of mental nausea. At others he decided to keep up his end of their childish exchange in the vague hope of forgetting himself for a while and perhaps talking himself into a more optimistic frame of mind.

"We can go to the opera and stroll around the Ringstraße, and I'll introduce you to my artist friends," he said cheerily, wondering if she were capable of opening her eyes to the great lie of it all. He willed himself on to more extreme performative excesses, flattered her in German, aware that these days he could barely patch together a sentence, and finally kissed her hand like an idiot. She blushed. Was he falling in love? Or was he merely acting a part? He imagined a comedy of manners performed over high tea on a rickety stage made out of corrugated iron and chicken wire.

"Paul," Laura said as he stared blankly down at the unfinished letter. Her long face, her light freckles and the dark eyebrows and hair against her fair skin struck him as lovely. Did he really want her to come to Vienna? How could he realise his own grandiose ambitions saddled with her and her mother? He looked up at her.

"Never mind," she said, returning to her novel, biting her lower lip. "It's just that I hope we do see each other again."

If her mother hadn't been there beside them — eyes peering up from her Baedeker's guide — he'd have touched her arm to reassure her.

## chapter sixteen

They parted company in Southampton, at which point Laura and her mother were heading to London and then on to Paris. Old Eleanor Thomas spoke longingly about Kensington or wherever it was they had letters of introduction. God help them, Paul thought. Laura kissed him sweetly and promised to come to "Wien" as soon as she could.

As he disembarked in Hamburg a day or so later the girl and her kiss were still with him. The steam of the ships billowed into a grey sky and trailed over the oily water of the port. He pictured a bleak Europe of industrial misery and feared that in it he'd never see her again. He pushed his way through crowds of Russian Jews waiting to sail for America. The sight of so many people clutching suitcases and staring out at the future with such tired expressions filled him with a sense of his own forlornness as he wandered over the wet cobblestones. With his suitcase in his hand he crossed a narrow walking bridge and gazed down a long canal weaving through a congested slum. It must have been low tide. The water had drained away, leaving an unctuous sludge that trailed off into the mist.

That night, having set himself down in a modest hotel, he was still thinking about her. To test his resolve he decided to walk back to the waterfront and through the infamous St Pauli. Sailors and workers loitered about the streets, drank in taverns and cavorted with prostitutes who looked hard and pitiless in the cold, damp air. He was about to give it up when Arthur Hume, the antiquarian book collector from the *Abendstern*, appeared at the next corner. He greeted Paul with a reticent, embarrassed grin, and claimed that he was heading off to some theatrical entertainment. Would he like to join him? Why not, Paul thought to himself, curious to see what an old lecher like that could get up to.

They walked to a theatrette a few streets away. Hume said something to the attendant about knowing a man called Wedelkind, but this was to no avail. The old man at the door insisted that they pay just the same, Wedelkind or no Wedelkind. Inside, the audience was seated at separate tables, not in rows as in a conventional theatre. It was a run-down place, full of people who looked to Paul like scions of aristocratic families, fallen dignitaries, and outcast, vagabond royals deprived of their kingdoms by an age of revolution. Men wore dinner suits that appeared as if they'd been slept in the night before while the women wore faded silks, old lace and even the odd tiara. They all reeked of stale cigar smoke. The place had the aura not of genteel poverty, but of fallen empires and historical anachronisms.

"An old friend of mine is performing," Hume said. "Max Wedelkind."

Before Paul could ask who he was, clashing cymbals and a run of notes on a double bass announced the commencement of the play. The curtain went up on a stage decked out to look like a hospital ward. In one corner sat a doctor, wearing a white coat and a greenish wig of thick, disordered hair. He was made up with ghoulish white face paint, glossy red lips and deep purplish shadows under his eyes. Paul couldn't decide whether he looked more like a mad scientist or a disinterred corpse. He was at a desk perusing some medical charts when two other men, evidently newspaper reporters, approached him armed with notepads. The doctor began to describe to them his revolutionary cure for madness and some garbled theories about the flow of the blood through the brain. He spoke very bad, comically-stilted German, as if he were imitating a foreigner's accent. Offstage the cries of lunatics and their ominous poundings grew gradually louder until finally they almost drowned him out. The doctor raised his voice to a scream and then collapsed into a fit of hysterical twitching, laughing to make light of it. The audience laughed as well while his body shook as if from repeated electrical shocks. It was outlandish. Paul had never seen anything so farcical.

"That's Wedelkind for you," Hume whispered to him. Paul smelt something distasteful, like sour milk or week-old flower water, on his breath.

As the doctor laughed the two reporters looked at each other suspiciously. To allay their fears the doctor called out to his attendants and staff, who began to parade like a menagerie of wild animals. Soon the doctor himself had joined in, leading a savage dance around the two journalists, who now realised the danger they were in. As the doctor whipped the attendants into a frenzy they pounced on one of the journalists and dismembered him on stage to the horrified shrieks of the audience. The whole scene was an inspired piece of visual trickery. The marauding lunatics crouched over the prone body, hiding it from the audience, as they seemed to hack into it with their hands and hurl pieces of what must have been butcher's meat and pulped paper soaked in red dye across the stage. In a moment, the set was strewn with gore, its white surfaces streaked with blood. When the lunatics turned to the second journalist all that remained of the first was a pile of torn clothes and raw body parts. The doctor danced a ridiculous jig and kicked a wax head off the edge of the stage, provoking fits of hysterical laughter. As the head hit the ground and rolled awkwardly across the wooden floor, Paul started in amazement. He stared at the doctor on the stage. Behind the wig, the make-up and the exaggerated antics, the actor was none other than Reuben Gines.

At that moment something gripped him and he too gave out, collapsing into a confused spasm of horror, hilarity and bewilderment. He turned to Hume, who was just about choking, and pointed at the stage.

"Wedelkind," Hume gasped back at Paul, his face red with the strain of it all. "Wedelkind."

Finally, some policemen appeared on stage and beat the lunatics back, saving the second reporter. With the menagerie cowering in the corner, the police chief revealed that the lunatics had taken over the madhouse and that the real Dr Goudron had been murdered and replaced by one of his patients. In a horrifying finale, one of the policemen produced the mutilated corpse of the real doctor, which from where Paul sat looked like a side of beef wearing a white coat and a stethoscope. The audience again howled as the curtain fell.

"Wedelkind," Hume said again, as if his vocabulary had been reduced to this single word, the mere utterance of which was enough to send him head over heels.

"Wedelkind," Paul repeated, obligingly. "Only that's not his name. It's Gines. Reuben Gines."

Hume blinked absurdly. "But I know him," he said, still cackling. "Wedelkind." He had to cough out the laughter before he could continue. "He came through Adelaide on a tour. About six months ago." He paused to catch his breath and repress the chuckles still mounting in him. "Tamer stuff then – comedy of manners, gentle melodrama, you know."

"Can we meet him?"

"By all means."

Hume stood up, still vibrating with the aftershock of the performance, and walked bravely backstage. In the meantime the audience settled down and the theatre assumed a semblance of order.

At any other time Paul might have been ready to thrash Gines or Wedelkind, or whatever his name was. But after such an extravagant performance he was completely purged. Every violent impulse in him, in fact every bit of strength, had leached out with his laughter. He was thoroughly relaxed and at peace.

A few minutes later Hume reappeared with Gines, who had removed the wig and cleaned off the make-up, but who still looked a bit insane anyway. Paul leapt to his feet and congratulated him on such a fine performance.

"Young Paul Walters," he declared shamelessly and with seemingly little surprise. "How good to see you. Fortune has brought you this far at least."

Paul was flabbergasted at the ease of his manner, but also vastly amused at the thought of such a versatile charlatan.

"Buy you a drink?" he asked, raising his almost hairless eyebrows (they'd been painted on for the play), and gesturing in futility to an absent waiter.

"You can buy me several," Paul said in the same spirit of high farce. "Don't you remember that you ruined me?"

"Oh please," he said with a laugh. "Much ado about nothing. A little levity."

Hume was all ears as the encounter unfolded.

"He calls you Gines, Max."

"Gines? Yes I was, once. Thought you'd get the joke. Gines, engines, something like that. It's literary. Eighteenth century. The distant past I suppose."

He thrust his hand out towards Paul and boldly proclaimed, by way of introduction, "Max Wedelkind. Pleased to meet you." Then he winced, twisting his face into a grimace of self-deprecation. "You're not still sore at me are you?"

"I don't much care now. It's all behind me. Just tell me what happened."

"Well, your friend played a little trick on you. Mind, it went a bit far, but that was your doing, your own enthusiasm. And his, I suppose. No one could have reckoned on either of you giving in to temptation and going at it with such determination."

"So, Arthur, Max is a sort of roving confidence man," Paul said.

"Not a bit of it," Wedelkind remonstrated. "I'm a reputable actor now, in a reputable company." And then, with an impish grin plastered on his blubbery face, he pulled a five-mark note from behind Paul's ear and gave it to him.

"The world of con men, drifters, itinerant showmen, vagabond magicians, and impersonators is fading. The Germans have a lovely word for a man of such callings – *Gaukler*. Today it means something wonderfully vague – juggler, charlatan, *Zauberkünstler*. The whole caboodle. But it's a world that is disappearing, which is a pity, but it's the truth. People just aren't gullible enough today. The age of realism has killed off our gullibility, our innocence. It did my old soul no end of good, Paul, to see you so willing to play along. I don't mind saying so. Perhaps there is hope for an old *Gaukler* yet, I told myself."

"All right then Max," Paul said, "just tell me who actually bought my painting, the one you paid for at the Gallery School."

"Why you know as well as I do. It was your friend. What's his name? Ralph."

"Ralph Matthews?"

"That's the one."

Paul was shocked, but in such a ludicrous way that he wouldn't have been offended to see Matthews walk in at that very moment and sit down with them. There was something so grandly bathetic in the conception of the plot, in Wedelkind himself and in his mesmerisingly absurd performance of insanity that he was overwhelmed with good humour and actually enthused by the air of trickery and the web of petty deceit in which he'd been so thoroughly caught. The thought of the fraud, coupled with the manifest grotesquerie of the play, both comic and horrifying, seemed to open up a new vista for Paul. He acknowledged that Max Wedelkind (and who was to say that that was really his name) was an artist – a bullshit artist – and in his own way a bit of a genius at it.

"How on earth did you get involved with a cleanskin like Ralph? Not at the Arcadia Club?"

"Good God no. I met him at the Melbourne Club, the week after you'd so mortally offended him in front of your sister."

"The Melbourne Club?" Paul was amazed. "Who let you in there?"

"I was dining with old what's-his-name, the one who brought out that family of acrobats. Or were they midgets? I don't quite recall."

A waiter finally appeared and Wedelkind demanded a bottle of brandy. "For my guests," he added brusquely. After a glass or two and a couple of cigarettes, Paul felt quite drunk. He told Wedelkind about his plans and soaked up his insincere delight. Finally, when it seemed that they would stay sitting in the deserted theatre till morning, Wedelkind bounced to his feet and declared that he and Hume had "business to attend to".

"Paul, I'll tell you what," he said, shaking his hand. "I've been a bit flippant about your little humiliation, haven't I? Mind, you could be toiling away on society portraits by now, so really you should be thanking me. Anyway, come tomorrow night, with old Arthur here, and I'll make amends."

The next evening Paul returned to the theatre where he met Hume, seated alongside an odd young man whom he introduced simply as Klessmann. As Paul sat down Klessmann stood up and offered his hand.

"Very pleased," he mumbled, with a slight bow. He squinted from under bushy black eyebrows and lids that looked as if they'd been encrusted with sleep picked off a few moments before. His face was thin and pale, with some patches of dry, flaking skin here and there. A pointed nose jutting out over a pinched little mouth created the unmistakable impression of a beak, ready to give you a peck for your trouble. Hume couldn't conceal a smile as Paul took in the strangeness of Klessmann's appearance.

"I understand you are returning to Vienna," he said to Paul, in somewhat stilted English.

"Returning? No, I'm going. For the first time."

"Yes," Klessmann said apologetically. "That's what I meant."

Hume, eager to get the formalities over and done with before the curtain went up, hurried things along. "Klessmann knows Vienna. Max thought he might be of help to you as you settle in."

"He did?" Paul said. "Very cordial of him."

"I'd be very pleased," Klessmann added.

Paul examined the blank bird-face. Klessmann's voice sounded wooden.

The band cranked up from the wings and the curtains parted on the same scene Paul and Hume had seen the previous evening. Wedelkind's performance lost nothing with repetition. His face contorted, his limbs trembled, his feet stamped, he threw his head back and waved his arms in spasms of dementia. Paul laughed less riotously than Hume. Klessmann, however, just smiled amusedly.

"You've already seen the play?" Paul asked him during a lull.

"Yes," he answered.

"You don't seem very interested."

"No, no. I am most interested."

Soon after, however, Paul noticed that Klessmann's eyes were closing and that his chin was falling onto his chest. As his neck bent forward, his head almost touching the table, he jerked himself back into an erect posture and opened his eyes. A second later his eyes began to close again and with the same wilting movement his head lowered itself towards the table. Hume, absorbed in the play, hadn't noticed at all, but Paul watched curiously out of the corner of his eye, eager not to give Klessmann the impression that he was being unduly scrutinised. Paul tried to guess his age. He couldn't be more than twenty-five, but there was a lethargy about him, a washed-out, sickly look that made him appear quite decrepit. Paul imagined that the dry patches around his nose and hairline were caused by an obscure industrial disease slowly eating away at his skin. The poor bloke looks exhausted, he thought, wondering at Hume's obliviousness. Finally he nudged the antiquarian and pointed to Klessmann, sound asleep as his head hit the table.

"Oh, all right," Hume whispered impatiently. "He said he'd already eaten something."

"You mean the poor bugger is starving?"

Hume waved off the question, trying to concentrate on the play. Wedelkind was leaping around in nervous consternation as the police lumbered across the stage in pursuit. Paul chuckled as he stood up and tapped Klessmann on the shoulder.

"Come on," he said, lifting him up by the arm. "We're going to get some food."

In his stupor he muttered something in rapid German that Paul didn't quite catch. Klessmann's eyes rolled back into his bony, angular head until, returning to his senses, he stood up by himself and groggily insisted that he was quite all right.

"Don't be stupid," Paul said. "You're a wreck."

"But Max?" he said, rubbing his eyes. "We must be here to present ourselves."

"We'll be back in a minute," Paul said, leading him out through the theatre onto the street, where the cold air of early winter caught them both full in the face.

In a tavern across the street Klessmann sat timidly while Paul ordered him bread, beer and soup. He lingered over the meal for a moment, embarrassed by his pitiful situation.

"Are you going to eat that?" Paul asked finally, as Klessmann picked at some crumbs with his fingertips. "I'll tell you what," he added impatiently, "I'll go back in and tell Hume where we are, and Max can come and meet us after the show."

Klessmann smiled wanly. Paul lingered on the street by the window just long enough to see him fall upon the food like a wolf, slurping up the soup in great spoonfuls that, too big for his narrow mouth, dribbled over his chin, which he hastily and unashamedly wiped clean with the cuff of his jacket. When Paul returned, Klessmann had sucked down the last of the beer. The soup bowl was mopped clean.

"I can't go on calling you Klessmann," he said. "What's your Christian name?"

"Theodore," he answered.

"And how is it that you are half-starving?"

"Don't overstate the case."

"Do they keep you locked up in a box somewhere, on a diet of thin air and darkness?"

"Who is 'they'?" He furrowed his brow at the question, as if it presented a grammatical quandary.

Paul shrugged. A fireplace in the corner cast a warm, flickering light over the plaster walls. Klessmann's face looked like a squashed cumquat in its glow.

"I have a nice place for you to stay in Vienna," Klessmann said.

"You don't say?"

"Very comfortable, in the heart of the city. I wired this morning. I hope it will suit you."

"I'm sure it will suit me wonderfully," Paul said. "But why take the trouble?"

Klessmann looked puzzled. "I don't understand."

Before Paul could say another word, Wedelkind came stumbling into the tavern, Hume close behind. He clamped his hands on Paul's shoulders and gave them a hearty shake.

"Now don't say I'm not trying to make amends," Wedelkind said as he sat down next to Paul.

He still had traces of make-up smeared over his face, and had forgotten to wipe off his lip paint altogether, giving his mouth a garish sensuality that Paul found repulsive.

"Klessmann is just the man to lead you through the maze of Viennese humbug, the decorative nonsense of the Habsburgs, the Pandora's box of God-only-knows-what, streets paved with culture and all the rest of it. And he knows the difference between a *Weib* and a *Frau*, if you catch my drift. Oh, Arthur, I wish I were young again."

Glancing at Klessmann, who sat dumb as Wedelkind babbled on incoherently, Paul doubted he'd be able to guide him as far as the end of the street.

"Klessmann is a protégé of mine, you might say," Wedelkind said, slowing himself down to catch his breath.

"Is that right?" Paul said. "You might feed him once in a while."

Wedelkind's eyes wandered to the empty soup bowl. "Don't tell me you haven't been eating?" His mouth dropped open as he looked imploringly at Klessmann. "Oh, Arthur, don't tell me you allowed this." He clutched his head. "You see, Paul, I've been taking care of Klessmann, and I take any criticism of my custodial duties quite to heart." He shook his head in disappointment, looking a bit exhausted, as if this final burst of histrionic nonsense had taken its toll.

"You'll have your work cut out with young Walters here," he said to Klessmann. "I expect you to take good care of him. And now, my friends, Arthur and I have business to attend to, don't we?"

"I'll say we do," Hume added with a grin.

"All the best to you both," Wedelkind said, bowing farewell as he stood up. "So glad I could make amends, Paul." He paused over the table. "We all even? Clean slate? What d'ya say?" He raised his hairless eyebrows, as if he needed an answer quick smart before he vanished into the smoke drift.

Paul couldn't help laughing.

"Never mind." He snapped his fingers and headed for the door, Hume at his heels.

The next day Klessmann was waiting on the street outside Paul's hotel, wearing a battered felt hat with a wide brim and pointed peak. He'd already ordered a cab to take them to the station.

"You don't mean to say that Wedelkind was serious last night, do you, Theodore?" Paul asked.

"Yes," he said with a lilt, as if the question were a bit obtuse. "I'm taking you to Vienna."

Paul's case was almost too much for Klessmann. He wrestled with it for a moment before Paul came to his aid and flung it into the cab.

Getting Klessmann to talk on the way to the station was difficult. He answered Paul's questions, but otherwise concealed himself behind his lethargy, as if he didn't have the strength to speak. Paul soon found his silence draining. On the train, as the cold, grey landscape rushed by, as other passengers came and went, lingering in the passageway outside the compartments to smoke or chat, Paul too was eager to distract himself. Having come so far with barely a second thought, he now felt momentarily disoriented, and longed for a conversation, the sound of his own voice, to stave off the sense of unreality growing within him. Klessmann was no help. Finally Paul lost patience and asked him bluntly how he got mixed up with Wedelkind.

"I can't easily explain," Klessmann said, closing his eyes.

Disappointed, Paul turned to the window, fixing on his own reflection in the glass, watching it floating through a blur of light and shadow.

"And you? How did you get mixed up with him?" Klessmann returned, eyes still closed.

"Just as you said," Paul said suddenly. "It's not that easy to explain."

He thought he saw Klessmann smile as he dozed off, letting the steady movement of the train rock him to sleep. Outside it was dark. Germany flashed by the window, frozen and desolate – dykes dug into the brown earth, patches of snow hardening into ice, the glow of fires burning on the horizon. Paul had never seen winter like this before, a winter in which everything dies away before it can be reborn.

Half an hour later Klessmann awoke with a sudden convulsion of his body that caught Paul's attention. The German scratched his eyes like a cat. Paul wondered that he didn't hack them right out of their sockets with his long, bony fingers and pointed fingernails.

"We must be nearing Berlin," Paul said. Klessmann's red eyes, now opening into their usual squint, rested on him from under those worryingly thick eyebrows.

"Are you hungry?" Paul asked, remembering that he had not seen him eat all day.

Klessmann shook his head.

"Cigarette then?"

Klessmann took the packet Paul offered him and rummaged in his pocket, hauling out some matches along with a length of cotton, a tiny needle kit, some lint, and a few stray coins.

"What are you reading?" Klessmann asked. He lit the cigarette and sucked in his hollow cheeks as he inhaled, coughing when the smoke hit his lungs.

Paul had his father's notebook on his lap. The landscape rushing by him had evoked the memory of the journey he had made with Albert to Ballarat. He remembered the sense of revelation as he surrendered his control of the pencil to the plunging movement of the train, the sense of wonder at being directed by the oblivious energy of the locomotive. And the German winter, he thought, was like one of the landscapes his father had invented as he sought refuge from the tedium of Melbourne. Dense forests, cottage dwellings rooted in a distant past, birds of ill-omen moving across the horizon, fleeing a catastrophe or hurrying to a new one.

"It's something my father wrote before he died," Paul said after a moment of hesitation.

"Was he a writer?"

"After a manner of speaking."

"May I?" Klessmann stretched his hand across to Paul who handed him the notebook and sank uncomfortably into his seat while the German's eyes wandered over the page.

"My father died of cholera," Klessmann said indifferently. "He always thought it was a worker's disease." It was as much as he had managed to say the whole trip.

Klessmann turned his attention to the notebook, studying the tiny handwriting with increasing intensity, taking in deep drags of his cigarette and letting the smoke float out through his open mouth. Paul in turn studied his responses, waiting for the slightest sign of criticism or approbation. He didn't know why it mattered to him, the response of this sickly German. But it did, very much. If a person as obscure and rootless as Klessmann couldn't see anything in the writing, then he'd have to ask himself again what he in fact saw, other than a dubious paternal inheritance, a wasted life and the spectral image of a waterlogged body drifting through the silty water of the Yarra.

Klessmann suddenly jerked his head over his left shoulder as he read. At first Paul thought the movement was merely the result of the train hitting a bump in the track that he hadn't quite felt. But then Klessmann did the same thing again, the same jerk to the left, this time accompanied by a slight contraction of his cheek. He seemed completely unaware. When it happened a third time he raised his eyes to find Paul looking at him curiously.

"It happens when I get excited," Klessmann said. "Or nervous." He jerked his head again and now his whole face contracted into a spasm. "They call it a tic. I ... I am going to need some medicine," he said, handing the notebook back to Paul as he jerked his head two or three times in rapid succession over his shoulder. Paul leant over and put his hand on Klessmann's shoulder, as if to steady him.

"It's not dangerous," he said. "But I'm going to need some medicine or I m-may end up being quite an embarrassment to you."

Fortunately the train was now on the outskirts of Berlin. At any other time, Paul would have been riveted by the city, but now Klessmann's condition was deteriorating. He jerked and grimaced and convulsed. He wasn't in pain and could still speak very calmly in between the spasms, but to Paul, it looked as though he was on the verge of losing complete control of his body.

When the train pulled into the station Paul was flustered. They had to wait overnight for a connection to Vienna, which left from the other side of the city, and needed to find a hotel. Paul had a porter take his suitcase and guided Klessmann by the arm onto the platform, where his spasms had people clearing a path for him, snickering, and looking mildly disturbed. Steam and the smell of burning brakes wafted along the walkway. It was already late in the day and the platform had a surreal gloom about it, as if the grime and dust of the station had managed to colour the air with a dirty brownish tinge.

Outside the station, Klessmann pointed at a street opposite them running towards a large church spire. As they made their way towards it, Paul tried to take in as much as he could. There were some street vendors, a huddle of urchins on a corner, the odd factory worker and a few shopgirls. A grubby man sold newspapers from under a stand. A fat woman fried sausages, her head wrapped in a scarf. Bitter cold, the smell of roasted chestnuts mingling with exhaust, blue sparks from a streetcar grinding to a halt along its tracks. Paul imagined all the streets of the city twisting towards them like parts of a great maze, concentrating their energy on this one spot, where a strange, dreamlike calm prevailed in the midst of all the activity.

"Where are we?" Paul asked, dazed.

"Z-Z-Zoo," Klessmann said. "I-I-I must ... to b-b-bed." He broke off, his whole body convulsing, and gestured towards a hotel on the corner in front of them. As Paul put his arm around him they made their way awkwardly across the road and into the foyer. Paul paid for a room and asked the concierge for a doctor. Klessmann shook his head, managed to extract a prescription from his pocket and explained in stuttering, broken speech that he needed the medicine right away. He handed it to the porter, his hand trembling. When the two of them were safely in the hotel room, Klessmann gave into the spasms racking his body and contorted horribly on the bed. He seemed to know what to do. He snatched a coaster off the bedstand and bit down on the corner, indicating with a wave and a jerk that Paul should hold it firmly in his mouth while they waited for the porter to return.

After he swallowed the medicine it took him half an hour to resume some semblance of normality. Paul watched the convulsions weaken as Klessmann fell into an exhausted sleep, a slight jerk and tic the only visible sign of his condition. When he was snoring lightly, hunched uncomfortably in his jacket, head cocked to one side, Paul too finally closed his eyes in a reading chair on the opposite side of the room.

He woke up sometime during the night with the power of old habit so strongly etched into his mind that he momentarily forgot where he was. He was sitting in a chair and had woken up stiff. Across the other side of a strange room, a young man with thin black hair and a sharp nose was bent over a book busily working away on something with a worn down stub of a pencil. Only an oil lamp illuminated the scene, creating deep pockets of shadow just out of the reach of its pale, greenish flicker. The young man held a cigarette in one hand. The thick smoke filling the room made Paul doubt he was awake at all. He rubbed his eyes. Where was he? For an instant he had the uncanny sensation of looking at himself sitting at the table opposite. He stirred in his chair.

Klessmann looked up at him.

"How are you?" Paul asked wearily. "It must be the middle of the night."

Klessmann still jerked his head over his shoulder, but now very slightly and at such intervals that it barely bothered him.

"I am well. Thank you." He seemed a bit embarrassed. "Thank you for your kindness. If your friend Max had seen that little performance he would never have let me leave."

The comment piqued Paul's curiosity. He stood up and walked over to the table.

"What do you mean?"

"He recruited me as an epileptic freak," Klessmann said. "He trawls the madhouses and hospitals of Hamburg like a body-snatcher. But with the medicine I can control my condition. I was no real use to him. Perhaps I can be of more use to you. I have taken a liberty with your father's work."

Albert's notebook was open on the table and Klessmann had started making notes in German on separate sheets of paper. The ashtray beside him was nearly full. Paul took one of his own cigarettes off the table. He'd never got the packet back from Klessmann and saw that it was almost empty. Klessmann pretended not to notice.

"Your father – how do I start with this, Paul? I think he was a genius misanthrope."

"What are you doing?" Paul said, still half asleep.

"With your permission, as executor of the literary estate, I'm translating."

Paul glanced at the notebook and at Klessmann's tentative renditions. His father had constructed an awful scene in which he was pulling a woman along a street. She was struggling to keep up with him, almost tripping. Then some curtains were drawn aside and they were standing against a dirty brick wall streaked with grime that stuck to their skin. There was a rank smell, like rotten meat. He put his hand to her cold cheek. "Please," she begged him, "not here."

It was a matter of a few lines, scratched neatly down the page, no punctuation, no sense of coherence. It was simply an image, a suggestion. Although Paul read it with some difficulty, Klessmann's German had done something wonderful with it. There were six lines of bare, brooding verse crafted with the care of an artisan. The other pages on the table indicated that he had been at this for some time, that he had gone through a number of drafts and that he was still not nearly done.

"You see," Klessmann said after a while, "my condition is aggravated by my excitement. I hold your father responsible."

Paul didn't say anything. It was almost three o'clock in the morning. He was suddenly nervous. He couldn't quite explain why. The city outside had come to a dead standstill. Everything was unreal. The clutter in front of him, the ashtray, the paper, the smoke, and most of all Klessmann — invalid, foundling, vagabond Klessmann — looking at him like a frail bird.

"Paul," he said, "I am to assume your father never published this?"

Paul nodded.

"So let me try to make something of it. In German. I have no notion of what passes in English, but in German I will bring it all to life, like ghosts rising from their graves."

Paul was uneasy about it, but he hadn't the heart or the energy to dampen Klessmann's resolve.

He continued to tinker away through the night. On the train the next morning he was still at it, spreading pieces of notepaper out around their compartment as they left the Eastern station. He was maniacal, Paul thought, as only a true artist is. It put him in mind of his own failure. Hadn't he felt the same irresistible urge, the same drive, the same impossible desire to quell a need that only grew with every brushstroke?

"Your mother," Klessmann said, looking up at Paul with a little jerk of the head. "I am very curious about her."

The train was picking up speed. Paul noticed that its movement was disturbing the cursive flourish of Klessmann's handwriting.

"You're going to have a hard time writing as we move," he said.

"Irrelevant. I'll type this out in Vienna. We'll need a machine. Fifty kronen, one hundred. I don't really know."

Klessmann twitched as the train jostled them in their seats. Outside it was grey. It felt to Paul as if they were on the edge of another Ice Age. If his father could have seen this country, he thought, what might he have been? What might he still be? Klessmann's image of ghosts rising up from their graves gripped him like two frozen hands closing around his spine.

## chapter seventeen

Klessmann worked virtually without a break throughout their journey. In Prague he needed more medicine. Paul left him alone with the family archive in a café near the station, grateful for an excuse to get away and wander intrepidly through the winding streets, marvelling at the masonry, the spires and the turrets. Melbourne might as well have never existed. It was unimaginable for him now and try as he might to retrieve it from his memory, it was mute and powerless against the splendour that surrounded him. I'll never go back there, he said to himself. I've shaken myself free. But he had to hurry back to Klessmann, who was working himself up into a frenzied state as he read through his father's notebooks. This was aggravating his tic as the medicine wore off and his nervous energy began to segue into more violent seizures.

When they finally arrived in Vienna there was still no rest for either of them. The family archive had saturated Klessmann so thoroughly that he couldn't think or talk about anything else. He hurried Paul along, almost stumbling on the cobblestones in his haste, nervously clutching a bundle of papers under his arm.

"The Ringstraße can wait," Klessmann said. "It can all wait. It will still be here tomorrow."

He hailed a cab and directed the driver to the hotel. Paul gazed out longingly at the foggy streets and sombre tenements. Yellow haloes floated in the cold, shadows stretched down alleyways, curving away into darkness.

The hotel apartment was four floors above the street. It consisted of an anteroom, a sitting room with a writing desk and a chaise longue, and a bedroom leading into a small, tiled bathroom. Paul was relieved to be there at last. Klessmann spread Albert's notebooks over the table, arranging things into an orderly work space, while Paul took stock in a more leisurely way.

"Paul, it's very late. If you are settled here I'll leave you now and return in the morning to continue the translation."

Klessmann stood up, hat in hand, and moved towards the door.

"What are you talking about? It's the middle of the night, where are you going to go? And in your state?"

"I am quite all right. *Bettgeher.* I have a place waiting."

Klessmann's eyes narrowed fractionally as they fixed upon Paul's.

"*Bettgeher?*" Paul didn't really know what he was talking about. He puzzled out the meaning of the word. "You have a place to sleep. Very well then."

"I'll return again tomorrow." He bowed with a jerk of his head and left.

It was almost midnight. For the first time in two days Paul was truly by himself. The room was eerie in the wake of Klessmann's sudden departure. Paul opened the door onto the hallway to make sure he wasn't crouching at the keyhole or sleeping bat-like in the rafters above the stairwell.

He closed the door, threw himself onto the bed and lit a cigarette. He was exhausted, too exhausted to sleep. He stood up and walked over to the desk where Klessmann had arranged the translations into a neat pile beside Albert's notebooks. He had left four pencils tied with a piece of cotton from his sewing kit between them, as if he were anxious that they not get confused in his absence. Paul sat down and, careful not to disturb the order of the table, glanced over Klessmann's translations. He could recognise his father's thoughts and images in a phrase here and there, and these served to evoke the rest of the sentence even when the German was of such complexity that he couldn't read it with ease. He remembered Klessmann saying he was curious about his mother. Paul saw his father dragging her down a feculent alleyway off Little Lonsdale Street where vermin scurried through the rubbish left to rot behind the dubious establishments that thrived along those backblocks. "Not here," she sobbed.

What did Klessmann know about that world? Where in God's name had he gone? Paul regretted that he had not been quick enough to follow him and imagined the German jerking his way into a nest hidden under the street. When he wasn't twitching, Klessmann had a gentle, almost scholarly air about him. But there was something off-putting in the black eyebrows and the sharp nose. Paul could imagine him studying in a library. He could just as readily imagine him burrowing under the ground with his sharp nails and crawling into some abysmal hollow for the night.

When he finally dozed off his dreams were overwhelmed by the city, though he'd barely set eyes on it. He explained to his sister how opulent, dark and lyrical it was, but his words sounded hollow, like something he might have read in a book. "Coming here is like returning to a place that I've always known in my heart," he said to her. She smiled. Matthews stood behind her, touching her somewhere that Paul couldn't quite see. "I don't mean that it actually looks familiar," he continued, "but you recognise its possibilities." Ondine closed her eyes, tilted her head back and breathed deeply as Matthews ran his hand up behind her ears. "The Ringstraße, for instance," he went on. Ondine was standing in a corset. There was something he wanted to tell her about the Ringstraße. How it circles the old city. How it is lined with grand public buildings, like the parliament, the opera house and the university. How the place looks wonderful, just wonderful. He hated the sound of his own voice, so trite, so bloody trite. His sister wasn't even looking at him now. She'd lost interest, but still his voice droned on. He couldn't shut up. He was rambling into one cliché after another, making an utter fool of himself. He felt sick with embarrassment. When he finally awoke into the wan light of his room, it was minutes before his mortification dissolved and he could leave the dream behind him.

He barely had time to dress when there was an abrupt knock at the door. Klessmann was standing in the hallway, hat in hand, his red eyes looking no better for a night's rest. Paul stepped back, already feeling wearied by the nervous energy Klessmann brought with him. As he stepped into the room and made his way over to the writing desk, he seemed to examine it for any sign that Paul might have disturbed his work during the night.

"You must think me an eccentric," he said as he sat down and opened Albert's notebook.

"No, but I'm damned anxious to get out of here and have a look around."

Klessmann's tic was under control, but to make sure he swallowed a handful of pills before he untied his pencils.

"Your father was an eccentric. How did he manage to survive out there?"

There was no hint of condescension in this. Klessmann spoke with complete indifference. The phrase "out there" had a peculiar hollowness to it, as if it had been emptied of all its possible connotations. Convicts, the massacres, gold rushes, doomed explorers, the violence of settlement – none of it had ever happened for Klessmann.

"Do you know what Oscar Wilde said about your colonies? Once is an adventure, twice is insanity. He's the only English author I read."

"Irish, actually, Ted," Paul said. Klessmann seemed not to hear him. "I would really like to get out a bit and look around. Maybe introduce myself at the academy. I'm a painter, you know."

"No, I didn't know."

"Can I leave you here?"

"Of course." Klessmann stood up and fumbled about in his coat pocket, finally producing a grubby piece of paper with an address written on it.

"I'll need a typewriter," he said. "Second-hand, of course."

The impudence of the fellow, Paul thought as he walked out onto the street. But in fact, he didn't care. The money was a matter of indifference to him. He was flush with Winton's funds and thrilled to be finally on the streets of Vienna. It was early. The city was still rousing itself. He walked wide-eyed along the Graben to the Stephansdom, and then headed down Kärntner Straße to the opera house and the Ringstraße. It was overwhelming – the detail and density of an imperial city draped in ornaments of its own authority.

Whereas Melbourne still had streets where glutinous yellow mud stuck to the soles of your shoes as you walked, the vistas that now confronted him put that sort of disorder at a convenient remove. A flow of automobiles, cabs, horse-drawn omnibuses and trams jolted over a wide expanse of cobblestones. Most of the tenements were higher than almost anything he had seen in Melbourne save the steeples of the churches and the dome of the Exhibition. The public façades were grander, the masonry was more elaborate, and the monuments were more resonant with the history they commemorated. Melbourne was a drab place by comparison. One reality quickly eclipsed the other. "*Ich bin hier, Ich bin hier*," Paul said to himself as he pushed his dream of the previous night well away and strolled off with the pleasure of his aimlessness evident in his gait.

It was late in the day when he got back to the hotel, overwhelmed by the splendour of the city but tired from so much walking and finally from having to lug the old Remington Klessmann had ordered back to the room. He was still hunched over the table when Paul opened the door and lumbered towards him, eager to unload the machine onto the desk. Klessmann waved him away.

"Over there in the corner if you please."

Pompous ass, Paul thought to himself. He sat down on the edge of his bed in a huff.

"Have you eaten anything?" Paul asked from the bedroom. "I'm anxious that you don't starve to death before you've finished."

"I'm fine, thank you," Klessmann said as he meticulously crossed out a word and corrected the line with another, written above it in a minuscule hand. On the page before him was a wall of words, cross-outs and corrections, connected by neat vertical, horizontal and diagonal lines that deviated into a curve only when the congestion on the page made a straight line impossible. The more curved lines there were, the more unworkable the page became, until finally Klessmann transcribed what he wanted from the maze, spacing the lines out across a clean page.

"Some coffee though," Klessmann said eventually, not even bothering to raise his eyes. "Some coffee and a cigarette would help me to concentrate."

The next day was the same. Paul realised Klessmann was working to a routine. He'd arrive at eight o'clock in the morning, as Paul was rousing himself. After a handful of pills he'd begin work, occupying the room while Paul sauntered around the Ringstraße, lingered in front of the fine public buildings and examined the artworks within.

Unable to take the Art Academy exam until the new year, Paul quickly got into the habit of spending the afternoon writing letters or slouching over a coffee in the Café Central. Past the alcoves and down a narrow hallway, the high glass roof of the main court reminded him of the arcades at home. Murky light filtered down over the green tablecloths. He had the same deep-sea feeling, and imagined he was sitting at the bottom of a lagoon watching the famed literary society of the city float past him. It was the middle of December. The cold was bracing, but it also invigorated him. As he stumbled out of the warm, smoky interior of the Café Central onto Herrengasse his tiredness left him and he could walk for hours more, finally arriving back at his room in time to see Klessmann ordering his writing materials and readying for his departure.

Day after day, this routine didn't vary. Paul was getting annoyed. Part of him wanted to throw the freeloader out onto the street and be done with him, and part of him wanted to take more of a hand in the translation of his father's writing. Paul felt that they had begun to develop an intimacy on the train journey and in Berlin, but this now seemed to fade away into Klessmann's obsession. When the German spoke to him, it was only to ask cryptic questions about his parents and his family, or to glean some obscure detail about Melbourne that might help him to round out a picture in his mind.

"Melbourne," he once said, as if he were thinking out loud. "I ought to go there and see it with my own eyes."

Paul longed for Hamish and the enthusiasms they used to share as they spoke about art and literature and lamented their isolation at the bottom of the world. It was the first pang of homesickness he'd felt since he'd been away.

Six o'clock. The table was put in order and Klessmann was ready to leave.

"Now I have only typing to do, Paul," he said, holding his hat humbly over his knees. "Then, it will be done, and I will be able to relax enough to dispense with these wretched pills."

"Ted," Paul said, "why don't we go out and have a drink?"

"It's nice of you to offer, Paul, but if I don't sleep I can't work and I have a long walk ahead of me."

"Suit yourself."

When Paul was confident that Klessmann would be halfway down the stairs he put his coat back on and went out after him. The streets were crowded enough that Paul could follow him unseen without much difficulty, and the familiar jerk of his head over his shoulder, occurring at regular intervals, ensured that he could pick him out at a distance. He fumbled for a cigarette as he walked. He now bought two packets a day, one for himself and one for Klessmann. The whole situation had something ludicrous about it.

It wouldn't be long before he was buying two sets of clothes and renting two identical hotel rooms on opposite sides of the hallway.

Klessmann walked through the part of the city that Paul knew: down Dorotheergasse, weaving his way through Michaelerplatz, and turning towards the Ringstraße. But soon he had crossed over into a poorer neighbourhood where the streets were narrow and squalid. The splendour of baroque and imperial façades gave way to smaller buildings of two and three storeys that had fallen into disrepair. Some of these had faces crammed into their doorways and bulging out of their windows, willing to brave the cold for a bit of fresh air. Glancing in through grimy and sometimes cracked glass, Paul could see indigent misery moving listlessly in the gloom. He imagined cramped rooms where people huddled together to stay warm, putting up with the smell, the overcrowding, the horror of the tubercular cough wheezing away through the night. Paul had had no idea that behind its glorious façades, the city housed such wretchedness. Beggars held out their gnarled hands. A man with no legs walked on his elbows as a couple of coiffed dandies flicked coins at his dirty fingertips. In front of him the movements of people returning from a day of labour were slow and he had to move briskly to keep sight of Klessmann, rudely dodging around bodies too sluggish to move out of his way.

"What about some company?" a young woman said to him, leaning out of the shadows as he hurried by her. He caught a glimpse of her shivering scarlet cheeks, the steam of her breath in the cold air, the shades of green and black around her eyes. She bent down to adjust a stocking, raising her skirt hem to reveal a lace-up boot. As he glanced at her, a day labourer rolled right into him, knocking him back a few steps, muttering to himself in a language Paul couldn't understand, and shaking his head.

When he recovered himself Paul had lost sight of Klessmann. He hurried along thinking that he could only be a step or two beyond his field of vision. But there were lanes and still smaller alleys snaking off at all angles and with the narrowness and congestion of the street his hopes of setting eyes on him plummeted. A cart dragged along by a donkey blocked his way. An old woman tumbled a sack full of potatoes over the cobblestones and a gang of urchins descended upon them as she tried to shoo them away. For a moment Paul thought he could see Klessmann's hat. He darted along the side of the street, but when he got closer his certainty quickly faded and he had to admit that Klessmann was gone.

Paul walked on to the end of the street. He'd come a long way and had no idea where he was. The crowd was sparser now. Annoyed with himself he turned back the way he had come only to find that he was lost and couldn't quite retrace his steps. He thought he knew the general direction, but after a while realised that he was walking aimlessly. He stopped outside a Wirtshaus and peered in through the window at a quartet – violins, a bass and a clarinet – playing on a stage, while men and women twirled each other around a dance floor. He felt the urge to go inside, but the scene in front of him looked too intimate, as if the people were all familiar with each other, one great big rollicking family to which he didn't belong. He walked on, despondently, wandering for what must have been hours. Sometimes he thought a street looked familiar, only to find it winding into an area he didn't recognise. He could see prostitutes on the corners, rugged up against the cold, coughing horribly into their hands, propped up in doorways like dummies. Finally, near a train station, he recognised Mariahilfer Straße from a map in his room and followed it back to the centre.

It was late by the time he made it back to the hotel. He was cold, exhausted and disheartened by the pitiless squalor of the streets Klessmann had dragged him through. The silence of the room filled him with a sense of his own loneliness. He longed for a conversation as much as he longed for the warm glow of the fireplace in the Montague or the familiar rattle of a tram along Bourke Street. Homesickness. It was childish. He pushed the sentiment away, recalled how badly Melbourne had used him, and resolved to make a better fist of things the next day.

He could only have been asleep for a few hours when a knock at the door awoke him. The deep blue light of another dawning winter's day had seeped into his room. He got up, still wearing the clothes he'd had on the night before. Hastily he smoothed over his hair with his hand and rubbed the blood back into his face, straightening himself as he opened the door to find Klessmann standing on the other side, hat, as usual, in hand.

"How in God's name do you do it?" Paul said.

Klessmann looked at him with puzzlement.

"Why don't you catch a bloody streetcar? You walk through the city, through that wretched slum and out into God-knows-where every night."

"The tram, the tram is fourteen heller," Klessmann said, looking embarrassed.

"Here then, take the money."

Paul rummaged about in a drawer and shoved a hundred kronen into Klessmann's pocket.

"No, I could not." He tried to return the gift.

"Take it," Paul said. He snatched the money and put it back into Klessmann's pocket.

"Very, very kind, Paul."

"When was the last time you ate properly?" he demanded.

Klessmann looked at the floor, and jerked his head. He's wasting away, Paul thought. He took him down to the dining room and ordered coffee and some rolls. Klessmann ate self-consciously, pecking at the food, a crumb at a time. It put Paul on edge.

"What is wrong with you, for God's sake? Are you trying to starve yourself to death?"

To silence him Klessmann took bigger mouthfuls, chewing more vigorously. Paul could see his bony jaw doing its best, but it wasn't used to such sustained activity. They ate in silence. Klessmann seemed ashamed of himself. His eyes wandered around the room with an uneasy, distracted look. It was only when he again broached the topic of Albert's writing that he began to reclaim his usual detachment.

"Paul, there is something your father has written. Can you tell me what it means?"

He took a crumpled piece of paper from his pocket and read:

"Hand over my mouth, eyes glistening, a silver blade in her white, blood-flecked hand. In Hanna Street, rats gnaw at the castrated carcass. '*Um Mitternacht*,' you said, but there was something else, a word, and I knew that we had met before."

Klessmann paused, as if he were letting the sense of the words take hold of him.

"What is Hanna Street?"

"I don't know," Paul said evasively, dunking a roll into his coffee. "I think it has a sewer or a drain opening."

"I see. There is no point in being too literal, with the rest of it. You have a sister, yes?"

Klessmann didn't wait for an answer. He returned his eyes to the page and felt around in his pocket for his pills.

"Paul, I'd appreciate it if you didn't follow me again."

Paul was angry that his hospitality had not been appreciated.

When they finished eating, he let Klessmann back into the apartment and left to recommence his wanderings through the city. In the foyer a clerk handed him a letter mailed from Paris. It was from Laura Thomas. Whimsically he'd sent her his address a day after arriving in Vienna. He put the letter into his pocket, touching it with his hand every other moment to make sure that it was still there. He walked quickly to a nearby café, ordered a concoction of coffee and whipped cream, and then tore the envelope open, barely able to contain himself.

Dear Paul,

I am so glad we met and that you had the time to write to me. I'm reading Balzac, since we are in Paris, and he says that the life of the true artist is a terrible thing, full of daily struggles and hardships that ordinary people can't imagine. So thank you for taking the time. It is wonderful here. I cannot even begin. Everything is wonderful. We have seen the Louvre and walked through the lovely gardens, and even though it is cold it is wonderful.

I am running my poor mother off her feet. But she is enjoying herself, she can't hide it, though she thought our people in London were condescending. She said that – "our people". It sounded odd to me, because they were so stuck-up that they couldn't possibly have been "our people". My cousin (I call him that, though he isn't a real cousin) treated me like a yokel and made snotty comments about the colonies. He thought I wouldn't take any offence, but I felt like slapping him, only he looked so sickly that I thought I might kill him if I did. Anyway, the good of it is that I think I've convinced my mother to give the Continent a proper go. And so we may come to see you. I hope you don't mind. I know I shouldn't if you were suddenly to appear here. I miss our talks and look forward to seeing you.

    Yours, Laura

Her handwriting was firm and controlled. Very adult, he thought. Very self-assured. For a moment he couldn't reconcile the maturity of the hand with the giddiness of the sentiments. Was she having him on with her line about the artist? He shrank from the memory of how Laura and her mother had embodied the shabby truth behind his hubris and pretension. Did she see through it as well? Had she been laughing at him the whole way out? He felt hollow, emptied of hope and inspiration.

While Klessmann worked like a maniac, his own energy seemed to ebb away, dissipating into a purposeless existence, where looking at culture had become an easy way to avoid making it. He slouched into his seat. The café was lively. People read newspapers and journals, chatted, drank and lingered idly. It was the life he had dreamt of, but it could do well enough without him. He was inconsequential and the thought of this insignificance oppressed him until it became intolerable. He'd kill himself sooner than accept it.

## chapter eighteen

Weeks slid by before Klessmann finished typing, then editing his manuscript. The manner of its completion was itself an oddity. Paul was on the verge of venting his frustration, of locking the invalid scribe out of his room, when one morning, as he sat by the window waiting for the usual knock at the door, he wandered over to the desk to take a look at Klessmann's progress. On top of the manuscript was a piece of paper bearing the name of a publisher and a Spittelberg address. Paul picked it up. Underneath it was the title page: *Romanze zur Nacht. Gedichte von Albert Walters.* The manuscript looked finished. Fifty-odd poems in all, distilled and translated from the notebooks which, Paul noticed to his dismay, were gone. Klessmann must have taken them with him, Paul thought. But why? He sat down and watched the clock tick past ten. Klessmann wasn't coming.

Paul felt as if a weight had been lifted from his shoulders. Finally now he might be able to reclaim control of his own life. But he was upset as well. The lack of ceremony in the German's departure and the fact of the missing notebooks left him confused and, he had to admit, offended. Was Klessmann prepared simply to vanish into the anonymous masses of the city after working with such obsessive dedication that his health had suffered as a result? And what did he want with the notebooks now that the manuscript was finished? Paul spent the day trying to retrace what he remembered of his steps the night he had followed Klessmann. When he got back to his hotel he was depressed and dispirited. The one person he knew in Vienna had left him. He was not even worthy of a proper farewell. He would have given anything to have Klessmann knock again at his door, and anything to sit him down again and try to make him articulate exactly what he saw between his father's notes and the poems he had fashioned out of them.

The next day he took the manuscript to the Spittelberg publisher. The place was in the basement of a run-down building, wider at the bottom than it was at the top, as if its foundations were swollen with water. Paul looked up at the façade. Shutters hung precariously on their hinges and layers of sky-blue paint were cracking and peeling off, revealing the grain of the stone underneath and the crumbling, weatherworn masonry.

In a dark room barely illuminated by a gas lantern, Herr Bressler blew a cloud of smoke over the pages as his eyes moved from line to line, skipping a page here and there, returning every so often to one he had already read. He was an earnest man, over fifty, balding with untidy whiskers hanging off his cheeks like red wisps of seaweed clinging to a rockface. All business, Paul thought. His officiousness was out of place in a room that looked as if it had been flooded once too often. The smell of damp lingering over the boxes of unmoved stock was overwhelming. Paul imagined rats nesting in old copies of cheap novelettes, books with titles like *Confessions of a Streetwalker* and *Erotic Berlin*.

His eyes wandered over the posters on the wall as he tried to ignore the smell and let Bressler concentrate on the manuscript. They were posters for the theatre. Strange, corpse-like forms, in which lines seemed to twist out of shape in response to some inner tension or aggravation. A skeletal woman with deep-set eyes and rotting teeth cradled a flayed body. In another, a man's profile shuddered so violently it threw off an after-image around it, as if the whole picture were vibrating.

Bressler glanced up at Paul as his eyes wandered over the illustrations.

"I devour you men and women. Half-waking listening children, the wild loving werewolf within you," he said in a chant. "Kokoschka," he added, and returned silently to the manuscript. "You can leave this with me? I'll give you a receipt. You know, there will be no money. Quite the contrary, I may need to ask for your assistance. A small subvention."

Paul waved off the sense of warning in his voice, as if money meant nothing to him. Winton's gold can pay for it, he thought sardonically. He wrote his address on a separate sheet of paper and handed it to Bressler.

"Who is the author?" Bressler asked. "Or are these your own poems?"

"No, they are my father's."

"Father?" Bressler raised his eyebrows. "Well then. And he is still living?"

"No. He drowned himself."

"Well. That's all to the good. I'll see what I can do for you."

Paul stood up to leave.

"These are very theatrical, you know," Bressler said. "Staged scenes, concealment, curtains. Did your father enjoy the theatre?"

"To my knowledge he never went."

"I have a theatre not far from here. You might be interested. Do you know much about Vienna?"

Paul knew next to nothing, and virtually nobody. Only Klessmann, he thought, the classic nobody, the original man of the crowd. The whole city was still a mystery to him. Every passer-by, every animated café conversation, every wonderful edifice or monument merely reminded him of how little he belonged.

"I'd planned to sit the Art Academy exam," Paul said.

"The Academy. A very conservative place. There are other options. Kokoschka went to the Arts and Craft School. I could introduce you if you like. There is something of him in these poems, I think. Expressionist."

Bressler pressed the manuscript into a briefcase and led Paul up the stairs back out onto the street, where he blinked at the winter sun as if he had never seen it before. Opposite them a young woman was hunched over the ground, coughing with such violence that her whole body shook. She was pretty, Paul thought. Bressler noticed him staring.

"Could you guess how many men in this city have syphilis, Herr Walters?" Bressler said, folding his arms over his chest and waiting for an answer. "One in five. And could you guess how many have tuberculosis?" he asked after a few more steps. "One in five. Or something like that. Now, I am sure you haven't come such a long way merely to encounter these Viennese plagues. At least wait until I see your father into print."

They walked along Siebensterngasse. It was late in the afternoon and the sun soon vanished behind thick, grey clouds, plunging the city into premature darkness.

"I hope your ambitions are not too grand, Herr Walters," Bressler said. "Vienna has become a place of small achievements. *Kleinkunst*. We like to think of ourselves as the world in miniature. Everything seems to be shrinking. People won't read a novel if they can read an essay. They won't watch five acts if they can watch one. Soon we'll have nothing but anecdotes. It's the pace of modern living. These days it's only the extremely rich or the extremely poor who have enough time to loiter in our cafés. I myself can seldom manage it. For everyone else, time has contracted too thoroughly. Why spend an afternoon if you can get the same result, read the same paper and gulp the same coffee in an hour or a minute or a few seconds. It is the beginning of the end."

Outside a Wirtshaus Bressler shook Paul's hand, then raised his briefcase and tapped it portentously as he made his way in. "Business, you understand."

Paul lingered for a moment, looking in at the workers drinking beer in a room thick with cigarette smoke. It was a grubby-looking scene. The men were rough and the women they cavorted with wore loose blouses, hanging down around their shoulders. Smoke, spilt beer and congestion. It seemed to Paul much cruder than anything he had seen in Melbourne, where good old Victorian morality still had a powerful enough hold on the city to keep its vices under wraps until they could be pursued with a secret, furtive pleasure.

He reached the Ringstraße and stood gazing at the Kunsthistorisches Museum. Was it possible to feel crushed by so much monumentality? If it were a city of small achievements now, that said nothing for its past. Paul felt its weight press on him. All he'd ever do here is look at things, he thought. The poverty of the streets through which he'd followed Klessmann was as picturesque to him as the buildings of the Ringstraße were grand. He looked at both with the tourist's pitiful longing for the beautiful and the sublime.

How many times had he rehearsed his response to Vienna? In a letter to Hamish he'd rattled on about the endless, grating friction between authority and rebellion, mind and body, the order of the man-made world and the chaos of nature, as if one needed a city of this scale to realise such things. How false it all sounded to him now as he made his lonely way through the mute splendour of the city, bustled by its traffic, withdrawing into himself, defeated by his own illusions. He couldn't write to Ondine like this. He couldn't possibly fool her. And he wasn't about to confess his unhappiness. On Herrengasse he caught his reflection in a window and imagined himself exposed to the impersonal gaze of the city. He'd become a type: the Australian abroad, the *faux* bohemian longing for culture, eager to shake off the dust of the new world. He saw himself realised as a caricature in some satirical *feuilleton*.

Back in his hotel he flipped through a copy of *Die Fackel* and was baffled by its busyness, the profusion of detail, names, scandal, the sense of a world that one was supposed to recognise behind the mask of satire. He lit a cigarette and read a paper, flinging it down after a while out of boredom. He wished again that Klessmann would show up to commandeer his room. He felt lost without the daily routine of being rudely brushed aside. He would have given anything to answer awkward, tactless questions about his mother and father. He looked at himself in the bathroom mirror, and remembered how enthusiastically he had chanted "*Ich bin hier*" only a few weeks earlier. Now he felt a numbness in his cheeks, a lethargy stealing over him. "Nothing, nothing, nothing," he repeated to his reflected image. He felt impotent – bereft of ideas, bereft of inspiration.

There was a knock outside the apartment. Klessmann, he thought. He could've almost hugged him. He rushed to the door, pulling it open to find a stranger, wrapped in a fur, staring back at him out of the half-light of the hallway. She was beautiful, he thought. A long pale face, glistening red lips, sparkling brown eyes and fine eyebrows. She wore a fashionable hat, with a broad brim, tilted to one side, which set off the elongated elegance of her face.

She took a bold stride past him, through the anteroom into the apartment, removing her hat and floating it about theatrically as she turned to face him.

"Surprised?" She was ready to explode with happiness. She had to purse her lips and tense her cheeks to keep it all inside her. "I've run away."

It was Laura Thomas, but it was only the slight nasal edge in her softer accent that gave her away.

"Aren't you pleased to see me?"

Paul took her hands and kissed the leather gloves she was wearing, making her laugh uproariously. He watched her eyes survey the apartment. She stretched her arms out as she turned, as if to test its dimensions, and then nodded approvingly.

"I think you'll find me a better conversationalist these days," she said as she sat down on his chaise longue.

"I think you'll find me a much worse one."

She glanced at a pamphlet next to her.

"*Der Prozeß Riehl*," she read haltingly, looking at the cover as she leant back on a cushion. "I love it here, Paul."

"Where did you leave your mother?" He sat down beside her and took her hand.

"Oh, don't be silly. I didn't really run away. She's downstairs in that lovely foyer."

Paul smiled to himself.

"Do you think I'm an idiot?" she asked, smiling as well.

He kissed her hand again.

"Mother is waiting. I thought you could walk us back to our hotel. What have you been doing?"

He thought about Klessmann. His time in Vienna had been all Klessmann. It seemed to Paul that he had no tangible experiences of his own. All he really knew of the place was the obsessive invalid, his strange habits and his disconcerting twitch.

"I met a very odd bloke in Hamburg, and we travelled here together," he said.

"Another artist?" Laura asked.

"I suppose you could call him that."

If Europe had transformed Laura, the same was true for her mother, but in the opposite direction. Eleanor Thomas looked older and crabbier than Paul had remembered. She wore a smock-like dress and had powdered her hair white as if it were the fashion. She waddled with the heaviness of her dress as they made their way out onto the street.

"You see, Paul, I've successfully worn Mother out," Laura said. "She's brow-beaten and subservient, aren't you? I told her that if we couldn't come here by Christmas I'd have to come alone. Of course we are later than I wanted to be. I thought it wretched that you'd be alone for Christmas. I imagined you starving in some garret, nibbling chestnuts by candlelight. Of course I didn't realise that you were so well off here."

"Stop it, Laura," her mother insisted, "you're babbling. She has babbled since we arrived in London, Paul. Talked my ear off. Ran me off my feet. I'm not as young as I once was."

"You don't say," Laura said with feigned astonishment and a gentle laugh. She linked arms with her mother and drew her closer as they walked.

They ate dinner in a restaurant on the Kohlmarkt after shivering through the twilight streets. Eleanor's eyes rested approvingly on the velvet upholstery and the pink marble of the tabletop as she flattened her dress behind her and sat down. They had an alcove to themselves, surrounded by large wall mirrors composed of individual panels that reflected and multiplied each of them to infinity. The chandeliers dangling from the ceiling filled the room with a soft yellow light that caught the gilt frames and furnishings. A potted palm tree in the middle of the room and some ferns artfully arranged in the corners gave the place the ambience of an exotic garden.

As they ate, Laura described the galleries she'd seen, and the young Englishmen and Americans, masquerading as artists, she'd met copying paintings in the Louvre. One of them acted as a guide for them, pointing out which works were worthy of their attention. She laughed as she described him, putting her hand over her mouth and blushing.

"He was very gentlemanly," Eleanor said.

"Oh, he was a pompous twit. Of course I told him that we know artists in Vienna, where the whole thing is taken a bit more seriously. That slowed him down a bit. And his paintings," she added, raising her eyebrows, "I couldn't believe he had the courage to try selling us one."

Laura and her mother exchanged affectionate taunts throughout dinner. Paul had never seen Laura look so wonderful. Surely she could see how idle he had been. The best he could offer them was a glorified tour. As the conversation ran on ahead of him, his thoughts wandered back to the folly of his plans and the despair he'd felt the moment before her arrival.

But he was happy she had come. When he could do so without being obvious, he let his eyes rest on the faint freckles running from her nose onto her cheeks and fading under her pale skin. He made an effort to look animated and to focus on the trivial currents of conversation flowing around him, picking up the drift with a comment here or a nod of the head there. Laura and her mother could talk tirelessly. They were staying for the winter and had planned to travel further when the weather got warmer. By then he'd be exhausted by the chatter. He thought he might have to coach Laura into a quieter, slightly more reserved manner. When she noticed the conversation getting too obscure she gave him a look of pained sympathy that told him to grin and bear it for her sake.

Slowly his mood improved under her benign influence. He wanted to touch her under the table, to push his hand up under her dress and rest it on her thigh, to see if she could keep a straight face. He noticed a man in the next alcove looking at her approvingly. Perhaps he was taken with her lightness of manner, which was so pleasingly out of place. The woman next to him looked dour by comparison. She barely spoke, edging around her food with a mild disdain for it as her partner's eyes continued to drift towards Laura.

After the meal Eleanor excused herself. As soon as she was out of sight Laura took Paul's hand.

"I'm sorry. Just humour us for a while."

He kissed her hand and said nothing, noticing a waiter standing silently beside them.

"*Chambre séparée?*" he asked with starched formality.

"Yes please," Laura said enthusiastically. Paul looked doubtful. He wondered if he'd heard him correctly and if Laura had understood.

When they remained sitting, the waiter had to wave them on. The man opposite smiled at Paul as Laura leapt out of her chair. The waiter led them through the dining room and down another hallway, presenting them with a white door and a gilt handle. Laura smiled and opened it, grabbing Paul by the cuff and dragging him in.

There was something immediately disturbing in the room's silence. It was cold and Paul could smell a trace of gas, mingling with perfume and stale smoke. It was all red velvet and gold. In the middle of the room was a cushioned couch surrounded by ferns draped over it to simulate a tropical canopy. There was a full-length mirror opposite and an ashtray perched on a stand. Nothing else.

Laura turned to him, biting her lower lip with embarrassment, then stretching it into something between a smile and a grimace, as if she'd just taken a wrong turn and led them to a dead-end.

"I think we had better go," she said, nodding as if he had suggested it.

"Yes," he said.

He took her hand as she walked past him to the door. She turned and he kissed her quickly on the lips. Even in the dim light of the room he could tell she was blushing. Her neck had suddenly rashed and she clutched it, trying to hide the discolouration.

"It's so depraved," she said. "Who would have thought?"

"Indeed. Who would have."

They made it back to the table just as Eleanor was reappearing. They all sat down together, Laura looking flustered, but Paul quietly pleased. Their unexpected brush with the other reality lurking behind the glittering façades of glass and gold promised her to him. They both knew it. He wondered how many trivial conversations and strolls around the Ringstraße lay between them and the *chambre séparée*. He was restless, but also found something wonderfully beguiling in the deferral. As long as he never lost sight of the still, silent room he could wait and wait with the pleasure of his expectations growing steadily beneath the formality.

When the time came Paul didn't even sit the entry exam for the Academy. He had tried to sketch in his room, but was unable to concentrate on his work, unable to shut out the city around him, and finally acknowledged that he had nothing worth submitting. He was annoyed with himself, but only mildly. Every day it seemed, he was walking with Laura and her mother, feeling trapped by the littleness of their conversation, yet glimpsing a wider field to which he and Laura might finally escape. He was happy to have company so constantly, yet he tightened up when, in this or that café, he could sense the animated discussions about literature and art going on around them. Yet he loved the subtle, seductive quality of being with Laura in a museum. The decorative grandeur of the spaces, the furtiveness of their glances, the play of concealment and the transport of meaning into the manner of their appreciation, filled him with excitement. When they went to the opera or the theatre the things they saw all had a terrific suggestiveness for him that he tried to impart to her. The cruelty of Strauss's *Salome* fired his imagination. He saw Laura showering the severed head with kisses, pushing her tongue into the dead mouth, closing her eyes, drifting into a mad trance with the taste of something bitter leaking through the skull. Back in his room the phantom-train of sleep slowly trained her innocence towards a shameless collaboration in the debaucheries that never failed to grip him in the dead of night.

Laura, pleasingly, began to learn German from a tutor. She sat in a café and went over grammatical rules and then studied the vocabulary in the newspaper. Later she would stumble through a few phrases with Paul, proud of her progress, and soon knew enough to discover the crude codes in the back page advertisements of the *Neue Freie Presse*.

"Fraulein Willing. Call at number 69."

She looked at it for a moment and then smiled.

In his apartment she glanced over some of the pamphlets on his desk, opening them at random and seizing on the start of a new paragraph.

"*Fort mit der Schamhaftigkeit, die die körperliche und geistige Gesundheit der Völker seit fast zwei Jahrtausenden untergräbt!*" She read it slowly, tripping over each syllable. She read it again to herself and then looked up at Paul, puzzled. "*Was bedeutet Schamhaftigkeit?* Oh, of course, it comes from shame. What about *untergraben?*"

He watched as the sense of the sentence sunk into her. She furrowed her eyebrows.

"Away with the shamefulness?"

"Yes," he answered.

"What is this?" She turned to the red cover and then flipped through it again. "Tell me what the rest of it says," she demanded as she opened the pamphlet back to the page from which she'd been reading and handed it to Paul.

He looked at it and shrugged his shoulders as if its contents were of little import to him.

"Nature gives women sensuality – *Sinnlichkeit* – which is the fountain at which men can renew themselves, intellectually speaking." He looked at her, studying her response.

"Go on please," she said, sucking in her lower lip.

"The founders of morality have..." He broke off, pretending to translate in his head, but deciding to give her his own loose summary. "The founders of morality have corrupted human sexuality, dammed it away, and as a result both beauty and mental vitality are drying up. Under these circumstances, under such repression, all a man can do is canalise the flow of female sensuality, and his brain is empty and uninspired as a result."

He watched her turn the thought over in her mind.

"It was written by a man called Karl Kraus, about the hypocrisy of modern morality and the way it makes us suffer the repression of our sensual selves."

Laura thought about the *chambre séparée*. Red velvet, deep shadows, fern leaves and gold. She recalled the detail of the room obscurely. She couldn't remember its dimensions or its arrangement, but the trappings stayed with her. Something inexplicable had winked back at her out of the light and shadow. Once, after an idle stroll, she found herself staring through the window of the same restaurant, momentarily mesmerised by the reflected glitter within.

As spring set in they all took longer walks through the Prater, looking at the panoramas and the sideshows, and spent lazy afternoons sitting in garden cafés planning trips to Prague, Budapest, Italy and the Alps. Occasionally Paul felt anxious at the thought of frittering away so much time, at feeling his ambition leaking away, choking in the silt of these endless diversions. Every now and then Laura would return to one of her pet themes: the Balzac novel in which the struggles of the artist were so vividly described. It merely reminded Paul of just how completely he had drifted from his own ideal. It occurred to him to look for Klessmann again, but he didn't know where to start. He wasn't even sure whether he would still be in Vienna.

"Look at that, Paul," Laura said, seizing him with one arm, her mother with the other, and dragging them both after her.

They were in the Prater, walking towards the Australian Panorama. It was too fantastic to believe. Paul had heard about whole African villages transported to European cities and exhibitions. Even Melbourne had imported a band of Maoris. But to see something like this in the middle of Vienna hardly seemed possible. They mingled with a crowd of spectators gathering around a large, enclosed area that housed a makeshift desert terrain of hard red earth and some huts made out of mud and straw.

"We could tell them a thing or two," said Eleanor. Laura had the good sense to nudge her mother into silence as they edged through the throng to see the inhabitants of the enclosure huddling around each other, protecting themselves from the mocking eyes peering in through the bars.

"*Sie sind wie Tiere*," said a woman standing next to them, wearing a neat summer frock with a blue shawl draped over her shoulders. "*Tiere, die unter der Erde graben.*"

Paul was stunned. He looked at Laura, who had turned pale, and took her hand.

"Barbarian," Laura said under her breath.

"*Genau*," said the woman in the summer frock, nodding.

"I mean you, you stupid, stupid woman."

She didn't understand her.

In front of them a pair of middle-aged men were talking quickly about the anthropology of the Stone Age, and the savage fear of incest.

"It's horrible, Paul," Laura said. "How can they do that?"

Paul couldn't answer her. He had a vivid image of Les Collins in his mind and regretted that his book on the Kulin had never come to pass, but he was at a loss for words.

Then Laura snapped, "Why don't we have anything to say? We just look at it and feel bad and then walk away and soon forget about it! What kind of society puts people in cages in order to speculate on world history?"

"Laura!" Eleanor seemed to rebuke her for the ability to express an independent thought.

"It's cruel, Mother."

For the second time she had the feeling of having led them down a cul-de-sac. Was she expecting the three of them to stand up and take responsibility for the cruelty, to shout down the crowd of onlookers or, more heroically, to put an end to the spectacle?

One of the middle-aged men turned to them quietly. He had a head of jet-black hair, a neatly trimmed beard and a silver pince-nez. He spoke as if he were explaining something quite complicated by way of justifying the display. Paul couldn't quite catch the detail above the noise of the crowd. Laura just shook her head. After a moment the man turned to one of the men inside the enclosure.

"What are you earning a day, my man?" he asked.

"None of your damned business," the crouching man answered, poking the ground with a stick.

"They are acting," the man with the pince-nez said patiently.

Paul looked more closely. It was hard to tell, but he guessed the people in the enclosure were wearing body paint. My God, he thought, is everything a trick?

"They are actors from Berlin," the man explained. "They do a different part of the world every day or so. Yesterday it was America. All money and humbug. Very funny. Can the conscience of the Antipodes rest a little easier?"

As if he had verbalised the transformation that was occurring in Laura at that very moment, she began sobbing and flung her arms around Paul, hiding her head on his shoulder. He could feel her chest heaving and heaving until she gradually regained some equilibrium. Eleanor Thomas had tactfully turned away.

Everything seemed farcical to Paul. They were lost in the surface of things, a prey to the most blatant kinds of deception and manipulation. He was becoming agitated. Laura still clung to him, wiping her tears away with the back of her hand, brimming with both relief and embarrassment. She looked at the figures in the enclosure. Of course they were actors. How could she not have seen it?

As they walked away she bit her lip. Did it matter that they were actors? How did it change the sense of inhumanity? The question puzzled her. It was as if something had happened, and then, suddenly, it hadn't. None of it was true. Or was it? Could it all be true despite the fact that they were actors? She felt as if she were being blown along by a breeze, about to be lifted up into the air and tossed about capriciously. She clutched Paul's arm as if it might help her ground herself. Would she ever go back to the country to live out her life on the land? She hoped not, but for the first time in her life she had no sense of where the wind was going to drop her. Nothing seemed certain, and no one was what they seemed to be, least of all herself.

## chapter nineteen

Paul had never ceased to think about Bressler. Every time he walked by the Café Central he went in to look for him. Once he found him deep in conversation with other coffee-house notables, but couldn't summon the courage to approach him in the guise of an unwanted interruption. Bressler had waved through the smoke and nodded to him with a confident twist of his nose, as if to suggest that the wheels were in motion.

One afternoon, Paul was sitting by the window of his room writing a letter to Hamish and considering where he and Laura might travel with the arrival of summer. There was a knock at the door. A porter handed him a parcel accompanied by a short note from Bressler inviting him to meet Otto Eisner, a well-known reviewer, at the Café Central the following afternoon. Paul tore off the paper to find a thin volume, brown letters on fawn-coloured cloth. His hands trembled as he opened the unturned pages and ran his fingers over the first lines. Strangely, Paul found that it didn't evoke the memory of his father. Instead, he saw Klessmann working away day after day, then vanishing into the obscurity of some far-flung suburb as dusk fell over the city. His excitement at finally having the book in his hands turned into the fear that somehow Klessmann might resurface to take his share of the credit or to accuse him of misappropriation. Was that why he had taken the notebooks? Paul had to admit that he had done much more than merely translate. But hadn't Klessmann himself typed his father's name on the title page?

That evening Paul showed Laura the poems and explained to her the secret of his father's notebooks. She could make out words, sometimes phrases here and there, but she needed Paul to explain each poem in its entirety if she were to understand it. Eleanor was sitting opposite them on a stool, pretending to busy herself with a letter to her sons, so Paul was reticent.

"Perhaps later," he whispered.

"Why?"

"Because my father was not always decent."

The next day Bressler slapped him on the back and ushered him through the smoke to meet a table full of journalists, writers and other coffee-house hacks in the arcade's court. Otto Eisner would have been about forty-five. His hair, perhaps once unruly, was brushed down flat over his forehead. He had full lips, a flat nose and, behind his spectacles, eyes with a slight purplish tinge around their lids. He shook Paul's hand and gestured to a seat with an open palm. Regulars at other tables couldn't help but turn their heads as they noticed the hitherto friendless Australian joining a table that was the envy of obscure writers and artists all over Vienna.

Paul felt faint. A wave of nervousness washed through him as he looked anxiously around the room, where eyes were either fixed upon him, or just as deliberately averted. His knees felt weak, his palms sweated. His first instinct was to run out into the street and call the whole thing off, to throw the book away and forget that it had ever been written.

"Your father has turned a damned whore into a virgin," Eisner said. The others at the table lowered their voices when he spoke and directed their attention towards him. "I understand he lived many years in Australia."

"Yes," said Paul. As soon as he spoke his panic dissipated, but his body remained tense. He still glanced over his shoulder every once in a while. The place had settled back into its usual repose, but Paul couldn't shake the sense that he was being watched from all directions. He glanced up at the high ceiling, half expecting to find a face gazing down at him through the glass.

"Well, that is probably what saved him from the rot," Eisner said. "You should write a little something about him – how he got there, what he did. A savage pilgrim," he added thoughtfully. "A German Rimbaud."

"Or a German Baudelaire," a younger man said. "Amazing. I wonder what Felix will think."

"And Kraus," said another.

The misconception under which his father's poems had been received was now clear to Paul. None of them had any idea that the poems had been translated from English. They had found the miracle of a German voice in exile, a vein of linguistic purity that had survived the decadence of Europe and the barbarity of the colonies to strike back at the centre with renewed force.

"Where did he come from originally?" Eisner asked.

"Boppard, on the Rhine," Paul said without hesitation. It was the town in which Anna's mother had been born.

"And why on earth Australia?" Eisner asked. "Did you see those clowns from Berlin in the Prater? Apparently a young Australian woman made a bit of a fuss until the whole thing was explained."

There were some sniggers around the table and Paul laughed as well. He ordered a coffee, lit a cigarette, and began to fill in the details of his father's life. Immigration, gold, poverty, the drudgery of Melbourne, the *danse macabre* of married life. They listened attentively. Someone made notes. It was Eisner's secretary, Bressler later told Paul as he shook his hand on the street.

"It has all worked out very nicely," he said. "A coup in fact. And a fine opening for you as well."

Paul had managed to lie flawlessly throughout the entire conversation. But now, as Bressler left him, he was again overcome by the nervousness that had seized him inside. He caught a glimpse of himself in the window of the Café Central. His exterior was unruffled. He held his face still, but noticed that it seemed a bit too stiff. He tried to practise a more relaxed posture. He let his shoulders hang a little lower, tried to relax the muscles in his neck, but still his face retained the same mask-like appearance – flat cheeks, loose mouth and dulled eyes. He tried to smile at himself, contorting his mouth into a grotesque wooden grin. He shook his hands at his side, as if he might be able to shake the stiffness from his frame. He had the comical sensation of having to play-act at being himself.

Nothing, nothing, nothing, a voice inside him echoed through his hollowness, keeping pace with his footfalls as he turned towards Michaelerplatz. His flesh prickled and he stopped cold. From the very instant Eisner had offered him a seat he had felt queer. The scene inside flashed before him. He turned back towards the Café Central, just as Klessmann was walking out onto the sidewalk, his beady eyes fixed accusingly on Paul.

"Why have you been ignoring me?" he said flatly. He was rake thin and his rough, unshaven cheeks were unhealthily red as he coughed ominously into his hand.

Paul rubbed his eyes. "What?"

"Every day I wait for you and you look right through me. Am I so thin that I've become invisible?" He didn't stop for an answer, turning his back on Paul and walking away.

"Now look here," Paul said, following him. "That's utter nonsense."

Klessmann shooed him away and kept walking, hunching his shoulders and drawing in his arms so that he could dart between the cracks in the pedestrian traffic like a mouse squeezing itself through narrow skirting-board crevices.

Paul went after him. Klessmann didn't turn around once, though his swift steps and skilful feints around slower pedestrians suggested that he sensed Paul's presence behind him. He walked in the direction opposite to that which he'd taken on the night Paul had followed him, and kept up the same frantic pace the whole way – through the city, over the canal, through crowds of peddlers, hawkers and day labourers, into the slums of Leopoldstadt, along the edge of the Augarten, finally turning into a street of tenements near the train station. Paul noted the building into which he vanished and waited outside for a few minutes. He was exhausted. Klessmann had done the whole journey, at least a mile Paul thought, at a freakish speed. He leant against a lamppost and caught his breath in the fading twilight, then walked over the road and into the building.

The place smelt horrible. The air was stagnant and the absence of lighting in the stairwell gave him the sense that it was choking on its own darkness. A few other stragglers were entering with him: an older woman with her hair held up in a net and her bare arms stained with a brown dye, and a youth whose face was black with soot. Paul followed them onto the second floor where the walls had been demolished to expand the floor space. What he saw staggered the senses. It was like a scene from the inferno. The interconnected rooms were dark, but for the bare illumination of the odd gas lamp hanging from a wall, and without furniture, but for the mattresses covering the floor. Paul stepped through a sea of exhausted bodies. Some rolled uneasily under filthy sheets and blankets, others coughed hideously or scratched away at scabious infestations. He covered his nose with his handkerchief and tried to breathe lightly.

Wedged up against a bit of wall he found Klessmann huddling into his jacket, panting with exhaustion. Paul picked him up. He was so light that he could carry him in his arms as if he were a small child. Klessmann's eyes resisted, but his body was too enervated to protest. In the cab, heading back over the canal, he looked at Paul coldly.

"I will try hard not to splutter over you," he said.

As he slouched in the corner, Paul noticed that his tic had vanished. It was as if his whole body were slowing down, drawing its last reserves of energy into itself, paring back to a few basic functions.

Paul carried him up to his room, put him down on the chaise longue and instantly wrote a note to Laura, asking her to bring a doctor. When she finally arrived with a Dr Hasek, he greeted her in the anteroom.

"What's wrong, Paul?" The concern in her voice made it evident that she thought he was ill.

"Not me." He gestured to the body on the lounge.

As Dr Hasek crouched over Klessmann, Laura edged closer, covering her mouth with her hands in disbelief. The blood drained from her face and her arm felt cold as Paul touched it. Klessmann opened his eyes and looked up at her, the hint of a smile creeping over his bird-like visage. He opened his mouth to wheeze and gulped at the air around him as the doctor pressed his chest and took his pulse. When Dr Hasek stood up and motioned to Paul confidentially, Laura quickly knelt down beside the invalid and took his hand, patting it calmly in hers.

"She is an angel," Klessmann mumbled in a dead monotone. "A good angel."

She looked at him, puzzled by the tone of his voice.

"*Aber Weib oder Frau?*" he said.

She didn't quite understand.

"Yes," she said softly.

When the doctor left, Paul touched her on the shoulder and lifted her away from Klessmann, who had closed his eyes as she sat beside him.

"He's going to die, isn't he?" she said.

Paul nodded.

"I'm going to stay here, Paul, and help you look after him. I'll send a note to Mother. Don't tell me otherwise."

During the night Klessmann mumbled. For the most part he was incoherent, though Paul thought he could hear traces of his father's poetry floating through the delirium, as if the poems had been dismantled and the phrases flung like bits of rubbish back into a formless babble.

In the middle of the night, while Laura slept in the bedroom, Klessmann raised himself on an elbow. "You cannot know how disappointed I am, Paul," he said. It was the first moment of clarity he'd shown for hours. "Disappointed," he repeated, the word sapping him of his energy as he sunk back down onto his back.

"Ted," Paul said as gently as he could, "what did you do with my father's notebooks?"

Klessmann turned to him and smiled. "I ate them."

Paul looked at him in disbelief. He noticed that Klessmann was clutching the book, holding it over his chest as he wheezed. How had he found it? Had Laura given it to him? Klessmann closed his eyes. The thing was like a gravestone, weighing him down, effacing him, pushing him into oblivion. His hands tightened around it as if he were trying with all his might to push it from him. Then his hands wilted a little. The book fell onto his chest and stayed there, perfectly still.

Paul had no idea how long he had been standing over the corpse. Finally, as the sky outside lightened, Laura touched his shoulder. Her hand sent a shudder from his skull down to the floor. She had glided across to him so silently that he'd had no sense of her presence beside him.

She looked down at the wasted face. Already Klessmann seemed inhuman to her, the skeleton pushing its way through the skin, moulding the worn flesh in its own image. She stood in front of Paul and took his hands, looking into his eyes. She had an image of Klessmann flung into the world like a delicate bird, buffeted by the wind and finally hurled to the ground, crushed against the stones of the city.

"We are just thrown out there," she said, a shiver running down her spine as she glimpsed the futility. "He was an artist, wasn't he?"

"He translated my father's poems."

"Yes, he told me."

She looked again at Klessmann. Paul followed her eyes as they wandered from the book, still lying on his chest, to his open mouth and the eyes sinking into their sockets.

It was an hour before they could get Klessmann's body moved to the morgue. The morgue attendant left the contents of Klessmann's pockets on the table beside the typewriter: some matches, some cigarette butts, a few loose coins and an old poster, folded into a small square and worn thin with time. It showed a photograph of Klessmann's face contorted into an expression of epileptic anguish. Underneath were the words "Hamburg's Theatre of Derangement", jagged across the page. Paul folded it into his pocket and cleaned up the other bits of detritus.

After the body was wrapped and hauled down into the street, Laura stood in the window niche, watching the men load it onto the back of a horse-drawn cart.

"Paul," she said. "The *chambre séparée*. I think I'd like to go there."

She remained motionless, still staring down onto the street. He walked up behind her and put his hands around her waist. She turned to him and he kissed her, but her lips were shut and her face unmoved.

"Not here," she said. "I want to go back to that place. The *chambre séparée*. Meet me in the foyer this evening at eight. Don't speak to me. Don't say anything to me. Not a word."

She pressed his hand and left him. The morning broke through the window and the sound of traffic on the street below grew gradually louder until the unreality of the night withered away and he was finally able to lie down. In his waking dreams he saw Klessmann buried in some obscure colonial grave while his father ghosted through the streets of Vienna, a posthumous celebrity extolled in the city's coffee houses and *feuilletons* as a modern master.

As he lay there he thought about the impression Klessmann had made on Laura. "He was an artist?" she'd asked, and he saw, behind the question, her secret admiration of the man's suffering as he lay dying before her eyes.

And their rendezvous that evening? He couldn't shake the idea that the thought of Klessmann had somehow led her to suggest it. Again he felt the emptiness open up within him. He had wasted more than six months playing at the fantasy of art with an increasingly sceptical attitude until he'd given it up altogether and degenerated into a flaccid dilettante, a tourist. It disgusted him. He couldn't go to Laura like that. He couldn't bear it. He got up and paced the room nervously, feeling his limbs tense as he pushed against the invisible wall that had closed around him.

He reached for his coat, pulling the poster of Klessmann out and rushing to his desk, where he folded it out flat in front of him. He saw Wedelkind's outlandish lunacy parading across the stage, arms waving, body convulsing, hair standing up on end. He saw a body hacked to pieces by a twitching maniac as the instinctual terror of the bestial and the perverted burst through onto the stage. It would be enough to unsettle the strongest will and the most rational mind. He put a piece of paper in the typewriter and started hammering away at the keys.

The epileptic maniac. The maniac of Hamburg. A poet drives himself into a homicidal frenzy. A twitching, jerking maniac prowling the streets of St Pauli. A murdered prostitute. A slashed throat. A bleeding body in a brothel. The *chambre séparée*. The poet's tic. Klessmann. The tic.

He stopped, looking down at the sheet, his heart beating with excitement. His mind was made up. Bressler would love it. He would call it "The Tic".

## chapter twenty

By the middle of 1913, Hamish McDermott was working at the offices of the *Melburnian* thanks to the intervention of Robert Walters, who was then chief editor. The two had met coincidentally at the Railway Hotel and Hamish had complained about his job in the hospital. Robert, fondly remembering him as a boy and conscious of the fact they had both loitered about St Vincent Place pining for lost loves, offered him work as a trainee reviewer and packed him off to a Rossini opera the very next week. Robert liked his first article (in fact he'd merely copied the enthusiastic, camp style of the *Table Talk* reviewer) and Hamish soon settled into a world of typewriters and cable machines, transcribing the workaday realities of the city. Court cases, the occasional society divorce, traffic accidents, reviews and pieces of urban trivia that took up a couple of lines here and there were the stuff of his working life now.

The lot of a journalist, he soon found, was not a glamorous one. If anything he was more mired in the mundane than ever before. But at least it promised him something better than illness and soiled linen. Hamish began a notebook in which he kept a private record of the city, hoping one day to synthesise these notes into something worthy of the name of art. He wrote a letter to Paul explaining his changed fortunes, aware that his writing seemed dull and plodding beside the exuberance of his younger friend.

He didn't receive a direct reply, but nearly six months later a small package from Vienna was delivered to his desk. He recognised Paul's hand in the address and tore it open to find a book of poems entitled *Romanze zur Nacht*. The author was Albert Walters. Accompanying the book was a short note:

Dear H,
   You have here the fruits of my labours. You deserve a good deal of the credit. Already the book has attracted a readership among critics and other literary types. My father is a minor revelation. Laura is here and has inveigled her mother into setting up house. She has grown up, thank God. And I've written a play, which will soon be performed, though it'll be away from the glamour. Not sure whether to send the book to St Vincent Place. What do you think? P

The familiarity, as if the two of them were involved in a conversation across a table at Fasoli's rather than one conducted from opposite ends of the world, left Hamish feeling warmly towards his friend. He opened the book and summoned what he remembered of his rudimentary German to find that poems literally unearthed from his own childhood had become impenetrable, foreign things that he couldn't read for the life of him.

Hamish envied Paul's adventurousness and his audacity. He imagined a golden city and the iconoclasm of an Ibsen, while he toiled away in the same dull Melbourne that Paul had left behind.

But only a few months later the news from Europe cast everything in another light. Hamish would never forget that first week in August, 1914. Fevered crowds gathered outside the offices of the city's major newspapers, expecting a cable at any moment declaring that Britain and Germany were at war. The entire city seemed to be twitching in anticipation of a call to arms. Men waving Union Jacks were hoisted onto the shoulders of the undulating masses and bounced along to the strains of *Rule Britannia* or *Soldiers of the King*. After a while the enthusiasm would ebb away and frustration would set in, sometimes spilling into petty scuffles over the details of one's patriotism. When it finally became clear that there was nothing new to report, the crowds would dwindle away, only to re-form in full voice that evening or the following morning. On the fifth of the month Point Nepean fired a shot over the bow of a German steamer, ordering it to stop before it left Port Phillip Bay. Later, patriotic Australians, eager for a place in history, would claim that this was the first shot fired in anger by British forces, forces in fact which had already been at war with Germany for the better part of an hour.

The shot was audible across the southern suburbs of Melbourne. At least people claimed to have heard it. When talk of it reached South Yarra, Ondine wondered if the war had already come to their doorstep. For two years she had resisted Ralph's desire to move back to the Monaro. Now with war a matter of course she was only too happy to leave the city and take refuge in the remoteness of the country. Already the atmosphere had begun to turn ugly. Louts had thrown a brick through the window of Spielvogel's pawnshop on

City Road and politicians talked about passing a *War Precautions Act*, which would provide for the instant imprisonment of Australians of German descent. She knew that Ralph wanted to join the Light Horse and she couldn't bear the thought of him leaving her to fight on the other side of the world. He had already dropped all talk of the Monaro, in preparation, she suspected, for the moment in which he'd appear before her dressed in khakis and brown leather. It was pointless child's play to her, child's play turned into a grotesque reality that had men marching through the streets in step, swinging their arms and their rifles for the most abstract of possible causes: the British Empire.

When she had married Ralph three years earlier, Ondine had experienced a moment of liberation as she left Paul behind for the unpretentious liberality of her husband's family. Ralph was a fine husband, a sensitive lover and had a constructive vision of a future in public life. He was working towards a career in politics. It didn't interest her in the slightest and for this reason his increasing involvement with it seemed to free her into a space which was entirely her own. But what to do with this space? She wasn't really sure. She could feel something gestating in her, though its fruition seemed a long way off.

Despite his political and military ambitions, Ralph remained committed to the land, at least in principle. He took her to his family's vast property and Ondine was overwhelmed by its immensity and the grandeur of the landscape, though the thought of staying there filled her with dread. When Ralph went out on the muster or inspected the place on horseback, leaving her alone in the huge sandstone homestead, she felt lost, swallowed up by another existence that was not her own. She knew she would never arrive at herself in such a place. It was too gigantic, too monumental, and she felt like an inconsequential speck cast against its enormity. She always returned to Melbourne with a sense of relief, instantly recognising the ground on which her own potential might unfold.

But now the war was threatening that sense of belonging. As the nation mobilised, issued edicts and drew thousands of young men into its armed ranks, violence, it seemed, had ceased to be an exceptional state. It had become universal, and sickeningly banal as a result. She couldn't understand how Ralph could be so eager to join up, how he could allow himself to be engulfed by it, obliterated as an individual and resurrected into the grinning masses arranged arbitrarily into nations and forced to march at the command of alien powers.

"You've always said you're an Australian, not a British subject," she remonstrated. "What does a war in Europe have to do with us? It's a million miles away."

"We're still British," he said. "At heart, I mean."

"I'm not," she said. "Nor is my mother. And Paul, for all I know, will be fighting for the Austro-Hungarians. Perhaps we'll all be locked up."

He took her hand. "Nobody is going to lock you up. You know that."

"Do I?"

For Ralph, in fact, enlisting was not a matter of loyalty to Britain or its empire. It was much simpler than that. The thought of other men, ordinary men like the ones who worked on his father's property or went to office jobs in the city, the thought of these men in the uniform of their country while he remained a civilian was mortifying. It was tantamount to being naked before them. He didn't dwell on abstract political ideals. He simply wanted to maintain his dignity. Nothing was more important to him. The ease with which he had taken Ondine away from her craven, degenerate brother and asserted their equality as the basis of their love would all count for nothing if he turned his back on that. But he hadn't reckoned on her resistance.

"I just don't see what this has to do with us," she said again.

"We can't simply stand aside when it's going on all around us, while others are sacrificing themselves. I couldn't live with that."

It meant nothing to her, the pride and the idea of sacrifice. She looked away from him, afraid of what was before them – the drab khaki terror of war, her mother sick with worry for her brother, the triteness of a women's campaign on the home-front, launched against all those brave enough to refuse the madness.

"We have to step up, both of us, as man and wife," he said.

"Well, why not step up for sanity? What good are you to me dead?"

"What good am I to you if I don't live up to myself?"

Her resistance didn't make him angry. He had made up his mind and was impervious to her arguments. He only wished he could articulate the imperative to fight, the imperative he felt so clearly, but could not explain.

In the August of 1914 Winton was sixty-six, but he looked like a man ten years older. He had grown gaunt, his hair had thinned and his skin had sallowed. He had arthritis in his knuckles and the beginnings of it in his knees, such that his cane was now no longer a piece of dandyish affectation, but a necessity for even for the briefest stroll about the gardens of St Vincent Place. His wife, then forty-four, was also much changed. Anna Winton was still handsome. In fact, in another context she may have been nearing her prime, demonstrating the calm self-confidence of a woman in control of her fate and capable of exerting a degree of influence on those around her.

But she hadn't heard from her son for almost six months, and with the outbreak of war, feared that he had been incarcerated in an Austrian prison. The uncertainty of the situation had eaten away at her. She lay awake at night imagining him caught in a firestorm or lined up against a wall. And, surely enough, the mood in Melbourne had turned against Germans. She heard stories about plans to build a detention camp at Langwarrin for internal dissidents, and the fear this aroused in her brought her back to her first days in Melbourne when she dreamt of leaving Australia for good.

One morning, a woman in her late-fifties paused on the corner of Montague Street and St Vincent Place South, trying to match a house number with the one she carried jotted on a calling card. She edged down the street, peering into each house until she found the right one, then marched onto the verandah and rang the doorbell. Mrs Norris answered.

"I'm looking for Mrs Charles Winton," the woman said in a stiff, formal voice.

"You'll find her opposite on that park bench," said the housekeeper, pointing across the road to the gardens where Anna and Winton sat in the warm morning sun.

The woman looked behind her into the deep shadows of the palms and oaks that lined the edge of the park. The pair was lost in forgetfulness, the woman thought, but she had no doubt that she could relieve the melancholy of the scene, so thanked the housekeeper and promptly strode across the road.

Winton gave a start as he noticed the woman marching towards them.

"Mrs Winton," the woman said, thrusting out her hand. "I'm Eleanor Thomas."

"Yes?" said Anna vaguely.

Winton sat up straight.

"I take it your son hasn't mentioned me," the woman continued.

"No," said Anna. "I've not heard from my son for a long time. Do you know of him? I'm very worried."

Winton stood up belatedly and shook the woman's hand.

"Charles Winton," he said, eager not to alienate her with a display of apathy or bad manners.

"I'm Laura's mother," Eleanor Thomas added by way of clarification.

"What of my son?" Anna asked, trying to rein in her impatience.

"Your son has seduced my daughter, Mrs Winton. Utterly ruined her."

"So he's alive?"

"Oh yes. Very much so. A little too much so."

"But where?"

"Zurich. They're living in sin in Zurich, where your son runs an outlandish theatre performing obscene plays."

Anna leapt up and hugged the woman. "Thank you. Thank you for the news." She embraced her again, tears of relief in her eyes. "Come in and have some tea."

Eleanor Thomas relaxed her manner only slightly when she realised the torments Anna had been put through on behalf of her son.

"Switzerland? Will he be safe in Switzerland?" Anna asked Winton.

"Armed neutrality, as I understand it," he answered. "He might be safe there if nothing changes."

"Come in and tell me everything," Anna said, turning to Eleanor once again and taking her arm, leaving Winton to hobble on his own.

Eleanor Thomas had come ready for a confrontation. She distrusted Paul and believed him to be a libertine at heart, though perhaps not a malicious one.

"Now I won't pretend I wasn't appalled, Mrs Winton. Imagine. Flaunting decency like that. It wasn't like Laura, not one bit." That said, she softened her attitude. "Is Paul a stable sort of chap?" she asked. "He'll do the right thing, won't he? By Laura, I mean."

"I'm afraid I can't reassure you," Anna said. "He's not the most stable son a mother could wish for."

Eleanor winced, sucking air in through her teeth as Anna dragged her enthusiastically across the road and up the steps to the door.

Winton made his own way, lagging behind a bit. The two women were on the verandah before he'd made it across the road. Anna deposited Eleanor on the doorstep like a parcel and motioned back towards him.

"No, no. I'm all right." He waved her on inside, but it was to no avail. Anna came back down the stairs and took her husband by the arm. She couldn't contain her happiness and the doctor smiled as well to see such lightness of spirit for the first time in weeks.

A figure moved in the park behind them.

"Who's that?" Anna said.

A man was looking at them from quite close to where they had been sitting a moment earlier. Winton turned awkwardly and saw a ragged-looking fellow moving into a patch of sunlight. He squinted, the better to make out the matted hair and brown, sun-worn skin.

"No idea," Winton said. "A beggar sleeping in the gardens perhaps."

Inside, Eleanor Thomas finally dropped her guard when she realised that Paul Walters was a well-provided-for young man. She now came to recognise, too, that her daughter was fortunate to be out of Austria. As she drank her tea she even got a bit carried away, regaling them with her dry gallows humour. She told them stories of Vienna, the outlandish *Grand Guignol* Paul had worked out with Bressler, and her daughter's stubbornness. She could not abide their life of sin, but she did acknowledge that there was a certain glamour to being a bohemian and that perhaps it might ultimately stand her daughter in better stead than a marriage to a Western Districts farmer.

"He's even tried to make Laura wear ghastly white paint and scream at the top of her voice," she said, seeing the humour in it. "Though the day my girl makes a goat of herself on stage will be the day I turn up my toes and die of shame. If you'd seen one of these plays you'd understand why. All screams and fainting fits they are — lunatics, killers, wife-beaters, a whole cavalcade. Should be banned of course, but the Europeans are so much lower in their moral standards."

"I'm sure it's not as bad as all that," Anna said.

"Oh it is. Worse. You've never seen anything like it. I'm as forward thinking as the next woman, but the scandal of it, Mrs Winton. Really. They've even written up one actress because she screams so well when they murder her. Deafening it was."

They laughed.

"It's funny to think how delighted I am to hear that my son has disgraced himself. But with the war none of it seems that bad. Just as long as they stay clear of it."

"I'm pleased we met, Mrs Winton. In normal circumstances I don't think I'd be taking all of this so lightly. But I'm pleased we met."

"Call me Anna."

"All right then. Anna. You will write to Paul and urge him to do the proper thing by my daughter, won't you?"

"Of course. I'm sure he will."

In response to her careful questioning, Eleanor gradually gave out enough information for Anna to get a sense of what had happened. Paul's play was popular with a certain class of people, but as war seemed inevitable Bressler thought they'd have a hard time keeping the crowds. And in Zurich they'd also be out of danger.

"That's when Laura made her stand," Eleanor said. "And I put my foot down. Of course, what chance did I have? She told me flatly that there was no use me being angry, because it was too late, if you know what I mean. So we all went to Zurich and I put up my white flag."

The doorbell rang. Winton insisted on getting up, moving towards the door with the aid of his walking cane. He shooed Mrs Norris away and opened the door himself to find Les Collins standing before him.

Winton thought the man looked abysmal, though in fact the vagabond author looked at least as robust as the doctor. Collins was brown with the sun but his eyes were bloodshot and his teeth yellow. His smell, moreover, was intolerable, and when he opened his mouth Winton could see, alongside the golden, misshapen stubs, shockingly ulcerated gums, as if his entire mouth had rotted out.

"Sorry to bother you, Doc," he said.

Winton's blood boiled.

"Could have come a lot earlier, mind you. It's a last resort."

"I don't suppose you've come to talk about the Bunurong?" Winton said.

"No."

"You can't come in."

"How we gonna negotiate, then?"

"I'll call the police," Winton said.

"So will I," Collins replied, grinding his teeth. "I remember that poor girl. I remember what you did to her."

At that moment Winton cracked. Fighting off the confused memory of darkness, blood and the filthy brown water of the river, he struck Collins with his cane, sending the man stumbling back down the steps into the yard. Collins steadied himself, clutching his forehead just above his eye.

"Are we clear then?" Winton said, hobbling forward with his cane raised.

"You'll fucking well regret that," Collins sneered at him and took off down the street muttering recriminations.

Winton already was. It was a foolhardy thing to do. The man held his fate in his hands. How hard would it have been to pay him off, Winton asked himself. He cringed at the thought of the bleeding girl dumped in the river and the headlines trumpeting the resolution of the mystery thirty years later. In an age of sensationalism he'd be hung out to dry, if not hanged quite literally in Russell Street's grim old gaol. He propped himself against the wall and caught his breath, wanting to crawl away to die like an old cat.

As he moved back down the hallway he could hear his wife's joy as she soaked up the detail of her son's fortunes and made the best of Laura Thomas's transgressions. She was truly happy for the first time in months. The contrast with his own situation was intolerable. His hands shook and he pictured himself as one of the madhouse neurotics in the play that Eleanor Thomas had just described to them.

After struggling to compose himself, he resumed his position in the sitting room, declared it was a charity worker at the door, and politely pursued the details of Eleanor's story. He sat stiffly, listening distractedly as they decided that when things settled down in Europe the two women would travel to Zurich to see their children.

"You've always wanted to go to Europe," Winton said, holding his wife's hand.

"And now we will."

Eleanor Thomas sat there for an eternity, drinking her way through two pots of tea, describing one city after another and still finding plenty of time to lament her daughter's lost innocence. When she was finally ready to leave Anna urged her to come again and then decided to walk her to the tram on Park Street, leaving Winton on the verandah searching the street for signs of Collins.

When the women were out of sight he went back inside, leaving the door open. He slowly climbed the staircase and dragged himself into his study, where he sat down at his writing desk and took a small revolver from the bottom drawer. As he stared at the gun he very deliberately thought the whole thing over, balancing his wife's horror against the pale face of the girl as her life bled away; his vision of her limp body hauled out of the river; Les Collins's rotted mouth accusing him and, lastly, his public humiliation in front of the woman he loved and depended upon. Sixty-six, he told himself, an old man with a young wife. He had already transferred some capital to Anna, and most of what remained was willed to her and the children. All his affairs were in order. Yes, he had done well by them. Nobody could complain about him. He had done well. All in order. As he put the barrel of the revolver into his mouth and slowly squeezed the trigger he wondered how Albert Walters could have plunged into the river with his house in such a state of disarray. But the man was mad, he told himself.

~

Charles Winton was buried with the terrible secret of his past. Everything else he could live down, but the thought of that one revelation was something he could not endure. The unsolved mystery of his suicide left Anna inconsolable. Its impenetrability was worse to her than anything she could imagine accounting for it. She remembered Sid Packard once said that the doctor reminded him of someone. Or was it that he recognised him from somewhere? The implication, the sense of the unknown, sapped her of her strength. She worked over everything she knew about Charles, and found no decisive answer, though behind the secure, scientific assumptions of social hygiene and sexual pathology, she glimpsed a dark form moving in and out of view, without betraying any of its detail.

During the war people in the area talked from time to time about poor, pale Anna and her two dead husbands. What had she done to them? There was something not right about it. Even Robert Walters stayed clear of St Vincent Place. The house developed a sickly, funereal calm, as if it were a mausoleum. Only Ondine came back, and after Ralph left for the fighting in France, the two women lived there like nuns attending the cult of their solitude.

# part FIVE

## chapter *Twenty-one*

Ondine could never quite imagine the war in Europe. She was conscious of this as a failure. Years after it was all over she'd lie awake at night and try to picture it. Trenches propped up with bodies, entrails spilling over the mud. She wanted to understand what had happened to Ralph and how he had died, but her need to evoke the horror went beyond that. She wanted to see if she was still capable of feeling.

The war had seemed unreal right from the start. The images of bitter, inveterate enemies, so prevalent in home-front propaganda as the conflict unfolded, bore no direct relationship to her own experience of people. She wondered if ordinary men, once they became soldiers, really felt that hatred, or whether they were simply and mechanically obeying their orders, running blindly out of the trenches at the command of something more remote than their own sense of injustice. They said it was the first war in history in which death had been thoroughly depersonalised. Did that mean that soldiers fought with no sense of themselves or that they were killed by machines? What had happened to the actuality of death? She couldn't imagine any of it. What had the war been but a vast puppet show in which individuals performed their roles in a largely unconscious fashion, with no sense of their own being realised in the terrible killing? There was no greater travesty, she thought, than to deprive men of their sense of self as they were killed, to turn them into automatons. It was as bad as leaving bodies unburied or desecrating graves in order to show that a man is simply the crude sum of his parts.

When she saw Ralph in his khaki Light Horse uniform before training camp in Broadmeadows, the foolery of military dress struck her as a sign of the impersonal death awaiting him. She'd been expecting it for weeks. It was as if the living soul of her husband had already been smothered under the khaki, the brown leather, the glistening gold buttons and insignia.

Eighteen months later Ralph was killed, along with almost two thousand other young Australians, in an overnight battle on a piece of French farmland. Not a single British soldier fell. The Australians were the front line. Dawn broke and the commanding officer surveyed the mess of broken bodies on the battlefield. Death, on such a scale, had already become routine, and the war was to drag on for another two years.

When it was over the soldiers who had survived returned to Melbourne and marched through the streets to the frantic cheers of the crowd. The city was festive and Ondine hoped the jubilation would begin to dissolve the impersonality of the war, as soldiers marched together, then one by one shed their uniforms and resumed their roles as people with homes and families, with loyalties and animosities so much more real than the obscure motivations and fantastic chimeras that had flung them out across the battlefields. She wondered what it meant to talk about "a national triumph" in that light. That's what the newspapers and politicians called it. What would triumph now was something far smaller and more intimate than the nation, which was nothing but a vast image-making machine, a magic lantern throwing up shadowy images on a wall, generating a hypnotic trance that could have millions of men going to meet their deaths as if they were zombies. She hated the nation, hated its cold, murderous malice. Its collective dream was the nightmare of modern times, and she had lain awake through it, eyes fixed on the darkness, while others around her restlessly tossed and turned at its bidding.

But in another sense her refusal to be drawn into the collective hysteria of the home-front also had something dreamlike about it. After Winton's death, before the war had even really caught on, her mother sank into a mild state of catalepsy. She continued with her routine of rose pruning and her sedate walks through the gardens, but now this domestic rhythm had the quality of a kind of ghost-seeing, serving not to distract her from her sorrow, but to bring her closer to it.

Early in 1915 Ondine tried to convince her mother to accompany her to the Matthews's property in New South Wales, but Anna was reluctant to leave and eventually Ondine gave up. After Ralph had left for the war, she moved back into the St Vincent Place house where she assumed the responsibility her mother had relinquished. Pruning the roses became more important than regular meals for Anna and her walks through the gardens continued even through torrential rain, such that she was frequently fighting off chills and fevers while her daughter fretted over her neglected and increasingly bedraggled appearance.

In this state of virtual isolation the two women were like a couple of ascetics inhabiting the still centre of a maelstrom. All around them the world swelled and burnt in constant, tumultuous anger. Whenever Ondine opened a paper she was confronted with it. The leaders had gotten suddenly bigger and threatened to outgrow the size of the broadsheet, and photographs of light and shadow and fire occupied entire pages. Her mother would sit down, glance negligently at the front page and then cast the paper aside, as if she were tired of reading or unconvinced of the reality. Ondine felt as if they were both being bleached by the lethargy of this static existence.

"You're white, Mother, white as a ghost," she said one day as they were reading on the upstairs verandah.

"Am I, dear?" Anna said vaguely.

It was too much for Ondine, the resigned indifference, the inane formalities of their conversation, the sense of slowly wasting away. She dropped her book on the bench beside her and went back inside, determined to assert herself against this vacuum of loneliness and protracted grief.

When the news of Ralph's death finally reached her, months after the battle of Fromelles, it was as if he had been dead since the beginning of the war. She chided herself for this lack of feeling. What had happened to her? The moments, years earlier, when she was so in love with him and felt her heart beating faster at the thought of meeting him at the opera, were like scenes coloured by the giddy lightness of childhood. Now her body had shut down. She saw her mother already existing in this almost vegetative state and, fearful of the same numbness, dreamt of flailing herself open to the world, letting her body be hacked at until the nerves tingled anew.

~

In 1916 the city was already full of casualties from the early years of the conflict. In the pubs, hotels, arcades and markets, one could see men with canes, crutches, prosthetic limbs or empty sleeves and trouser legs limping through their tragedy in various degrees of drunkenness and stupefaction. The first time Ondine walked through the city after Ralph's death she was struck by the motley collection of war veterans shuffling about the city.

She had walked towards the Yarra and over Princess Bridge with the vague intent of reanimating something in her, of escaping the moribund atmosphere of St Vincent Place. But the city was not made for a single woman out on her own. It was a grey, drizzling day in October, the kind of day when winter rain and summer humidity seem indistinguishable and the city sinks into its own foul atmosphere of sweat and steam. Shop interiors had fogged up and beads of condensation ran down the insides of the windows. Stepping into the Block Arcade Ondine felt as if she were entering a hothouse. Her blouse was wet, whether from rain or her own body she couldn't tell. Some women in Red Cross uniforms were sitting in the window of the Hopetoun Tea Rooms. There was a poster for the All British League on the wall. A walrus-moustached officer gazed at her approvingly as he leant back smoking a cigar. For a moment she felt affronted by the frankness of his stare, but quickly collected herself and walked off towards Block Place.

She didn't really know where she was going. She was just walking aimlessly. She imagined the officer in the tea rooms following her, accosting her and offering her money for sex. What would she have done? Perhaps she would have refused the money and given herself to him just the same in some greasy alleyway. At that moment it would have been of no consequence to her. She felt nothing except the thin film of moisture on her body. In an effort to provoke herself she imagined squatting like an animal on the wet cobblestones in front of him, performing a parody of desire aroused by the squalor of the streets. Could she excite herself by walking with the dead, by giving herself to the low-life of the city? The thought didn't disgust her. It simply came down to the choices one made, and these struck her as a matter of indifference. Several times she walked through the arcades, or through the Eastern Market, glancing at the men loitering outside the peepshows. She wondered what she was capable of doing in her numbed state amidst the smells of rotting vegetables and the ragged, vagabond characters that gathered about these parts of the city like creatures homing towards the shadows.

And still, when she tried to picture the horror of war all she could grasp was horror in the abstract. She imagined the carnage of modern times reduced to the sordid comedy of stagecraft, histrionics and special effects engineered by her brother. The letters and cuttings Paul sent back to South Melbourne from Zurich described his success in the theatre. Even while the war was still being fought, while men were being slaughtered across Europe in their tens of thousands, Paul wrote plays about a military asylum overrun by its inmates, and a shell-shocked maniac unleashed on the home-front to seek a terrible revenge upon his adulterous wife. The plays struck her as vulgar, turning horror into farce.

Paul also sent her photographs. There was one of him looking contemplative as he smoked a cigarette and edited a script, and another of him and Laura, soon after they were married. Paul wore a dark suit and a tie, Laura a long, striped frock. They both smiled with a self-assurance that Ondine found disingenuous. Behind them were some tenements with shops along the street. The background was tranquil. No people, no traffic, no sign of the war. It was as if they'd found their way into an idyllic place safely beyond its reach, as if they'd managed to escape from history. Ondine didn't believe it. She threw the picture down on the table with a fit of temper, and once again tried to conjure the nightmare of her husband's death.

## chapter Twenty-Two

In the *chambre séparée* they didn't say a word to each other, just as she'd insisted. Laura closed her eyes. Paul leant over her. His hands were on her hips. She could tell he was fumbling, trying to be considerate, so she moved her legs apart to help him. She wanted to get it over with, but it all happened more easily than she had imagined. The movement of Paul's body and the rhythm of his breathing prompted her responses. When he was finished she covered her body and looked at him as he lit a cigarette. He was heavier than she'd imagined. His stomach had a thickness to it and his chest sagged.

"*Weib oder Frau?*" Klessmann's voice followed her now. It was like a tune she couldn't get out of her head. The next day, when Paul showed her the play he was working on, she knew straightaway that the main character was Klessmann. She was certain of it. The image of the skull pushing through his skin was indelible.

When the play opened she could hardly bring herself to watch it. The man at the door raised his cap to her. The theatre was a run-down firetrap: smoke, hot lights and bodies jamming in, one upon the other. Afterwards, they went to the American Bar to celebrate with Bressler. She found it difficult to be her usual bright self, but she made a good fist of it. She wondered how Paul could write such a horrible play and still be the same person she'd fallen in love with. She suspected him of hiding behind a façade and imagined she had seen beyond it in the dreadful violence of the Hamburg maniac on a killing spree across Europe. When they got back to his apartment he kissed her neck and eyes. He was trying to make her feel comfortable, but it felt false to her.

"Do you love me, Paul?"

"How can you doubt it?" he said.

"Because your play is about Theodore Klessmann, isn't it?"

"What makes you say that?"

Paul was sure she hadn't seen the poster of Klessmann in Wedelkind's "Theatre of Derangement".

"I just have a sense of it."

At the mention of Klessmann Paul was overcome with guilt. He wondered, as he'd often done since the night of his death, whether he had said anything to Laura about the book. Paul would have given anything to wipe that bird-face from his mind. It haunted him. It accused him. It gnawed away at his resolve.

"You didn't like the play, then?" he asked.

"It was frightening. That's what you wanted though, wasn't it?" She kissed him. "I think you're very clever."

She decided to leave Paul's play alone. She was happy with him as long as she could keep at arm's length the disquiet she felt at the thought of it. After all, the press had written the play up and people had paid money to see it. Moreover, she liked Herman Bressler a great deal. He struck her as avuncular, not the sort to go about compromising himself.

It was Bressler's idea to take them all to Zurich. He was being prudent, she thought, and had an eye for their welfare. Paul married her six months after they arrived there. Her mother had already left Europe and her absence was a huge relief for them both. They were settled together, at last.

Laura liked Zurich. She met unusual people there – artists and eccentrics who'd come to avoid the war. Paul was often with Bressler, writing scripts and building sets, so she had time to wander about on her own. She met a German woman – Hilda Meyerhold – who took her to a cabaret tucked away in a basement under the Spiegelgasse. The two of them went there often. People wore outrageous costumes, read nonsense poetry on stage, played imaginary violins, rambled on about the end of art and generally played the fool. It was bizarre, but beside Paul's plays she found it all very innocent. She felt civilised now, urbane. It pleased her no end and for a while it gave her a feeling of security that she hadn't known before.

Still, when she yielded, as she occasionally did, and went to see one of her husband's plays, she was deeply troubled. They seemed to threaten the stability of their life together, to mock it in a way that she didn't fully understand. Paul talked about being part of the avant-garde. He took it all very seriously. She didn't understand how he could keep this seriousness up amid howling lunatics and hacked-up bodies. Next to the horror of his plays everything else looked two-dimensional.

One night she decided to test him. They'd come back from a café and both of them were pleasantly light-headed from the wine.

She waited for him to get affectionate. She knew the formula: hands in the hair, kisses on the neck, a deliberate, gentle stroking of her arms and back.

"No, Paul," she said. "Don't treat me like a piece of porcelain. I'm not about to break."

But that night he made love to her with more restraint than ever before. It was as if her demand had tamed whatever she sensed lurking within him, and for a while at least she felt relieved, though it left her still empty and unfulfilled.

It took months before the formalities of their marriage really began to drop away. At first, Paul merely paid less attention to her pleasure and got through with his more quickly. It made little difference to her. Then he began to change. It was around the time he began to translate his father's book back into English. He was more erratic and impetuous. He made her do things she'd never dreamt of doing, guided her to them in a way she sometimes found thoughtless. At first it shocked her. She couldn't believe it was her. Sometimes she felt ill. Sometimes she found the theatrics curious, even laughable. The question *Weib* or *Frau* had ceased to matter to her. She was neither. She was something else entirely, in her own *chambre séparée*, the place she went to when she needed to be free of him.

She thought about Hilda Meyerhold, who sometimes wore trousers and a jacket. She thought about the first time she saw Paul on board the *Abendstern* and imagined he was the height of sophistication. At the cabaret she had a cigarette, her first, but when the war was finally over Hilda went back to Berlin and Laura's world began to contract. One by one people left Zurich and filtered back across Europe. Paul and Bressler hung on for two more years. Laura felt like the last girl at the dance, hanging around after everyone else had left. She knew she'd missed her chance.

There was talk of going to America, but finally Bressler went back to Vienna and Paul decided it was time to return to Melbourne. While the Swiss audiences had been constant, interest had begun to drop off after the fighting had ended and the novelty had run its course. Those last years in Zurich were trying. The theatre lost money and without an audience to fill the place, the plays were pointless. Paul couldn't put them on only for a handful of devotees; the screams from the floor, the laughter and the sense of mass panic were so integral to the overall effect. When Laura saw how hard Paul was working she did her best to help him and finally got her hands dirty working backstage, filling trick knives with fake blood and making up the actors. By then she found the plays more tedious than shocking. As the crowds diminished, so did Paul's enthusiasm.

They both knew it was time to move on, but Paul was not completely discouraged. He now dreamt of success in Melbourne that would efface once and for all his failure a decade earlier. He was confident he could do something wonderful. As they boarded a steamer in Bremen he was already feverishly jotting down notes for a new play to be set in the Eastern Arcade – *The Cabinet of Anatomical Curiosities*.

During the six-week voyage, Laura scrutinised Paul with renewed intensity. It was the first time in years, probably since Vienna, that they'd been in each other's company so constantly. In Zurich, Paul had been absorbed in his plays. For long periods of time he seemed to think of nothing else. But as the ship neared Australia, Paul became more self-conscious, more concerned with the dubious stature of his achievement, and this also began to consume him. Laura noted that he had changed physically as well during the voyage. Somehow his body had become even thicker and his skin a touch greyer. There was the beginning of a liver spot on his temple. Once, when she saw him sitting in the dining room chatting amicably with a steward, she was shocked to find that she almost didn't recognise him. His stomach was like a round melon, the skin under his chin had doubled and his fingers were like plump chipolatas. How odd, she thought, remembering the thin, rakish young man she'd fallen in love with on their voyage out. She chided herself for her superficiality and sat down beside him. He talked confidently about his plans for Melbourne and boasted about Zurich with all the gaudy aplomb of a practised showman. It had never really occurred to her that he was an entertainer, not an artist, but his brashness now convinced her of it. She had given up her romantic view of things years ago, but as the ship approached Australia she couldn't help but suspect the disillusioning effects of the country's pitiless realism.

At night, as the ship swayed with the motion of the sea, her husband's body rocked away on top of her in a manner that would have been comical if it had not been so oblivious. The cabin was small, and the heat reminded her of country Victoria — the farm, the sheep dung, the swarms of blowflies humming through the long, dry summers. His hands always held her down, pushing into her shoulderblades. She'd just lie there on her stomach and try to relax. Afterwards he was always kind. But in the musty cabin, feeling the undulating ocean beneath them, she found the rankness of their bodies hanging in the hot air humiliating.

By the time Anna and Ondine greeted them on the verandah of the family home, Paul had developed into the epitome of condescension. At another time this might have been amusing, but right now Laura felt he'd shattered the ease of their arrival. After almost a decade away — the most momentous decade in recent memory at that – Paul sauntered into the house on St Vincent Place like a jaunty prodigal son. His flippancy was abrasive. Laura cringed as she watched him greet his family with a throwaway familiarity that jarred with the sombre habits of solitude that so clearly hung over the house.

Mrs Norris roasted a leg of lamb in honour of the occasion and Anna welcomed her new daughter-in-law with as much warmth as she could muster. The conversation at dinner rambled over trivialities, the details of the voyage and European anecdotes which Paul dispensed as if he were scattering rare jewels of culture and erudition over the table.

"You simply must go, Mother. You too, Ondine. Imagine how much easier it is to live in the midst of noble cathedrals, great museums, gigantic libraries, and the accumulated effects of the centuries in such ancient cities."

"We might have gone, but your return is certain to keep us here a bit longer," Ondine said.

"In Europe one can breathe freely. One need only open one's eyes to be inspired."

"It's a wonder you came back," Anna said, smiling.

"Well, I'd imagine that we will go back sooner or later. Wouldn't you say so, darling?"

"Yes, it's quite likely," Laura answered.

"But what about the war?" Ondine asked. "I'd imagine that half of Europe lies in ashes."

"Three years have made a world of difference. And besides, everything is pretty much as it was. It was the countryside that saw the fighting. The cities are largely untouched."

Later, in the sitting room, Laura noticed that Paul appeared anxious when he spoke to his sister. He seemed a bit unbecoming, stumbling to express himself, tripping over complicated sentences and catching himself out in the convoluted meandering of his own eccentric ideas about life and art.

"I don't know about popular entertainment, Paul," Ondine said as she poured the tea. "It surprised me to hear that you'd embraced the popular mood so thoroughly."

"Embraced it? Rubbish. I've shaped it. Made it modern and done away with all that lyrical nonsense."

"Made it modern? What are you talking about?"

"Well, I mean contemporary – the shattered psyche of the age. You know what I mean. The war and all that."

Ondine said nothing. She was aware of how constantly neglectful Paul had been of Ralph's death.

"Look, Ond, my point is that entertainment, what you so derisively would call amusement, can be relevant. It can capture the spirit of the age and express something new."

"Well," Ondine said calmly and without a hint of animosity in her voice, "I think you could be accused of making light of it."

"Not at all. There is a profundity there."

"Paul, I'm led to believe that the *Grand Guignol* is the very opposite. Cheap effects, sensationalism, and painfully obvious gestures. Bathos and bluster. A child's theatre really, as the name suggests."

Paul bristled. He glanced at Laura, who sat impassively, well aware that she too was being indicted by these comments.

"And what about you, Laura?" Anna asked with no clear idea of the information she was requesting.

"Yes, what about you?" Ondine turned to her solicitously. "We've heard enough from Paul. Has the *Grand Guignol* been as unequivocally fulfilling for you as it has for my brother?"

Laura blinked at the question, revealing long dark eyelashes and what Ondine thought a touching reserve.

"Well, yes," she said finally, a bit hopelessly, not wanting to be disloyal to Paul. But as Ondine raised her eyebrows quizzically, she realised that this reply could do her no credit in her sister-in-law's eyes. "In Zurich people were talking about the plays all the time." She tried to sound authoritative but sank into her chair as she spoke, letting her shoulders drop in unconscious acknowledgment of how unprepossessing she was.

"What people?" Ondine demanded.

"The public," Paul put in.

"A beastly thing, the public," Ondine said. "A vulgar thing. I can't bear it."

"Don't tell me you're going to refuse to come along to my plays, just because they appeal to the public?"

"Of course I'll come."

"Good. They'll be a sensation. You'll hear the screams across the bay."

It occurred to Ondine that she was not overly fond of her brother right now, even though he had a right to expect some warmth from her after his long absence. She felt that Laura was withdrawn and a bit insipid. Paul, she suspected, had robbed this girl of her will, turned her into something pliable and lifeless. In Europe she must have been completely dependent on him – as dependent as a child or a slave. The thought of it put her on edge. A vague, destructive impulse welled within her as she contemplated the apathy that was expected of her own sex in the service of male creativity.

Laura imagined she could sense her sister-in-law's disdain for her. It was evident in Ondine's impatience with Paul. And in perceiving the new and revealing light in which Paul was cast by his sister's sober questioning and lack of sympathy, Laura found her own confidence diminishing. She did not find the sorority she had expected in her husband's home and she felt as if she had been left to fend for herself. Ondine was like some vision of the ideals for which men fight. Even at that point Laura suspected her fear and admiration would mingle in equal parts, but now she felt like a tortoise without its shell, and couldn't wait to escape the penetrating gaze of Ondine's clear, blue eyes.

It was almost midnight when Anna retired. Paul swirled a glass of aromatic, orange liqueur. It was the moment he had been waiting for. Ondine stood up and stretched drowsily. When they kissed goodnight on the landing outside their old rooms, Paul gave her a small parcel wrapped in gold paper.

"A gift from the old world," Paul said. "Don't show it off to Mother."

"Why?" Ondine asked with a shrug of her shoulders, questioning the shape of the book inside the paper with her hands. "Is it the forbidden yellow book? How predictably decadent of you."

"Better than that. It's the family archive. I was lucky to get it through customs."

Laura stood awkwardly beside her husband. She wanted to add something prescient in front of Ondine, but all she could think of was Klessmann. The merest mention of him in conjunction with the book was sure to irritate Paul. They never talked about him now. He was a secret they shared in silence.

"What is the family archive? Never mind. I'm about to find out." She kissed her brother again, chastely, and then, unexpectedly, gave Laura a hug.

As Laura followed Paul into his old room, which had now been made up for the two of them, and watched Ondine glide into hers, this brief physical impression was rounding itself out in her mind and she brimmed with adoration.

"Your sister is dazzling," she said to him as she sat down on the bed.

"Yes. Dazzling like white light, or the rays of the sun reflected in the snow," Paul said affectedly. "But she doesn't understand that men prefer to prey on garbage."

Laura turned away from this comment. Paul had once explained the meaning of the line from *Hamlet* in which garbage might be taken to mean entrails.

"I'm going to sleep," she said. And with that put on her nightgown and then, ill at ease, watched Paul undress on the opposite side of the room.

In her own room Ondine tore off the gold wrapping paper and found a volume of poetry. The Gothic lettering on the title page read *Nocturnes* by Albert Walters. Translated from the German. As she tried to fathom the mystery of this revelation she was already reading the first page.

A child wrapped in a white shawl stood on the sand. The writing lingered lasciviously over the detail of her mouth, her red tongue, and her white teeth. The water sparkled as the sun set. The toxic waste of the city leaked into the spongy depths of the bay. A magician, expert in French letters, stalked the streets. The sky slowly burned itself out, shadows danced by the lamplight and the mouths of painted women dripped with blood.

She turned the pages one after the other, barely aware that she was reading at all. In her father's sick imagination faces leered out of the darkness, velvet curtains concealed freaks and monstrosities of a sexual nature, poisonous flowers gave off noxious fumes, the abortions of the ocean dragged themselves from the water to rot in gutters, and bodies decomposed outside the walls of the city. The orange lights of the markets and the arcades conjured the obscure properties of the night. The God of Christianity was dead, usurped by the evil powers and savage retributions of primitive religions. The world was made of ash and blood, the heathen fear of darkness, strange shapes trembling in the sky. At times it all read like gibberish as the images proliferated in an uncontrolled, hysterical outpouring of depravity and perversity which circled around visions of prostitutes, gutter-crawlers, strangers lost in shadows, shameful encounters and violent crimes in a city collapsing into its own foundations.

Ondine imagined her father's secret and disgraceful life. She closed her eyes for a moment and remembered her own wanderings through the city of crippled soldiers. The cult of the prostitute. Her father worshipped these women as if they were deities, the mystical bearers of desire and death. She wondered about her mother. She wondered about Paul, and half suspected him of concocting the whole thing either as some elaborate literary hoax or as a ridiculous exercise in self-aggrandisement.

What Paul called the family archive was a web of symbols, obscene clichés and obscure confessions that alluded to a great, but unnameable, crime. The whore pointed to the corpse, the corpse pointed to the killer, the killer gave way to the drunken wanderer, the wanderer was himself a madman or a poet who demanded punishment by mutilation or blinding at the hands of terrible, omniscient forces presiding over the city since the beginning of time. All of these moments bled into one another, all circled around the transgression that festered behind the words like an infection.

Ondine felt the darkness pressing around her. She shuddered as she read, remembering her father's eyes fixed on her with a mysterious intent. "My daughter's wanton eyes shine like razor blades as the burning curtain falls." She wanted to feel disgust or hatred, but there was something contrived to her in that. In fact she felt queer, sensing the way in which the words robbed her of herself. That was the only way she could describe it.

That night she dreamt of the house on Brooke Street. Underneath the rotting floorboards she could see pupae clinging to the wooden bearers and joists. When they hatched, darkly-coloured moths — blood-red, purple and black — flew into the house and hovered in front of dusty dressing-table mirrors. The house was full of mirrors so that each moth threw off a host of reflected images as it hurtled about. But the moths all had damaged wings and, one by one, they dropped to the floor, where they twitched and struggled against the force of gravity until the remaining floorboards were thick with them. Ondine struggled out of her dream to warn her father that his heavy boots were going to crush the moths, making a bloody mess that she wouldn't want to look at. Already her bare feet had squashed some of the dying creatures into a thick brown pulp. She couldn't endure it. She had to warn her father, but with every step she took towards him, she killed more moths until, finally, the whole house was strewn with crushed bodies and torn wings and the soles of her feet were wet with blood. The dream gripped her until the killing was over. When she finally awoke, she knew that she had been the guilty one. In the first confused moment of consciousness she imagined that the savage judge would come for her as well.

## chapter twenty-three

The war had passed by Hamish McDermott. Overweight and suffering from what the military doctor described as collapsed arches, he was initially ruled out of active service. He hadn't wanted to fight anyway, sensing something sycophantic in the Australian response to a European crisis, especially with the Americans keeping well clear. But that was a difficult thing to admit to in a climate of frantic mobilisation and mounting national sentiment. For a few weeks in 1915, after reporting on a meeting of Irish nationalists for the *Melburnian*, he was placed under investigation by the police as a potential Sinn Fein sympathiser and was even threatened with incarceration at Langwarrin until the investigating officers realised that they were barking up the wrong tree. He never received a white feather in the mail, but when uniformed men brushed past him in the street, or women glanced disparagingly, he always felt that he was being accused. Galled by these perceived insults and feeling a kind of anxiousness that he didn't doubt would finally have a physiological effect on him, he thought he might as well put on a uniform, for the sake of appearances. As the army gradually eased up on its exclusion of unfit recruits, Hamish was posted to an administrative office in the St Kilda Road barracks, where he spent his time drawing up futile lists of resources for the military to commandeer.

He saw Ondine only once during those years. It was shortly after he had joined up. She was standing on the corner of Bourke and Elizabeth Streets, outside the post office, wearing a grey skirt and matching jacket. Hamish had just left the Royal Arcade and was standing on the other side of the street. He recognised her in an instant and was about to cross the road to greet her when a man in uniform appeared beside her. Without saying a word to each other, they crossed the road and walked right past Hamish into the arcade. Ondine's eyes were fixed in front of her with an apathy that reminded him of the deadness in her mother's eyes, the deadness he had never ceased to yearn for. The young man in the uniform was an officer who walked with a slight limp and the aid of a cane. Hamish watched them head towards the Little Collins Street end of the arcade and decided to follow them. They crossed into Block Place and, from the corner of Little Collins Street, Hamish saw Ondine unlock a red wooden door about halfway down the narrow lane, into which the two of them disappeared.

He stood on the corner wounded by what he'd seen. Perhaps he felt betrayed. Perhaps he felt simply jealous. He could have waited for her to reappear and offered her money to fuck him, or beaten the man she was with until he confessed everything. He waited for almost an hour. The afternoon faded into twilight and still neither Ondine nor the soldier reappeared. Finally Hamish dragged himself back to his flat on Flinders Lane feeling sullied by the prurience of his own curiosity. His penis was still hard when he lay down on his bed and imagined that he was the soldier she'd led through the mysterious red door. Often after that he walked through Block Place, casting an inquisitive glance at the red door, or lingered around the Royal Arcade feeling his heart beat faster with anticipation. But his efforts were in vain. He didn't see Ondine again until well after the war was over.

It was the opening night of Paul's play. Laura was backstage, reluctantly painting faces with carmine and rice powder, Anna had shown no inclination to venture out, so Ondine was alone. She was pleased to see Hamish, kissed him on the cheek and insisted that they sit together, for old times' sake. In the vestibule they walked past a booth behind which sat a doctor in a white coat offering to take people's pulses and check their blood pressure in case they doubted their ability to withstand the shock of what they were about to witness.

"This ought to be an interesting experiment," Hamish said as they made their way towards the front of the theatre and sat down.

"Oh, experiment nothing. I'm sure people will love it. My brother has become much shrewder than when we used to know him."

Hamish noticed the muted cynicism in her voice.

"I meant to ask you, Hamish, did Paul ever show you a book by my father – *Romanze zur Nacht* or *Nocturnes*?"

"I have both of them." He blushed as he said this, aware that his possession of these volumes had given him something over her.

The lights dimmed and a double bass player among a small group of accompanists plucked out an eerily disjointed sequence of notes.

"And what do you think?" she asked, still looking straight ahead.

"I think your father was an inspired writer."

"You do?"

She seemed to want him to say more, so he obliged.

"That book is very well regarded in Germany and Austria, I hear."

"Who would have thought it? All the time my father was a German poet, pretending to be an Australian madman. Just goes to show you."

The curtain went up on a set designed to evoke a cross-section of the Eastern Arcade. One could see along the centre of the arcade, and into the interiors of a bordello on one side and the Cabinet of Anatomical Curiosities on the other, both of which were pushed out on slight angles so that they protruded towards the audience. The Cabinet of Anatomical Curiosities was crowded with body parts and model corpses half-hidden behind black veils. A drumbeat joined the double bass and a roundish man, characteristically made-up with white face paint and dark, purplish rings under his eyes, sauntered through the displays towards the door just as a pair of unsuspecting women were making their way down the centre of the arcade. The music stopped with a clash of cymbals. The man welcomed them into the museum, gave them a short speech about the educational benefits of the display and proceeded to reveal the models as, one by one, he flung the black veils into the air, giving a description of the particular sexual disease depicted each time. The two women screamed and drew back in horror with each new revelation of sickness and malformation. At the same time the audience mimicked their hysteria in a raucous cacophony of shrieks and laughter.

"They do have good lungs, I'll give them that," Ondine said over the noise of the crowd.

When the two women had regained some composure the man, who called himself Dr Podmore, blew on a whistle summoning half-a-dozen flunkeys from the wings – dwarfs, hunchbacks and other grotesques. Again the women screamed at the top of their lungs, and the audience roared with laughter as the withered little men grabbed at their legs and hands, snarling like vicious dogs.

"Now, my dears," the doctor said ominously, "I invite you to join my little show."

He drew a scalpel out of his jacket and twirled it expertly, suggesting a deft hand in foul play. One of the women wrenched herself free of the homicidal flunkeys and raced back into the arcade, her eyes searching vainly for help. But it was too late for her companion. As the double bass player tried to imitate the sound of a beating heart, the retracting blade of the fake scalpel sliced into the neck of the captured woman. The other woman ran to the front of the stage where she stood facing the audience, and let out an ear-splitting scream that vibrated through the fittings around the walls of the auditorium. The scream hung in the air for what seemed like a full minute as Dr Podmore butchered his victim. People wailed and hid their eyes. At the very moment when they could take no more, when horrified laughter and genuine terror had pushed the shuddering audience to the limit of its endurance, the scream stopped, the curtain fell on Act One and the lights went up, leaving the usually staid theatre-goers of Melbourne convulsed in their seats, afraid to look each other in the eye.

Even Ondine was red with laughter, though she quickly regained her composure and resumed her cynical air. Hamish was already making notes for the review he'd write the following day.

"Well then, what do you think?" Ondine said as people stood up, still recovering their senses of balance and proportion. "It's trashy, but I'll grant it a certain primal dignity. The screaming at least. I feel for these women though. I don't know how Paul gets them to do it. He's even tried to talk his own wife into it. Imagine."

"All I have to do is describe it," Hamish replied. "A plot summary and a brief account of how a few old women fainted and I've done my job. Don't you read the papers these days?"

"Not really."

"Well they don't give you much scope for an opinion."

"But if you had one what would it be? You're evading me, Hamish."

"If you want my opinion then here it is. *Grand Guignol* is not art in any conventional sense. It's not simply entertainment either. It's an expression, a clumsy expression perhaps, of the *thing*. The thing that underpins us – us as decent, orderly citizens, I mean. There."

"Yes. I understand you perfectly. The thing. If we wanted to be even more perverse we could call it *das Ding*. But even better to phrase it in some utterly unintelligible, inhuman language. The language of things themselves. Anyway, that's all very well. It's just that I don't believe you, unless by 'thing' you mean woman, some man's fantasy of eternal night, like in my father's awful poetry. It's all academic. I suppose if people want bread and circuses they can have them, though we have too much of both if you ask me."

She cut herself short as the lights dimmed again and the curtain went up. In The Cabinet of Anatomical Curiosities Dr Podmore unveiled his latest exhibit to his gang of deformed helpers. It was the body of the woman he had just murdered in Act One, cut open and displayed as an anatomical Venus.

"How on earth?" a voice whispered in the audience.

The doctor turned his attentions to the flunkeys who let the woman from the first act get away, whipping them with a long piece of cane as they cowered into the corners of the set. At the same time two policemen walked down the centre of the arcade and knocked on his door. The doctor gave some hasty hand signals and the horde of dwarfs and hunchbacks quickly concealed itself behind the models and display cases.

"How can I help you, officers?" the doctor said, welcoming them in.

"You're under arrest, Dr Podmore."

"Don't you find it prosaic?" Ondine whispered to Hamish. "It's dull, plodding stuff."

"But, officers, surely you have a warrant?"

"Under arrest for the abduction and assault of Miss Pixie Franklin."

"Abduction and assault?" said the doctor. "I can show you her body if you like. Then you'll have a bit more to go on than the say-so of a scatterbrained girl."

He gestured towards the anatomical Venus and the policemen both craned their heads to get a better look. The doctor beckoned and they followed him deeper inside. The door closed behind them. As the accompanists cranked out a few frenetically disjointed flurries, a multitude of tiny hands and angry mouths fastened upon the policemen, dragging them to the ground amidst desperate, panicked cries and groans.

Paul used the stage trick he first saw performed by Wedelkind in Hamburg. With their backs to the audience the dwarfs tossed up little pieces of raw meat and bits of papier-mâché soaked in red wax and dye, creating the impression that the two policemen were being torn to pieces. The audience screamed and shrank in revulsion from the carnage in front of it. In the background the steady beat of a drum created the atmosphere of a primitive ritual. The doctor capered with glee.

Meanwhile, in the bordello opposite, which had hitherto been shrouded in darkness, a dim lamp lit up a luxuriously appointed sitting room. A buxom brothel madam, hair swept up into a pompadour, presided over a harem of women draped upon velvet-covered couches.

Suddenly the woman from Act One appeared again at the top of the stage, in the centre of the arcade, leading a mob of concerned citizens, which included a priest, a tram conductor and some armed soldiers. They ran to the front of the stage, pausing before the audience in a posture of collective alarm, as if startled by the last groans of the mutilated policemen, who were now revealed to the audience as a mound of torn uniforms and bleeding body parts.

The woman banged on the door of the Cabinet of Anatomical Curiosities. The flunkeys scattered, retreating and exiting unnoticed by the audience, whose attention was now focused on the bodies and the startled Dr Podmore, who sniffed danger in the air. The mob burst into the room, sparking a mad chase around the models, which sent bodies tumbling in a comically arranged sequence of choreographed mayhem. Finally the pursued doctor managed to escape into the arcade, where he flew directly to the door of the brothel.

"Madam Mazel," he cried. "Please. Mercy."

The door opened and the doctor fell panting onto the scarlet carpet at the feet of the four women.

Meanwhile the mob spilled back into the arcade. The priest banged on the brothel door, demanding the fugitive.

"Why should we listen to you?" the madam said stubbornly.

"Listen to me then," said the woman from Act One boldly, assuming command once again. "The man you harbour is a brutal murderer, responsible for countless mysterious deaths in this very arcade. Can't you smell the blood on him?"

The madam sniffed the air, catching something rank that had her twisting her face and recoiling in disgust. The doctor cowered in fear.

"No, don't listen," he implored. "They're a rabble."

"Smell it!" the woman cried.

The light changed to a lurid green, highlighting the pale faces of the actors and exaggerating their gestures.

The three prostitutes stood up lazily and formed a circle around the doctor. He tried to get to his feet, but was pushed back down.

"No," he shuddered, his voice faltering.

The women closed in. As the lights went dead and a cacophony of piercing shrieks rang out over the audience, the dim outline of flailing limbs could be seen hacking away at the darkness.

When the lights went up again several minutes later, the violence of the screams still echoed through the theatre. The curtain had fallen and the shaken audience was white with shock.

The next evening two separate articles in the *Melburnian* made mention of the play:

# The Theatre of Fear Comes to Melbourne

Those of us who experienced the opening of Melbourne's own *Grand Guignol* at the Bijoux Theatre on Bourke Street will be left in no doubt that the theatrical culture of the city has shifted decisively. No longer will it be possible to produce romantic melodramas or even thrillers, such as the recent adaptations of Conan Doyle, without a distinct sense of anachronism. *The Cabinet of Anatomical Curiosities*, written and directed by Paul Walters, has established the theatre of fear in our city. Last night theatre-goers shuddered, screamed, and fainted with fright as they watched the bestial side of human nature dragged out of the shadows and displayed in full view. The play adapts a long tradition of Gothic horror to the local scene. Readers of Poe and his more extreme French disciples will recognise elements of this tradition in this play about a mad doctor who murders the patrons of his anatomical museum to enhance his collection with their corpses.

The popular spectacles of history have not been without their share of gore. Those of us who think that these modern times have dispensed with the need for a bit of public blood-letting need only step into the Bijoux Theatre to see that the old desires die hard. Our respectable theatre patrons, who only a week ago might have been content to debate Hamlet's madness until they were blue in the face, will today be recovering their battered senses. It will remain for the prudish and hypocritical among them to insist that *Grand Guignol* is theatre for the masses. The truth is that even the most moralistic of us seek out violent, prurient entertainment where fear and revulsion merely veil a secret desire to witness the unthinkable.

# Eastern Arcade, or Passage of Crime?

Anyone who has walked the length of the Eastern Arcade of late will be in no doubt as to its unsavoury qualities. Running between Little Collins and Bourke Streets behind the Eastern Market, itself a perpetual eyesore on the face of the city, the Eastern Arcade is a haven of vice where gamesters, pornographers, prostitutes and petty criminals of every imaginable ilk congregate to hatch their sordid schemes. Among the dubious businesses operating there we found a wine saloon, a billiard hall, a bookshop specialising in obscene publications, a photographer's studio, a phrenologist, a palm reader and no less than three brothels, barely concealed behind soiled sheets of red velvet hanging in their windows. Prostitutes, moreover, feel no disinclination to solicit in the arcade itself and no doubt the procession of shadowy characters constantly making their way through it are drawn by this market in human flesh.

Melbourne's arcades were once a symbol of the city's prosperity, and every bit the equal of the Burlington Arcade in London. How regrettable it is that they have fallen into such disrepair and neglect, and are now infested with the detritus of the city. The Eastern Arcade has become a breeding ground for the miscreants from which all good parents should hope to shield their young. A sensational play now doing the rounds could not have been closer to the mark in imagining the arcade as the home of obscenities dredged out of the gutters of modern life. We urge the board of city planning, currently addressing the issue of slum housing in Carlton and Fitzroy, to turn its attention to this blight and consider correctives before its moral influence is irrevocable.

By the middle of the next week *The Cabinet of Anatomical Curiosities* had warranted write-ups in the city's leading dailies:

## THEATRE OF TERROR

*The Cabinet of Anatomical Curiosities* has somehow slipped past the moral censors of the city and is drawing packed houses. Apparently the public is only too willing to be deceived by the trickery of red wax, retracting blades, and the odd piece of butcher's meat thrown in for good measure. A quack doctor in the foyer pretends to check hearts before the performance and is apparently on hand in case of heart failure during it. The show is a curiosity in its own right. Grotesquely exaggerated performances by a talentless and justifiably unknown cast would merely be amusing if the content were not so horrific. A pack of bloodthirsty dwarfs, whose fate is still unresolved at the end of the play, is too ridiculous to comment upon, and the amount of deafening screaming is only matched by the carnage. The final scene of the play, where the special nastiness of the playwright's imagination comes to the fore, is a particular outrage to public decency. The thought of young people or women being exposed to the Bacchanalian obscenity of this conclusion is enough to suggest that the play itself should be shut down without further notice. We refer it, without further ado, to the city's Indecent Literature Committee, and imagine prosecution pending.

And a day later in the *Argus*:

## The French Malady

*Grand Guignol* is not new. The French, with their own particular flair for the depraved, have been performing these plays since the close of the last century. Regrettably, the taste for public obscenity is now catching on here, especially among ex-Diggers whose overly excited nerves have failed to readjust to the tranquillity of peacetime. A Yarra Bend doctor is even recommending a trip to the Bijoux as a therapy for his shell-shocked patients. Notwithstanding, the French malady is a deplorable influence on the moral fibre of the city. But we are loath to say too much on this score for fear that the very thought of such an obscene production will be like a red rag to a bull, attracting larrikins and blackguards from far and wide to its door. It is worth noting that the playwright and director, one Paul Walters, who claims to hail from Zurich, the better to beguile a public of hapless colonials no doubt, is none other than the Paul Walters of Melbourne whose crude paintings disgraced the city a decade ago. A stint in the cesspools of Europe has apparently prepared him for a second assault on the taste and decency of the public with his third-rate plagiarisms of second-rate French plays. We trust that discerning and rational theatre patrons will not stand for it and will vote with their feet.

By the end of the week, when the *Melburnian* responded to these damning reviews, *The Cabinet of Anatomical Curiosities* was a hit and Paul Walters was infamous.

# Grand Guignol and Public Morality

Fortunately Melbourne's theatre-going public is quite able to recognise the difference between fiction and reality, quite able to distinguish between a mere play and a genuinely criminal or immoral act. Theatrical spectacles have always toyed with the boundary between the two. Unfortunately, reviewers at our two major newspapers seem incapable of making this simple distinction and believe that the play currently being performed at the Bijoux Theatre is a sufficient threat to civic order to warrant legal intervention. Perhaps they have failed to read their own publications, where they'd find enough real life tales of murder and madness to produce a hundred plays of much greater terror. The real horror of the age is not being performed on the stage, but on our streets and if one has the stomach one can read about it in the pages of our dailies. It is probably too much to expect the writers at the *Peacock* and the *Screechowl*, who have directed opinion and taste almost since the founding of this city, to acknowledge the datedness of their predilection for the theatre of insipid bourgeois compromise, in which a touch of danger gently dissipates in the working out of a conventionally uplifting conclusion.

*The Cabinet of Anatomical Curiosities* pushes into territory that will be unfamiliar to Melburnians, because it presents the dark places of the imagination rather than any directly recognisable reality. It shows us what the cult of realism in our national culture has hitherto disallowed and dismissed – the psychological. To wed morality and art in the name of public respectability, as is so often our want, is to travesty both.

Hamish McDermott was in the Eastern Arcade a few weeks after the play was banned by the Melbourne City Court in a special sitting convened to expedite a decision and conclude the whole affair before Christmas. Paul was fined fifty pounds and all copies of the play were confiscated under the *Obscene Publications Act*. Robert Walters, anxious that his paper's defence of the play might lead to the discovery that the *Melburnian*'s chief editor was in fact the uncle of the defendant in a public obscenity hearing, had decided to reassign Hamish before the debate over *The Cabinet of Anatomical Curiosities* got any more vitriolic. Disapproving of his nephew's efforts, which offended his own sense of social hygiene, but at the same time unwilling to undermine Paul's interests, Robert had allowed Hamish considerable latitude in the play's defence. But by the time legal proceedings were launched, things were becoming overly heated and he decided to redirect Hamish's fervour towards a cause that was closer to his heart.

So at the end of 1921, December 30 in fact, it happened that Hamish was in the Eastern Arcade, thinking about a series of articles on the decline of "marvellous Melbourne". He had just come from a screening of a travel documentary, *Sir Ross Smith's Flight from England to Australia*, and was struggling to reconcile the aerial camera work – its abstract, joyously dislocated omniscience – with the tangible sense of location he was confronted with now. Once people got used to seeing things from the sky, he thought, the tiny details that distinguish one place from another would be lost to them.

He was supposed to be exploring the moral and physical degradation of what had once been a splendid Victorian city, writing sketches of locations like the arcade, the Eastern Market, and Little Lonsdale Street. Robert held up his own article "Eastern Arcade, or Passage of Crime?" as an indication of the general tone he wanted to convey, but the moralising of the piece was alien enough to Hamish to make him doubt his ability to manufacture it. He went to the arcade hoping to find the "miscreants" of a declining city, and seemed to be loitering himself, watching the odd person slip into one of the brothels or emerge from the stationer's clutching a brown paper bag or a parcel squirrelled away under a folded jacket. He felt quite purposeless, as if he were waiting for something to hold his attention, and the slow meanderings of the arcade seemed to be lulling him further into this blankness when a large, loutish man with conspicuous gold teeth glistening like nuggets half-buried in his red gums brushed past him, waking him from his daydreaming.

That was when he saw the girl. At least he thought he saw her. When he thought about it afterwards, he really couldn't be sure. In the following weeks the newspapers were full of such detailed descriptions of her that practically anybody could have accurately visualised Alma Tirtschke gazing longingly through the plate-glass window of a fancy dress shop as she paused on her way through the arcade. She would have looked like any other schoolgirl had not her fate transformed her white cambric blouse, pleated navy-blue tunic and panama hat into symbols of an innocence devoured by the jaws of the city. If he had seen her, Hamish thought, he probably wouldn't have noticed the exact details of her dress until the newspapers jogged his memory. But in the days and weeks that followed there she was just the same, standing before him in the arcade, the twelve-year-old schoolgirl with pale, freckled skin and auburn hair, clutching the package of butcher's meat she had just picked up for her aunt.

By the next morning the girl was dead. It was just after dawn when a rag-picker, a veteran down on his luck, stumbled into Gun Alley, a cobbled cul-de-sac running off Little Collins Street opposite the entrance to the arcade. The man scanned the cobblestones for bottles until the bend of the alley led him to the body. In the days that followed, the details of this discovery were not left to anyone's imagination:

### Girl of Twelve Brutally Murdered. Body Found in City Lane. Strangling Cord and Clothes Removed from Body

One of the most horrible murders that has ever been committed in Melbourne was discovered early last Saturday morning when the nude body of a child of twelve – Alma Tirtschke – was found in an alleyway off Little Collins Street. She had been outraged, strangled with a thin cord, stripped of all her clothing, borne from the death chamber, and dumped onto the street, where the body was found.

The spot is a narrow alleyway at the rear of shops in Little Collins Street near Exhibition Street. This lane runs east and west off Gun Alley, alongside Lane's motor garage. Few people use the lane, and probably nobody would be in it after midnight, as an ordinary rule, though during the daytime it is always under observation by men employed in the neighbourhood.

While walking along Gun Alley, shortly after six o'clock on Saturday morning, Henry David Errington, a bottle gatherer, saw the corpse of the murdered girl. She was lying on her back, with her legs doubled beneath her. Errington immediately ran to the butcher's shop of Watkins and Co. in Bourke Street and telephoned the news of his gruesome discovery to the police, and Senior Constable Salts went to the scene. The girl's auburn hair was spread out on the ground, and the position of the body suggested that she had been carefully laid down on the granite pitchers.

People who previously had not bothered much with the news of the day certainly read the papers now. As the investigation into the murder gathered pace the pages of the city's dailies came alive with the grim details of the crime and still grimmer speculation about it. Not since the Crimea Street murder thirty years earlier had a crime aroused such public concern. The papers introduced the phrase "lust murder" into the popular vocabulary, recounting a history that ran from Jack the Ripper to Gun Alley. "What sort of fiendish person could perpetrate this sort of crime?" The question was the subject of endless speculation. The papers were almost unanimous in their conviction that the killer would strike again and could even be hiding behind the veneer of public respectability. Sex maniacs, one prominent alienist claimed, are often "respectable" citizens or even saintly, churchgoing types with a reputation for piety. Still, it didn't take long for public fear to turn to the arcade itself, and the maze of little alleyways associated with it.

As Hamish read the papers, the girl's naked body was constantly before him – hair spread out on the stones, legs folded beneath her, bruised skin around the slender, white neck. At night, when he masturbated, he couldn't help but imagine her posing in the arcade and the killer's hands trembling around her neck. Afterwards he felt sickened. This fleeting identification with the killer, the merest possibility of it, left him feeling polluted by his own touch. He looked at his hands – obscene lumps of flesh they were. Sometimes he imagined they'd been dug up and sewn on. The smell of them – sweat, semen and the grime of the city – repulsed him.

But when he tried to moralise about the arcade and the murder for the paper, he found his own increasingly florid prose ill-adapted to the task. The daily papers had descended into the most mundane form of journalese. Semiliterate stuff, he thought. But next to their simple clarity his writing seemed tainted. Twice Robert withdrew Hamish's articles and finally referred him, chidingly, to the *Herald*'s damning evocations of the market area. Hamish ran his eyes over the articles which pitted the menace of the evil-smelling arcade against the longing for clean, modern structures, where the sweet smell of fruit and flowers was not strangled by the reek of old, dirt-begrimed buildings. Hamish understood the metaphor perfectly. Fruit and flowers, dirt and grime. He again looked at his hands and wondered, shamefully, what they were capable of.

## chapter twenty-four

On the day Alma Tirtschke was buried, crowds of weeping women laid wreaths of flowers in Gun Alley, and then besieged the arcade with such fervour that a police barricade had to be thrown up around the Little Collins Street entrance. The demonstration quickly died down, but a large crowd remained outside as flower-bearers continued to pay homage to the corpse of the city's innocence.

Paul Walters made his way down Little Collins Street, sardonically pleased at the sight of the mob his banned play had envisioned with such accuracy. He'd heard rumours that the police were close to an arrest and that the suspect was in the arcade itself, so, like hundreds of other Melburnians since the murder, he thought he'd have a look at a genuine crime scene.

He was in need of distraction. The banning of the play had left him at a loose end, and his sister and wife had subsequently formed a conspiracy of the just against him. Under Ondine's influence Laura had become stubborn and assertive. By the time the court case concluded she seemed glad that the play had been stopped. He suspected his sister of coaching her resentment.

"Why do women only appear as corpses and whores?" Laura asked him.

"It's not supposed to be realism," he replied.

"Still, I think I've almost had enough, as if I've overeaten and am now feeling a bit sick."

He looked at her suspiciously. "My sister has got to you," he said.

"Rubbish."

Paul was already tired of the two of them. He could see they were intent on establishing their own enclave and was happy to get out of the house. He quickly forgot himself in the comforting bustle of the streets and the commotion as he approached Gun Alley.

"Makes me think of Little Nell," a voice said at his shoulder as he walked towards the arcade entrance. "Who wouldn't be moved to tears?"

The voice belonged to an impish old man whose eyes were firmly fixed on the crowd of women. He had raised his walking stick slightly in readiness, as if he expected to have to fight his way through.

"How's a fellow supposed to conduct a business with such a kafuffle going on?"

Paul looked at the man intently. He was older, more wrinkled and a bit smaller, as if he'd shrunk with age. But the same bulbous eyes and round bald head were there under the brim of the flat straw hat.

"Max? Max Wedelkind?" Paul said, astonished.

"Good God, boy. Nobody has called me that for years."

"It's Paul Walters. You remember."

Wedelkind paused on the pavement, put on his glasses and pushed his face closer to Paul's.

"Paul Walters. So it is," he said. "I suppose you'll be coming to me for a bit of help now that your play is bust? I thought you would have been smarter than to try it on back here."

"What on earth are you doing here?"

"Oh, I just turn up where I'm needed."

The police outside the arcade shepherded Paul and Wedelkind through the crowd.

"You see that bloke behind the bar in the wine saloon?" Wedelkind said, pointing to a large fellow with gold teeth. "He's the one who'll hang for that girl's death."

"How the hell do you know that?" asked Paul.

"It's my job to know these things." He stopped outside a shopfront. "Oscar Kismet – Phrenologist" was painted in red letters on the door.

Wedelkind dangled some keys, fiddled with the lock, and led Paul into an office where he slung himself into an old chair and lit a cigarette. There were astrological charts on the wall, weird symbols from Eastern mysticism and some ornately illustrated tarot cards, one of which depicted the grim reaper as a skeleton concealed behind the mask of a smiling young woman.

Wedelkind noticed Paul's eyes resting on the card.

"You show them death, let them think you can see death, and they'll believe anything. It's the oldest trick in the book. That's how I know about poor Ross down there in the wine saloon. He's a bit simple, really. He watched his mates mangled in the trenches. Now he sleeps in the same room as his brother and screams at night.

Maybe even pisses himself and could have a touch of the syph as well. All those country brothels in France, you know. I told him he might do someone in if he couldn't control his urges and sure enough the bloke has been true to my word. There are half-a-dozen whores here who'll see him hang sure as the sun will rise."

Paul stared in amazement at the aged impostor in front of him. For a moment it was all too fantastic to be real.

"And now you're a phrenologist? What on earth is that?"

"It's nothing really. An ambiguous kind of calling I'll admit, a hangover from last century, though I've always had a bit of a talent with other people's heads." Wedelkind smiled mischievously. "Now, I suppose you'd like me to tell you your future, wouldn't you?"

"No, not at all," Paul said, aghast.

"Well, what else are you doing here?"

Paul looked stunned. Had the man really forgotten that he had almost single-handedly moulded Paul's fate?

"Who are you?" Paul said.

"Who am I? Didn't you read the door?"

"Kismet. Fate. What nonsense. I must be dreaming."

"Dreaming? Oh, I like that." Wedelkind looked thoughtful for a moment. "You know," he said, pointing his smouldering cigarette at Paul, "I bet you could do a good job with poor old Ross down in the wine saloon. Was there ever a better subject for one of your horrible little plays? And think of the controversy. You'll probably burn in hell for it, to use a dated metaphor, but your name will burn much brighter than that in the inflamed imagination of posterity."

Paul was on the verge of wringing his neck or dragging him out into the arcade and unmasking him, but felt sufficiently light-headed that he let the moment pass and simply sat there breathing in the pungent, scented smoke of Wedelkind's cigarette.

"You know," Wedelkind continued, "these are the last days of the Eastern Arcade. We can all read the writing on the wall. Soon they'll raze the place and turn it into some sterile department store or office block. A shame really. The last little bit of devilry will be gone. That will be a sad day, my friend. You, who have been such a part of it all, should appreciate that. There'll be nothing left for the likes of you or me when places like this are gone. There'll be horror, to be sure. But of a blander, less appealing variety. So make the most of it, that's what I say. Make the most of it, Paul Walters. You come from a famous literary family, after all."

He leant back in his chair, cigarette in hand, and pulled a book down from the shelf behind him. It was the English version of *Romanze zur Nacht*. Wedelkind opened a marked page and read, "'In the Eastern Arcade I met a man who said that I would sell myself, or reap profit from the dead.' You see," he added, "this is such a wonderful book because everything is in it. Everything is written. What ever did become of my young friend Klessmann? Never mind." He closed the book and gestured to the door. "Good day then, Mr Walters. May Kismet smile on you."

Paul stood up, stunned. When he re-entered the arcade the light had turned a murky green. The crowd was still gathered at the Little Collins Street end, but was thinning. Amongst the women emerging from Gun Alley, where the floral tribute to the dead girl now covered the ground, he noticed his own mother, looking pale and tired in the steady movement of pedestrians up and down the narrow street. He turned away from her, confident she hadn't seen him, and walked the other way.

Wedelkind's voice echoed in his ears. It was as if the old charlatan were still speaking to him, insinuating himself into his consciousness until Paul couldn't quite distinguish his own thoughts from the words that drifted about him on clouds of clove-scented smoke. As the fumes overwhelmed him, he felt himself go dizzy and then a bit blank. The nauseating fog rushed to his brain. He had to grip the wall beside him.

"Who wouldn't be moved to tears?" a voice whispered.

He looked around, but there was no one there. He regained his composure and it occurred to him then and there that he would write a play about the murder, and shock the city to its very foundations. Why not? What did he have to lose? The audacity of it. It was brilliant.

He had visions of a madman with gold teeth, a shell-shocked veteran shaking with fear as he stalked the child, watching her innocent movements as she looked with wonder at the sights of the arcade and the subterranean figures emerging from its depths. He saw the old rag-picker stumbling over her body, falling in love with the corpse as the whole city had done, and the vengeful mob prowling the arcade for the killer. The play would slice through the consciousness of the city like a burning knife, etching his own bleeding initials indelibly in its memory.

When he got back to St Vincent Place Laura and Ondine were seated opposite each other in the sitting room, each nursing a different volume of Balzac's *Human Comedy*. It was hot outside, and when Paul entered he was sweating. He flew to Laura and dropped himself down beside her. "I've had a wonderful idea," he said. He was already clutching his wife's hands. "We can perform the Alma Tirtschke murder. Call it 'The Gun Alley Atrocity'. It will send the place into convulsions."

Ondine stood up, book in hand, glanced at Laura and left the room. Paul, in his fervour, barely noticed her exit. Laura looked down into the folds of her dress.

"You don't think it's a good idea?' he asked. "It will make us here. It will put us on the map and show up those prudes for the idiots they are."

"I think it's touching something too raw," Laura said gently.

"Nonsense. It's merely topical."

"Won't it be construed as bad taste? What about the relatives of that poor girl?"

"What do we care if we stir up a bit of controversy? It's all good publicity."

"You've turned into quite a pragmatist, haven't you?"

"That sounds like my sister talking. Since when have you worried about that?"

Laura looked back into her lap, trying to avoid eye contact. "I don't think it's decent, Paul," she said without looking up. "A little girl being murdered like that is a terrible, terrible thing."

"My sister has hypnotised you with all her high moral seriousness," he accused.

"I am capable of thinking for myself, you know."

"Since when?"

"Since always. Since now. Since you've hit upon the idea of turning your silly theatre into a source of such callous disregard. It's awful."

"Oh, please." Paul stood up. "If you're not interested I'll do it alone. I'll find my own Alma Tirtschke to strangle and we'll be the talk of the town." He laughed to himself.

"Where will you find your Alma Tirtschke? They'll all keep clear of you after the last debacle."

"Oh, I know my way around Melbourne pretty well."

Paul threw himself down on the couch opposite her, looking like a limp rag doll.

"My sister is a devil in her own right, you know. Where do you think she is going to lead you?"

"Oh, shut up, Paul. You're being moronic."

Laura took her book, stood up abruptly and left him alone in the room. She walked upstairs to Ondine's room. The door was ajar. She pushed it open and entered without knocking.

Ondine was sitting at one end of her canopy bed reading. She looked up from her book and met Laura's eyes as the latter calmly sat down at the other end of the bed and opened her book as well. The two women were cross-legged, backs against opposite ends of the bedstead, necks craned over Balzac like a couple of bookends turned around the wrong way.

"I wonder if Paul will finish up mad as well," Ondine said without raising her eyes. "Like our father, I mean."

"It would be awkward, wouldn't it?" Laura replied.

Ondine smiled to herself. She loved her sister-in-law's capacity for such miscalculated remarks.

Laura lowered her eyes again and resumed her reading. Ondine raised hers, ever so slightly, fixing on the waves of jet-black hair tumbling over Laura's white shoulders, and her mouth narrowing into a pout of concentration which seemed to be speaking the words she read as if she were trying to memorise a part in a play.

Neither Ondine nor Laura attended the opening of *The Gun Alley Atrocity*. That afternoon the two of them had played tennis on the courts at the far end of St Vincent Place. When they returned to the house they were both pleasantly flushed from their exertions as the cool, dark air of the old stone house greeted them. Paul was waiting for them in the downstairs sitting room. He had been frantic for the last few weeks writing, casting and refurbishing the set of *The*

*Cabinet of Anatomical Curiosities*. He hadn't grown thinner in that time, as one might expect with all that nervous exertion. On the contrary, his stomach had become softer and rounder and his face had begun to sag. He seemed more anxious than he had ever been and looked tired and haggard. He knew Ondine wouldn't go to the premiere, but still imagined that his wife would be loyal to him even though she, too, clearly disapproved of the play.

"Laura, darling," he said, taking her arm as he emerged from the sitting room. "You will be coming tonight, won't you? Hamish will take you if you like."

"Paul, you know I'm not going to come. I don't think it's right, this play."

He gripped her arm tighter. "Laura, darling, you must come. It would mean so much to me."

He spoke with a staged irony that she found repugnant. She could smell the back rooms of the theatre on his tattered suit. She imagined old posters of chorus girls peeling off the walls and traces of cat piss stained into the floorboards.

"Don't," she said angrily, wriggling out of his sweaty grip. "I'm going to shower."

Ondine had already mounted the stairs. Paul cast a glance at her. She had turned and was watching the scene below with what seemed to him a smile curled into the wrinkle of a lip.

"You're in love with my sister, aren't you?" he said under his breath.

"Don't be silly." Laura blushed as she spoke. She abruptly followed Ondine up the stairs, hoping that she hadn't heard Paul's accusation.

Paul followed a few paces behind, the feeling of betrayal mounting in him. When he and Laura were in their own room he seized her arm again and shook her.

"What?" she implored.

The smell of her perspiration aroused him and he sniffed her neck like an animal. For a moment she stood there in the middle of the room, motionless, listening to his heavy breathing, imagining his nostrils dilating.

"Have you kissed her?" he hissed.

She turned away from him.

Suddenly enraged, he twisted her slender wrists behind her back and pushed her onto the bed. He pulled her tennis skirt up over her back, yanked her drawers down around her knees and pushed his fingers in between her buttocks, touching the edge of her anus. The stunned terror in her silence as she clung to the counterpane returned him to himself. He stood back. She pulled her skirt down, staring at him in horror as she pushed past him through the hallway into Ondine's room. Paul choked back his anger, rearranged himself, and followed her out. He listened at his sister's door for a moment before going back downstairs. A few minutes later he was out in the street, driving towards the city, cursing the two women with such vehemence that his body shook.

## chapter twenty-five

It was late February and Melbourne felt as if a sirocco had been blowing its hot breath along the city's dusty streets for the best part of a week. The place was parched, withering in the heat of the country's vast, interior deserts. The police had arrested the bartender at the Australian Wine Shop for the murder of Alma Tirtschke. Within a week of the trial beginning a cast of prostitutes and spiritualists from the arcade had come out in force to testify against Colin Ross, who gaped at the court with his glistening gold teeth and pleaded his innocence with a sad, hang-dog look on his rough, unshaven face. Paul didn't need to wait for the verdict to finish his play. He could already divine its end and envisioned Ross going to the gallows haunted by his satanic prompter, Wedelkind, whom he imagined rubbing his hands with glee at the fulfilment of his prognostication.

As evening fell, the play looked as if it would be well attended despite the soaring temperature. Still angry at his wife, Paul stood in the vestibule of the Bijoux under the whirling blades of a ceiling fan as patrons, befuddled by the heat, stumbled in from the brutal clamour of Bourke Street.

"I think that man will certainly hang," one woman said shrilly.

"But who would trust the likes of a Madam Gurkha?" said another.

"What about the father? Shot in a hunting accident just the other week. Doesn't that make you suspicious?"

Paul hadn't noticed Hamish standing beside him.

"Truth of it is," Hamish said, "that poor fool from the wine bar is probably innocent."

"How do you know that?" asked Paul. "In this play he's as guilty as hell. I'll stake my reputation on it."

"Besides the most dubious of testimonies nothing connects him to the girl."

As they watched the crowd file into the theatre Paul thought about Wedelkind and wondered what role he had played in the affair.

"And they all know that tonight they'll see Alma Tirtschke die a second time," said Hamish. "Why do they need to see that?"

"Because the good burghers of Melbourne like a bit of sadism. Always have. If we were allowed to throw Christians to the lions they'd be showing up in droves."

As eight o'clock approached Paul retreated to the wings and Hamish took his seat near the front of the stage.

A large man with a double chin and a few tufts of black hair on his onion-shaped head leant over towards him.

"Can bet on a bit of strife tonight. You're from the press, ain't ya?"

"Yes," said Hamish. "The *Melburnian*."

"Well ya can bet there'll be a bit of trouble. Look over there."

He pointed to the end of the aisle at a thin, bespectacled man neatly attired, despite the heat, in a dark suit concealing a vicar's collar.

"That's Percy Gambell. Any Saturday night you can hear him preaching on Little Bourke and Little Lon at the whores and Chinks. A right one he is. A real fanatic for good Christian virtue."

The curtain went up, revealing one side of the Eastern Arcade, which ran on a diagonal from the top of the slanting stage down into a darkened space at the very front.

A balding old man, wearing a monocle and a dark cloak, escorted a large, oafish chap with ugly metal teeth down the length of the arcade, past a fancy dress shop, a photographer's studio, a tattoo parlour and a peepshow.

"Now listen here, my good man," the old man said, by way of offering advice. "If I had your charms I wouldn't be hiding them away. You're an ex-Digger after all, and the women respect that."

A woman, evidently a prostitute, exited a door into the centre of the arcade. The oafish man looked her up and down. At the urging of the old man in the cloak he moved closer, blubbering something inaudible to himself.

"Get away from me, you beast!" the woman shouted, giving him a good kick, which sent him scampering back towards the front of the stage.

"This is what our fighting men get," the old man told the audience. "They've seen their mates killed in the mud of France and on the cliffs of Gallipoli. They've fought for their country and the empire. They've witnessed their mates blown to pieces."

A few members of the audience laughed. The vicar at the end of the aisle coughed loudly.

"Cut the palaver and let's have some blood," someone said impatiently.

"Shut up," said another voice.

A crowd of ragged-looking figures appeared at the top of the arcade and made its way through to the end, finally clearing to reveal a solitary figure. The audience fell silent at the sight of the little girl carrying a gas balloon. She had long auburn hair that shone under the stage lights, and wore a white cambric blouse with blue spots, a navy-blue tunic and a panama hat with a red band, just like the real Alma Tirtschke had worn on the day of her murder.

"Oh, yes," said the old man as the oaf eyed her eagerly. "She is Innocence itself."

The girl looked into the shop windows, oblivious to the two men in the foreground.

Hamish squirmed uncomfortably in his seat.

"Will they do her in onstage?" the man next to him whispered with evident relish.

Hamish wondered what Paul was capable of. He imagined the girl stripped naked in a filthy back room and then, a moment later, her body draped theatrically over the cobblestones.

"I can't watch this," a woman behind him said as the actress strolled down the arcade, pausing in front of a window to look at herself. She posed coquettishly, pushing her auburn hair over her shoulder, and then turned back the way she had come.

"Oh yes," said the old man as the girl vanished at the top of the stage. "A real little jewel."

Percy Gambell stood up, as if on cue, and shouted at the audience. "It's an outrage! They've made that innocent little girl into the whore of Babylon. It's despicable. A sin against decency, an insult to us all!"

The audience's attention was now diverted just as the lights were dimmed further and the oaf scampered off after the girl.

"An outrage!" the man shouted again.

There was a deafening shriek from the stage. The girl was being dragged into the foreground by the man with the glistening metal teeth, who fumbled at her tunic.

"Stop it!" someone shouted.

"I can't watch!"

Someone from the audience leapt up onto the stage and kicked the would-be murderer away, pulling the girl clear of him.

Gambell waved his clenched fist in the air as if it were a hammer, and in response a group of young men climbed up onto the stage and began demolishing the set. Cardboard walls and frames tumbled like gigantic playing cards revealing the confused innards of the theatre – props, costumes and ropes dangling backstage – as actors and stagehands fled into the wings. The stunned audience was now on its feet. Some people stood transfixed, reeling with the shock of it all, while others made for the exit.

At first Paul thought the commotion was merely the audience's predictable response to the theatre of terror. But when he saw the sets falling apart and the actors fleeing backstage he too took a few quick steps towards a rear exit. He feared the turmoil of the mob and the possibility of his public humiliation more than the indignity of slinking away like the cowardly captain of a sinking ship. He was on the threshold of the exit when a few burly ushers reasserted control of the theatre, kicking the small band of rioters offstage in a flurry of fists and flailing boots.

To Hamish, still in his seat, this finale looked like a marvellously directed piece of onstage violence. Bodies moved in the half-light and faces were blank with the effort of concentrated savagery. One of the rioters clutched his broken nose as blood gushed over his chin, only to be knocked to the ground before he'd made it back into the aisles. The young woman playing Alma Tirtschke gave him a kick in the balls as she confidently resumed control of the stage, strutting about with a look of brazen defiance.

"Fuck youse all!" she screamed.

I can always go back to Europe, Paul said to himself, feeling the utter hopelessness of the situation. He assumed a manful air of proprietorial authority and approached the actress with his hand outstretched in a gesture of consolation.

"Fuck you too!" she screamed at him. Make-up ran down her face and her dishevelled auburn wig slid off to one side.

"That's telling him, love," someone in the crowd called out.

Egged on by this the would-be Alma Tirtschke seized the last remnant of her professional dignity and launched into Paul, pounding his chest with her fists and kicking him in the shins.

"Fuck you! I shoulda known better. Pervert! They all said you was a fucking pervert!"

"Bravo," the crowd yelled. "Good for you, love. Let him have it!"

Hamish was still stuck to his seat. As he wiped the moisture from his upper lip he could again smell something, his own stale skin perhaps, or traces of dry semen. He looked at the little brown freckles on the backs of his hands as the lights came up. He had the hands of a savage, made for working the land or digging coal from the earth. He remembered how, years ago, they had made him self-conscious in front of Ondine. He felt dirty, unfit for human society, a creature stitched together out of other people's nightmares, a patchwork of desires that bled at the seams.

He watched Paul fend off the enraged acrtress and finally crawl away defeated to the wings as the crowd continued to jeer him. His friend looked worse than simply shaken.

Finally Hamish dragged himself through the stifling air of the Bijoux out onto the street. A crowd had leaked out of the building and was assembled on the pavement, angry and still harbouring the potential for further mayhem. Someone had kicked in a glass panel advertising the play, but the heat was quickly sapping the mob's energy. By the time the police arrived there was only a handful of patrons remaining. The rapturous tones of their outrage amply indicated that, all up, the ruin of Paul Walters had supplied them with a highly satisfying night out.

Later Hamish tried to write a review, but the words refused to come. He lingered at his desk, distracted by the humidity. Finally, in the small hours of the morning, watching fluttering moths throw shadows on the wall, he put a piece of paper into his old typewriter and lethargically began to tap away at the keys, conscious of the thickness of his fingers, barely aware of what he was writing.

It was hours later when Paul eventually left the Bijoux. He had been sitting in the bowels of the building drinking Scotch from a bottle until he was confident that the cast members and stagehands had left. He couldn't bear the thought of confronting them again. The would-be Alma Tirtschke had quit and now there would be interminable arguments about contracts, terms and payments. The theatre alone had been booked until the end of March.

Sitting under an old stage light, he caught a glimpse of himself in a dust-covered mirror opposite him. He was pale and bloated. His black hair, plastered to his scalp with sweat, was thinning, and his skin had turned pasty. For the first time he noticed that his jowls had become fleshy and swollen and that his stomach had turned into a round gut. He took another swig of Scotch, stood up, unsteady on his feet, and walked out through the wreckage of *The Gun Alley Atrocity*.

Outside, Bourke Street was stifling, but quiet, as if the city had been drugged into a deep, torpid sleep by the asphyxiating darkness. There were sounds of music and debauchery somewhere in the distance, but these were remote and mysterious, merely serving to highlight the eerie stillness of the night. Paul clutched the Scotch, which he poured down his throat every few steps, and staggered in the direction of the Arcadia Club, the last refuge of the ruined. He had been brought low a third time by the cursed colony and was now ready either to leave for good or to sink lower still into the ranks of the destitute and forgotten, the casualties of the city who drink themselves into oblivion after it has hacked away all hope.

When he got to where the Arcadia had been a decade earlier he found the headquarters of a theosophical society selling cheap pamphlets about the way to God. But he was drunk and doubted that he had come along the right part of Little Lon. He tottered back up the alley and tried to reorient himself.

"Bad luck there," a voice said to him out of the shadows.

He turned sluggishly to find Max Wedelkind stepping out into the glow of a streetlight. The man was dressed in a buttoned-up suit and still wore his straw hat. Insects of a thousand different shapes swarmed about him, attracted by the light, but he barely seemed to notice.

"I'm glad my acting days are long gone," he said. "Mighty tough audiences nowadays."

"Go to hell," Paul slurred.

"But I was flattered to see that you hadn't forgotten me in your little drama."

Paul could barely stand and suddenly felt as if he were about to vomit. His jaw went slack and his mouth filled with warm saliva.

"Oh, very nice," Wedelkind snickered.

Paul propped himself up against a wall, and slowly slipped down into a sitting position, his legs splayed out on the pavement.

"The problem was that your Alma Tirtschke was too cheap. Completely ill-suited. Where in the devil's name did you find her?"

Paul eyed him suspiciously. Wasn't it Wedelkind who sucked him into the theatre in the first place? Wasn't it Wedelkind who held the strings that guided him through all his botched endeavours, Wedelkind who was the presiding genius of his ruin? Paul closed his eyes, trying to get it all straight in his mind, trying to unravel the tangled knot of decisions and motivations that had led him to this wretched impasse. In his drunken state he saw his wife melting into his sister's arms, kissing her with a passion that she had never shown him, giving herself over to the power of cold blood and still, limpid eyes.

"I'm telling you, the problem was with your Alma Tirtschke."

"Don't say her name again," Paul said, "or I'll thrash you."

"Alma Tirtschke," Wedelkind dared him, his eyes almost popping out of his head.

Paul blinked. Wedelkind was holding the child by the hand. She was wearing the same tunic and the spotted blouse the actress had worn earlier that night.

Paul blinked again, then closed his eyes and shook his head. When he looked up the girl was still standing in front of him.

"What is this?" he said. "Take her away from me!"

But the girl bent over him and let him smell the floral scent of her innocence. Her cheek brushed his, her hair fell into his eyes, and her lips touched his so softly that he doubted they were human. She helped him to his feet and led him across the road to a warped little house which opened into a warren of rooms and connecting hallways. The air was hot, almost too hot to inhale. In the darkness there were other forms, little more than blurs, moving languidly as if slowed by the heat. Paul thought he could see a slender white body slip out of its tunic and blouse. But he could barely breathe and his eyes were already heavy as he felt the soft lips again brushing his and the gentle, beguiling hands pulling him down.

He slept for what felt like years, through vast tracts of time stretching him across the ages of man. He was giddy with the incalculable, with huge numbers measuring his mortification, the empty depths of his own soul, the infinity of his nothingness brimming with the bitterness of humiliation.

Slowly the rottenness of the place worked its way into his dreams and he forced himself awake to find that he was lying in the arms of a much older woman. His head ached. He felt as if acid were coursing through his veins, burning him from the inside out. He was still too drunk to move off the mattress. He must have fallen asleep again when he heard the woman's voice whispering to him. He had the dim sensation of her breath on his ear, but heard the voice as if it were crawling about inside him. "I've always hated you. We all do. All of us hate all of you."

He roused himself again and pulled himself clear of the twisted sheets. He fumbled for his clothes on the floor and dressed as the anonymous sleeper flopped herself over onto her back. In the half-light he recognised Roxanne. Something in him broke and he went back to her, studying the lines on her face, recalling the paintings that were never bought and the brief period, a matter of weeks, when his idealism had been boundless. She still had traces of youth, but time had worn away her slender, serpentine features.

"Is that you, darling?" she said drowsily as Paul touched her face.

But this moment of recognition revolted him, and he fled the room, stumbling back out onto the street where another bright morning was already working its way towards blazing midday heat.

Again Paul caught a glimpse of himself in the brothel window. He was indeed haggard and old, booze-bloated as if, like the picture of Dorian Gray, he were aging before his very eyes.

He walked towards the Eastern Arcade, thinking that he might find Wedelkind and beat him to within an inch of his life. But when he got there the phrenologist's door was closed and a sign on the window indicated that the space was for rent. It was cooler in the arcade, out of the sun, but still the air was musty and in want of circulation. Paul stood gazing at the "For Rent" sign wondering whether he had dreamt the whole encounter the night before. The man is a phantom, he told himself. I can kill him at a stroke. He confidently turned away from the window and walked back towards Bourke Street.

He bought a copy of the *Argus* from the stationer and checked the reviews, pausing just inside the arcade entrance to read the headline: "Gun Alley Debacle". His aching eyes moved quickly over the article.

> Last night at the Bijoux Mr Paul Walters, whose play *The Cabinet of Anatomical Curiosities* was banned shortly before Christmas, was back before the public eye with yet another obscene and insulting piece of grotesquerie. Citizens of the city will not need to be reminded of the shocking particulars of the Gun Alley murder, which are currently being replayed at the trial of Colin Ross. As if

the public were not already sick with these details, Mr Walters has seen fit to rub salt into the wound, as it were, with a callous and offensive rendition of these shocking events. Fortunately, this time the audience was in no mood to be insulted. Many people left at the first appearance of a lascivious Alma Tirtschke, others shouted their dismay and a few even leapt up onstage to physically put an end to the performance. We are not in the habit of praising such outbursts of public disorder, but he who lives by the fickleness of the mob should be prepared to die by it. With any luck, public outrage will put an end to *The Gun Alley Atrocity* before Paul Walters again finds himself before the courts.

He threw the paper away and wandered off towards the market. The stalls looked cooler than the street. Paul veered into their shade only to discover that the promise of relief was illusory. What he found were sweating bodies and stagnant air, the stench of bestial humanity tinged with the rankness of overripe fruit and day-old fish. The people looked bigger and uglier than any he had ever seen. Flabby arms trembled before him, hairy armpits gaped, and sagging bellies pushed him into rotting, ulcerated flesh, torn open by the sun. He decided to hurry out of the place when a man with a large beer belly bounced him back into the crowd.

"Say, ain't you that bloke?" the man said. "Hey, youse. It's that bloke."

Paul tried to get past him, but the man was insistent, knocking him back with his fat, meaty arms. Paul turned away and began to walk in the opposite direction straight into a wall of sweating flesh that wrapped itself around him with the same insistence.

"It *is* that bloke," said another voice.

"It most certainly is," a voice, more mellow and insinuating, chimed in.

Paul searched around him and saw Wedelkind's merry old face smiling through the crowd. He seemed to wink at him just before the first man with the meaty arms slapped him across the face. Paul wriggled like a fish but the mob had him in its wet, fleshy hands. He could smell the bodies closing around him. The odour made him gag more than did the threat of violence.

At that moment he had a vision of Wedelkind bobbing up and down like a jack-in-the-box. He would have torn the old man limb from limb if only he could have found his way clear of the blows and kicks. Someone spat on him. With his arms and legs pinned to the filthy floor of the market a steady stream of warm saliva, phlegm and mucus rained down on him.

Finally he got back on his feet, wiping the slime off his face. "It's the old man!" he cried on the verge of tears. "The *Gaukler!*"

But Wedelkind was nowhere to be seen. The crowd stood back at the sight of what it now took to be a raving lunatic. Passers-by who hadn't seen the incident unfold would have sworn that Paul Walters was a vagrant or a madman. As the initial perpetrators of his humiliation vanished, the tone turned from hostility to fear. People shrank away from him in revulsion, clearing a wide path as he made his way out of the market towards the river, where he did his level best to clean himself up and wash away his humiliation.

When he got back to St Vincent Place Ondine and Laura were seated silently in the downstairs sitting room. The papers had been delivered and now lay on the polished walnut table.

"So," he said, throwing his coat onto the arm of the couch and standing before the two amazed women like a bloated scarecrow. "So!"

But embarrassed silence greeted him as neither one was game enough to say the first word.

"Bitches," Paul muttered under his breath.

He snatched up the papers, knocking over a teacup in his haste, and hurled them ineffectively across the room, sending pages fluttering to the floor.

Ondine's eyes darted towards Laura.

"I told you it was daft," Laura said to Paul.

Paul looked at her, dumbfounded. "You told me it was daft?" he said and threw his arms into the air. "Neither of you have the right to accuse me!"

Laura stood up and took his hand, but he shook her off.

"Sit down Paul," she said, "and try to be civil."

"You're in love with my sister."

For a moment there was dead silence.

"Don't be silly," she said. She looked into his red eyes, then at his pale, unshaven cheeks and dry, cracked lips.

"Say it. You're in love with my sister!" he repeated.

Finally Ondine stirred. "Perhaps your sister is in love with your wife. At any rate, what business do wives and sisters have falling in love with anyone?"

As Paul listened to his sister he felt something black and heavy drop within him and then squirm around in the pit of his stomach.

"Then I am nothing," he said.

He pushed Laura away from him, caught between violence and melodrama.

"You're being stupid, Paul," she remonstrated.

"Stupid?" he screamed.

Like a madman he lunged at his coat on the arm of the couch and drew out a knife which he held up to the light.

"Stupid?" he wailed again at the top of his voice.

In response to the racket coming from downstairs Anna had appeared at the door of the sitting room in time to see her son plunge the knife into his chest right up to its ebony handle. His face turned red and as he staggered towards the couch he withdrew the blade and plunged it in a second time. Anna screamed as Paul stumbled forward onto his knees, blood drenching his white shirt and dribbling onto the floorboards.

"Oh my God!" his mother shrieked.

Paul tumbled to the floor. Ondine and Laura flew to him, rolling him onto his back. He was still. He had stopped breathing. His hand still clutched the knife lodged in his heart.

Laura felt his cheek and then his neck. Then she dabbed the tip of her index finger in the blood forming a puddle around him and rubbed it on her thumb, studying its consistency. Paul was still motionless. She looked at Ondine and smiled.

"Dead?" Ondine asked, raising her eyebrows.

"Hardly."

Laura pulled the bloody fingers away from the handle of the knife one by one, letting the hollow, retractable blade spring back out as it fell to the floor. She picked up the stage prop and squeezed the handle, which in fact was made of black rubber, spraying a jet of watery red liquid into the air. Both women laughed. Ondine touched Laura's hand just as Paul opened his eyes and stared blankly at the ceiling.

Anna, recovering from the initial shock, looked at her son with incomprehension. "What is wrong with you?" she said angrily. For a moment all she could see was the image of his father. She sat down on the couch and closed her eyes, hoping to dispel the memory of those miserable years in Brooke Street.

"Me? What is wrong with *me*?" Paul cried in disbelief as he got to his feet. He strode past the two younger women, snatched his coat from the couch, walked into the hallway and back out onto the burning bitumen of St Vincent Place.

# epilogue

Colin Ross insisted that he was innocent right until the end. Some strands of reddish hair and a shred of blue material, apparently from the dead girl's tunic, were uncovered in his Footscray home. It was this evidence that finally convicted him. He was executed at Pentridge Gaol in the April of 1922. The same week the city council met to consider the future of the Eastern Arcade and Market, discussing plans for urban renewal that promised to transform Melbourne into an orderly, modern metropolis.

For some, however, the case was not over. Ross's lawyer claimed to have received letters from the real killer, describing the crime in graphic detail, and then wrote a pamphlet expressing his outrage at the verdict. A spiritualist in the arcade, Madam Gurkha, responded with another, portraying Ross as a syphilitic, predatory maniac. But for most people the murder, the most notorious in the city's history, quickly passed into the realm of anecdote. Grandmothers told their grandchildren that they were there to lay flowers on the cobblestones where the body had been found, and local personalities briefly mentioned the scandal of Gun Alley in their pithy memoirs and nostalgic evocations of old Melbourne. Years later, when the crime had been almost completely forgotten, curious researchers began to stumble across its traces in the basements of libraries and wonder what capital they could make out of it. Eventually one of these sleuths managed to test the forensic evidence in the case, comparing DNA from different strands of hair, proving that Ross was probably innocent.

When the arcade was finally demolished Hamish McDermott was still living in a flat above Flinders Lane. The place was small and had become cluttered with the detritus of his years as a bachelor. He imagined he was living in a time capsule that historians would rummage through after his death, sorting through shelves of dog-eared books by obscure writers, newspaper cuttings of the city's most macabre crimes, six paintings by an unknown Australian artist, bought years before at a pawnbroker's, and the effusions of a journalistic hack with just enough insight to recognise his own mediocrity. For the first time he felt dated. Perhaps this meant he was ready to die, he told himself. But what did it matter? It's a curious thing about cities. People linger on for years in the same old haunts, stubbornly refusing to vacate. Finally their ghosts are exorcised when enough buildings and streets are demolished that they cease to recognise their surroundings. When the Eastern Arcade and Market were destroyed, generations of ghosts disappeared into the ether.

Sometime in the early-twenties, after the furore around the Gun Alley murder had died down, a place called Walters's Magic Shop opened in the arcade. It quickly became a magnet for young children, and its oddity guaranteed its popularity. Children who couldn't afford any other amusement would congregate there and run amok through its dusty aisles of curiosities.

Of particular interest was the collection of stage props, which included fake limbs, frightening masks, a couple of life-sized corpses, a skeleton, an imitation iron maiden and a whole range of devices capable of producing weird sound effects, like the wind in the trees, or the rattle of chains. The children would stab each other with the retractable daggers and swords, and sometimes even make themselves up with fake blood and a bit of mutilated tissue before running out into the arcade to scare passers-by. The place also stocked a variety of magic tricks including hats with false bottoms, miniature guillotines with trick blades, unsolvable puzzles involving interlocking hoops and triangles, and tiny boxes that could makes coins disappear. As the years went by Walters's Magic Shop also accumulated no end of other useless bits and pieces. A couple of discarded mannequins, entwined like Quasimodo and Esmeralda, stretched their dead limbs through piles of terracotta cupids, plaster sphinxes, Chinese lanterns, religious icons, rusted surgical instruments and yellowing newspapers, such that the children almost had to dig them out of the rubbish. The debris of deceased estates from every corner of the city somehow found its way into the back of the store where a multitude of odds and ends bred like mosquitoes on the muddy banks of a sluggish, tropical river.

The owner of the store, as well, was something of a local attraction. He had a decrepit gentility about him, as if he couldn't be bothered washing his clothes or cutting his thinning black hair, but dressed expensively just the same, at least by the standards of the day. His heavy, sallow face was usually unshaven and his stomach bulged against a grubby vest. He was an apathetic businessman and let the place run to rack and ruin. The children treated him with a combination of camaraderie – as if he were one of them, the king of the kids – and derision – as if he were a bit touched in the head. For the most part he'd talk to them as equals and tolerate their rummagings. He'd even tell them stories about his past and, when he had the energy, warn them against the blandishments of a capricious figure called the *Gaukler*, whose trickery, he said, had been the secret of both his making and his unmaking. Sometimes the children would listen attentively, sometimes they'd snigger under their breath. The older ones, already rubbing shoulders with the larrikin pushes of Collingwood or Fitzroy, found stories about the *Gaukler* lingering around the old arcades of Melbourne too eccentric to be taken with a straight face and mocked the old man as a kind of freak, a laughing-stock.

There was something eerily melancholic in these stories, a touch of madness, the desperation of loneliness and solitude, the strange life of a city full of cracked tunes and tainted visions. There was one particular circumstance in all of this that people still claim to remember with great clarity. Once a week, two graceful ladies would walk arm in arm through the arcade to the magic shop. When Mr Walters saw them outside his window he'd scurry to the door and lock it, leaving these poor women tapping on the glass with their parasols, or whatever it was women carried in those days. After a moment or two they'd give up and walk away, only to return the next week, to be rebuffed in the same fashion.

The children who hung around the shop looked upon these two mysterious women with awe, envisaging them floating in the sooty half-light of the arcade like a pair of radiant apparitions, their feet barely touching the flagstones. Nobody doubted that, had they wanted to, the two of them could have drifted right through the glass to the counter where Mr Walters sat, sullenly clinging to a bag of old tricks.

"Perhaps I'll go to Europe," he'd mutter to himself. "I can always go back to Europe."

# NOTES AND ACKNOWLEDGMENTS

The verse at the beginning of the book comes from "Sunsets" by Richard Aldington as found in *The Complete Poems of Richard Aldington* (London: Allan Wingate, 1948). It is reproduced here with kind permission from the Estate of Richard Aldington.

The Karl Kraus essay discussed in Chapter 18 is 'Der Prozeß Riehl' in *Die Fackel* 211, November 1906 pp 1–28, quoted in Edward Timms's *Karl Kraus, Apocalyptic Satirist: Culture and Catastrophe in Habsburg Vienna* (New Haven: Yale University Press, 1986), pp 84–5.

The newspaper article describing the Gun Alley murder that appears in Chapter 23 was excerpted from an article originally published in the *Weekly Times*, 7 January 1922.

In addition, there are a number of historical reference works that have helped me a great deal in the course of writing this book.

They are Gerhard Fischer's *Enemy Aliens: Internment and the Homefront Experience in Australia, 1914–1920* (St Lucia: University of Queensland Press, 1989); Mel Gordon's *The Grand Guignol: Theatre of Fear and Terror* (New York: Da Capo Books, 1997); James Grant and Geoffrey Serle's *The Melbourne Scene, 1803–1956* (Melbourne: Melbourne University Press, 1957); Susan Priestley's *South Melbourne: a History* (Melbourne: Melbourne University Press, 1995); Alan Sharpe's *Crimes that Shocked Australia* (Milson's Point: Currawong Press, 1982); Carl E. Schorske's *Fin-De-Siècle Vienna: Politics and Culture* (New York: Alfred A. Knopf, 1980); Jüngen Tampke's *Wunderbar Country: Germans Look at Australia, 1850–1914* (Sydney: Hale and Ironmonger, 1982) and Edward Timms's *Karl Kraus, Apocalyptic Satirist: Culture and Catastrophe in Habsburg Vienna* (New Haven: Yale University Press, 1986).

Finally, Siegfried Kracauer's wonderful essay "Abschied von der Lindenpassage", in *Straßen in Berlin und anderswo* (Frankfurt am Main: Suhrkamp Verlag, 1964), has shaped my view of Melbourne's arcades for so long that I'd be hard pressed to know exactly where the Lindenpassage ended and the Eastern Arcade began.

A number of people have been very generous with their support and expertise throughout the completion of this book. I would like to thank Rod Morrison, not only for his initial faith in the manuscript, but for his constant and careful attention to its editing and production. Belinda Lee and Carl Harrison-Ford also read the manuscript and contributed valuable editorial advice. The stunning cover design, something the novel will have to live up to, is the work of Katie Mitchell. Finally, without the support (patient and impatient) of Rachel and Rosa, my own fragile ego might not have stood up to it all. I owe them the greatest debt.

# THE BREAD
*with*
SEVEN CRUSTS

*Also available*

# THE BREAD WITH SEVEN CRUSTS

## SUSAN TEMBY

In the autumn of 1943 Giuseppe Lazaro, an Italian prisoner of war, is dropped into a small rural outpost on the edge of the West Australian wheatbelt. He has never seen a place so colourless and flat. He has never met anyone like Max Nash, the young and struggling owner of the farm.

The Nashes slowly accept Giuseppe – or Joe, as they call him – into their home, but he discovers there are limits. Max's sister, Eddy, back from nursing Australian soldiers overseas, bitterly resents 'the enemy' eating at her family's table.

The enforced isolation and intimacy of the farm gradually push Eddy and Giuseppe into an uneasy truce. As the months pass, Giuseppe's feelings for the prickly young woman grow stronger, bringing him into conflict with not only the family and the community, but also with Hal, a neighbour and family friend.

In Italy, 'the bread with seven crusts' is the hardest crust you will ever earn. This is a story about identity and exile, passion and conflicting loyalties. *The Bread with Seven Crusts* marks the arrival of a major new voice in Australian fiction.

ISBN 0 7322 7426 5

*Coldwater*

**MARDI McCONNOCHIE**

*Also available*

# COLDWATER

## Mardi McConnochie

In 1847, three sisters — Charlotte, Emily and Anne — live with their father on the island of Coldwater off the coast of the colony of New South Wales. The island is a prison, in every sense. The sisters' father is Governor Wolf, in charge of the island's penal settlement containing some of the most hardened convicts in the colony.

Aware of their vulnerability as unmarried women, particularly should their father die, the sisters must find a means to earn a living in the outside world. To this end they start writing novels.

Within its shores, Coldwater contains both the passionate and romantic imaginations of the sisters and the brutal realities of convict life. It can only be a matter of time before these two worlds collide, and the dangers of the heart meet the dangers of armed revolt.

Taking the few seeds that history reveals about Charlotte, Anne and Emily Brontë, Mardi McConnochie has skilfully reimagined their lives to create a work of fiction as psychologically riveting as any contemporary thriller. *Coldwater* is a powerful and daring literary debut from a compelling new voice.

ISBN 0 7322 6954 7